The 31
Near Death
Experiences
of Jenny Black

A novel

F.E. Shearer

PUMPJACK PRESS

To /CH, always
Thank you

ONE

Loretta Sparkman looks through the window at a pair of winter finches perched on the wooden bird feeder, a light snow dusting their feathers, and waits for the reaction from Matthias to the news she is becoming a zombie. He hasn't said anything for close to a minute and she wonders if maybe she should have phrased her announcement differently, if another word choice could have crystallized her intent more sharply. Had she gone the right way with the simple, straightforward 'Matthias, I'm becoming a zombie?' The birds flutter off. She turns to face Matthias. He's sitting in the big red chair, the one that's hard to get out of because of the broken springs. He was reading, but no longer. He closes the book and sets it on his lap.

"Right this second?" he asks.

"That's a fair question, and no, not right this second. It started a while ago, and it's a work in progress, but I'd say it's pretty close to done."

"What exactly does 'becoming a zombie' mean?"

"Another reasonable question. Suffice it to say the

sense of who I am, my identity, is disappearing, barely there anymore, to be honest," she says, wishing she could slow her words down. They are coming out at the speed of early summer rain, too fast.

He leans back in the chair and locks his long fingers behind his head. The book slides from his lap onto the carpet. The cover is pale blue, the pages are dog-eared; she can't quite make out the title, something about life on Mars?

"Go on, you've got my full attention," he says.

His tender response calms her, and she takes a breath, thinks about how to best describe what's been happening, how to explain that the zombie is a useful albeit imperfect proxy for her state of being, or rather, absence of being, and how despite certain cartoonish limitations, in particular the brain-eating part, she is impressed by its metaphorical prowess, the insidiously clever way a zombie prioritizes reaction over intent in the consideration of self.

"I'm certainly not hungry for brains. And it's not that my ability to think and be smart and read and talk and love and so on is gone. It's just, I'm no longer sure who's doing that stuff anymore. Like, there's no 'I' inside me."

"You don't feel anything?"

"I feel things but in an instinctive way, a reaction to whatever is happening around me, without having any sense, or minimal sense, of who or what is doing the reacting."

"Who then is having this conversation with me?"

"Try not to take this too literally. I'm not making some lofty philosophical argument about identity," she says. "But I need to be honest with you about what's happening because while you recognize me, I don't, except as it relates to the present moment. I mean, I know who I am relative to you and to my job, and as Sally-Anne's mother, of course, and I'm sure when

Jenny gets here, I'll slip into a pre-constructed Jenny-module."

"So, 'you' have become situational?" he asks.

"That's close, but not exactly. Better to say an 'I' isn't needed to do the things that need doing. Instead, it's straight-up reaction to stimuli like, well, a zombie that slumps along responding to whatever it is they respond to," she says. "Of course, there are gray zones, it's not that all of me is simply gone. But here's the most important part, the kicker..."

She pauses. Loretta isn't intentionally trying to build suspense but it's clear Matthias is taking it that way. His eyes widen as he raises his naked eyebrows.

"I don't miss me," Loretta says.

"Not at all?"

"Not at all. Turns out, life works fine in reaction mode, everything is simpler. Frankly, it's liberating."

"I see the attraction of a simpler life, but I suspect there's more going on. Do you think maybe this could be a precursor to a coming bout of depression?" he asks. He keeps his voice even, wanting his question to land gently.

Loretta has been depressed once or twice—well, more than that, if she's honest, which isn't always easy when it comes to depression. The last time she stayed in bed for a full week and ate only tomato soup and dry sourdough toast, but that's not what's going on now. Still, it's sweet he's checking. Matthias is kind that way, she thinks, kindness is his default setting. She's lucky he sticks with her.

"I'm not depressed, I'm the opposite of depressed," she says. "I'm neutral. If there's no one home inside anymore, who would have those feelings?"

"Seems the opposite of depressed might be joyful, not neutral," he says.

"I don't think anyone would say zombies are known for feelings of joyfulness."

He smiles and it still gives Loretta a flutter in her stomach, even now, after twenty-three years, seven months and seventeen days of marriage, even in her zombie state of mind. Or lack of mind.

"Here's one more possibility, but don't take it the wrong way," he says.

"Go on."

"Maybe this is a midlife crisis. You're the right age, going through some hard stuff with me, you're burned out at your job, your nest is newly empty."

"That's a shallow narrative, Matthias, and you know it. Zombie fits the evidence and situation far better."

Loretta crosses her legs at the ankles, and then uncrosses them. She wonders if this confession was a mistake but she needs him to understand. It's crucial for his well-being.

He says, "You're always tired from work, plus taking care of me. You don't have to dress it up with zombies. I can help, I want to help. Or we can get you help from someone else. We can figure this out together."

She says, "There's nothing to figure out, that's the entire point. I'm not upset about this and you shouldn't be either."

They startle at the sound of the almost-broken doorbell, a stretched-out corrugated noise, as if the sounds are trying but failing to convey meaning.

"You ready?"

"Zombies are always ready. That's the beauty of it. No need to plan, no thought, every moment is pure reaction."

Loretta stands and raises her arms, groaning and stumbling into the hallway. Matthias laughs, but without conviction. She ends the zombie mimicry before opening the front door.

Seconds later, Jenny Black explodes into the house in a whirl of frosted air. She shrugs a damp backpack off her tiny body onto the floor. Matthias's cheerful hello is drowned out as the women hug and share news at a hyper speed—what have you been up to, are you seeing anyone, how's your health, how is Sally-Anne, has it really been six years, how time flies, yes, yes, I am starving, how did you guess?

They keep talking, interrupting each other and then laughing about that, and circling seamlessly back to pick up the orphaned threads. Loretta hangs Jenny's coat in the hall closet and Matthias carries her pack upstairs after calling in their takeout order. Loretta waits while Jenny freshens up, dabbing on pink lipstick and face powder to tone down her chilled red cheeks. When she finishes, they hug again, longer this time. Loretta grabs a box of wine from the fridge and leads Jenny into the back room that used to be an outside porch until two years ago when Matthias put up walls and glass and turned it into a sunroom. A drafty sunroom—the east wall isn't quite level with the floor and cold air streams through baseboard cracks. The windows look out over a postage-stamp yard—two sides are wire-fenced and divide their tiny parcel of land from two other tiny parcels belonging to neighbors on either side; the third is the brick backside of a low-rise apartment building. A cherry tree, bare this time of year, rises alone from the center, its bark shimmering against the angled sunlight. The snowfall has slowed, delicate lace-flakes appearing and disappearing in the evening air, floating, never seeming to reach the ground, evident only by the shallow muddiness left behind.

Loretta and Jenny sit face to face on a brown velvet sofa, the arms worn bald. Loretta spreads a plaid blanket over their laps to ward off the chill. Jenny tucks her legs beneath her body as Loretta stretches her legs out straight because they don't bend like that anymore.

"It is good to have you here, Jenny. It's been way too long."

"I'm relieved to be here."

Relieved is an interesting word, Loretta thinks. "I like your short hair, it's a nice style on you. You look beautiful and, well, luminous," Loretta says. "You're lit up like a movie star, but from the inside out."

"Thanks, that's a nice thing to hear."

"Ready for a glass of wine?"

"I'm not drinking, Lolo," Jenny says, lapsing into Loretta's childhood nickname. "And I know you won't mind if I'm honest, but you don't look so great. Kind of exhausted, and your eyes are all puffy. I mean, you're still beautiful, but what's going on?"

Loretta leans over the coffee table, the one she painted canary yellow this past summer with leftover paint she found outside the hardware store, and fills her own wine glass nearly to the rim. She considers telling Jenny about becoming a zombie. But she isn't sure Jenny will understand, and while understanding isn't paramount, the chore of explanation is more than she's ready to undertake, and so Loretta redirects.

"Time and gravity catching up with me, I suppose. Now come on, tell me everything, world traveler. Let's hear the details of your latest adventure and your plans for the coming year," she says. Loretta raises her glass. "Cheers to a new year, even if we are a few months late celebrating. May this new decade be the most perfect either of us have ever experienced. Here's to 2020."

The wail of an ambulance pierces her one-sided toast. As they wait for the sound to pass, Loretta looks through the window at a bird flying low across the late-day sky; its distant body creates an exacting line of punctuation against the flat winter clouds. The siren fades into the background.

"A crow?" Jenny asks.

"Could be a hawk," Loretta says.

Jenny chews on her lower lip and then says, "I do have one adventure to talk about."

"I'm all ears," Loretta says. "Spill."

"Brace yourself, this is big."

Loretta takes a long sip of wine, finishing nearly a third of the glass in one swallow. "I'm braced."

"Have you ever had a near death experience?"

Loretta is expecting a story about a new lover or a stint in rehab or an exotic destination, but she manages to keep the surprise off her face and answers Jenny's question. "The last time I was on a plane, a few months ago, we hit a turbulent patch, and I was sure I was going to die, and then one time…"

"No, no, not that, not having a bad scare or thinking you might die. The other thing. When you go through a tunnel, float above your body, see dead relatives, your life flashes before you."

"People who come back from the dead and say they've seen heaven or something?"

"Yes, that."

"I've never had one," Loretta says. "Have you?" She finishes her wine, sets the empty glass down on the floor and cracks her knuckles.

"Twenty-two."

"When you were twenty-two?"

"No, I've had twenty-two near death experiences."

"I don't understand. Have you almost died twenty-two times?" Loretta asks, confused.

"I wasn't dead, or even almost dead, during any of them."

"But don't these things require being almost dead, or even really dead for a bit, hence their name?"

"It's not that way for me. I'm just sitting around going about my life, or doing nothing, hanging out, then with no warning, boom, I fall through all the way to the other side, the other side of death."

"The other side of death?"

Jenny's words tumble out. "I know it sounds nuts but when it happens, I go to this place, not a physical place, it's different, everything is there and also nothing.

It's hard to describe but each time I travel to the other side of, well, it must be the other side of death, what else could it be, because I'm flying through a tunnel—"

Loretta moves close to Jenny, as if extreme proximity will help fathom her meaning. Their shared blanket slips to the floor. "Flying to the other side of death? Jenny, what the hell are you talking about?"

"Not flying like on a plane, more like a bird, but not even that … shit, I wish I were better at describing this. It's fuzzy like a dream. Once I get through the tunnel and beyond the light and see people I know from before they died, when I get past all that, that's when it all happens. It's beautiful, so much love is there, time stops. I'm blessed, it's everything I've ever wanted, like my entire life's journey has been worth it. But still, even though I'm happy about this, I'm not sure what's going on. Why do I keep having these things without dying?"

Jenny stops talking. She takes in a deep breath, exhaling slowly. Loretta leans back into the sofa cushions, not speaking, the mechanical purr of the electric space heater the only sound fastening their silence. Loretta stares at the orange coils, wondering if Jenny is sick, like maybe she has a rare neurological disease or has had a bunch of silent strokes, or maybe living such a solitary life has taken a toll on her mental health.

Finally, Loretta breaks their quiet. "Twenty-two?"

"Yes," Jenny says.

"Have you seen a doctor?"

"After the third one, but he didn't understand, or more likely didn't believe me. I asked him to do a full physical and whatever brain scans he needed. Had to pay out of pocket."

"And?"

"Totally healthy."

"Are you scared?" Loretta asks.

"I'm not scared so much as blown away," Jenny

says, picking at the cuticle around her thumb. "Well, maybe a little scared."

"Food's here," Matthias calls.

Loretta stands and pulls Jenny up by her small hands with their bitten-down fingernails. "Wow. I'm not sure how else to react yet."

"Yeah, like I said, it's big."

Loretta wraps her arms around Jenny's shoulders, and despite a rising unease for her friend's state of mind, or perhaps because of it, falls effortlessly into the familiarity of Jenny's body, and images of the long-ago girls they once were unlock from her memory, agile and awkward children playing together, emotions at the surface, reacting to the freshness of each moment, blissfully free of the burden of time or purpose.

Loretta has a flash: maybe her zombieness means she has come full circle, maybe this is what it means to get old?

A few minutes later, Matthias, Loretta and Jenny sit around the dining room table, scratched up by two decades of a mostly happy family life, a space now infrequently used after Sally-Anne left for college three years ago. Now, when they are alone, Matthias and Loretta eat on trays in front of the television and watch old westerns, true-crime shows or BBC mysteries.

Tonight, the friends slide into an easy enough banter. They trade Chinese takeout cartons and Jenny fills them in on where she's been living the last few years. Jenny loves to swim—she is a strong swimmer and was competitive enough for an Olympic trial before she broke her shoulder goofing on a trampoline in high school. She has always seen the world, and describes her travels, through the lens of coastlines and lakes and rivers, and the ease, or not, of swimming in their waters. After finishing a rambling story about the buoyancy of the Aegean Sea on the Izmir side of Turkey, Jenny stops talking, fixes her eyes on Matthias and asks about his health. He is bald and very thin, so different from the last time she visited.

Loretta would love more than anything not to talk about this, but Matthias can't be stopped and launches into his diagnosis and the months of treatment. He tries hard to make them laugh, and succeeds when he goes into way too much detail about his vomit-diary as they finish up the tofu stir-fry.

"He's fine now," Loretta insists. "Totally fine. There is zero to worry about. Except his persistent need to describe the most disgusting parts."

"You look very distinguished bald," Jenny says.

"Liar." Matthias runs his hand over his bare chalky-white scalp. "But I do consider it my own personal work of art."

He says this because eleven months ago, two days before the first chemo, Matthias announced—using a fake high-pitched voice to imitate an imaginary museum director or art critic—he would shave his own head, a form of performance art, rather than be turned into a passive symbol of medical deconstructionism. Standing naked in the bathtub, Loretta lathered his head, giggling at his silliness, but really pantomiming courage.

"How about we get back to near death experiences," Loretta says, interrupting Matthias because she can tell he is on the verge of telling that story to Jenny.

"Near death experiences?" Matthias asks.

"Jenny is having a lot of them."

"How interesting," he says, cocking his head to the left.

"Start at the beginning," Loretta says.

Uncertainty washes across Jenny's face, and a furrow deepens between her eyebrows.

"Where does anything begin? How far back? To our childhood? The beginning could be anywhere. I can't see from the future into the past where maybe there was a trigger, a decision I made, something I ate—"

"Let's not complicate this," Loretta says. "Describe the first one you had."

Jenny places her hands palms up on the table, as if an interrogation she has long been expecting is finally getting underway. "It was early last year. At the beach, you know, the one we went to as kids."

"I remember," Loretta says. She smells suntan lotion and vinegary French fries and hears the drawn-out cry of seagulls.

"It was dusk. Off-season. I was alone, sitting at the surf with the boardwalk behind me. I had broken up with this guy, whose name I can't remember now, maybe Dan, no, it was Derrick, yeah, Derrick, anyway, I was feeling this super strong sense of peace and beauty, one of those crazy-perfect moments that sometimes come out of nowhere, you know?"

Loretta and Matthias nod.

"I was happy, really happy. And right then, when I felt like I couldn't be any happier, at the peak of this bliss, the first one hit me. For a split second, I thought I was falling, like the world was literally dropping from under me, and then I thought, goddamn it, I'm having a stroke and I cursed myself for being careless with my health."

Loretta takes Jenny's hand and feels a tremble.

"But then the fear passed and it became something else, something amazing. There was a tunnel filled with beautiful golden light, and pieces of my life shuttled through my mind, but not my mind as you might think of it. I could see myself from above, and at the same time, I was spread out like a layer of fine sand. I was a grain and also the beach."

"You float above your body?" Loretta asks.

"Yes," Jenny says. "And like I said earlier, time stands still. I'm part of something bigger than me alone, another dimension or something, as ridiculous as that sounds, my whole self dissolves. It's mystical."

"Your whole self dissolves, sort of like a zombie?" Matthias asks, eyeing Loretta. She shakes her head at him mouthing *no*.

"I wouldn't describe it quite like that," Jenny says.

"How many times has this happened?" he asks.

"Twenty-two," Loretta and Jenny answer together.

Matthias does the math in his head. "That's one near death experience every two weeks."

"They're not so regular. Sometimes I go for months, other times they're an hour apart. And each one is a little different but also the same."

Matthias stands, grabs a bottle of Jameson from the counter and pours two fingers into a coffee mug. He looks at Loretta. She nods and he hands it to her and then he pours three fingers into another cup. Jenny shakes her head so he keeps it.

"That's a lot to process," Matthias says.

"Will you help me?" Jenny asks.

"Help you how?" Loretta asks. The whiskey burns going down.

"Ask around at your University, all those experts. You're important. I see your name all over the Internet. Loretta Sparkman, University spokesperson. With you, they'll listen if you ask about near death experiences. Me, they'll think I'm crazy. Maybe commit me."

"That's why you came here? Because I work at a University?"

"Partly," Jenny says. "I mean, it was a factor because you know smart people, but mostly I came because it's you. I need someone to help me. To help figure out what's happening to me and what I should do about it."

Loretta finishes the whiskey; she is tired and a little drunk. Ever since her descent into zombieness, she gets drunk faster. It's an upside to joining the ranks of the living dead.

"Let me think it through a little," Loretta says.

Later, after Loretta hauls out clean sheets and a quilt for Jenny and sets her up in Sally-Anne's old bedroom, Loretta and Matthias talk softly in their own bed, a habit forged during the worst days of chemotherapy when whispered pillowtop assurances and limbs blindly intertwined in the darkness were all that steadied them. Eventually, as the cancer receded, relief flowed into the ragged space that fear had carved open, and now, almost a year later, the rough edges are smoothed over like polished marble and the same nighttime moments have been transformed into the most intimate of their present lives.

"This has been a strange day," Matthias says.

"Do you believe her?" Loretta asks.

"I hadn't thought of not believing her. Don't you believe her?"

"I'm not entirely sure. She's always been a wanderer, a self-described seeker, never had a real job. Well, once back when she was a teenager as a camp counselor for a couple of summers. She lives off an inheritance from her uncle, traveling around, looking for answers to questions most people give up on in their twenties."

"Maybe they shouldn't give up."

"What do you mean?"

"Maybe persistence is why she's found something."

The light snow of earlier has given way to a steady rain. They are quiet, listening to the water land on the rooftop. Loretta imagines each droplet as a different color of bright paint, and then pictures the splatter as a Pollock-style canvas that nearly as fast as it's created devolves into color-muddied ribbons running down the shingles, overflowing the leaf-stuffed gutters, streaming down the sides of the house.

"Will you help her?" he asks.

"I'll certainly help her find a better doctor."

He pulls her close. "Listen, this is your chance, don't ignore it."

"Chance for what?"

"To use all that knowledge at the University for something interesting, to give your brain a break from your job, but mostly, to give yourself a new purpose."

"Why would I want Jenny's near death experiences, assuming that's what they are, as my purpose?"

"There's a symmetry here, don't you see? Her self dissolving into a near death experience and you saying the same, the zombie thing."

"They're very different," she says. "Totally not the same. And that's an odd thing for you to say."

"Are they different, though? No, wait, don't answer, it doesn't matter. What matters is she's your best friend. You have to help her."

"You're my best friend."

"She was your best friend before I came on the scene. No one has known you longer. Do her this favor. Dig in, figure out what's happening, talk to the experts. Don't let her become isolated or get put on some drug regimen or whatever just because they don't understand. Maybe helping her will kill two birds with one stone."

"You're being a little melodramatic and I hate that saying," Loretta says. "Why would anyone want to kill any birds, much less two birds, at the same time, and how would that be possible with one stone? Birds are too nimble. Unless it's a really big stone, like a boulder, but that doesn't make any sense."

He laughs. "I won't say it again, but to my point, you can help Jenny and navigate out of your midlife crisis."

"I'm not having a midlife crisis, I was clear on that."

"Sorry," he says. "I meant to say your zombieness."

TWO

In the morning, over black coffee with sugar, Matthias and Loretta decide the best course of action is to discuss Jenny's situation with the Dean. Matthias still can't work, so he agrees to stay home with Jenny who, they both think, shouldn't be left alone.

As she leaves, Matthias hands Loretta a brown paper bag containing a Swiss cheese, mayo and ketchup sandwich on sourdough bread, a small Ziploc of raw almonds and a mini-can of Diet Coke. He kisses her and the taste of his toothpaste makes her think of a peppermint schnapps snow cone.

"Don't run away with the Dean today," he says.

"Don't be silly," she says. "Never on a Monday."

It's an old joke between them and he always laughs, but this time his laughter is cut short by a rasping cough. Loretta fills a glass from the tap, insisting he drink. She fusses over him, not wanting to leave, but he pushes her toward the door. "I'll be fine, just a little something caught in my throat."

Loretta backs the car out of the garage. The pink

curtains covering the window on the second floor pull apart. Jenny waves from between the cleave.

The drive takes eleven minutes, two minutes faster than usual. Easing the car into her parking space in the lower section of the University by the river, she hears a sharp pop as she runs over something. She gets out, relieved it's just a smashed beer can—Bud Light—and tosses it into the back seat; it's worth ten cents as a return.

The University campus has two parts; one half is nestled alongside the river and buzzes with life: food carts, a gym, dormitories. Students zip around—on bikes, scooters, skateboards, on foot—through a sleek labyrinth of classrooms constructed over the past few decades. One building is under construction, squeezed into the last free lot next to a rusty shipyard, the legacy of an industrial waterfront, now overshadowed by modern academic towers of glass and brushed steel.

The other half of the University, the dowdy part, is perched on an anomalous volcanic upwelling that, in its ancient resistance to weathering, sits a thousand feet above the bustling riverside campus. The hilltop is home to century-old academic buildings with degrading lead pipes and fussy HVAC systems, along with the University hospital and executive suites.

An aerial tram connects the upper and lower halves of the University, bridging old and new with thick cables and a pair of gleaming aluminum cabins shaped like teardrops.

The day is clear but cold. Loretta walks from the parking lot to the lower tram terminal, thoughts focused on the conversation from the night before, rehearsing how she will present the information to the Dean. She talks to herself, a lifelong habit that's more pronounced now in her zombie state, stopping every now and again to search out the perfect words, willing them from idleness.

At the terminal, she steps into the waiting cabin seconds before lift-off, sloughed into the thicket of people for the three-minute ride. As the tram slides up the braided metal cable, the river gets smaller and falls behind. Close to the upper terminus, Loretta looks for the eagle she spotted two weeks ago on the top branches of a Douglas fir but doesn't find it today. Maybe it's flown somewhere warmer, looking for food. The tram lurches left then right, bumping its way into the dock. Loretta ducks her head away from a tall man in blue scrubs coughing into his elbow.

After walking the few minutes more to her office, she reconciles to the genial volley of how-was-your-weekend and oh-my-god-how-did-it-get-to-be-Monday-so-fast greetings from the staff. Over the next few hours, the gears of the morning grind forward until Loretta finds the right moment, in between meetings, to poke her head into the Dean's office.

"Time for a quick question?" she asks.

The Dean steps out from behind a giant mahogany desk. He is white, pushing sixty, with the stocky build and confidence of a once-athletic man.

"Sure, Loretta, come on in. What's happening with my public relations director?"

Even now, after more than a decade, it jolts Loretta to hear her name attached to the words "public relations." She'll never get used to it. Twelve years ago, Loretta was scratching out a living as a feature article freelancer and in her down time working on a novel about volcanoes. Matthias had a job as a security guard at the community college. That May, Sally-Anne turned ten. Nothing unusual about a birthday, but somehow their daughter reaching double digits forced Matthias and Loretta to acknowledge they had no hope of paying for Sally-Anne's college education on their current trajectory. No magical influx of money was going to plop down in their collective lap, they weren't going to win the lottery, her unfinished novel probably would never hit the best seller list, and their debt was now up to three-alarm levels. They promised each other they would find a better way. Loretta agreed to look for a nine-to-five type of job with benefits. Matthias would take on a second job. Before they had the time to act on those promises, the economy crashed and Matthias was laid off. They had enough in the bank to cover their mortgage for two months but replacing the health insurance from Matthias's lost job was out of the question. Then, Loretta was in a fender-bender and they couldn't afford to fix their car. In response to their low-key but obvious panic, Sally-Anne asked if they were going to become homeless.

Loretta kicked her job search into high gear and got a lucky break. There was an opening at the University for a writer. Then, two more things broke her way: her predecessor quit abruptly so the University was desperate and the Dean, who had the final say, was new to his role and didn't know enough to realize the depth, or implications, of Loretta's inexperience. When she came up with a killer argument to mitigate that gap—all writers are, at heart, public relations experts—he bought it. She was so relieved she broke into tears on the drive home while shout-singing to an ABBA song on the radio.

She worked hard, and after a few embarrassing years of on-the-job learning, Loretta figured out how information, along with egos and money, flows within the power dynamics of the University. She also discovered that her interview pitch, which she built out of desperation and bullshit, was true. The basics of storytelling were the same whether one did it on behalf of a University, a Fortune-500 company or millions of imaginary readers of a now never-to-be-finished lava novel. (So, maybe the Dean wasn't so naïve after all.) Some days, even after so many years, maybe especially after so many years, she despises herself for how good she is at her job and how quick she was to give up on her dreams. But most days she is too damn busy doing the work that she doesn't have time to think about that. Plus, the family has health insurance, thank god, given this cancer scare, and Sally-Anne is doing well in college. So, Loretta is grateful, but the scar of the close call they avoided years ago never quite healed.

"I need to ask you something not work-related, do you mind?"

"Of course not," the Dean says. "Please, sit."

The relationship between Loretta and the Dean, like her public relations success, is a fluke. If pressed, neither Loretta nor the Dean could articulate how it came to be so strong so fast. At first, it seemed a function of proximity and happenstance, which led to cautious curiosity and then hesitant intentionality, until they hit bedrock—and now each is silently so grateful for the small miracle of their unlikely friendship that neither would risk its existence by examining it too closely.

Not many people understand their bond—Matthias is one of the few, thank goodness—and certainly no one at the University seems to get it. There are whispers, of course; completely ill-founded. Loretta doesn't find the Dean especially attractive and is sure he feels the same about her. She knows next to nothing about the Dean's life outside of work except that he loves his wife and has three grown children (or is it two, she can never remember). He could be a weekend cross-dresser with rage issues, for all she knows. And Loretta could be a chain-smoking video poker addict, but none of it matters because theirs is an intellectual relationship, an unrestrained, perpetually self-enlarging exchange of ideas.

For this reason, she's a little nervous that discussing Jenny's unusual situation could breach their unspoken parameters. But during her earlier rehearsal as she walked to the tram, when her pleasantly plain, worry-free zombie brain pre-reacted to multiple scenarios, the words came to her that will keep the conversation, she hopes, in the isn't-this-a-curious-phenomenon realm, providing the safe harbor they both need.

"Do you know about near death experiences?"

With a startled expression of concern, he asks, "Is something wrong?"

"No, not with me."

He pauses, clears his throat, and then speaks loudly, like he always does. Her office is next door, and she can always hear his meetings through the plasterboard wall, or at least his side of the meetings. Luckily for him, she keeps secrets well, and that he doesn't share a wall with anyone else.

"I know enough to make me dangerous," he says, chuckling. "Why do you ask?"

"I had a visit from a friend last night, a childhood friend," Loretta continues. "She's had a few near death experiences, at least that's what she's calling them. She describes a tunnel, a golden light, a sense of oneness. She floats above her body."

"That must have been an interesting and alarming conversation," the Dean says, his tone now more serious. "She cites multiple events?"

"A few, yes."

Loretta isn't sure why she is glossing over the fact that Jenny has had twenty-two near death experiences, but trusts her instinct to keep that information out of their conversation.

"Does she live a risky life?"

"Not that I'm aware of. But the thing is, she's skipping the part about being dead or almost dying."

"What do you mean?"

"Her episodes aren't associated with dying, there is no death to be near. They come out of nowhere, with no apparent trigger."

"Is she experiencing medical distress?"

"Not that I can tell. She seems healthy, kind of radiant, even."

"Age?" he asks. He's lapsed into fact-finding, they're on steady ground now.

"Same as me."

He looks at her curiously, as if the information had never entered his consideration.

"Mid-fifties," Loretta says. A strand of hair slips from behind her ear and she tucks it back into place. The hasty ponytail she shoved her hair into this morning won't hold much longer. "So, are near death experiences a real thing?"

"There have been a few peer-reviewed publications on this topic. One was some time ago from a Dutch team," the Dean says. He fishes around on his laptop and sends a link to Loretta's phone. "Go on, read it. I'll wait."

She scans the study abstract.[1]

Ten hospitals admitted 344 patients, all clinically dead, all resuscitated. Each was asked if they had a near death experience, which they defined as a "special state of consciousness, including specific elements such as an out-of-body experience, pleasant feelings, and seeing a tunnel, a light, deceased relatives or a life review." A small number said yes. At a two-year follow-up, those who said yes believed more in an afterlife and had less fear of death compared with the people who said no.

Loretta looks up from her phone screen. "So, they are definitely a real thing?"

"These cases are medically documented, although self-reported, which makes their descriptions unreliable to a degree. And even though this Dutch study is rather old now and has always been a bit controversial, it marked a pivotal moment in the scientific community in accepting the phenomenon."

"Why controversial?"

"The assumption had always been that oxygen deprivation causes near death experiences. This study revealed a problem with that explanation."

"I see the problem," Loretta says. "All the patients should have had one because all of them experienced oxygen loss at the instant of clinical death."

"Right. That fact caused the researchers to conclude that oxygen deprivation was an insufficient explanation, causing a minor stir in people who believe, or hope, that near death experiences have mystical import."

"Proof of an after-death realm, I suppose," she says, thinking of Jenny's description. "Or heaven, whatever that means."

"Exactly."

"Maybe they weren't really dead, the ones who didn't report having a near death experience."

"Death is a complex biological phenomenon and it's possible that the parameters used across all individuals in the study to define clinical death, such as heart rate and respiration activity, were inadequate. However, they all experienced the loss of oxygen that presumably initiates the near death experience," he says. "And beyond this study, there's also information coming out of epilepsy research that shows an unexpected side effect when stimulating the brain to reduce seizures. Some patients report floating above their own body."[2]

"Like what happens in a near death experience," Loretta says.

"But the core question remains unresolved."

"You think that's key? Figuring out why only certain people have them?"

"We don't have enough data to draw a conclusion. But even so, we can conclude that these people are anomalous. Anomalous data or experiences can lead to new ways of looking at the world when compared against a baseline agreed upon as normal. Arbitrarily,

I'll add because baselines are by definition arbitrary. Nevertheless, it's safe to say a near death experience is anomalous relative to pretty much any baseline."

As is often the case, Loretta is amazed by the Dean's breadth of knowledge, wishing she were more like him. Sometimes, she wonders how her life would have turned out if she had pursued a University life due to youthful intellectual curiosity rather than late-life financial desperation because even though she complains a lot about her job, the pettiness of faculty, the stress of students, and so on, her personality is suited to the academic environment. Well, her pre-zombie personality was. Now, in theory, her non-personality is suited for anywhere, more or less.

"How is it you know so much about near death experiences?" Loretta asks.

"Can't remember why I read up on the subject, but it was a while ago. Something caught my eye and I ran it down. Looks like whatever it was came in handy today, eh?"

He laughs, a booming sound that echoes through the entire floor.

"How should I help her?" Loretta asks, despite now recognizing the unfairness of asking him what to do about Jenny. What were she and Matthias thinking when they hatched this plan? How could the Dean know what she should do?

Still, she hopes he has an answer. She crosses her fingers under the table.

"You said your friend isn't in any immediate health jeopardy?"

"She seems fine," Loretta says.

"If I were you, I'd gather more information so she can make an informed decision about next steps. I'm sure many of our University scholars have knowledge of the topic as it cuts across disciplines. You'll need to contact several departments. I'll give you a list. Tell the chairs I sent you."

Just what Matthias suggested she do, she thinks, as the Dean scribbles down a list of departments. Her phone vibrates. She reads the incoming text. Oh no, she thinks. What is it this time?

"Mona is calling an emergency meeting," she says. "Do you know what this is about?"

"I do, but it's best to hear the details from Mona," the Dean says. "Buckle up, you'll have your hands full. Interviewing the department chairs about near death experiences will seem like a vacation by comparison."

Before leaving for Mona's office, Loretta asks her assistant, Caron, to arrange meetings with the chairs.

"What do I say the meetings are about?" Caron asks.

Loretta pauses. Academics are a suspicious lot, even when—maybe especially when—the Dean's name is invoked. How should she frame the request? She doesn't want to tell them about Jenny, not yet anyway. She's still feeling unexpectedly protective—in the same way she didn't want to tell the Dean about how many episodes Jenny has had. A story pops into her head, fully formed, and before she can stop herself, she says, "Tell them it's about appearing on *60 Minutes* for a segment on near death experiences and I want to talk to the chairs about being an on-camera expert."

"Oh cool. I'd watch that for sure," Caron says.

THREE

Loretta sits at the sole table in the University public relations conference room. The room is small; more chairs circle the table than can fit, mismatched extras dragged in and left behind over years to accommodate a team that seems to grow or shrink—as far as Loretta can tell—at the same rate as threats to the University's funding. Now, when the room is full of staffers, they sit elbow to elbow and breathe in each other's body odor, perfume, deodorant and breath mints that usually, by the end of a meeting, all blend into a not horribly unpleasant aroma.

Today, it's just two people. Across from Loretta is Mona, her boss. Mona has exceptionally long eyelashes. Most days, Loretta thinks they are fake but some days, typically in the late afternoon when the fluorescent lighting is strongest, she wavers, thinking they might be real and that Mona really does have the world's longest eyelashes. Today, she's convinced they are fake and watching Mona blink three times, wonders if the fake lashes brushing against her face feel like dead butterfly wings. That thought makes her wonder what fake eyelashes are made of. Do people donate eyelashes the way they donate real hair for post-chemotherapy wigs? Or maybe they're rat hairs. Seems about the right size. Nah, they must be synthetic.

"This one is going to knock your socks off," Mona says.

"I'm not wearing socks," Loretta says.

Her stomach growls, and it feels like pebbles sloshing around in acid down there. She should not have skipped breakfast.

"Get ready," Mona says.

"I'm ready."

"Really ready?"

Loretta puts her coffee mug on the table, watching as the vibration ripples form on the liquid surface, like a tiny stone has been tossed into her tiny brown caffeine lake. "I'm always ready," she says aloud. I'm a zombie for fuck's sake, she thinks.

"The wrong sperm was inserted into a patient at the University fertility clinic," Mona says.

"When did this happen?"

"About a year ago."

The implication of the timing sinks in and Loretta says, "A baby got made."

Mona nods. "And there's more."

Loretta waits. Mona tugs her left ear lobe. "The sperm donor is white. The recipient is Black."

"Why does that matter?" Loretta asks.

Mona, who is white and about fifteen years younger than Loretta, looks at her blankly, as if she has asked why the sun seems brighter on cloudless days. "It shouldn't matter, of course, but it will matter, and you know it will. This is America."

Loretta glances out of the conference room window, letting this ugly truth settle or, more accurately, dredging up this truth from the place she buries ugly things she only faces when forced. Two students on the quad are tossing a Frisbee, despite the chilly weather. It flies over the girl's head and lands in the street. A truck slams on its brakes and a screeching sound cuts across the green space slightly out of sync from the action as the driver stops for the twenty-something blonde rushing heedlessly to retrieve the plastic disc. She grins and waves an apology. Loretta wonders if she was ever like that young woman, so certain traffic would stop. It's hard to remember.

"Are you listening?"

"Yes," Loretta says.

Loretta casts about for a name for this situation, a private catchphrase she alone will use, as she always does at the start of a public relations crisis because it helps focus her thinking; titling is an upstream tributary to controlling. *The Case of the Misplaced Sperm.* That will do. Even though the sperm was not misplaced—it's clear where it ended up—she likes it well enough to use it as the prism through which her ideas will coalesce and hopefully combine into a story that best protects the University's reputation, because that's what she is paid to do.

"I'll give you the basics," Mona says.

Loretta listens and doesn't take notes.

"A white man and his white fiancée became patients at the clinic about a year ago. They were having trouble conceiving and hoped technology might improve their odds. The fiancée was in her early forties, and her age was their clinical challenge."

"So, unmarried?" Loretta asks.

"Correct. The Black woman was married and her husband's sperm was the obstacle. They selected sperm from an anonymous donor, a Black medical student. Both women had appointments at the clinic, fifteen minutes apart. The white woman was at the clinic for the third try with her fiancé's sperm. The Black woman was there for her first try with the medical student's sperm."

Loretta visualizes the events, embellishing details as Mona speaks, the women in side-by-side treatment rooms at the fertility clinic, separated by a layer of thin drywall covered with daffodil-colored wallpaper, both on their backs with heels in stirrups, each nervous and dreading the cold instruments and intrusion. She unconsciously squeezes her thighs together.

"The physician took the wrong vial from his assistant and inserted its contents into the Black woman," Mona says.

Loretta sees a graying physician, his right eye cloudy, maybe from undiagnosed macular degeneration. As he performs the procedure, the woman gazes up at the photos of cumulus clouds on the ceiling of Loretta's imagination.

"Fifteen minutes later in the exam room next door, the doctor inserted the sperm from the Black medical student into the white woman."

Loretta pictures a rainbow on the ceiling of this clinic room. And then she thinks about what might have happened afterward. Maybe after staying still for the requisite period, giving the sperm the needed travel time, the two women bumped into each other as they were leaving the office, nodding pleasantly, oblivious to their soon-to-be forever-intertwined futures.

"The Black woman conceived. The white woman did not," Mona says. "Once he realized his error, the physician did the right thing and admitted it to clinic administrators, but by then a full month had passed."

"That timing is going to be a problem for us," Loretta says. "Presumably, then, everyone affected was informed about the mix-up?"

"Yes. The man demanded that the baby made with his sperm be aborted. The woman refused."

"Her prerogative," Loretta says.

"A child was born, although the University didn't tell the man. The clinic let him assume, without directly saying so one way or the other, an abortion had been performed, because the woman didn't want anyone to know she had the baby, and the University must abide by patient privacy laws. Are you still tracking?"

"I am."

"You don't need notes?"

"No," Loretta says.

"Why not?"

"I'm good at remembering things."

"Okay. Everything probably would have been fine, or as fine as these things can ever be, if the man had let it go," Mona says. "But he didn't. Somehow, no one is sure how, he got a scent of the truth and now the University has been informed by his attorney that he is filing a lawsuit demanding a child, if one was born, be presented for a paternity test. If it is his child, he wants partial, maybe even full custody."

"When will the lawsuit be filed?"

"Assume soon. Maybe tomorrow."

"The identity of the man and woman?"

"Anonymous," Mona says. "It's Jane Doe versus John Doe. They don't even know each other's identities, although we know both, of course. And I'll tell you, confidentially, the man is prominent."

"How prominent?"

"Very. Tom Thomas."

"Jeez, Mona, talk about burying the lead. You should have told me first thing that the sperm donor is a racist radio shock jock."

"Shock jock?" Mona says, letting out a laugh that sounds like a toddler with a wet cough. "You're dating yourself. Today, we call them MAGA assholes with social media platforms."

"Does Thomas know his sperm was used to make this baby?"

"He's guessing."

"Yet somehow he's landed on the truth. Funny how that happens." Loretta slips down a few inches in her chair, thinking out loud. "He's got the money and media savvy to hire his own public relations team, or his attorney will. He's got a brand to protect and he'll find a way to leverage this situation to expand his brand, maybe take it national. Possibly his entire motivation." Loretta does a quick check of his Twitter feed. "He's got more than a million followers."

"Maybe he's desperate to be a dad. For real. It's another possibility. Prospective parenthood does weird things to people," Mona says.

"I suppose it could be that, but we have to assume otherwise for practical reasons. If I were advising him, I'd run with an injured-hero-doing-the-right-thing story for the media, which will paint the University as the villain, and then I'd tell him to use that opening to make this political because it's so damn easy these days. Shout something about University elites stealing babies into the right-wing echo chamber and he'd win the first battle, hands down. Next, although I wouldn't suggest this because I'm not an asshole, once he finds out the woman and baby are Black, he could use that fact to pump up his followers, say something ridiculous about playing the race card. Totally meaningless but a reliable trigger for his audience." Loretta's mind is moving quickly, spinning through the facts, weaving stories, trying them on like jeans, deciding which might work, which are comfortable, and which to immediately discard.

"That's all worst-case scenario stuff. Hopefully it won't come to that," Mona says. "So now, what's *our* story?"

"I'm working on it."

"Work faster. We need your magic here."

"It's not magic, Mona. It's straight-up storytelling

and it requires just a little time to process."

Back in her windowless office, Loretta continues working, considering characters and motivation to frame the University's initial reaction to the lawsuit. Is the doctor who misplaced the sperm a villain? A villain could focus public anger away from the University, but casting the doctor in this role, even indirectly, means throwing one of the University's own under the bus, an act that would undoubtedly rile the faculty. The always easily riled faculty. She'll need to do some digging into the doctor's standing and online presence before making that call. Maybe the bad guy is Tom Thomas, the sperm donor himself. That could work but how? No matter what, she'll still need an out-of-the-gate preemptive pushback against his inevitable hardball tactics. Or could it be that this story has no villain and is instead a damsel-in-distress narrative, with the University galloping in for the rescue. That's probably sexist, she thinks. And effective. She'll think about the racial element later, how to add it into the mix if she has to. Maybe that part will stay quiet.

Her phone vibrates. She reads Matthias's text.

Jenny had a near death experience in the bathtub.

Shit. She calls Matthias. "What happened? Is she okay?"

"Yes, but it was very odd. I'm rattled to be honest."

"Tell me everything," Loretta whispers into the phone, even though she is alone in her office.

"She wanted to take a bath, but was nervous of, I don't know, drowning—"

"In a bathtub?"

"It can happen. It only takes a few inches. I offered to wait outside. I was sitting in the hallway reading the news on my phone, trying not to be obtrusive, when suddenly she moaned and I heard water splashing, then nothing. I called through the door, but she didn't answer. After three times more, I went in. She was

31

flailing around like she was having a seizure. I thought she was going to crack her head open and I yelled again, trying to get her attention. 'Wake up, Jenny, wake up!' Then her eyes rolled back in her head, and all I could see were the whites. She stopped moving, went dead quiet, totally still."

"Did you call an ambulance?"

"No, it all happened so fast and just as I was pulling her out of the tub, she came around. There was a golden light, Loretta, it was all around her."

"A light? *You* could see it?"

"What did you say? I can't hear you."

She repeats the question, louder. "You could see the light?"

"It felt that way, absolutely, but when you ask me now, I'm not sure. It's fading, like a dream. Something is happening to her. I don't know if it's a near death experience or what, but I saw something. Or felt something. This is real."

"Where is she now?"

"Upstairs, resting."

"What did she say about it?"

"That it was number twenty-three."

"Was it awkward, seeing her naked?"

"What? No. Don't be stupid."

Matthias's breathing is labored, ragged and amplified by the phone speaker.

"Are you having trouble getting air?"

"I'm okay, allergies I guess," he says. "But like I said, I'm a little rattled."

"I should come home."

"No, it's fine. I just wanted you to know."

"Promise me you'll rest and not let all this wipe you out."

"I promise," Matthias says. "So, what about you? How's your zombieness?"

"Convenient."

"Does that mean something new, something big?"

"Huge. You won't believe this one. I'll fill you in tonight."

"Are you going to help Jenny?"

"Yes," Loretta says. "The Dean gave me a plan."

After Loretta disconnects, she tilts back in the chair, imagining the scene at home. As she does, she is overtaken by a sense of urgency, her head pulses and her fingertips tingle, electrified. She doesn't understand why but knows with absolute certainty that speed is of the utmost importance in getting to the bottom of Jenny's near death experiences, and with this knowledge her thinking crystallizes; she feels the same when she tackles a new University communication crisis—name the story and build the narrative.

She needs a title.

Loretta pulls out a fresh spiral-bound notebook from a desk drawer overstocked with blank notebooks; using a red marker, she writes in bold letters across the cover *The 23 Near Death Experiences of Jenny Black*. She turns the first page and dates it, then selects a purple pen, deciding to write the results from each department in a different color. Maybe in the end, the opposite effect of light refraction will occur: The rainbow colors will reunite into a single beam of understanding.

Caron sticks her head in the door.

"Your first meeting on near death experiences is in fifteen minutes. The Department of Religion. The chair rearranged his schedule to see you right away."

FOUR

The Department of Religion is located in the oldest part of campus—a nucleus from which the University drifted outward over the past century. The buildings and grounds are unkempt, overlooked by maintenance staff for years, a fact Loretta attributes to the decline of tuition-paying students in the disciplines of antiquity. But even after such neglect, Loretta can still see an old-world charm peeking through the maze of crumbling courtyards and rowdy gardens, like sugar cubes degrading in a tumbler of fine gin.

Loretta reaches into her coat pocket and pulls out the list of departments the Dean wrote for her. It's a curious list, with little overlap on the face of it. As she walks, she thinks, maybe for the first time, about the whole concept of a 'department.' At her University, at any academic institution really, the department exists so completely in the background that it escapes consideration, like white noise. Loretta realizes she too has casually assumed its relevance, never examining the origins, accepting it as a logical edifice defining and containing the borders of knowledge.

But how is a body of knowledge categorized and designated a department? Who or what determines its existence in the academic hierarchy? Some are obvious, like math and music departments, but why does a Department of Religion exist, for example, but not a Department of Kindness? Why Physics but not Time? Who decides what discipline, what focus area, is worthy? What philosophers, what books or theories, what historical events get canonized within those departments and why? A collection of knowledge isn't a biological thing that grows to some tipping point after which it gets bumped up to the department category. People choose the categories, along with their contents, of course, but who, exactly, from ancient times all the way to today, this present moment, has done the choosing, and why do they get to choose?

Well, she thinks, that's clear—whoever has the power to choose does the choosing. But that doesn't explain why one body of knowledge is crowned a department over another. What agenda is being advanced? Or perhaps more accurately, whose agenda? Answering that question would require looking across centuries to identify who gained from knowledge being prioritized, or slanted, a certain way.

And now that's she thinking about this, or more likely, overthinking, she sees so many oversights. Why a Department of History but not a Department of Sex? Sex has had way more influence on the trajectory of human civilization than history. Then again, maybe a history department is, by proxy, a sex department. And, my god, she thinks, why doesn't every University in the entire world have a Department of Death, given that denying or dealing with mortality in one form or another is the common denominator underlying pretty much every human impulse? Although, one could argue that's accounted for, to a degree, by a Department of

Religion, she supposes, and also the Department of Philosophy. But why be so contorted about it? Why not just a straight-up death department?

A bird, a finch maybe, lands on the pathway a few yards ahead, pecks at the lightly frosted earth and flies off.

Loretta wants to keep thinking about departments, about the ripple impact of this hierarchical way of choosing and categorizing and then blessing some knowledge, but time has run out. She has arrived at the building that houses religion. She watches her breath condensing in the chill of the afternoon and then pulls open the heavy wooden door and steps inside the stone building. The lobby is empty. A janitor's wide broom leans against the far wall. To the right, at the end of a short corridor, is an open door. A tall lanky man stands there, his features obscured by the brightness of the fluorescent halo emanating from behind.

"Dr. Orr?" she asks.

He steps forward and his celestial backlighting slips away.

"You found religion," he says, grinning at his joke.

Loretta follows the department chair into his office, a small space cluttered with papers, folders and books. He points to a plump purple easy chair; when she sits, dust flutters up. She asks and receives permission to record the interview and confirms he understands the purpose of their meeting.

"You are lucky," he says.

"How so?"

"Near death experiences are not something most academics care about. Generally, scholars categorize them as wishful thinking or pseudoscience, but they are tangential to my research on the intersection of religion and human consciousness."

Well, that's not even close to the direction Loretta assumed an interview with the religion chair would take, but maybe it would turn out to be a good thing.

"That is lucky," she says. "For me and *60 Minutes*."

Dr. Orr sits across from Loretta, nothing between them; their knees almost touching. A ruddy white man, he wears a vintage red and blue bowling shirt and Birkenstock sandals with striped athletic socks. He has a long, thin beard that reaches nearly to his chest, brown flecked with gray. She notices a few crumbs trapped in his beard. Peanuts? Popcorn? Toast?

"Are near death experiences a real thing?" she asks, deciding on the fly this will be the first question for all the departmental interviews.

"We would have to arrive at a common definition of reality for me to respond meaningfully, but for the sake of simplicity, I'll answer yes."

Definitely peanuts.

"What do they signify?" she asks. "For example, do you consider them proof of heaven?"

Loretta leans back to avoid the scent of his breath.

"There are books, bestsellers even, that suggest near-deathers have flown to heaven, bounced on God's knee and so on. But your question is, frankly, naïve, even for the *60 Minutes* audience."

She knows on some level his response should irritate her, and it might have in the recent past, her pre-zombie days, but Loretta doesn't feel the sting of his arrogance. Instead, she watches Dr. Orr stroke his scraggly beard curious if the motion will dislodge the peanut crumbs. It doesn't. She waits for him to talk, knowing he will eventually even without her prompt. Silence does not make Loretta uncomfortable the way it does most people, and that's not a zombie thing. She's always been that way.

"Let's see if I can frame this productively for us," he says after a minute or so, his tone now kinder. "People who have a near death experience generally describe common elements. A tunnel of light, a life review, out-of-body events, typically defaulting to an interpretation of these phenomena through the lens of the familiar symbols of their own religious tribe. Christians mention angels and the actions of a loving male deity, but a Buddhist will describe a journey into the Bardo and an ancient Swede would likely describe the great halls of Asgard."

Loretta says, "It makes sense that the experience would be colored by familiar icons."

He asks, "But does it? If this place where people go is real, why would it appear differently to people?" He uses his fingers to put air quotes around the word 'real.' His fingernails are raggedly chewed with a scab on the right thumb's cuticle. "Would this room you and I are sitting in this moment appear different to an old-god Swede, a Buddhist or a modern Christian? You can see the chicken and egg problem with this observation."

She checks to make sure the phone is still recording because she thinks this is important, even if she's not sure why and does not see a chicken or an egg problem.

"Would you elaborate on that point?"

"Is this something you think the producers will ask?"

"Producers?"

"Of *60 Minutes*," he says.

"*60 Minutes*, right, yes, of course. It's too soon to know, so I'm casting a wide net. They're in the early stages of concepting the story, looking for articulate camera-ready scholars with new ideas about near death experiences." Loretta pauses to let this lie settle around her. "You'll be great, lots of character. The camera loves that."

"Excellent, good to know," he says, straightening his collar and sitting up a bit taller. Three barely-there peanut crumbs come loose and fall onto his lap. He doesn't notice. Loretta wonders how often that happens to men with beards.

"You were talking about a chicken and egg?"

"Have you heard of cosmic consciousness?"

"No."

"As described by several scholars, including myself, it's the third and highest level of three types of consciousness.[3] The first is simple consciousness, what animals have to varying degrees. Self-consciousness, common to humans, like you, me, everyone, is the second type. The third is cosmic consciousness, the higher form, possessed by very few people across history, an evolved consciousness defined by profound mystical events. When in this mystical state, individuals with cosmic consciousness experience the world differently, uniquely, they sense and feel connections between all sentient life, what's often called a oneness with the universe. They touch the divine, as it were."

Dr. Orr stands and walks over to his desk, picks up a water bottle and takes a sip. She senses he is choosing his words carefully.

"Do you know the story of Saint Paul?" he asks.

"He was struck down by light or something and heard the voice of Jesus, or maybe it was God, on some rural road in Louisiana," Loretta says. "Wait, no. Sorry, I don't know where that came from. In some biblical place, and that light or voice gave him instructions to start a new religion." Why did she say Louisiana? Maybe because last week she started reading a vampire novel set in New Orleans?

He laughs. "Close enough, except for the Louisiana part," he says. "The important part is that during this revelation, Paul's perspective on the world shifted. Some believe this is because he experienced cosmic consciousness. And from that moment forward, Paul dedicated his life to spreading the word about what he experienced, describing it as a new religion."

"Was the light Paul experienced the same light at the end of the tunnel in a near death experience?" Loretta asks, hopefully.

"My suspicion is near death experiences are related to cosmic consciousness, a cousin, so to speak. Those who have a near death experience provide one strand of evidence of the steady evolution of humanity toward this higher state of cosmic consciousness, away from our current lower form. Most of these near-death people, not all, but most, speak of becoming one with the universe and lose their fear of death because they have seen something they interpret as a life beyond death. That something is the experience of cosmic consciousness."

"This seems like a jargon-filled academic way, no offense, of saying near death experiences *are* proof of heaven."

"Not quite. What I am asking you to consider are the origins and nature of the hypothesis of heaven itself."

Loretta struggles to understand the meaning of Professor Orr's words but before she can formulate a question, he asks one.

"Are you an atheist?"

"I don't believe one way or the other."

"Choosing not to believe is a belief."

She starts to say that's a bullshit statement because it isn't possible for anything to be an anti-choice, but instead Loretta checks once more that her phone is still recording.

"A not uncommon misunderstanding among non-believers, including many who work in this esteemed institution who have transferred their belief systems to the congregation of scientism—"

"The congregation of what?"

"Scientism. Individuals whose faith is in science."

Loretta likes this word, scientism; it feels fresh and important, even if she doesn't agree with what she thinks Dr. Orr is implying about science. While there is undoubtedly subjectivity involved in interpreting data, at the root of what counts for science, and scientific advancement, is a commitment to empirical evidence. She wants to ask him about this, but he barrels on.

"Some people think scientism is as bad, as blinding, as religious fundamentalism," he says. "But perhaps worse, I believe, is the core misunderstanding of scientists about religion."

After taking another bird-like sip of water, he puts the bottle down and paces the small office, arms locked behind his back at the elbows.

"This misunderstanding about religion, really, the disdain from contemporary scientists toward religion, shapes the questions asked, or more accurately, not asked, from a scientific standpoint, which is a shame because the persistent faith that humans have is curious. Within the scientific realm, this should be considered evidence. But evidence of what, you ask? That requires research. Why do humans believe in gods, and why do they believe in heaven? Why have various gods come and gone?"

"People need to believe in something. It gives life meaning, gives people a feeling that they can escape death," Loretta says. "Right?"

He stops pacing and stands in front of her, gazing down. He is tall and from her perspective, looms. The feeling of being a supplicant takes form as a reaction to their positions. Does he know he is being physically overbearing, and if so, does he care?

"A common belief but intellectually dissatisfying and illogical," he says. "Given what science has reasonably demonstrated about our world and, on the reverse side, has quite thoroughly refuted about creation stories and the like in the bible and other canonical sources, what rational person could continue to believe? Yet many do continue to believe."

"Okay, so why do humans continue to believe?" she

asks, hoping that at some point, with enough latitude, he will circle back to near death experiences, and this first departmental interview will not be the tangled waste it's shaping up to be.

He takes his seat, and they are again face to face, knee to knee, breath to peanut breath. She flutters a hand over her mouth, not wanting to breathe directly on him. Why is he so close?

"Here's my point. If you trace religions backward, and not only to Saint Paul, but all of them, you land on a mystical experience at their root that the founder or the disciple experienced, subsequently described in words that essentially mean the same thing, a sense of oneness with a great power. This is followed by the creation of stories and metaphors to capture what they experienced in that instant of cosmic consciousness to explain to us lesser mortals, those still stuck ignorantly, blissfully, tortuously, at the second consciousness level.

"God, heaven, eternal life, souls, the resurrection, the Holy Spirit and the love that is the bedrock of Christianity—and let's stick with Christianity because its symbols are culturally familiar—are metaphors for aspects of the cosmic consciousness that Jesus and certain acolytes, like Paul, experienced. These stories, in their original form, provide a guidebook, a blueprint, a trail of evidence, for the rest of us on how to achieve cosmic consciousness. They resonate on a deep human level because of their mystical origins, which is what allows unscrupulous types throughout history to distort their original meaning to satisfy earthly power and wealth dynamics."[4]

"You are saying religious stories that are discredited factually by science speak to people on a different level, in some sort of secret mystically coded language ..."

"That's going a bit far," he says.

"I'll try again. How about this? Insights from people experiencing cosmic consciousness are told in the language of stories, which reaches something in the believers, I don't know what you would call it ..."

"Soul is a reasonable placeholder," he says.

"Okay, soul. The stories reach their souls, and the soul as you're defining it is unreachable by the facts of science, but still responds to stories and their mystical wordings, which is why religion stays powerful. And what allows people to be brainwashed by people who understand this but are up to no good."

This is making an odd sort of sense to Loretta.

"That's correct but it's not the most important aspect of what I'm saying."

Loretta gets she's being quizzed. She sifts through his prior words. "You think the concept of heaven is a manifestation of something happening in the brains of the people across time who have experienced this higher state, cosmic consciousness, and they spread the knowledge about it through stories?"

"That's close. But it's premature to identify the source of the mystical experience," he says. "I suspect the brain may play a role, but whether as interpreter or creator remains to be seen."

Loretta looks at the ceiling, reacting to his words and escaping from the intensity of his eyes.

"A part of my research is to study occurrences of cosmic consciousness throughout history. The data so far suggest this phenomenon is increasing in frequency with statistically significant degree of acceleration in the twenty-first century, particularly in the reporting of near death experiences," he says.

The arrangement of water stains above, all the same shade of gray, reminds her of a map of the continents, but before they all migrated on their tectonic plates. What was that called? Panera? No, that's not right, that's the restaurant that serves soup in bread bowls. Pangaea, that's it. The stains look like the ancient supercontinent Pangaea. This makes her think about those poor women looking up at the photos on the ceiling of the fertility clinic patient rooms while they got the wrong sperm injected into their bodies.

"A punchy line for *60 Minutes* might be to start with the idea that the crucifixion and resurrection could represent a near death experience," Professor Orr says. "The light and the tunnel are fairly common elements in the way this event is pictured, especially in the visual art of the early era of Christianity."

She looks down from Pangaea, meeting his eyes. "This is very fascinating and gives me a great deal to consider. Thank you. Now, if you don't mind switching gears, what would you say about someone having multiple near death experiences without the specter of death?"

"I don't understand."

"That's one of the what-if scenarios the producers want to consider." She is surprised by how easy it is to tell the lie about *60 Minutes*.

He looks at her curiously, as if he might be deciding that she's not a believable person. His tone is tempered. "That's never been documented. Even people having more than one in a lifetime is extremely rare, although repetitive out-of-body experiences are less rare. That can occur as an escape from severe pain or emotional distress. It's an unexpected angle for *60 Minutes* to pursue."

"They are thorough at these network shows," she says. "So, let's say having these experiences weekly, or even daily, would be unusual? I'm asking so I can give the producers feedback."

He doesn't answer. He continues to look at her askance. She is unconcerned. Over her years in public relations, she has learned that the lure of media fame is powerful for scientists, especially the national-level kind of fame that *60 Minutes* offers. It's the reason she's using this cover story. He'll come around, he'll keep talking, they all do. Researchers correctly understand that celebrity is an increasingly important route to catch the eye of a billionaire looking for a pet project. And they need the money.

"It likely would signal something other than a strict near death experience, I venture," he says after a full minute passes. His eyes light up and he claps his hands together softly, and then holds them palm-to-palm, like in prayer. "We could speculate that such a person is a new point on the spectrum of our evolution toward cosmic consciousness. Maybe this person would be having something similar to, but in a different form, the mystical insights that started the religions of the past."

Jenny? A modern mystic. That would please her so much.

"It would help me if I sum up what you've said to be sure I understand," Loretta says. "And so that I can accurately share with the producers, of course."

"Yes, by all means, please, go right ahead," he says. "You know the saying, I'm sure, if you can't paraphrase something, you don't really understand it."

She nods. "Near death experiences are real, and may or may not be proof of heaven, but to understand if they are, one needs to first consider what heaven is."

"Correct so far."

"You suggest that heaven may be a representation, no, hold on, reflection is a better word, of a type of human consciousness, an advanced type, called cosmic consciousness that the people who start religions, you used the example of Saint Paul, experienced during a mystical event where they saw into a different form of reality."

"Not bad," he says, a hint of surprise in his voice. "You've been listening."

"What is that different form of reality?"

"This requires study. We would need to research, as a start, the commonalities across religions and mystical experiences. There is sadly precious little funding for this type of academic work although I hope to secure the attentions of private philanthropists interested in human consciousness. I can envision a link between this research and artificial intelligence efforts."

There it is. That siren call of *60 Minutes*. She finds it sad that brilliant scholars have to audition for scraps from billionaires. Oh well, this is not something she can solve except to do her part by delivering to as many scientists as possible their fifteen minutes of fame.

"And as part of that AI research, you'd also study near death experiences, because these people might be seeing into that different form of reality too?" she asks. "That one-with-the-universe thing."

"I believe so, yes," he says.

Loretta's phone vibrates. A text from the University media on-call staffer. *KGWN calling about medical error related to sperm. Do you know anything?*

Here we go, she thinks. The shit storm begins, just when this discussion with religion was getting weirdly relevant. Loretta stands. "I'm sorry, Professor, a media issue has come up. I need to cut this short. I've really enjoyed hearing your perspective. Thank you."

"I've enjoyed it as well," he says. "It's not often I get to talk about this work so openly and with a receptive audience. But we didn't get to LSD or monks."

She sits back down. "How can I walk away from that? Can you give me the elevator pitch?"

The story spills out, as if he is approaching the final minutes of a class, knowing the students are about to power down their laptops and race for the auditorium doors.

"Studies happening at Hopkins, Harvard, not here, not yet, in which LSD, or more accurately, psilocybin, do you know what that is, yes, of course you do, you're the right age, is given to religious leaders to stimulate mystical experiences, a recapitulation of the infamous

Good Friday experiments."

"And the monks?"

"I could spend hours talking about Buddhism.[5] To make a fascinating story too short, some monks can breach the mind-body barrier with intense meditation, reaching what they also call oneness with the universe. They are being studied by researchers."

"What kind of studies?"

"Neurological imaging with MRIs before and after. Their brain patterns are altered, extreme neural hyper-connection."

Loretta stands again and slips into her coat. "I'll need to learn more about that for sure."

"Come back anytime," he says, shaking her hand. "And, if you don't mind saying, who else is on your list for *60 Minutes*?"

Loretta hands him the Dean's list of departments. He scans it, assessing his competition. "Will all of these department chairs appear on the show? That seems a bit crowded."

"I'll know more after I talk with each."

"Be prepared to hear the story of Phineas Gage over and over from the bioscience-type departments, the Adam of materialism," he says. "It's their own origin story."

FIVE

Back in her office, Loretta stands at her desk, reads the message from the media on-call staffer again and then punches in the callback number, praying she will catch Jamie, the KGWN reporter, before she goes live. The worst possible start to Loretta's management of *The Case of the Misplaced Sperm* would be for a reporter to break it before Loretta has a chance to plant the University narrative, still unwritten but percolating, on the beachhead of public opinion.

Jamie picks up and jumps right in, not bothering to say hello. "I'm posting a promo to my story in an hour. Consider this a friendly warning, along with my formal request for comment."

"Exactly what story are you talking about?" Loretta asks, to be sure Jamie has really been tipped off. She learned that the hard way. Twice.

"Don't even. You know. The fertility clinic mix-up."

Jamie and Loretta met six years ago when Jamie joined the local Fox news channel as an on-air reporter after a three-year stint in a rural Arkansas market. Most of the time, Loretta and her team try to persuade Jamie to report on the good goings-on at the University— research breakthroughs, student honors, patient lives saved, therapy dogs (although dogs don't take much pitching; they always get the clicks) and football (which also doesn't take much persuasion). Jamie usually picks up their pitches. After so many years, they've settled into a routine of making each other's jobs a little easier by being collegial, even friendly. But things won't be friendly now. While this is only the latest of too-many-to-count public relations crises for Loretta, it's a career-making story for Jamie.

Loretta launches into what they both know from experience is a negotiation, one in which information is the currency, by asking Jamie to wait until morning for an official statement from the University before saying anything on social or broadcast about the situation.

"Situation? That's rich. Nice spin you're auditioning. Medical error seems more accurate," Jamie says. "Or multimillion-dollar lawsuit? 'Situation' sounds, I don't know, so sterile."

"How is it that you even know anything about this *situation*?" Loretta asks.

Jamie says, "Confidential."

Loretta again asks her to wait until morning for the statement, which she admits is not ready yet, but could Jamie please do her a favor this one time. Jamie refuses, knowing she has all the leverage. "I'll say the University has no comment at this time. That's my favor. Tell you what, I'll go ahead and say you couldn't be reached for comment. That's nicer, right?"

"How about I share the official University media statement with you two hours before any other reporter gets it and before we post it on our website. You'll break the story."

"When?"

"By noon tomorrow."

"Well, now, this has been a revealing conversation. You're clearly worried. You never give exclusives. Fine. You have until noon."

They disconnect.

Loretta isn't worried, she is never worried, but some "situations" take more energy than others. This is one of them and she's short on energy. Also time. The deal with Jamie bought her some time though. She has a little less than nineteen hours to write the statement, get it approved by the University higher-ups, and get some sleep. And of course, there's Jenny and her near death experiences, which is her number one priority.

For the next hour, Loretta listens to the playback from the interview with Professor Orr and covers four pages of the notebook in a messy, cursive scribble. As she is writing out the last bit and thinking through the different threads Dr. Orr presented, she is startled by a booming "hello" and swivels at the sound of the Dean's voice behind her.

"Loretta, didn't mean to surprise you, but here's someone I want you to meet," he says. "Cyrus Thrush, our new director of the Division of Evolution."

"Division?"

"If Cyrus can attract a healthy philanthropic gift, maybe we'll turn it into a full-fledged department," he says, clapping Cyrus on the back. "Cyrus, meet Loretta Sparkman, our public relations director extraordinaire."

Loretta flashes on her earlier thoughts about how a body of knowledge becomes a department. Is that how it works these days? A fat-cat wealthy donor prioritizes the knowledge, supports its accumulation and slaps their name on a department. Or institute. Or school. Well, I'm being naïve, she thinks. It's probably always worked that way, but what constituted wealth—or power—has shifted over the decades and centuries. Once it was the clergy or a monarch or enlightenment-age titled families who defined acceptable knowledge categories. Later it was the self-appointed academic aristocracy. Today, a tech wizard or pharmaceutical executive or oil magnate or some other obscenely rich oligarch makes the call.

Cyrus Thrush is young, by academic standards, white with red hair and freckled skin that makes her think of the soft underside of a deer. Loretta shakes his hand and when he says hello, she hears a faint accent, maybe Irish. Or Scottish. Could be British, some specific neighborhood in England. Maybe it's where the Beatles came from, Liverpool. Who knows? It's impossible to tell all those accents apart. Half of them she can't even understand.

"Cyrus may have insight into your research on near death experiences," the Dean says, turning and walking back toward his own office. His assistant trails behind him with a stack of papers to sign.

"That was awkward," Dr. Thrush says. "I like how he dumped me on you."

"He has a way about him," she says.

"An intimidating way."

"Confidence blended with persistent distraction," she says. "Dr. Thrush, or perhaps you prefer Professor Thrush?"

"Either is fine," he says.

"Dr. Thrush, it's late and we don't need to talk now. I'll make an appointment—"

"Happy to chat," he says, dropping into the spare orange chair in her small office. "I've got nowhere to go. I've not been assigned an office yet." He looks around as if coveting her space.

Loretta tells the lie about *60 Minutes*, careful to mention that the Dean knows nothing about it, no reason to bother him, stuff like this is below his level, she says. "So, how about I ask you some questions like a reporter and you can answer them? For practice, so I can see how you'll do."

"Fire away," he says.

She flips to a clean page in the near death notebook, picks up a green pen and writes *Division of Evolution*, underlining it twice. She wonders why evolution is not already at the department level, given how long the theory has been around. Perhaps because everything, every piece of knowledge, including religion, would be subsumed beneath it, a full reorganization of the taxonomy of human thought. That would take a lot of money. Maybe there's not enough money in the world for that intellectual overhaul, or maybe the people who have the money don't believe in evolution. Or don't care for its implications.

"Are near death experiences real?" she asks.

"I've never had one so I can't say personally, but sure, why not?"

"What does a near death experience signify?"

"It's an interesting question and I'm not sure that the evolutionary paradigm has an easy answer. But let me try," he says. "Wait, that's not a good opening, is it?"

Loretta shakes her head.

"Reverse tape." He twirls his finger. "Commencing again," he says, sinking his voice into a melodramatic tone. "Evolution can explain everything, even near death experiences. Just ask this one question. How does it, whatever 'it' is, help make babies? This is the lens through which modern scholars view human history, the clever ones at least, by evaluating if this attribute or that development moves genes more efficaciously into the next generation. If it helps make babies or extends reproductive life and the concurrent potential to make future babies, it survives. If it hinders baby-making, it gets left behind or otherwise rendered irrelevant."

"It's hard to see how a near death experience would be influential in reproduction," Loretta says.

"Quite right. But consider this one word: free riders.

Pardon, that's two words." He smiles broadly, crooked teeth surrounded by crusty sun-chapped lips, like maybe he's been skiing recently. "There are free-rider genes acting on the forces of evolution, things we don't understand that have persisted through eons and have no ready explanation."

"Male nipples."

He smiles again. "Everyone uses that example, and for good reason. And evolution does in fact provide an explanation for the infamous male nipple conundrum. In an embryonic state before genders differentiate, awash in a heady mix of testosterone and progesterone, less developmental energy is needed to create nipples in both genders and then leave them useless in boys than it is to create those nubby little devils uniquely in girls after gender differentiation."

"Evolution conveniently explains everything."

"Does that make you suspicious?"

"A little."

"Nothing wrong with that. Suspicion is the flip side of curiosity. All knowledge is, to a degree, provisional. But here's a better example of what I mean by free riders. Why does schizophrenia exist? Why hasn't it been weaned out of the gene pool? These men and women are not prime partners for reproduction and often die young. Yet, it has not disappeared. What does this tell us?"

"You're good," Loretta says, thinking that while he's a tad long-winded, he is better than most. "You've done media training, I can tell."

"Media training by dumpster fire," he says. "Worst, most humiliating experience of my life."

Loretta scribbles a margin note to search his name later to find out what debacle got him. It's probably funny. Dr. Thrush clears his throat and then balls up his fingers beneath his chin, like Rodin's *The Thinker*, pretending to be on camera. She's holding back a laugh, and it's obvious that pleases him, he beams a little. Loretta wonders if he's flirting with her. It's been a long time since anyone flirted with her. She isn't sure she would recognize flirting anymore. Or has she forgotten how to pick up on it? Do zombies "get" flirting?

She refocuses on their free-rider discussion. He asks, "Could certain genes, or attributes, be protected for some reason becoming permanently part of the human genome or biome or connectome or whatever-ome? And could these protected genes continue to be passed along generation after generation because they play an important role in evolution that we have yet to identify?"

"Meaning free riders help make babies in ways we don't yet understand," she says.

"Reproduction but considered at a larger meta-scale, the survival of the species rather than the individual."

Loretta thinks about Professor Orr and his cosmic consciousness. Could cosmic consciousness, if it exists, stem from a protected free-rider gene? "If free-rider genes are acting on troubled brains, like those suffering from schizophrenia, if they cause these people to see the world in a different way—"

"Well done," he interrupts. "That's precisely where I was headed. Perhaps these afflicted men and women are seeing something about reality that is impenetrable to the rest of us but essential in some way for our collective survival. Consider how a schizophrenic vision could, from time to time, cause people to split from their tribes and pull away with a few stragglers to form new tribes, and then someone in that new tribe goes on to discover, I don't know, fire or tools or a cure for cancer, whatever.[6] Wouldn't this suggest schizophrenic voices and visions play an undiscovered but beneficial role in evolution, at that meta-scale, thus explaining why they have survived?"

"How would you ever prove that?"

"A great deal of time and money would be required for the requisite data generation," he says.

"Along with a lot of schizophrenics," she says.

"Indeed."

"Are you telling me a near death experience and schizophrenia are the same?"

"An argument can be made that they fall into the same categorical consideration, meaning expressions of genetic free riders of indeterminate purpose," he says. "But there's another, easier explanation and we always prefer the easiest explanation. Occam's razor and all."

"Would you mind explaining Occam's razor?" Loretta knows what it means, but for the sake of inquiry, and Jenny, she wants to understand how Dr. Thrush is applying this concept.

"Occam's razor. Cut and flay, as one might do with a razor, until you hit bone. To put it in scientific terms, the simplest, most elegant theory, the most plainly beautiful, is more likely to be a truer representation of reality than a bloated, contorted theory with lots of steps."

A subjective decision about beauty doesn't sound particularly scientific to Loretta, but who is she to judge. She prefers the first description and asks, "What's a theory in which near death experiences are cut and flayed to the bone?"

"Our personality, our elusive sense of self, dissolves at death, and the heaven-like hallucinations of a near death experience have evolved to ease the trauma of biological extermination, so we don't resist. Or resist less. And therefore suffer less."

"Biological extermination. You mean death?"

"Yes, of course. Death."

"How would easing the passage to death help in reproduction?" Loretta asks.

He shrugs. "Beats me. But the evolutionary model gives us guardrails to parse out these types of questions.

Although now that I'm thinking on this, I can come up with a simpler explanation for near death experiences," he says.

"I'm all ears," she says. Before she is aware of her actions, Loretta is smoothing her hair down around both ears, giving them maximum exposure.

"Forget about easing any suffering. The biological shutdown produces random and utterly purposeless hallucinations. But no matter if the hallucinations are random or purposeful, the people coming back from the brink of death, after they regain their sense of a self, they ascribe meaning to the hallucinations, as humans are wont to do."

That is simple, she thinks, but it doesn't answer the question of why not all people who return from death report having one. Doubtful this young evolutionist will be able to address this point, Loretta instead decides to push on the question of self.

"What's the purpose of the sense of self from an evolutionary standpoint? Animals reproduce but they don't have selves, as far as we know," she asks.

"The jury is out on your excellent question, but scholars across multiple disciplines are beginning to coalesce around the idea that the self develops as a means to facilitate collaboration, which in turn—"

"Allows for better reproduction," Loretta says.

His eyes sparkle. "Bingo!"

"Maybe a self isn't needed anymore for people past the age of reproduction. At least for women."

"A post-menopausal woman would presumably not need a self from a strictly evolutionary standpoint. But, if that theory holds, it's likely the self would linger because its deconstruction is not a good use of biological energy, like male nipples in reverse."

Loretta finds it amusing for her reproductive status to be compared to male nipples, but doesn't let it show. Instead, she says, "Assuming the self does linger." The evolutionist looks puzzled. She moves on. "Is there a difference between self and human consciousness?"

"Same thing, more or less. What we call the 'self' is that which experiences consciousness, and vice versa. And getting back to that concept of free riders, here's an interesting little fact. Schizophrenics appear to have no bedrock sense of self, no version of what we refer to as identity, no 'I.' Why is that?"

"I presume you'll tell me," Loretta says.

"Since you asked so nicely," he says, with a lopsided grin. "Perhaps the absence or presence of self are polar positions of identity on a spectrum of selves that shifts throughout our lives, in a way similar to what we are discovering about gender identity."

"Meaning there's no core, unchanging self?"

"I wouldn't go quite that far, not yet. But maybe the idea of a unifying self, a rigid defining personality that persists eternally, is a story we tell ourselves to feel like we have control over our lives, to—"

"Make more babies," she says.

He smiles broadly. "You get me."

"I wonder what would happen to society, culture, the world, if we embraced the idea of a fluctuating self?"

"Anarchy!" he says, and winks. He winks. At her. And then looks down at his watch. "Oh, bloody hell, I've got to jet. I have an appointment at an apartment I want to rent. Housing in this town is hellish. To be continued, maybe over coffee?"

Sure, maybe, she says, thanking him for his time as he walks out. She turns back to the notebook about Jenny's near death experiences, wanting to record the main points of this impromptu interview. She looks up when Professor Thrush pokes his head back through her office door a few seconds later.

"I forgot to ask, how did I do? Think you'll be able to get me a slot on *60 Minutes*?"

"You did great. It looks like you learned a lot from whatever trial by fire scorched you. I'll let you know about the show."

He gives her two thumbs-up and leaves again.

Loretta starts writing. The evolutionary framework, she scribbles, offers three scenarios.

First, a near death experience is a free-rider, possibly protecting some big-picture but as-yet mysterious aspect of species survival. This presents a dead stop in terms of explaining what's happening to Jenny, even though it opens up the possibility of filling that void with any story she likes. Because as far as she can tell, categorizing something as a free-rider is a way of saying evolution can't provide an explanation yet, so go on and fill in the blank with whatever fits your immediate need.

Second, a near death experience could be nature's way of easing the terror a person feels while actively dying. This makes intuitive sense but connecting it to reproduction is a stretch, and the bigger strike against it is that evolution isn't a thing that cares, it's not an empathetic force being applied at the instant of biological extermination (and why didn't he just say death)?

Third, a near death experience is simply part of what happens during the biological shutdown of the body as it dies, and even though she thinks this explanation makes a certain sense, it still doesn't answer the core question: Why doesn't everyone who comes back from death report one?

She closes the notebook and shuts off the light in her office. Sitting in the dark, she thinks back to the question about what might happen if we all embraced the idea of a fluctuating self. The professor thought it would lead to anarchy. She's not so sure. Giving up the idea of a time-resistant and impermeable self would require that we also give up, or loosen our attachment to, the concept of individuality. She thinks that might not be so bad. Maybe, at least in the American story, there would be more "we" and less "I."

A janitor knocks on the door, an older Black man, thin and tall, with a close cut beard. "Okay to grab the trash now?"

"Sure thing," Loretta says, "and thanks."

A few minutes later, when she walks by the Dean's office, she sees through his open door that he's still at his desk, head down, reading. She says goodnight. He waves without looking up or speaking. Outside, it's almost dark and the upper campus is quiet; faculty, students and staff have mostly gone home for the day.

She stops to look at three crows doing barrel rolls in the air above the University library. As she watches their twilight playfulness, Loretta abruptly becomes aware of her awareness, as a thing, an entity that exists. She ponders the fact that her mind is thinking about her mind watching the crows, even as she doesn't know who—or what—is doing the thinking, and then she gets caught inside that thought, circling and barrel-rolling like the birds, as observer and observed collapse into each other, over and over, back and forth, and for an instant, she slips into infinity.

SIX

Loretta dumps her overstuffed shoulder bag onto the hallway bench and peels off her black puff jacket. Jenny is sitting at the kitchen counter, elbows propped up, chin in her hands, wearing faded jeans and one of Matthias's plaid flannel shirts, swimming in its size like an elfin lumberjack. Matthias stands next to the stove, stirring a pot; he holds out a spoon for Loretta to taste.

"Delicious, as always," Loretta says. "Are you playing with the recipe?"

"No, why?"

"Tastes a little more peppery than usual."

"Is it okay?"

"More than okay," she says.

He wipes his hands on the apron, leaving a smear of blood-red marinara sauce, and pours Loretta a glass of white wine. Loretta sits on the stool next to Jenny; both watch as Matthias drops pasta into the boiling water.

"How was your day?" Jenny asks.

"Nuts," Loretta says, staring at the rolling steam. "And you?"

"Matthias told you, right?"

"He did. How are you feeling?"

"I'm usually alone when it happens."

"Was it better to be with someone?"

"Yes."

"You're not alone now. We're going to help you. But I have to ask you something first. Please don't get mad."

"I won't, I promise."

Loretta thinks about how to phrase the question that's been floating through her mind ever since Dr. Orr mentioned psilocybin. She decides to be direct.

"Have you been using drugs, legal or otherwise?"

"No. Absolutely not. I haven't done anything like that since our wild days," Jenny says.

"Wild days?" Matthias asks.

"I've told you about that," Loretta says.

"Um, I don't think so."

Loretta persists. "Nothing at all? I'm about to go out on a limb here with my job. I'm willing to help, more than willing, but it will be hard if I'm sharing wrong information. It counts if the mind-altering substances are *natural*." She makes air quotes around the word. "No Carlos Castaneda kind of questing?"

"Especially not him. He's been discredited. Well, not completely, but most people don't think Castaneda studied under Don Juan at all."

"That must have been disappointing for you."

"For a few minutes."

Steam swirls into a vortex from the boiling pasta water. Loretta refills her wine glass and sips. Jenny adds a teaspoon of sugar to her mug of tea and stirs. The spoon clinks against the edge of the ceramic as she circles the cup. Matthias interrupts the quiet.

"Come on, if you're not going to spill the beans about your wild, misspent youth, at least tell us about your wild, misspent day."

Loretta gives them a broad-strokes overview of *The*

Case of the Misplaced Sperm, keeping the identity of the sperm donor confidential but, relaxed from the wine, she succumbs to the temptation to embellish enough of the salacious details to entertain them.

Later, over dinner, Loretta tells them about the conversation with the Dean and her plan to interview the department chairs, explaining how if all goes well, it should provide Jenny with enough information to make an informed decision about next steps. Loretta leafs through the notebook so far, paraphrasing what she's learned, reading choice quotes and describing Dr. Orr's ideas on cosmic consciousness as the mystical basis of all religions as well as the interview with the Irish evolutionist, who isn't a department chair but for the purposes of the notebook she plans to treat as such.

"I like how you've titled the notebook *The 23 Near Death Experiences of Jenny Black,*" Jenny says. "But what will you do if I have another one?"

"Change the title," Loretta says.

Matthias uncorks a second bottle of wine and tops off Loretta's glass. "Jenny, maybe you'll start a brand new religion. The Jen-tecostals."

"More likely I'm expressing a weird schizophrenia."

"You don't need to worry about that. Schizophrenia affects people when they're young. You're too old," Loretta says.

"That's comforting," Jenny says. "In a depressing sort of way."

"Let's stick to my prediction," Matthias says, waving away the discussion about schizophrenia. "And to clarify, religion might be the wrong word, spiritual is better. I know I'm stating the obvious, but people are turning away from mainstream religion, from the community-building role of churches, but they still long for a place to belong, to be seen, a community, a new kind of church ..."

Loretta holds up her hand to stop him from talking,

"Matthias, please. What's happening in this country relative to churches and religion illustrates pretty much exactly what Dr. Orr was saying, that leaders bending them for earthly agendas distort the mystical origin stories. These people don't care about godly principles or values. They care about power for their tribe, the primacy of their beliefs and a justification for their greed."

"There is more to religion than those people," Jenny says, at a near whisper. "You weren't raised with God, I was, and while I don't follow anymore, I know the comfort it can bring, the sense of purpose."

"Yes, I understand that, but it's the political religious types who make noise these days," Loretta says. "And pray to god, no pun intended, after the presidential election next year, we won't have to suffer through all the hypocrisy anymore."

"The time is right for a new story for humanity, not just for America but for everyone," Matthias says. "A story that values our differences, a story that atones for the past without crippling the future. Why don't you help frame that story?"

"You must have been drinking before I got home. A lot," Loretta says.

"How about kindness?" Jenny suggests. "Maybe that's the basis of a new religion, or story, or whatever. Maybe we don't even call it religion."

"That's not the same," Matthias says, slugging back the last of the second bottle of wine. "Kindness isn't a story about who we are or what we believe, it's a behavior. What people want is to belong to something, to be part of a story that defines us and inspires us." He turns to his wife. "Come on, Loretta. Go for it."

"My attention is about to be necessarily focused on another kind of story, one much less grand and that I get paid to do, and in this case, it's a story explaining a sticky situation."

Matthias laughs, and it comes out as a snort with a little wine spit. Loretta stands, grabs her laptop and, after apologizing for cutting their evening short, climbs the coffee-stained carpeted stairs alone.

Spreading out on the unmade bed, she stares at the screen coming to life. She yawns. She is a little drunk, and a little drunk is a good place to be for this kind of pseudo-creative work. She reaches for a months-old unread *New Yorker* magazine, flips through it and tosses it on the floor. She stares at the ceiling, tugs on the quilt, rearranges the pillows. She puts her fingers on the laptop keyboard and types out *The Case of the Misplaced Sperm*. Nothing. Dammit. She checks her phone for messages. She checks her phone for news. She checks Twitter. She stands and makes the bed then sits back down on top of the blankets and stares at the screen.

And then it happens. Loretta has never understood this small miracle of creation—when words drop out of nothingness—and in these moments, sometimes, wonders if she's a conduit, like those old-time tent revivalists, channeling public relations messages instead of speaking in spirit-tongues, transcribing rather than shouting, but she only wonders this after the fact, never in the moment when she is consumed.

She pounds at the keyboard without pausing for twenty minutes straight. Then she reads the draft media statement out loud in the empty room. She smiles at that recognizable sense of rightness when something she has written is exceptionally good, even if it's only a little story in which misplaced sperm is the main character.

Satisfied, she punches a number in her phone, trying for the third time to reach the misplacing sperm doctor who appears to be avoiding her calls. A gravelly old-man voice invites her to leave a message.

"This is Loretta Sparkman from University public relations. We need to talk, urgently. Ten minutes, I'll call back in ten minutes," she says, her tone sounding more imperial than she intends, but whatever it takes.

Loretta uses the time to look up information about the Good Friday experiments Dr. Orr mentioned earlier today. Out of hundreds of hits, she picks an academic article[7] describing the experiment conducted in 1962 on, of course, Good Friday.

Walter Pahnke, a doctor and minister, gave small capsules to 12 advanced divinity students at Harvard. Half contained psilocybin, an extract of psychoactive mushrooms, and the other half was a placebo. Nobody knew who got what, making it a classic double-blind experiment, the gold standard of research. "Thus began the most scientific experiment in the literature designed to investigate the potential of psychedelic drugs to facilitate mystical experiences." She is surprised to learn that Timothy Leary was Pahnke's academic advisor at Harvard. "There are no experiments known to me in the history of scientific study better designed or clearer in their conclusions than this one..."[8] She reads farther down the paper, realizing it's a summary of follow-up interviews with the divinity students who took the original psilocybin, from twenty years later in the 1980s. Several of the participants, even after all that time, vividly recalled their experience.

"It left me with a completely unquestioned certainty that there is an environment bigger than the one I am conscious of."

"All of a sudden I felt like I was drawn out into infinity, a blending, the main thing about it was this sense of timelessness."

"The inner awareness and feelings I had during the drug experience were the dropping away of the external world...a sudden sense of singleness, oneness, this inner core of oneness was more authentic than normal consciousness..."

She thinks back to her discussion with Dr. Orr, wondering now if the psilocybin was responsible for opening a pathway into this oneness-place or if the drugs created an illusion of a oneness-place. How could anyone ever prove the difference?

Her phone vibrates. "Loretta Sparkman here."

"Elizabeth Stork here," the caller says. Aptly named, Professor Stork is the chair of the Department of Obstetrics and Gynecology, and the boss of the faculty physician who misplaced the sperm.

"Dr. Stork, I wasn't expecting to hear from you. Has something new happened?"

"I wish the circumstances were different, Loretta. But we need to talk."

Loretta finds it curious how often University faculty members call her by her first name without asking, even as she addresses them by a formal title. She hears in these interactions the echo of a foundational narrative of hierarchy and superiority, which is now collapsing into dust around these scholars, and they can't see it. Or maybe they do see it and still believe they'll dodge the bullet of change, as they have across centuries.

"I am waiting to hear back from Dr. Walker. I have a few questions for him before we finalize our media strategy," Loretta says.

"He texted me that you called. I'm returning the call on his behalf. I've sent him on a short vacation. Dr. Walker is devastated by this turn of events, as you can imagine. He needs green tea, yoga and meditation."

A vacation from the fact that he's responsible for a potentially multimillion-dollar sperm insertion fuckup? Sounds more like a reward, she thinks. "Will you be the spokesperson in his absence?" she asks, her voice flat.

"We will look to you for guidance."

"My guidance would be not to send the main actor out of town. It looks like we have something to hide."

"Trust me when I say his interaction with the media

would not work in our favor."

"Fine," Loretta says, knowing there's little to be gained by pushing this point and that Dr. Stork may be right. In any case, the low-vision, aging, wrong-sperm-injecting doctor is not coming back from vacation on her command. She has a crisis to manage, she needs to stay focused. "Do you know if he has a social media presence?"

"Not unless his grandchildren help him log into Facebook."

Well, that makes things a little easier, Loretta thinks. Nothing on social means nothing controversial to add fuel to this fire. She moves on. "I need to be sure nothing else pops up, no surprises. Let's rough out the details and the timeline so we are all on the same page."

Dr. Stork runs through the timeline as Loretta builds an alignment document to share with the University public relations team. Loretta confirms that only a small circle—Dr. Stork, the physician, the University general counsel, the patient advocate, and now Loretta and Mona—know a child was born. "And the mother, of course," Dr. Stork adds.

"Let's do our best to keep this knowledge circle small." Loretta reads the media statement she has just written to Dr. Stork.

"That's a new direction for the University."

"It's the only play we have," Loretta says.

"It will be interesting to hear Legal's perspective on this approach." And then Dr. Stork says she has to go now, and disconnects. Abruptly, in Loretta's view. Oh well. It doesn't make any difference.

Loretta plows into writing the step-by-step crisis communications plan. The evening grinds into the past and she leaves the bedroom only long enough to say goodnight to Jenny. Later, Loretta clears the bed of papers and her laptop, and does a final check of emails while Matthias brushes his teeth.

"Did you get it all worked out?" he asks, coming into the bedroom.

She nods. He sits on the edge of the bed and she runs her hand over his scalp, forehead to back; his head is mostly smooth, with a few bumps and a concave area about the size of a half-dollar on top, along with a bony ridge rimming his right ear. When he had hair, she never noticed these details, of course.

"Wonder why it never came back," she asks.

"Probably mortally offended that I shaved it," he says. "But let's discuss my cue ball another day."

The bedroom is overheated—the furnace is acting up again. They undress and stretch out on top of the sheets, the crisp cotton cool against their skin.

"Your wild days," he says.

"I'm one hundred percent sure I told you this."

"I wouldn't have forgotten."

"It was a long time ago, we were fifteen. We tried acid—"

"You and Jenny were dropping acid at fifteen?"

"It was the eighties. People did stuff like that."

"Fifteen-year old people? Wait, never mind. At this point, that is irrelevant. Tell me, what was it like?"

"I remember time standing still, completely still, and I loved that when I moved my finger, or any part of my body, there were trails, so many versions, replicas, of my finger emanating from my real finger, like there was an infinity of universes inside my hand. I spent almost the entire time, a few hours, watching my hand as I wiggled and waved my fingers, but there was no lasting impact. I napped after and went to school the next day, like any other day."

"And Jenny?"

"Her most intense moments were floating around in space, untethered, like a stranded astronaut."

"That sounds awful."

The room is too hot now. Loretta gets out of bed to

crack open a window. They listen to two people outside arguing, a man and woman, something about getting a job and flirting with her sister. Loretta turns on a fan sitting on top of the dresser to block the noise. When she lies back down, she curls onto her side and tucks her head into the curve between his head and shoulder. A dog barks, the sound amplified by their stillness. A door slams. The arguing couple goes silent.

"Was there anything from today you kept back?" Matthias asks.

"No, not really, but you were right—"

"Wait, did I hear you correctly, you said I was right? Ouch, stop pinching me."

"You were right that looking into Jenny's near death experiences might help, what was it you said, fill up my zombie brain? Everything felt new, and a little exciting even though the core mystery is still there."

"Who it felt new to?"

"Right," she says.

"It's a start, I suppose."

"Remember, I'm not worried about this, and you shouldn't be either."

"I didn't say I was worried."

Loretta listens to his breathing, which is deep and slow tonight; ever since the diagnosis, she is attentive to his breathing patterns. Deep and slow generally means he is feeling well, or well enough. She relaxes.

"How about answering my other question. Was there anything from the interviews I should know?"

"The Irish-sounding evolutionist said the sense of self might not be firm, that maybe it's always in flux."

"I see how you might find that intriguing, maybe even comforting, in your current state."

"Have you heard of Occam's razor?" she asks.

"The idea that the simplest theory is the right one." He coughs and untangles himself from Loretta's arms long enough to take a sip from the cup of day-old chamomile tea on the bedside table.

"Isn't it weird to think the whole of science assumes simplicity is a core attribute of reality?" Loretta asks, slipping a leg between his bare thighs. "It feels like a form of, I don't know, bias. Like the opposite of what science is supposed to be."

"To me it makes sense because the principle of simplicity is at play in nature. Think about how water flows, following the path of least resistance."

"That's a superficial observation. You don't know that whatever makes up the flow is simple. A car looks sleek on the outside but the engine beneath is anything but. Occam's razor would never let anyone figure out what lies beneath a Buick."

"To take your example, a theory of the Buick would start with the simple and build up, like recognizing flammable things release energy, which in turn drives pistons. A car is built on a series of simple assumptions that culminate in the theory of a combustion engine."

"But you're coming at it from the inside. What if all you can see is the outside of the Buick?"

"Buicks don't exist in nature," he says, yawning. "This is pretty smart stuff. I thought zombies didn't have brains."

She smiles in the darkness; the conversation falls off. They slip into their decades-old sleeping positions, back to back, on their sides. Loretta sleeps heavily and does not dream. But at some time in the middle of the night, or even later, when dawn is closer than not, she wakes up, her head scrambled with unconnected thoughts— mystical religions, the backyard birdfeeder, what to wear to work the next day, near death experiences, how frequently Dr. Orr washes his beard.

The confetti word-parade ricochets around her mind. Not wanting to wake Matthias, Loretta doesn't move for what feels like hours but might just be a few minutes. Finally, she gives in to the insomnia and gets up. She pads into Jenny's room and stands over her, envying the peaceful sleep, the steady undulation of life washing across her face every few seconds like a baby.

Loretta's heart speeds up a notch and her mind goes into the past. She remembers when, as a new parent, she obsessed over the idea of bearing witness to the instant baby Sally-Anne recognized her own face. She can't remember why she was so focused on this, nor what she was trying to learn. Multiple times a day, Loretta held Sally-Anne up to her reflection: a hand mirror as she nursed, her tiny breaths slightly fogging the glass; after her bath, swaddled tight, pausing in front of the mirror over the sink; in front of a store pane in the bright noonday sun, Loretta scrutinizing Sally-Anne's reaction.

But there was never a single instant when Sally-Anne woke to her own image with a gleeful gurgle, pointing at the mirror as Loretta expected, or hoped. Instead, one day Sally-Anne's gaze lingered a little longer, she pulled on her tiny ponytail, turned her head to look at the orange toothbrush on the sink and then fixed her eyes on the ring on Loretta's left hand—curious about her own face but also newly intrigued by everything in her field of senses. It was as if the moment Sally-Anne realized who she was, when the glimmers of self materialized, she also brought the world around her into being.

Loretta looks down at Jenny and feels a flash of despair at the emptiness clutching her insides, and it doesn't feel like she's a zombie or anything so clever, it just feels dark and deep and hollow. Just then, Jenny opens her eyes. She smiles, and then reaches out to pulls Loretta into the bed and under the quilt.

Lying there next to Jenny, Loretta's heart slows into the unencumbered rhythm of their childhood, and together they slip beneath the surface into the quiet sea of sleep.

SEVEN

The public relations conference room is filled elbow to elbow: the general counsel, a representative from risk management, the patient advocate, the fertility clinic administrator, five staffers from the communications team. And long-lashed Mona, of course. The room is packed with morning smells—coffee, fresh deodorant, breath mints that aren't up to the job, possibly an egg sandwich—all marinating in the swirl of the century-old building's erratic heating.

Mona tilts her head slightly, signaling for Loretta to start the meeting. Loretta passes out copies of the draft media statement. "We will apologize, we will say we're sorry. That's our lead."

Loretta has determined that *The Case of the Misplaced Sperm* is a story of redemption, a journey to forgiveness in which the hero recognizes that absolution can only be conditioned on humble self-sacrifice and a renewed commitment to protect those upon whom they have inflicted damage. She sees it as a cross between the motifs of Jean Valjean and Han Solo. Sort of.

Loretta leans back to watch. The short statement won't take long to read. A few heads bob. No startled glances, no sour faces. The risk management staffer pulls out a pen and makes an edit (the intentional spelling error Loretta slipped in because so many people need to make edits). Finally, Antoinette, the general counsel, slides her glasses off and sets them on the table.

"I appreciate what is obviously a great deal of hard work and consideration that went into this," she says.

And a great deal of wine, Loretta thinks.

Antoinette is somewhere in her fifties. A white woman with silver shoulder-length hair, she's tall and thin with yoga-defined arms, the type of woman who looks glamorous in a slinky black sleeveless gown dancing across a buffed-up ballroom floor; at least Loretta imagines it in this way—she has never actually seen Antoinette in a formal dress. Her professional voice is soft and emotionless, like a motorized purr, and her smile is always a few beats behind her words, creating a gap of anxiety as people wait to find out which direction her lips are headed.

Loretta and Antoinette have worked together for five years and like each other well enough, although their professional roles don't overlap enough for acting on that impulse. But it doesn't really matter because Loretta's life doesn't leave time for friendship with attorneys or anyone other than public relations types, who are the only ones who can appreciate the mental exhaustion that comes with this territory.

A few years into her job, after Loretta was promoted to her current position, Matthias developed a rubric to evaluate each day: Was it a whiplash kind of day? After realizing her answer was yes 98 percent of the time, he developed a ranking scale: How *many* whiplashes on a scale of one to ten? Usually it's about five or six, but on her very worst day two years ago, she hit eleven.

A faculty member was accused of sexual misconduct and someone leaked it to the media, and then she learned *Nature* would be announcing a retraction the next day of an article from one of their research labs due to plagiarism while she was in the middle of fast-tracking the creation of an emergency communications plan for a possible federal government shutdown slash pissing match that would halt the flow of student loans, research grants and who knew what other funding, upending thousands of lives. At the end of that already awful day, she was called into a meeting to advise on how to inform the campus community a student had thrown himself off a highway overpass the night before. What does the family want us to do, she asked while holding back tears.

But it wasn't all bad, she told Matthias that night. The University student council was busily organizing a resume-writing clinic for homeless vets and the Dean won a new award, but she couldn't remember what for even though she had written his acceptance speech that morning. So, it netted out to a nine-whiplash day. Matthias fixed her a double gin martini. Then another. She went to bed at eight o'clock.

"I remind us all we are facing, among other things, a negligence lawsuit," Antoinette says.

Loretta watches Antoinette's eyes, the pupils slightly dilated, and sifts through her flat tone; it doesn't contain any tinges of 'I'm about to destroy your day.' This combined with Antoinette not making any edits on the statement bolsters Loretta's confidence that the lawyer can be persuaded.

"Are we denying the event occurred?" Loretta asks, careful not to call it an error.

"I'm not at liberty to discuss our legal strategy," Antoinette answers. "Nevertheless, please explain why you conclude that the University publicly saying 'we are sorry' is a good media strategy."

"This approach puts us on the moral high ground, aligns us with the aggrieved patients and, under cover of our goal to protect them, is a clean rationale for never providing specific details. No who, what, when, or how, only the where."

"It's the only play," Mona adds. "Unless, as Loretta asked, we intend to deny the event."

"What happens after we issue this statement?"

"That's it. Like the statement says. We won't comment again because what the rest of the statement says is true, right? We *are* sorry. It *is* an ethically complex situation. Our role now is to make amends, to do the best we can to support the involved parties, including their wish to remain anonymous."

"Who signs?" Antoinette asks.

Loretta looks to the far end of the table.

"Babs."

Babs glances up from reading the statement. "Me?"

A former nurse turned patient advocate, Babs is a white woman who, in the conference room light, looks more pink than white, seventy-something. She's been involved in *The Case of the Misplaced Sperm* since the start, tasked with breaking the news to recipient and donor about the mix-up, even before anyone knew anyone was pregnant. Part of her success as a patient advocate is because her face—with its clear gray eyes and rosy cheeks—combined with a soft body and gentle tone of voice seem like what a person would imagine a patient advocate to be, like she could play the role in a movie.

"Babs, you won't have to actually talk to the media, just lend the gravity of your title to the statement," Mona says.

"And your image. We'll send your photo with it," Loretta adds.

Babs says, "Sure, I'm happy to help."

Watching her now, Loretta remembers Babs is a faculty member in the Department of Medicine, one on the Dean's list for a near death experience interview. Loretta decides to try to grab her after this meeting.

"And there will be no comment other than this statement? You can guarantee that?" Antoinette asks.

"No one can guarantee anything in a crisis media situation, but we can do our best," Loretta says.

Loretta is feeling spry today after last night's restful sleep with Jenny. It's been some time since she's slept so soundly.

The lawyer looks at the representative from risk management, also white, who Loretta has met a few times before. But this time, she notices the lovely brown mole above her upper lip. Maybe it's the morning light bringing the mole into focus or maybe her bright red lipstick makes it stand out. Loretta rummages through her brain trying to remember the supermodel who has the same thing. Mindy? Vanya? Carmen?

The risk manager nods at the lawyer and says, "It's not ideal but we can work with this."

Antoinette approves the plan; it's a hesitant approval but this is not a game of horseshoes—there are no degrees of approval. It's done. Mona hands out copies of the full communications plan, outlining timing and staff duties.

"It would be good to have some positive media stories during this," Mona says. "To balance out the coming negative crush. It's a heavy lift but let's give it a shot. Options?"

Kevin, the senior media coordinator on the team and a former reporter, speaks up. "I'm ready to pitch a story about the new medical school curriculum."

"And?" Mona asks.

"If we change how doctors are educated, we can change the health care system from the ground up and give new docs the tools they need to make it a more humane and accessible system."

"Like what happened at Harvard with the MBA program," Loretta says. "But the opposite."

"Exactly," Kevin says. "For those of you who don't know, a new curriculum was introduced at Harvard in the 1980s for business degrees that focused on shareholders and stock value as the primary metrics of success for CEOs, shifting away from worker and community well-being. My point is that the Harvard example is a real-world demonstration of the ripple effect of educational programs. We want to do the same thing for doctors, but it won't be evil like the MBA program shift at Harvard."[9]

"I went to Harvard," Antoinette says.

Kevin looks like a deer caught in large headlights. Loretta laughs inside at his terrified expression.

Antoinette says, "I don't disagree. It was a terrible curriculum change. Basically, it taught that greed was desirable, even admirable. Disastrous societal effects are still playing out although it wasn't created in isolation. Harvard had a lot of help from people who stood to benefit, people with a long-term libertarian vision for the country. You need to understand more about what was happening in the banking sectors at the time, learn about the who and why—"

She stops herself and looks around the table. "Sorry. An unnecessary digression. Let's focus on our medical school curriculum."

Mona jumps in. "Helpful information, thank you, and illustrates the point that this is too complicated for most daily editors. Kevin, probably best to pitch it as a magazine feature, which won't help for what we need this week to offset our current situation. What else?"

"I've got one about a research breakthrough related to breast cancer genetics," says a young man wearing a plaid flannel shirt beneath a light-blue denim jacket. He's brand new to the team and Loretta doesn't remember his name. "The scientist has a cool story about how her mother's death from breast cancer inspired her research."

Cool is not a word Loretta would put next to cancer, still she gets his point. It humanizes the research.

"It's a long shot, but that might work to offset the fertility clinic story, even if for just one news cycle. Find a breast cancer patient, get some quotes about how the breakthrough could change her future and hit the death of the scientist's mother angle hard," Mona says. "A headline like 'University breakthrough research shows promise in curing breast cancer.'"

"Was the research in humans?" Loretta asks.

"GEMMs. Genetically-engineered mouse models," the plaid-shirt man says.

Loretta says, "That should be in the headline too. 'This cool cancer research that was done in mice has potential.' Something along those lines."

Heads swivel in her direction like a flock of curious birds; no one challenges Mona on media decisions.

"Implying that something discovered in mice, or any animal, will lead to human treatments is misleading," Loretta adds quickly.

The group moves its flock-gaze back to Mona.

"But it might. Lead to treatments, that is," Mona says, her voice overtly neutral.

"Maybe, and let's hope so." Loretta knocks on the wooden table. The faces pivot again. If Loretta wasn't focused on choosing her words so carefully, she would laugh at the synchronous heads. But she is choosing her words carefully, and says, "But even if it does, it will take decades, and won't help any breast cancer patient we dig up today, who will undoubtedly, and tragically, die before the mice discovery moves into human trials. By giving people false hope, we're putting another nail in our coffin as trusted experts."

"That sounds so sinister."

"You know what I mean, Mona. We're nothing if we

lose public trust. And this kind of shitty storytelling—"
Everyone's eyes widen a little at Loretta's word choice.
Except attorney Antoinette, who smiles. "It erodes the
University's credibility. Why do you think so many
people don't trust science anymore?"

"Because a bunch of Fox News personalities tell
them not to," Mona says.

"And every time we put out a story like this, we are
giving those Fox people and others more ammunition,
because from their standpoint, it's another lie in the
making. Drink coffee, don't drink coffee. Eggs are bad,
wait, they're okay after all. Take baby aspirin to prevent
heart disease, no wait, scratch that, might cause
excessive bleeding. We found a cure for breast cancer,
whoops, we didn't mean that your aunty dying of
cancer would be saved, just some genetically-altered
mice we engineered to have cancer in the first place."

Antoinette tries to interrupt, probably to tell Mona
and Loretta to shut the hell up, Loretta thinks, which
would be the right move. It's not the time or place for
this discussion and Loretta is now regretting her words,
even if they are pretty good ones but Mona barrels over
Antoinette.

"Our job is to get positive media attention for our
academic institution. Ours," she says, stabbing her
chest. "Not others. This enhances our reputation, helps
us get funding from the legislature, gets the attention of
philanthropists, keeps everyone employed and keeps
those mouse *and* human breakthroughs humming
along. People love a winner, and today we need a
headline that says we are a winner. Discussion closed."

Mona turns back to the plaid-shirted young man
whose name Loretta still can't remember. "No mice in
the headline. Focus on the human implications in the
pitch and get it out today. Oh, one more thing, find a
Black breast cancer patient. Now, what else have we
got?"

Did Loretta really hear Mona ask Mr. Plaid Shirt to find a Black patient? Loretta looks around the room for reactions. Three staffers look uncomfortable. Another is leaning forward, palms on the table. The clinic director is nodding. Antoinette and Babs check their phones. Mr. Plaid Shirt's head is down, furiously taking notes. Mona, savvy leader that she is, senses the tension and adds, "It's strategic to be focused on diversity in our media outreach at the moment."

Antoinette nods and says "That's the right approach. Kill two birds with one stone."

Ugh, Loretta thinks, again with that phrase? But she doesn't say anything as a block of silence builds. Mona doesn't let it gain structure.

"Okay, what else? Oh, and anyone outside of the media team, feel free to leave. You might not want to see all this sausage-making."

The mole-supermodel risk manager and the clinic administrator gather their papers and technology and make for the door. Antoinette stays. Babs too.

"Okay, people, round robin. Keep on pitching me."

"The political science department is running an online fundraiser to buy art supplies for children living at the downtown homeless shelter," the social media director says.

"Some chemistry faculty are lobbying the legislature tomorrow about limiting pesticide use around schools," a purple-haired junior staffer says.

"A patient painted a portrait of her doctor," Mr. Plaid Shirt says. "And it's pretty good, really."

"They're small, and won't overshadow the clinic story, but maybe with enough of these feel-good pieces it could dampen the impact," Mona says. "Anything else?"

Loretta's attention wanders as the staffers continue to pitch their story ideas in a minor frenzy, hoping to get Mona's approval. Looking around, Loretta realizes that every single person in the room is white. How had it come to be that there are no Black people or people of color on the public relations team, a University that has been in existence for more than a century?

Loretta is jolted back into the meeting when Toni asks, "Do we need an all-employee message before the fertility clinic story hits?" Hailing from Wisconsin farm roots, Toni is a twenty-something staffer on Loretta's direct-report team. Her last job was public relations for the city zoo. Her question about internal comms means the group is done with the media-pitching part of this meeting. After a few more minutes of back and forth, Mona calls the meeting to a close.

Loretta shoves papers into her bag and fast-walks down the corridor to catch up with Babs.

"Tough meeting," Babs says.

Loretta shrugs. "You mean the mice thing? Not a big deal. Mona knows what she's doing."

"For what it's worth, I agree with you."

"You do?"

"I've worked here almost forty years and during that time, the way people look at universities has changed. It used to be our communities respected and trusted us to always do the right thing on their behalf, but now it's different, as if we've stayed still while everything around us changed, or maybe we spend so much time chasing money that this chase has become our purpose. All things are possible if the public is with us and nothing is possible if we lose them. It's going to come back to haunt us if something terrible happens and experts aren't trusted. Everything should be on the table to ensure we maintain that trust, including mice."

Loretta is glad of Babs's support, but finds it a little odd she doesn't mention the thing about Mona asking for a Black patient. Should Loretta say something about it? Should she have said something in the meeting? What should she have said? Well, it could be I overreacted, Loretta thinks, persuading herself it was probably okay to say nothing about that.

They stand side by side in front of the elevator. The doors slide open. A young white man with a handlebar mustache and a killer smile sits in a wheelchair inside. Babs takes a step forward.

"Do you have time to talk to me on another topic?" Loretta asks, putting her hand out to stop the doors from closing.

"Of course, what do you need?" Babs nods to the man and steps back. Loretta lets the doors close and simultaneously she lets go of thinking anymore about the meeting or what she should have done.

"How many years were you a nurse in the University hospital?"

"About thirty, in the Department of Medicine, in the division of Palliative Care for most of that time, and now a patient advocate for about ten years. Why do you ask?"

"I've got a request from *60 Minutes*. They are doing a story on near death experiences. Are you familiar?"

The lie about *60 Minutes* feels heavier with Babs but she's in too deep now to backtrack. But really, what difference does one lie make? She'll tell everyone later that the producers changed their minds. No one will ever know.

"Oh yes, very much so," Babs says.

"Are they real?"

"Without question."

"I wasn't expecting such a certain response."

Babs doesn't add anything more. Loretta continues. "What do they signify?"

"All I know is what my patients have told me."

"Will you tell me?"

Babs gestures at a nearby empty alcove with three beat-up chairs and a small table next to a trash can overflowing with water bottles and pizza boxes. The room smells like pepperoni. Babs sits down across from Loretta and takes her hands, like they are about to pray together.

"Angels, tunnels, a glorious light, being welcomed by relatives, floating above their bodies and profoundly, a sense of oneness with all things, of being at peace. This is what some of my patients say, often in strained whispers, in the moments before death. But there are others, not many but some, who return from death with a similar story. One patient I remember well. An older man who underwent emergency heart surgery. After describing the tunnel and lights, he said he rose out of his body to the ceiling, drawn to the corner of the room and watched as doctors and nurses worked on him."

"You believed him?"

"I might not have except for what happened next." Babs releases Loretta's hands. "He arrived unconscious at the emergency room and, as required by protocol, a nurse removed his dentures. The next day, he was in a room on the wards, recovering, after the acute situation subsided. He asked me for his dentures. I went to the ER to ask around. The attending nurse wasn't on shift, so I looked for the dentures myself but couldn't find them. When I came back to his room empty-handed, he told me the exact place where they were. I went back and they were there, in the drawer of the cart next to the cot in the ER. When I asked him how he knew, he said he watched from above when the nurse took them out, even though he was unconscious at the time, clinically dead. I know that because later I found that nurse and asked if he was truly unconscious."[10]

"You don't find that odd?"

"Of course I do. But odd or not, it happened. And every nurse has similar stories. Every single one."

"Do you think near death experiences are proof of heaven?"

"I'm not qualified to answer questions about proof of anything, and certainly not heaven," Babs says. "I encourage you to talk to the hospital chaplain. He's an expert on this topic."

"I don't need an expert, just your opinion."

Babs looks away, gathering her thoughts. Loretta notices a small gold cross hanging around her neck. Turning back, Babs says, "The experience helps my patients lose their fear of death, and this gives them peace in their last moments. That's a kind of heaven, as far as I'm concerned."

Later, back in her office, Loretta puts aside *The Case of the Misplaced Sperm* to update the Jenny notebook, writing with a red pen this time.

Babs said good feelings from near death experiences helped her patients, a positive thing. Maybe all those soothing feelings are nature's way of easing passage into death, of feeling less terrified, like the Irish evolutionist speculated. But this doesn't explain the tunnel, the welcome crew of dead relatives or the life review, not to mention the floating-above-your-body phenomenon. Nor does it explain why Jenny is having so many. For argument's sake, she writes in a red flourish, let's assume a near death experience gets switched on as the body is dying for what is, in effect, a palliative purpose. This could mean that Jenny's wiring is simply off and her body is activating that death sequence incorrectly. If so, Jenny could get it fixed. But what if it's not fixable? Where do Jenny's near death experiences end? Loretta doesn't like the scenario that slides into her mind.

Caron pops her head into the office. "I'm heading to the cafeteria. Would you like a sandwich?"

"No thanks, Matthias packed me a lunch. He always packs me a lunch."

Caron smiles. "Wish my husband packed me lunch. And hey, a reminder, your next departmental interview is in thirty minutes. Biology this time."

EIGHT

Beneath the upper campus is a warren of old tunnels built at the same time as the first University buildings. Their original purpose was to contain water and sewage pipes, and also transport food and supplies by foot and wheelbarrow and, later, by mini-golf cart. In the 1980s, the tunnels were transformed into a modern pulsating circulatory system of wires and cables. Today, they give cover and protection to computer servers and an assortment of high-tech medical equipment humming along, next to the now-ancient but still in-service water and sewage pipes. Throughout their existence, those in the know have used the underground maze, especially on rainy days, as weather-protected pathways between buildings. Sometimes, when Loretta walks through the tunnels, she slows down, trying to imagine the people who also walked through over the past century, wanting to feel the shadowy presence of past lives shuttling through the same constrained space. But not today, she doesn't have enough time. There is no map for this underground space, it's a dead spot for reception, so familiarity is the only way-finding guide. And she is lost. For the third time, she stops at an unmarked juncture, hopes a right turn is the correct choice, ducks her head, walks fifty or so yards through the tunnel, realizes she was wrong because the door she was told to expect isn't there, retraces her steps, this time taking the left fork and after another forty yards, she is relieved to spot the olive-green metal door Caron told her to look for.

Passing through, she leaves the tunnels, climbs the metal stairs to another door opening to a hallway lined with rows of refrigerators and freezers. Some have glass doors and hold vials and jars with murky contents. Others open from the top, and she half expects them to be full of ice cream sandwiches and popsicles as if they were from the corner store near where she grew up. Reaching the far end of the corridor, Loretta passes three sleek, brushed metal floor-to-ceiling refrigerators; one is padlocked with a scribbled note taped on its door: *If the power goes out, call the poison center immediately.*

She opens the last door, the only door at the end of the hallway and steps into the Department of Biology. Dozens of potted plants hang from the ceiling in macramé rope casings, grow-lights near each; a human-sized terrarium. A young Black man, dressed in khaki slacks, a denim shirt and a polka-dot bow tie, looks up from his monitor with a smile that spreads easily across his face. "You must be Ms. Sparkman from the Dean's office. I'm Derrick, Dr. Mitchell's assistant. I spoke with Caron a few minutes ago."

"She was checking on me, I bet. She didn't think I'd find my way."

"I'll let her know you did," he says, leading her into the small conference room next to the reception area. "Dr. Mitchell will be in straight away."

Loretta examines Dr. Mitchell's degrees and honors, framed and decorating the perimeter of the room. She is a highly educated neurobiologist, attending only the top schools. Hopkins. Berkeley. Scripps. Loretta takes a seat at the table, and within seconds, the door swings open.

"Okay, Dean's office person, what can I do for you?" Dr. Mitchell asks, breezing in and slipping into a chair opposite Loretta.

She is forty-something, white and wears no makeup. None. Not even to cover a faint spray of acne across forehead.

"Hopefully my assistant mentioned why I'm here?" Loretta asks.

"*60 Minutes* and near death experiences."

"They are planning, or thinking of, not so much planning yet, it's in the early stages—"

"I get it. Paranormal pseudoscience stuff gets good ratings. What do you want to know?"

"Are near death experiences real?" Loretta ticks off the first question.

"Many people report them. Many people also report alien abductions."

That is clever, Loretta thinks. Dr. Mitchell would be great on a real *60 Minutes*.

"What do they signify?"

"There are two theories about near death experiences. The afterlife theory and dying brain theory. Neither term originated with me, and you should get the correct citations before sharing."[11] She's curt but not demeaning. "Do you want me to explain them?"

"Yes, please."

"Okay, first the afterlife theory. Let me start by saying it's a kindness to categorize it as a theory. It posits that near death experiences are evidence of life after death. The tunnel is a passageway to heaven, or Valhalla, or whatever celestial vision the experiencer's cultural affinity prescribes. A few people move beyond their personal domains and refer to another realm, an undiscovered spatial-temporal dimension. Nevertheless, common to all the interpretations is a place where dead people congregate for eternity. One would think it must be awfully crowded by this point."

She looks at Loretta for a reaction, testing the waters of her beliefs and the latitude they offer. Wanting to grant the widest berth, Loretta asks, "Are pets allowed, do you think?"

It is enough to pass Loretta off as an intellectual ally and Professor Mitchell continues. "Presumably, only in off-leash areas," she says with a smile. "More seriously, though, while the afterlife theory offers comfort in the face of mortality, it's not a tidy way to fit facts, nor is it a theory in any meaningful sense." She pauses and then asks, "You do understand what it means to call something a theory, right?"

"Pretend I don't and explain. Let's see how it might play for the *60 Minutes* audience."

"Right. Practice. Good advice. Thanks."

Her voice takes on a softer, patient tone, a bedtime-story melody. Must be a mom to still-young children, Loretta thinks.

"A theory is a construct that can explain empirical evidence. This construct, once established, then guides the process of collecting and categorizing knowledge and data for the purposes of affirming, or not, its legitimacy. There are two aspects of theories that are important for our discussion. First is simplicity and the second is predictive power. By simplicity I mean if two theories compete to explain the same set of facts, the one that is simpler, with the fewest steps, the fewest suppositions, the least number of gaps, is preferred."

"Occam's razor," Loretta says, still mistrustful of this tenet but who is she to refute a foundation of the entire scientific enterprise.

"Correct. But the second may be more important. Predictive power. A theory is only as useful as it is reliably predictive, if it gives us something to test, a way to prove it, expand it or, if needed, replace it. If it's not testable, it's philosophy."

She smirks, just slightly, and Loretta realizes she intends this as a slight to philosophy but she doesn't let the pause linger.

"Both these criteria are problematic for the afterlife theory, but the second part is pivotal. The afterlife explanation offers no testable way to prove or disprove it. Heaven as an explanatory concept, and by extension God, is a hard boundary for knowledge acquisition."

"Are you saying that if a concept doesn't allow for follow-up questions, science categorizes it as untrue?"

"Not quite. For your television audience, it's better to say the concept lacks usefulness in the way that science is conducted. If it isn't useful, it isn't relevant."

"I'm guessing those two attributes are in play for the second theory, the dying brain theory."

"You'd be guessing correctly but before we get to that, we need to consider the sense of self. Much more research is needed on this topic but for our purpose in engaging this largely non-scientific *60 Minutes* audience, we will simply accept that for each of us, a sense of self exists. Do you agree?"

"Well, sure, I can agree to that."

"You sound hesitant."

"No, not hesitant." But Loretta is a little hesitant, of course, given the currently tenuous contours of her degraded zombie self.

Dr. Mitchell continues. "It's okay to be doubtful. Skepticism is a foundation of science. Nevertheless, for our purposes, let's agree the self is a concept created by our biology that allows us to effectively use incoming sensory data to facilitate collaboration between humans. It allows us to interact and, most importantly, to predict the behavior of other people and the world around us."

"So, as you're using it, the self is another word for

personality. Or identity."

"Sort of, but not really. The self is more akin to a story, or metaphor may be more apt, that our brain creates about personal identity and agency to distract us so our body can go on about its business without the need for conscious awareness of every little thing."

"Are you saying the sense of self is manufactured by the brain, all on its own?"

"Exactly. Think about how the brain instructs the body to breathe, without any conscious awareness of that action. It's doing the same with the creation of a self, although the process is likely more complicated."

"So you're saying there isn't really a self then? It's all a fabrication?" Loretta asks.

"That's not quite the correct way to frame it, and frankly we're straying from the near death experience topic. For our discussion, we need only agree there is a sense of self, not about how it's created."

Still, this is something definitely worth looking into later, Loretta thinks, because it would mean everyone is a zombie, kind of. Maybe instead of her being the aberrant one, instead she's being honest about the state of non-selfness.

She realizes Dr. Mitchell is still talking.

"… the dying brain theory posits that as the brain approaches death, this story of self falls apart because it's superfluous to what's happening, and the body ceases to expend the biological energy needed to maintain it. For most of us, this occurs at the instant of death and that's that, we start to die, our sense of self evaporates and then we do die and aren't around to tell the story of what happened to us in that instant. But for people lucky enough to be resuscitated on that brink, they remember that microsecond of no longer having a personality or identity, and in turn, they try to make sense of this experience of nonexistence and tell themselves a new story, they translate it into a mystical state of oneness. But really, it's a simple shutdown of the body and its embodied self, which is an illusion to begin with."

This is similar to what the maybe-flirty evolutionist said yesterday, but Dr. Mitchell is explaining it more lucidly. "How does biology create the elements of the near death experience?" Loretta asks.

"The bright light and the tunnel are a breakdown of the visual cortex and narrowing of sensory inputs. The out-of-body experience is the brain's vestibular canal system going haywire."

"What about meeting old friends and loved ones?"

"The biological residue of memories escaping their neuronal foundations as the brain dies."

"How would our biology selectively release only the memories of dead people? I mean, how does biology keep track of who is dead and who isn't?"

Professor Mitchell purses her lips and then says, "Good question. And something that requires more study, but that proves my point. We can ask questions and conduct research to answer questions within the paradigm of the dying brain theory. The afterlife theory is a dead stop." Her expression verges on a smile but it doesn't quite materialize, although her eyes brighten. "Pun not intended but I'll use that if you put me on *60 Minutes*. That kind of exposure could help bump up my research funding."

"You are for sure in the running. Now, let me make sure I get the dying brain theory. It assumes, or better to say, it requires that the sense of self, and by extension, human consciousness, is a construction of biology, probably the brain."

"Yes, it does, because this is true."

"This is considered unequivocal?"

"Not yet unequivocal but inevitable. What else could it be other than our biology?"

"Do we know how biology creates the self?"

91

"No, that isn't known yet, and as I implied earlier, a complicated question, one I doubt *60 Minutes* would pursue," Dr. Mitchell says. "But maybe this will help. Do you know the story of Phineas Gage?"

Score one for Professor Orr's predictive abilities.

"It's known as the American Crowbar Case," Dr. Mitchell says. "This would be great stuff for a television audience. I'm picturing some cool animation or old black and white photos running with my narration."

She describes a railroad construction accident in 1848 when an explosion sent a crowbar through the forehead of a young worker, Phineas Gage, piercing his brain. His mother was called to his bedside, as all expectations were that he had only hours to live.

"Defying all odds, he fully recovered. Well, perhaps 'fully' is the wrong word, because something curious happened to Phineas Gage. Prior to the injury, he was considered a nice-enough man by all reports, but afterward he became surly, irresponsible, took to the bottle. His personality was altered by the injury to his brain.

"These observations of the first man documented to live through a traumatic brain injury became medical ground zero for the idea that the brain is enough to create the mind, or what we now call the sense of self. His brain was damaged and his personality, his sense of self, changed. Because of this, scientists started to realize that nothing else was needed to make the self. No ethereal substance lingering outside the body. No transmutation of the soul through the pineal gland. No souls at all in fact."[12]

"Meaning, the brain is the mind?"

"Full stop. And you've stumbled onto the shortcut words used to refer to this theory. Brain-is-mind."

Dr. Mitchell looks down at her wristwatch before continuing.

"Soon, we may have better evidence of this. I read a

paper last week on some brilliant new research in which human brain matter is being grown in the lab from stem cells. It's early days but there's already talk about the possibility of implanting these proto-brains into non-human primates and this would provide enormous insight into the development of consciousness."[13]

"You mean apes?"

"We don't do research anymore on apes or, for that matter, chimps. Too close to humans, but another primate species will do."

An image of a monkey recognizing its face in front of the mirror pops into Loretta's mind, followed quickly by monkeys drinking tea, writing poetry, bemoaning the meaning of existence. These cartoons are then quickly supplanted by a precursor picture, gruesomely realistic, of a surgical team hovering over an anesthetized monkey as its brain is removed from its skull and replaced with the lab-grown human proto-brain, a modern Frankenstein.

"Are you okay?" Dr. Mitchell asks. "You have an odd expression."

"You're kidding."

"About your expression? Oh, sorry, of course not, you meant the lab brain business. No, not kidding. It's an extremely elegant technique to learn a great deal about human consciousness."

Elegant? Loretta pushes the monkey brain surgery from her mind, and for a brief second, wonders if she is pushing too much from her mind lately. Is *that* what becoming a zombie is really all about? Has she created an elaborate avoidance technique?

She shakes her head faintly and moves on.

"How about I try to paraphrase what you've explained so far about near death experiences to be sure I can explain it all to *60 Minutes*?" Loretta asks.

"Good idea."

Loretta gathers the threads of the conversation. "If

we accept that near death experiences are an expression of self, or consciousness, whatever you call it, and also accept these are functions of biology—in other words, brain-is-mind—then near death experiences are, by logical extension, also a function of biology."

"You've got it. And to further clarify, I'll share another example from research on vestibular systems, which as I mentioned before can explain out-of-body experiences."[14]

"Vestibular, that's ear?"

"Correct again. Micro-canals in the inner ear. Working with other senses and the brain, a function of the inner ear is to help track your location in physical space."

"It keeps you balanced," Loretta says. "And we are talking about humans, right?"

"Yes, humans. I'm drawing from memory so don't quote me on this, but in the study about fifteen percent of people with inner-ear infections report having out-of-body experiences. But in people without these ear infections, only about five percent have out-of-body experiences."

"So, when people die, some part of their vestibular system might go awry, akin to an ear infection, and cause the out-of-body part of a near death experience?" Loretta asks.

"That's the supposition."

Again, as she did with the Irish evolutionist, Loretta thinks back to the central question the Dean identified but this time asks it. "Wouldn't it be simpler, and give the theory better predictive value, if everyone with ear infections had out-of-body experiences, not just fifteen percent?"

"You catch on quickly. And you call out what will undoubtedly be the focus of follow-up studies. Why do some people love cilantro and others think it tastes like soap? We're all people, with the same set of biological tools, so why the variance? In the latter case, it's likely genetic. Could be something like that for near death experiences, or a function of nutrition. Maybe certain people die faster than others or some are genetically predisposed to come back from clinical death. Who knows? But this is how science works. Data show that a prior conclusion was wrong, and this leads to a reversal when a piece of knowledge, or even a theory, is proven incorrect due to the development of new knowledge."

Loretta understands the role of reversals in scientific progress—one step forward, three steps back, because knowledge is always provisional, always building on and replacing what's come before—but what she doesn't say to Dr. Mitchell is that she suspects non-academic people call reversals by another name: mistakes.

While on the face of it this might seem a simple difference of vocabulary, Loretta sees this as another factor explaining why so much of the public no longer understands, or trusts, what Universities do, at least the really big ones like hers, other than provide a path to a white-collar job if you can afford the tuition. Because in their quest for funding, to be seen as the top of the intellectual heap, they put out media releases and celebratory messages about research breakthroughs and discoveries that give desperately ill people hope, or give new information about what to eat, how to lose weight, how much to sleep and then some other University puts out a media release about a newer experiment that reverses that knowledge without ever explaining that the other "breakthrough" was always provisional to begin with.

Whose job is it to insist that academic institutions stop doing this? Whose job is it to find a different way to tell the story, the purpose of a University? That's the question she and Mona are wrestling with, the fight that spilled into their staff meeting earlier today, with the poor little GEMM mice serving as proxies. Loretta says it should be people like them in academic public relations because they are the voice of the University writ large and have the tools, but Mona argues that's not what they get paid to do. They're paid to get their University, and *only* their University, the good sort of attention while suppressing bad stories. That's what helps make the University competitive for government funding and attracts billionaire philanthropists. Mona says that in today's media landscape, you don't get good attention by telling boring stories about academic purpose and provisional knowledge. You dazzle them with cutting-edge, first-in-show research breakthroughs and the like. And if the information is reversed in the next news cycle, or if the discovery is relevant only to mice, who will ever remember?

But they do remember, Loretta keeps arguing to Mona, they do. That's the whole of the problem.

Once again, Loretta pushes away these errant thoughts, trying to stay focused on Dr. Mitchell, but then another one pops up: Who or what is shoving away all these thoughts?

Derrick slips in the conference room with a note, which Dr. Mitchell pauses to read. "I need to wind this down."

"Do you have time for me to finish up connecting the dots on this discussion?"

"Yes, please go ahead, sorry to have interrupted." She looks at her watch again.

Loretta talks fast. "Near death experiences are real but what is likely happening is that the sense of self, which is another way of saying human consciousness, which is in turn a construction of biology, disappears at death. When a dying process is disrupted and someone returns, they have a memory of that selfless state and misinterpret it as being one with the universe, or heaven, or whatever, because their boundaries of self were gone for a little while."

"What you have said is good. It's the brain shutting down, much like a computer shuts down. Or an avatar in a virtual game ceasing to exist."

Loretta now thinks she must also be a mother of adolescent gaming kids, not just bedtime-story kids.

"A sample is arriving in five minutes. Are we done?"

Loretta scans her notes, wondering what she has missed, knowing there will be something. But before she can answer, Dr. Mitchell says, "Actually, just come along with me. The brain lab could be a great location for a *60 Minutes* interview."

NINE

They sit close to the water's edge on the isolated and rocky coastline, wrapped together in a woolen blanket. Matthias wears a black skull cap, protecting his bald head from the wind and chill. Jenny has a floppy red knit hat pulled down over her ears. They are enjoying a sunbreak through the winter ocean mist. Flashes of blue cut across the dull gray sky.

"Not the greatest weather, but it's good to get out," Matthias says.

"Thanks for bringing me here. It's lovely."

The rowdy waves crash in, collapsing against each other and leaving behind shells and rocks and detritus at their apex, dragging back murky ribbons of sand as they return to the ocean. A band of toothpick-legged shorebirds trots after the receding waves, looking for bits of crab and insects and other edible fodder, and then scurries back to drier sand when the next wave rolls in. Overhead, seagulls wheel and chastise.

"Tell me something I don't know about Loretta's past, her childhood," Matthias says, tugging the blanket tighter. "She says she doesn't remember much of it. But only if it doesn't make you uncomfortable."

"It doesn't make me uncomfortable. I doubt she keeps much from you by intent. Probably blocking parts of it out. She had a happy childhood until it ended unexpectedly when her mom died."

"That much I know."

"Her mother was seventeen when she had Loretta, so they were kind of like sisters. They lived in a tiny one-bedroom house down by the community center, a shack really, and they loved being with each other, always hanging out, except when she was in school or her mom was at work. They did tons of stuff together."

"Like what?"

"Well, normal things. Reading. Eating. Talking. And laughing, lots of laughing. Plus, Loretta's mother was an artist, super creative. Most every Sunday they took the bus downtown to the museums. Oh, and her mom was very pretty."

"Like Loretta. I've seen a few photos," he says.

"Yeah, and like Loretta, never cared much about it."

Matthias thinks about something Loretta said a year or so ago as she looked in their bathroom mirror after his first round of chemotherapy. Aging, she said, forces you to confront the illusion of permanence and, given that, why have faith anything is real or steady? Any insights he may have offered were lost as he jumped up from the bed to throw up for the third time that hour. Later, she refused to discuss what she meant, saying there was time when he was feeling better to delve into what was probably an overly intellectual way to justify simple vanity. Looking back now, Matthias wonders if this was the beginning of her zombie story.

He unscrews the top of a thermos, pours tea and passes the cup, billowing in a cloud of steam, to Jenny.

"Did you ever meet her father?" he asks.

"No, she doesn't know who he is or was. Or if she

does, she never told me. We used to make up stories about him, thinking maybe he was married, or maybe a CIA agent—"

They both laugh at that.

"We gave up that game after her mother died."

"She talks about her mother once in a while."

"It was a brutal loss. The cancer chewed her up in a few months." She looks at Matthias. "Sorry. Bad topic."

"I'm doing all right, don't worry about it. Cancer sucks for everybody."

"Loretta was with her every second, even when she took her last breath. She went from a mostly carefree childhood, wrapped in support and love, to being, in effect, an orphan. She had nothing. No family. No money. No one looking out for her. She moved into our basement after the funeral but disappeared four months later. Must have felt chaotic to her, with my brothers always running around the house and yelling. I was worried sick, and so were my parents, but we got a postcard from her a year or so later, after she landed here. She was eighteen. Said thanks for the help and not to worry about her."

Jenny wraps her hands around the thermos cup of tea, blowing at the steam, rising stark against the cool air. The blanket slides off her shoulder.

"When she claims not to remember her childhood, I think she's mostly telling the truth. Grief blew it all up, pulled the entire thing out from under her. I'm all that's left standing from those years."

"She says she's turning into a zombie."

Jenny laughs, and the sound rushes into the curl of a crashing wave. "She's eating brains?"

"More like, feeling her own brain dissolve. She says she reacts to things in the moment, no past, no future. That her thoughts and sense of self are disconnected."

"Not such a bad strategy."

"How so?"

Jenny takes a sip of tea, but the liquid is still too hot to drink so she balances the cup on her knees.

"The zombie story might be an excuse to freeze time, to live only in the present."

"Because of my illness?" Matthias asks.

"That's my guess. Less painful that way."

"I called it a midlife crisis."

"Ouch. I bet she loved that. Is this zombie stuff why you sent Loretta on this quest?"

"Quest?"

"You know, about near death experiences."

"Your condition sent her on this quest, not me."

"She wouldn't have done it without your push."

He shrugs. "It's not the worst idea I've ever had. Help you and find herself in the process."

"I hope you're right. Anyway, thank you."

He uses his fingers to break the top wet layer of packed sand, grabs a fistful and opens his hand enough to let the dry sand pass, as if through an hourglass, building a small hill next to his right foot.

"Tell me a story I don't know from her childhood."

Jenny ponders for a few seconds. "Here's one. We had just started high school, and a teacher fell in love with Loretta. He was like twenty years older, maybe more. Anyway, he professed his mad love for her and then slept in the yard behind their house all night, pulling a dysfunctional Cyrano or something."

"What did Loretta do?"

"Ignored him because she was embarrassed. But in the morning, her mother invited him inside, gave him some coffee and then said if he ever came back, she would call the police. And that if he ever touched her daughter, she would kill him with the pistol she had in her nightstand drawer."

"Did she?"

"Have a pistol? I don't know, I never looked inside her nightstand."

"Sounds like a tough lady."

"She was fiercely protective of Loretta. For good reason. It was clear early on there was something about Loretta that attracted, well, odd people. Like they felt she could save them somehow."

Matthias laughs. "Not sure how I should take that."

"With gratitude. I sure have. For the people she lets in, Loretta has always also had that protective tendency, lucky for me. Here's another story. Once in junior high, the teachers were trying to get the girls to play kickball with the boys, wanting us to do things outside our comfort zone or whatever. The boys were taunting us ferociously, saying really mean things about our looks, and stupid sex stuff. One chubby kid was the worst. It was enough to make most of us refuse to play, a few cried. He was especially mean to me, said I looked like a troll, I must live under a bridge, that kind of stuff. But then Loretta came up to kick. I still remember the determination on her face, how she looked over at him and smiled. And things weren't easy for her then. She developed early, with those big boobs showing up almost overnight. But when that red rubber ball came rolling toward her, she kicked it with everything she had right smack into that asshole. She kicked so hard it knocked him down when he tried to catch it, making everybody laugh. I don't think she ever played kickball again, she doesn't even like sports—"

"But she wanted to make a point."

"Exactly."

"Why didn't your brothers pound that mean kid?"

"They didn't have to because of Loretta. That's what she said after, 'we can take care of each other.'"

Matthias knocks over the little sand hill he's built and runs his hand across the ground, smoothing, until it's flat again, like nothing was ever there.

"You know what's funny? I told her that story last time I was here, years ago, and she had zero memory of it," Jenny says. "To me, it's so vivid, a turning point. Seeing her stand up to that bully gave me the courage to live, to really live, as I wanted, not how people thought I should. But to Loretta, it was a total blank. She wondered if I made it up or if it was some other girl who kicked the ball."

They watch a boat labor offshore, a fishing dory bouncing on the waves. A dog bounds into the surf, chasing a tennis ball thrown by a tall man bundled up in a red parka. They laugh at the unbridled joy of the dog. After a couple of minutes, the man and dog walk on.

"What about you? What was your life like as a kid?"

"Not much to tell. Like Loretta, I was on my own young, at seventeen. My parents were ranchers, and we didn't get along very well. They didn't try to stop me from leaving."

"Liberating. And sad."

"It was a long time ago, a lifetime really. I don't think about it much."

"Maybe that's why you two understand each other so well, because you were both on your own so young."

"Could be."

"What did you do when you left the ranch?"

"I lived with my nice high school music teacher in the little Wyoming town where I was born, stayed with her for a year until I was old enough to enlist."

"Did you see your parents again?"

"Not often."

"Where were you stationed?"

"Germany. Drank a lot of beer, smoked a lot of weed and loaded a lot of boxes onto cargo planes."

"Doesn't sound like a bad life. Then what?"

"I never really liked working. I mean, who does, but I never found, or fell into, a career. I took odd jobs. Security guard, dishwasher, whatever I could find. Loretta and I met when I was bartending where she was a waitress. About the time we got married, I landed a security gig at a restaurant supplier. I lost the job awhile back, but it was okay because Sally-Anne needed one of us at home, and Loretta has her hot shot University job now. It's been a good life, a great life. Until this little detour into cancer-town."

"Sorry. I know it sucks." She is silent for a moment. "Are you afraid of dying?" she asks at last.

"Not really. I mean, I don't want to, and I hope it's not anytime soon, but I'm not too concerned about it."

"Trust me when I say you don't need to be scared."

"I do worry about Loretta and Sally-Anne. When I'm gone, I won't care anymore, but they'll be wrecked, at least for a while. I mean, I know they'll get over it. Everybody does. But it breaks my heart to think about how rough it will be for them at first."

Jenny perks up her chin to look out toward the horizon, her eyes tracking a black dot above the water line. "Is that a whale?"

Matthias follows her gaze and lands on the dark oval spot. "Hard to say. Dammit, I should have brought the binoculars."

The water ebbs and flows around the anomaly. Jenny stares so hard her eyes begin to water, and she lets the tears slide freely, as if even dabbing her eyes might frighten the whale off. They breathe the damp air in and out, in and out; for a brief instant, the misty coldness breaches the margins between them and the landscape.

"I think it's a rock," Matthias says.

Jenny pushes out her bottom lip in a mock pout. "Boo. I wanted to see a whale."

"We'll come back in the spring when they migrate."

A wave washes up close to their feet and they scuttle backward like crabs, low against the sand. The tide is coming in.

TEN

Loretta follows Dr. Mitchell through another freezer-lined corridor to a barely visible door. The professor punches in a code to unlock the door and once inside the dimly lit space, Loretta hears a mechanical hum and the gurgle of circulating liquids. As her eyes adjust to the low light, she peers at a wall of what looks like glass cinder blocks. Dozens and dozens of striped fish wiggle inside each miniature aquarium.

"What are they?" Loretta asks.

"Zebrafish. Their bodies are nearly transparent, and with magnification their internal organs, many of which are similar to humans, are visible."

"Fish are like humans?"

"Yes, at the level we're studying," she says. "Seventy percent of human genes are shared with these fish."

"How do you use them?"

"We do things to the fish and observe the response, this gives us insight into how the same event might play out in humans. Also, the fish embryos grow outside mom's body, allowing us to track development in close to real time."

Loretta wonders what she means when she says they 'do things to the fish' but doesn't ask, she's still trying to erase the monkey-brain surgical images from her own brain.

"Why so dark?"

"Sunlight is their environmental cue to reproduce. We fluctuate light to maintain the population at desired levels. With University budgets the way they are, they're swimming in the dark most days now."

Behind the third row of stacked fish, Dr. Mitchell opens another door. They pass through and walk up a staircase and enter a bigger room, filled with floor-to-ceiling shelves and lined with rows of file-sized plastic containers, an arrangement similar to the zebra fish aquariums but on a larger scale. A young woman, likely a student, skin as pale as blackboard chalk, looks up from a microscope. Dr. Mitchell asks her to fetch someone named Marcus. Within a minute, a man in a knee-length lab white coat arrives, presumably Marcus. He is old, older than Loretta by easily two decades, and bent at the waist. Loretta wonders why age bends some people. She stands straighter.

"Could you give Loretta a quick tour, please? Ten minutes, and we'll be ready," Dr. Mitchell says, adding in an undertone to caution him, "She's from the Dean's office."

Marcus motions Loretta to follow him down one aisle and up another. She parses her own stride into toddler-step lengths to match his pace. On either side, hundreds, maybe thousands of identical plastic tubs— Loretta can't tell how deep the wall shelves go—nest together, each exterior-facing side marked with Sharpie hand-scribbled letters and numbers. Just when she thinks maybe this is a silent tour, in the middle of the third aisle Marcus turns his pasty white liver-stained face around.

"Inside each of these containers is a human brain," he says, in monotone. "Therefore, in this room there are more than one thousand human brains." His voice is deep and gravelly, not the dusky fragments she was expecting. "The next part of the tour is to ask if you want to see one. Do you want to see a human brain inside a plastic box?"

"Yes, most definitely."

Marcus leans over the counter and after three pulls slides a stubborn container from the bottom shelf. Loretta wants to help, but is afraid he'll be offended. He opens the box, an unfamiliar chemical smell races out. She peers inside to examine the ribbed, grooved miracle. Loretta has never seen a brain. To her, it looks like a congealed cauliflower folding in on itself. "You have my permission to touch it," Marcus says. "This is the left hemisphere. The matching right hemisphere is freezer-stored."

She presses her fingers tenderly, cautiously, and the surface gives way beneath her touch, lightly springing back like an under-inflated rubber kickball covered by a sheet of satin sandpaper. She flattens her palm against the half-brain and simultaneously touches the top of her head with her other hand.

"It is curious how often people do that," he says, ready with a paper towel so she can wipe the liquid off her hand. A brain butler, she thinks.

"Okay, people, let's get to work," Dr. Mitchell says.

Marcus snaps the lid back into place, and Loretta follows him slowly back to the front of the lab where he joins another tech, a twenty-something man with wavy hair who looks like Ryan Gosling. The Gosling twin stands in front of a stainless-steel countertop that reminds Loretta of the kitchen in the restaurant where she waitressed for a few years, where she met Matthias. Their first kiss was in that restaurant, inside a walk-in refrigerator between a tray of fresh-caught barely dead salmon and a bucket of chunky blue cheese dressing.

Marcus and Ryan Gosling, probably four decades between them, push their hands into blue plastic gloves and hold them up like surgeons, clearly a familiar routine. Ryan asks, "Ready, Captain?" and Marcus says, "All systems go, Ensign." They grin and turn their attention to the cardboard box on the counter between them.

"Did you get filled in?" Dr. Mitchell asks, slipping up behind Loretta.

"I touched a brain."

"Well, that's nice for you, I suppose. Let me tell you more about what's going on here. This is the University brain bank. We have two main research projects. One is to understand the molecular basis, if any, for suicide. The other is to understand the aging brain. Particularly why some people live into their eighties and nineties, even longer, with little neurodegenerative decline. We maintain a database correlating each brain, or tissue sample, with demographic, clinical and developmental histories, and send samples to scientists around the world researching similar questions."

"Do you have normal brains here?"

"Normal is a relative term and a culturally defined baseline, but yes, we do. We need control brains against which to compare our lab brains to detect aberrations."

"Let me guess, they're in short supply."

She smiles, big this time, and it's lovely, washing across her face like a delighted young girl. "Might we sign you up as a donor?"

"It probably wouldn't be for the normal group. But I'll consider it. Who pays for this?"

"Wealthy people with family members or friends who've committed suicide, people who fantasize about living forever, combined with an anchor federal grant for operations. It's a knife's edge budget-wise. Public funding has gone down precipitously this past decade, as you know, with all the frenzy to cut taxes." Dr. Mitchell sighs. "Sometimes, I fear the hidden goal of all this tax cutting is to slowly strangle elite universities out of existence entirely."

"Not so sure it's hidden," Loretta says.

"But why?"

"The same reason something gets to become a department, I guess. The human need to control things, especially knowledge, to be in charge of the big story of all of humanity, to have power," Loretta says, surprising herself that somewhere in the recesses of her zombie mind this past day, she continued to unconsciously think about the meaning of a department.

"I'm not quite following you, but no matter. I don't have any ability to affect these kinds of problems. I've got my hands full doing science."

Loretta knows what the professor says is wrong, that there is a great deal the faculty at this University and every university, especially the big well-endowed ones, could do about their funding situation. (For starters, stop talking about research results in mice like they are people.)

Sometimes she just wants to shout at the ostrich-like faculty—*Pull your head out of the sand, go out into the world, rub elbows with folks you serve, the people who live around the University, the students in public schools and community colleges, help them build stuff, be visible, throw pot-lucks and block parties, move beyond your peers, beyond the tech millionaires and drug manufacturers who give you money and take you to fancy parties, beyond your self-congratulatory academic conferences. Let your communities know you personally, what you do, why you do it. Redefine yourself not as an academic but as a public servant. Show up!*

Now it's Loretta's turn to sigh. She has been saying these things for years. Nobody listens and she's tired of repeating herself. "Is there a brain in this collection that has had a near death experience?"

"That isn't something we track, although maybe we should. I'll query our database on the chance someone entered the descriptor and ask my colleagues at other brain banks to do the same. It will take a little while, but I'll let you know if anything turns up."

Loretta wonders what an autopsy of Jenny's brain would show.

"Would you like to watch us section off the latest sample? A man committed suicide last night. He slit his wrists, so the brain remained intact. Many suicides, bridge jumpers, shooters and the like, don't leave behind useable material. John Doe here was very considerate of science."

Loretta is taken aback by the chair's casualness, but it's offset by a mental picture of the communications team developing a marketing brochure aimed at people contemplating suicide: *Don't do the unthinkable, but if you do, please consider using poison or razor blades rather than guns as your last act. Allow science to use your despair to help prevent future suicides.* Okay, that's gross. She definitely has been working too hard.

"Yes, I'd like to watch, thank you," she says.

Dr. Mitchell nods at the two men and they begin. Marcus pulls the brain from its storage box filled with dry ice and sets it in the large sink. Ryan selects a clean knife, at least Loretta assumes it is clean; maybe he sliced his cheese sandwich with it at lunch. Just as he's poised to cut, the knife hanging mid-air, he asks, "Are you familiar with brain anatomy?"

"No," Loretta says.

"Do you want to be?"

"Sure."

"The terminology shifts a little depending on which discipline is asking the questions but at the most basic level, the brain is composed of three parts. First, this is the brainstem." He points to the base of the specimen where a nub of material pokes out from the bottom like a Thanksgiving turkey neck. "Next to the stem, nestled below the gray bowling-ball-like mass where the neck connects with the skull, is the cerebellum. The biggest part by far is the cerebrum, comprised of everything other than the stem and cerebellum. With me so far?"

Loretta nods.

"Typically, the cerebrum is divided into four lobes. The frontal, parietal, occipital and temporal," he says, pointing to the back, middle front, bottom front and the area just above the cerebellum.

Ryan brings the knife down confidently and firmly, slicing the brain, with only a little back and forth sawing, right down the central ridge, separating the left and the right sides, using this natural line as his butchering guide. The brain falls into halves.

"Well done," Dr. Mitchell says.

He nods, acknowledging her praise, and then lifts the left side up, continuing Loretta's tutorial. "My most excellent assistant will take this half and place in its own plastic container on the shelves," he says, handing it to Marcus who walks off, left hemisphere held up in his palms like an offering. "This other half, we'll section."

"Section?"

"Slice it into samples and put those into formalin for storage and shipment out to other labs. Formalin is embalming fluid. Kind of toxic in high doses but this is diluted. It's what all the brains here are stored in."

"Who is, I mean, was this?"

"That's confidential information but given you're with the Dean's office and presumably covered by our global agreement for confidentiality..." He pauses to give Loretta a chance to refute his assumption. She doesn't and Dr. Mitchell offers no objection, so he continues. "A twenty-six-year-old man diagnosed with cancer who decided to end his life before it metastasized to the brain, as he was told it would."

She feels the cold, familiar vise under her ribs,

clamping down on her heart and momentarily trapping her breath. The oncologist treating Matthias last year told them he would be watching for exactly that—metastasis to the brain.

"Bit premature on his part, I'd say," he says. "Taking his own life. There's no sign of cancer in this brain. Why not wait and see how it turns out?"

"What does cancer of the brain look like?"

"We don't get brains like that in here," Dr. Mitchell says. "Not usable for our purposes. Check with the cancer institute. They might have something in their freezers."

"Where's the rest of the body?" Loretta asks.

"We removed the brain and then returned the body to the funeral home. After tidying him up," Ryan says.

"His funeral is this afternoon. Typically, we send a representative, but the timing didn't work out today," Dr. Mitchell says.

"A funeral for a zombie," Loretta says.

Ryan places the right hemisphere on the blue cutting board and flays with practiced precision—like a sushi chef—and by the time he finishes, a dozen thin slices of brain lay on the board like medallions, each a half-inch thick.

He points to the runt of the fine cuts. "Even in this little section there are about four billion neurons, also known as brain cells, with another forty billion helper cells."

Loretta counts the slices, multiplies them by two to capture both hemispheres, and gets to about 100 billion neurons and 400 billion support cells, numbers so vast it's hard to put them into a meaningful perspective; how could anything be so small to fit so many of them into a brain?

"Want to touch a slice?"

"May I?"

"Sure. He won't mind."

Loretta steps forward. It looks like food when it's sliced like this, thick meat, like the Spam her mom used to cook for dinner, which she supposes is exactly what it is now that it's lifeless. Human meat. She brushes her fingers along the edge of the dead rubbery matter.

Dr. Mitchell hands her a towel. As Loretta wipes her hand, Dr. Mitchell asks, "Well, what do you think of our little lab as a backdrop for the *60 Minutes* piece on near death experiences? Might be pretty cool."

ELEVEN

Loretta reads the media statement one last time. She is looking for typos or grammar errors, knowing there will be none at this late stage, but checking anyway. This must be perfect; a mistake will elicit an unconscious reaction of mistrust—how can anyone believe the University really cares if it doesn't even care about typos? And it can't be too smooth sounding. It needs to be informal, a little folksy even.

The University is deeply sorry for the situation. We take full responsibility for this ethically complicated circumstance and will do whatever is necessary to make the situation right. We will be steadfast in supporting our patients, protecting the privacy of everyone involved and following the direction of those affected. Although nothing like this has happened before in the history of the University Fertility Clinic, we have put into place new protocols to ensure it never does again. As part of our commitment to privacy and the support of our patients, we will not comment beyond this written statement. Again, we are very sorry.

She pauses, forces herself not to read it yet again, and hits send. Figuring she has about a minute, two at most, she finds the Vaseline in her desk drawer, swipes some across her lips and pops open a mini-can of Diet Coke. She drains half the can in one sip.

The desk phone rings. Jamie from KGWN.

At the same instant, a text comes in from Matthias with a photo of Jenny at the beach; birds fly behind the backlit silhouette, frozen against the cloudy gray sky. Puffins? That would make sense. But maybe not at this time of year. Gulls. Plain old screechy gulls, probably.

The phone keeps ringing. One more and it will go to voicemail. Ready, set, go.

She picks up the receiver. "Loretta Sparkman."

"That's it? You're sorry? You made me wait twenty-four hours for this?"

"That's it."

"What about the baby? Are you confirming the birth of a baby?"

"We cannot by law comment on our patients. You know that."

"Are you denying a child was born?"

"This is an ethically complex situation, and our goal is to protect the privacy of everyone involved." Stick to the talking points; focus on the story of redemption, the hero's contrition and service to those who have been damaged, those who need protection.

"Stop bullshitting me. Off the record, was a child born?"

"No comment. And no comment doesn't mean I'm confirming or denying the birth of a child. Please, these people have the right to privacy."

"Not if one of them is filing a lawsuit."

"We don't know what's in that filing yet," Loretta says, although it's tough to argue that point. Later, she may need to modify the statement to focus exclusively on the woman's privacy.

"I'm sending a crew over. We'll broadcast live from the University hospital this afternoon. I *will* get the full story, and I won't be so accommodating next time."

"I'll have someone meet your crew to be sure you have what you need. But come on, play straight here. How did you find out about this? You knew yesterday. You owe me. I gave you an exclusive."

"You call that an exclusive? This bullshit soft-serve vanilla statement? I could have beaten everyone else by a day, now it's only going to be by a couple of hours."

"Jamie, please emphasize the part of the statement where it says we are sorry. We really are," Loretta says, keeping her voice tactically calm.

"I want to interview the sperm doctor."

"He's a gynecologist, not a sperm doctor. And we are not providing spokespeople for this story."

"What about Babs Meekam? The person on the statement. The patient advocate, whoever the hell she is. Is she camera-ready?"

"You can use her name for the statement, as well as her photograph, but we are firm on this point. No interviews."

"Huh. You think that's clever? That you going quiet will make me go quiet? You'd better hold on tight, Loretta." Jamie hangs up.

Loretta calls Mona to brief her on the conversation, letting her know they're in for, at a minimum, a bunch of sound and fury from Jamie that will likely play out as short-term posturing for ratings. Given she has no actual content, her reporting shouldn't be much of a hit to the University. Still, predicting the full sweep of media coverage and associated social media response isn't possible yet—she needs to wait for the statement to hit the inboxes of everyone on their list, but her sense is to go ahead with an all-employee message to preempt any public relations push the sperm donor might have ready to launch.

Mona tells her that the filing has dropped at the courthouse. "Can you get to there today?"

"Sure, no problem."

Loretta reviews the draft all-employee message, makes a few minor edits, and sends it to Mona for final approval. The Dean knocks on her door.

"What's next in this saga?" he asks, settling into her visitor's chair.

"Depends on what's in the filing."

"Seems like the attorney will want to make the man out to be as sympathetic as possible, and to do that—"

"They need to make everyone else look bad," she says, finishing his sentence.

The Dean wears blue scrubs, which means he is just back from the hospital surgical suite. Loretta glances at his fingernails clipped short and clean for surgery, his hands pale and smooth like the hands of a child overly tended by a doting mother. She will never admit it to anyone, not even Matthias, but something about his fingernails never fails to make her feel safe in the world, if only for the few seconds it takes to notice them.

He looks at the ceiling.

She waits, not talking, knowing he has something to say, but isn't sure how to say it.

After a few seconds, he looks at her. "Have I ever told you about an error I made once during surgery?"

"Only one?" Loretta asks, then winces. "Sorry, that came out wrong. I meant, you know, you've done so many surgeries, it seems inevitable."

He smiles, without reproach, understanding there's no malice in her awkwardness.

"I imagine situations like at the fertility clinic bring up difficult memories for doctors," she says, trying again. "Nurses too, all of you. PTSD of a sort."

"Errors happen all the time, and to call them errors isn't entirely fair. More often than not, they're system breakdowns, poor communication or, increasingly, a

117

technology problem, sometimes just bad luck." He twists around to push the door shut. "I was a resident surgeon in pre-fellowship training, my last year."

The Dean isn't an eloquent man, even with all his education, and in his public appearances Loretta has established the narrative of an authentic man, a humble leader, a narrative framing to cover his rough edges and many stumbles, a story that took root easily because in his case, it is one hundred percent true.

"My patient was in for a routine hysterectomy and everything went as planned. She was healthy, other than the endometriosis. I removed her uterus and ovaries, cleaned up the fibrous tumors, and closed. The nurses wheeled her into the recovery room. I had some tea. I remember to this day that the tea was so hot I burned my tongue. Earl Grey. Odd, isn't it, the little details that scorch their way into our memory banks."

Loretta stays quiet, waiting.

"After a short time in recovery, the patient started screaming, sobbing. The recovery nurses paged me to come quick." He shakes his head. "Turns out, she was awake the whole time, the anesthesia froze her muscles, including her facial muscles, she couldn't speak, but it didn't knock her out, didn't dull the pain."

"My god," Loretta whispers.

"No one understands how or why anesthesia works. We pump it into patients and out they go. But now and again, rarely, whatever mysterious biological interaction that causes ninety-nine point nine percent of people to black out doesn't happen. And those patients undergo the excruciating ordeal of being operated on while fully conscious."

"You couldn't have known."

"That's what the lawyers argued. And we prevailed. An award for pain and suffering only. No negligence. But still, her life was changed forever by the experience. Mine too. Since then, I've implemented new protocols.

We undertake a more rigorous screening before I make the first cut, monitoring for tears, because even with frozen muscles, that's the tell, people can still cry. Now, I assign a tech to watch a patient's eyes, their only job, to watch for tears."

"How is it possible we don't understand how those drugs work?"

"If we don't know what makes a person conscious, it's not surprising that we don't know what makes them unconscious."

"Nobody knows why we sleep?"

"Nope, not yet, although there's a great deal of research happening on that subject. It's dumb luck, an accident, that decades ago someone stumbled on the fact that these meds knock a person out, most people, anyway. It's perfect for surgery."

On the surface, this seems an odd story for the Dean to share, but then she understands why he is telling her this: He wants her to see *The Case of the Misplaced Sperm* from a physician's point of view, the shame and sorrow of hurting someone, and is using his own experience to be sure it is meaningful for her.

"Thanks," Loretta says. "It's good perspective."

Watching his back as he leaves, Loretta sees in the slump of his shoulders—pushed down now by the weight of a decades-old scream—a man determined to do good in the world. The realization wrestles a tired sense of gratitude from her.

TWELVE

Loretta punches the elevator button for the fifth floor, pushing out all thoughts of misplaced sperm, and spins the treadle of her mind, weaving together information from religion, the hopefully-flirty Irish evolutionist, Babs, brain biology and Ryan Gosling's tutorial. She lands on three scenarios to explain Jenny's near death experiences. Maybe.

One: Jenny has some never-before-seen disease that periodically tricks her brain into thinking she is dying, probably by oxygen starvation, which in turn jumpstarts the near death experiences. This is the most plausible, and the scariest. Also, Loretta thinks this scenario would disappoint Jenny. It would reduce her feelings of oneness-with-the-universe to the simple result of a medical condition, a fevered delusion. Pure biology, nothing mystical, nothing external. An elaborate sneeze.

Two: Jenny is expressing some sort of dormant free-rider genes with no (current) explanation, making the near death experiences like male nipples of the mind. That's possible and a better outcome for Jenny, as long as the hitchhiking genes are harmless. The unanswered questions in this scenario, though, are why does Jenny have these genes and is she experiencing something "real," as in access to a hidden realm of existence, or is it created by her brain, a hallucination?

Three is an expansion of two: Jenny is manifesting the theory of Dr. Orr, chair of the Department of Religion, about evolving human consciousness, having already attained the third level, what he called cosmic consciousness, putting her in the company of mystics from across history who started religions. Maybe at some point, Jenny would be the progenitor of a new religion, maybe that's already happening, like Matthias joked last night. As utterly ridiculous as this seems, logically Loretta can't dismiss it out of hand. If not for his cognitive peculiarities—divine gifts being the preferred term among adherents—Jesus would have been the forgotten son of a carpenter and his unfaithful wife, lost to history.

The elevator lurches to a stop and the doors open into the Department of Philosophy, which is in the same building as the Department of Religion. Religion is on the ground floor, philosophy on the top. A Department of Death would fit well right in between the floors, she thinks, stepping out of the elevator. No one is around. She walks over to a fish aquarium that extends across the length of the far wall. The base of the aquarium is lined with turquoise-colored gravel; three leafy blue-green plants flutter as water and oxygen flow from the small bubbling pipe hanging over the edge. Bright green mold stains the glass.

Two fish circle. One is large and red and glamorous, with bright yellow spots shaped like human eyes on its side and fins like ruffled taffeta. It pauses, pushing up against the glass with an open-mouthed kissy-face. The second fish is small and glittery and golden, swimming quickly, almost frantically, around the perimeter, nearly touching the edge of the tank with each pass, closer every time but never breaching the gap, a fish dance with infinity.

The door from an inner office pops opens and Professor Thill—a ruddy middle-aged white man, tall and thin save for a protruding belly, enters. He is wearing round John Lennon glasses.

"Loretta Sparkman from the Dean's office?"

"Yes. Thanks for seeing me on such short notice," she says, sticking out her hand. His grip is firm and dry.

"I didn't expect you to make this meeting," he says.

"Oh? Why not?"

"An email message just came out from the Dean about the lawsuit against the fertility clinic. I would imagine this topic would be keeping those in your line of work busy."

"Was the email clear?" Might as well do double duty and see how the story she developed for *The Case of the Misplaced Sperm* is landing with the faculty.

"It was clear, and the apology seems sincere, but it left open the possibility that another shoe may drop. Or a baby. A baby shoe may drop. Is there a baby?"

"Best not to talk about it. Patient confidentiality and all." Loretta looks down at her bright yellow shoes.

The last time she was home, Sally-Anne convinced Loretta to add color to her wardrobe, to move away from black and gray. "Shake things up, Mom. Start with a pair of shoes. That's easy enough." She picked out a pair of shiny faux-leather canary yellow flats. Loretta has not worn any other shoes, except trail runners on the weekends, since she bought them over the holidays. The tips are scuffed up.

"Why else would anyone go to the trouble of filing a lawsuit?" he asks.

She doesn't answer. He waits, watches her watching her yellow shoes. She waits longer. She looks up from the floor into his eyes. He blinks behind his John

Lennon frames. He speaks. She wins.

"The weather app says the rain will hold off for the next hour or so. Not sure how much we can trust that, but can we walk while we talk?" He pats his belly. "My husband is relentless about my daily steps. Kill two birds with one stone."

What the hell is up with people and that saying? She winces at the image of two birds being hit by a boulder as she follows him down five flights and onto a gravel path that winds behind the building. She spins out the *60 Minutes* ruse, says she will be asking the kinds of questions he might get from their reporters.

"Are near death experiences real?"

"Enough have been reported, one would certainly think so."

"What do they signify?"

"Could you contextualize that question?"

Loretta doles out a summary of what she has learned so far about near death experiences. He nods like a bobble head, taking in her words, glasses sliding down and back up his long skinny nose with each head jerk.

"The perspective of my department requires taking a few steps back," he says, emphasizing the word *my*. He fiddles with his fitness watch, mutters something about needing to prove the steps to his husband; satisfied it is working, he strides forward, posture erect, an apostle of philosophy and fitness.

"Darwin in his day answered the greatest puzzle of the enlightenment, the origins of the diversity of species. The greatest puzzle of our contemporary era is the origin of consciousness. Discoveries in this research area will render some scholar as important as Darwin himself, or some other luminary, maybe Einstein or Oppenheimer."

Intellectual immortality, academics would choose it over bodily immortality in a heartbeat, she thinks, or many of them at least.

"And a path back to relevance for philosophers as we leap into the debate, pointing out the gaps and assumptions of the scientific inquiry. Philosophers are once again equal to scientists," he says with a hint of triumph in his tone.

She looks down at the muddy path. He has a long stride and for every step he takes, Loretta's short legs require nearly two.

"Am I walking too fast for you?"

"I'm fine," she says, as her breathing ratchets up to a near-pant.

"Have you heard of Phineas Gage?"

Before she can answer, a squirrel plops down in front of them, falling from the crown of a gnarly old oak. The little creature looks up, shakes its bushy tail, makes a clicking noise and disappears back up the tree.

"Poor thing," Loretta says.

"Bookmark that tumble," says Professor Thill as he launches into his version of the Phineas Gage story. He gives Phineas a head of unruly red hair, a loving family and petulant mistress. But even so, his end is the same as what Professor Mitchell said. The personality of Phineas changed drastically after the crowbar smashed through his head. Loretta waits for Dr. Thill to say that the saga of Phineas proves brain-is-mind. And he does say that, but then also more.

"Before the crowbar burst through that poor man's skull, piercing his frontal lobe, our friend Phineas didn't know what it was like to be a bat.[15] Nor did he after."

"Be a bat? What? I have no idea what that means."

His brisk walking hinders the phone recording, and her own heartbeat is now a dull thumping undercurrent to Dr. Thill's words. Loretta pushes the phone closer to his mouth as they walk, imagining how they look; a tall philosopher marching purposefully across campus, a black scarf flapping behind him in the damp wind, trailed by a middle-aged woman, hair unkempt, wearing scuffed yellow shoes and a puffy black fake-down coat, holding a phone to his face as she struggles to keep up.

"Let's put the bat question aside for a moment. Tell me, what do you think it was like to be that squirrel back there as it fell from the tree?" he asks.

"Surprised, probably embarrassed."

"A projection perhaps. Because if we are crisp in our thinking, all we can fairly and logically conclude on behalf of the squirrel is that it was 'like' something, something unique to the little rodent, a subjective experience. Do you agree?"

"I guess so. What's not to agree with," she says, half-jogging now. "Dr. Thill, could we slow down?"

"Of course." He calibrates his pace to Loretta. She gives up on the recording—too much ambient noise—and tucks the phone in her pocket. Her breathing begins to steady.

"If you think about it, you have no way of knowing what it's like to experience the world as a squirrel," he says. "Or a bat."

But still she tries, and now imagines flying through the darkness, hanging upside down, using the bat's ability to sense a position based on how sound bounces from nearby cave walls or the water down below. But her imagined experience is only what she would feel if she, a human, were inside a small, fuzzy, winged body doing all the things a bat does. That is, if the bat experiences anything at all beyond immediate sensation. Does a bat have a sense of self, she wonders? Or is it all reaction, like a zombie?

"Okay, I don't know what it's like to be a squirrel, or a bat. And so?"

"What color was that squirrel?"

"Brown."

"What *is* the color brown to you?"

"Milk chocolate, my husband's eyes, a latte. It's like—"

He interrupts. "It's *like* something. Your version of brown is something I can't access, much less agree on or even describe. Experiences that can only be described as being *like* something are subjective, in turn, a function of human consciousness."

"Or bat consciousness," she says. "And squirrel."

"These creatures are proxies to simplify the example and provide an entry point to the more complex aspects of the discussion," he says. "Let's transition to the human application of this phenomenon. Is that all right?"

"Sure, of course."

"There's nothing more familiar and about which we are more knowledgeable than our own experiences. We call these experiences qualia, because, well, I suppose jargon makes people who use it feel like they're in a special club ..."

He pauses as if he has lost the thread of his thought, but then reconnects and continues.

"Do you like cherry pie?"

"Especially warm with vanilla ice cream."

"It's my favorite as well," he says. "Now, since we're both fans, tell me how cherry pie tastes to you so we can determine if it tastes the same to me."

"Sweet and tart and ..." She can't describe it, not in any way that would enable him to say they are tasting the same thing. He smiles, knowing his point has been made.

"The taste you experience for cherry pie and what I experience are qualia, wholly unique or maybe identical or possibly something in between, but there is no way to measure this. Nor is it possible for you and I to know if we are experiencing brown in the same way. I cannot know, based on any objective measurement tool available to us today, how you experience brown. So, these qualia are different than the objective things in our world, like the size or weight of the squirrel, or its heart rate as it fell, all of which can be measured in ways that allow us to agree on their attributes."

"I mostly get what you are saying but I'm not tracking the connection to near death experiences."

"A near death experience is an aberrant artifact of the sense of self and thus provides an intriguing lens into the workings of consciousness. This is what I meant by taking a few steps back from simply discussing the significance of near death experiences. One cannot understand a near death experience without understanding human consciousness."

They round a curve in the trail. A crow squawks loudly, four times. Loretta looks in the air but cannot locate the bird.

"Vocabulary is important for our discussion. Let's break down consciousness into two layers. First, the functional layer. Awareness, pain, cognition, what we categorize as instinctive reactions, wakefulness and sleep. Perhaps emotions. We aren't sure about that yet, but likely. Presumably, these functions are the product of biology, probably the brain in interplay with other body parts."

The footpath turns to mud mixed with wet bark dust. A crosshatched pattern of tread is embossed in the soil, the vestiges of students and faculty walking, running, skipping. Future fossils pressed into the dirt.

"Consider zombies."

"Zombies," Loretta says, surprised. "How so?"

"Everything we do at the functional level to survive does not require the subjective experience of it, does not require qualia. One can theorize that our bodies would react in ways that would avoid pain, pursue desire, perhaps even develop language, all without the need for a conscious self to experience or interpret these phenomena. We could all be zombies, or meat sacks to use a colloquialism, going about our business successfully enough for continued existence, without the subjective lens of our experiences. What then is the need for self?"

What *is* the need for self? That's exactly what she's been trying to explain to Matthias. Who needs a self? But she knows that's not the answer the professor is fishing for now.

"To make babies," she says, remembering what the probably-not-flirty Irish evolutionist said. "With a self, I can predict how other 'selves' experience the world. And while it might not be exact, because how can I really know what they are experiencing, like with the cherry pie, it's close enough to allow humans to plan for the future, to protect and nurture babies, to share cherry pie recipes."

"That is a common argument. Collaboration does provide an explanation for why consciousness may have evolved. Another argument is that consciousness is a trait that got out of hand. We evolved what we needed for baby-making, along with a bunch of junk, such as prolonged grief, depression, obsessive introspection, suicidal tendencies, a passion for dominance. There are examples of human attributes stemming from consciousness that make life hard, if not downright unbearable."

Free riders, she thinks. Human consciousness is like male nipples. Maybe evolution backfired? Or overshot the intended mark. Way overshot.

"But that's not my primary point. Most philosophers and scientists agree on the first lesson of Phineas Gage. With tenacity and technology, along with truckloads of money, the functional layer of consciousness can be mapped. Just as scientists linked blood flow to the beating of the heart, we can figure out how our biology creates physical pain, emotions and the like. In other words, this functional layer is approachable by the methods of science because the items in this category can be objectively measured."

The trail transitions from flat to a modest downhill. The rosebushes along the path are scraggly with dried pink and white flowers; no one pruned them back for winter.

"This brings us to the second layer of consciousness and what is referred to as the hard problem."[16]

"Does this have something to do with you asking me about being a bat?" Loretta asks.

"Yes. The hard problem is sometimes referred to in shorthand with the question *What's it like to be a bat?*' What this means, at root, is this: Most scientists and philosophers believe this second layer, this problem of purely subjective experience—the qualia, the taste of cherry pies—which cannot be objectively categorized or measured, is also a function of biology and will ultimately be excavated in the same way as the first layer. It may be an extremely difficult problem, but the objective measurement-based methods of science will triumph, slowly but steadily."

"But not everyone believes this?"

"Not everyone."

Loretta surmises from his tone that he's in the not-everyone camp.

He continues. "The experience of Phineas Gage and countless others who have been changed by strokes or brain injuries supports the theory that our sense of self is a construction of our biology and that anyone who thinks otherwise is either a closet non-atheist—"

Non-atheist? Loretta's mind detours into a groove that processes the implication of wide adoption of this term. I am no longer not-religious. The religious person is non-atheist. She makes a mental note to start using the phrase.

Dr. Thill is still talking. "Can we get to a satisfying answer about subjective experience with the third-person objectivity of science if one can never know what it's like to be a bat? Or more accurately for our discussion, what it's like to experience the world as another human?"

He trips over a tree root. Loretta throws out her arm, as one does with a child in a car abruptly braking, and he regains his balance. He bends down to brush off his shoes before walking and then talking again. They both ignore her instinctive maternal reaction.

"No matter how far we travel in unlocking the secrets of the first functional layer of consciousness, we can never be sure that our mind is not tricking us at the second layer, because we cannot experience the world through another person's perspective. It's challenging to envision a method to measure the brown I see through my eyes and have confidence that it precisely measures the brown you see through your eyes."

The footpath ends at the University's test garden where horticultural, plant biology and genetics students conduct cross-pollination and other experiments.

"Seems like the people who believe in the hard problem of consciousness are not far off from people who believe in a soul," Loretta says. "Like they want to find a way to reserve something, hold it back, and say science can't access it."

"That's correct, and insightful."

"But still a belief, right?"

He sighs. "If we are brutally honest, at this stage in the study of self and consciousness there is precious little that isn't a belief. Rather, it's a massive jockeying for intellectual position across the academic world."

"Even the whole brain-is-mind thing?"

"We don't know how atoms become measurable things—furniture, a rosebush, our squirrel friend, you, me—much less how they become, or generate, qualia. Many assume, probably reasonably, that consciousness will end up being governed by the same rules of atoms and their subparts coming together to create matter, those rules playing out in the brain, but we don't know what those rules are so that assumption is by definition a belief. It's rather like the wild west of scientific inquiry. And while there are no literal shoot-outs, there are reputational dustups regularly. Quite a bit of rudeness, actually." He shrugs. "It's an age-old battle, matter versus mind. We used to call it science versus religion, but even as these paradigms shift, the driving force remains the same, a search for meaning by unmasking the bedrock of our reality."

They stroll around the small garden, following an old labyrinth path; half the burnished stones are pushed deep into the dirt and nearly invisible, the other half are missing. He pulls out a weed struggling up through a row of boxwood.

"Could you let the Dean know the horrid condition of this garden? It's an embarrassment." Loretta doesn't answer. There is no money for a gardener, the days of the Dean snapping his fingers and money materializing are long gone, lost in a past when people believed in—and funded—education as something other than a pipeline for winning the lottery of white-collar jobs. Before the world, at least this country, fell into battle over collective identity and national narrative, a battle that seems to require taking the academic world hostage, because that's where history gets written, more or less. Which, now that she thinks about it, is of course related to her question about how something becomes a department.

Suddenly, a new question pops into Loretta's head, forcefully, like a slap to the cheek. Is the underlying battle about America's collective identity, including the truth of what it was and the promise of what it will be, an outgrowth of a parallel struggle to make sense of the concept of the self, to agree on a new definition?

"Here's the thing," he says, standing and leaving behind muddy handprints on his khaki pants. "Proving unequivocally that our mind derives from our biology has become rather urgent. Because what if we can't? What if it turns out we can't penetrate the subjective nature of consciousness with the objective tools of science? The consequences of being unable to prove the brain-is-mind model would require a revisiting of our accumulated understanding of our world."

He starts walking. Loretta follows, thinking about how Jenny describes the indivisibility of her near death experiences. And she thinks about Professor Mitchell's explanation that a theory must be both useful in terms of its testability and predictive value. According to the Dean, anesthesia is both those things but still no one knows how it works. Meaning, the underlying reality of anesthesia is unknown. Is this philosophy department chair implying that the underlying reality of, well, reality might be something other than what people assume?

She is breathing hard again. She needs to start working out, she will as soon as Matthias is ready and they can exercise together. The philosophy department building comes into view from the opposite side of where they started, a back door into the deteriorating brick and stone structure.

"Where do you stand on all of this?" she asks.

"I fear a rush to accept the brain-as-mind model could lead us to ignore the very real implications of the hard question for the entire scientific enterprise. And that could be our undoing." He looks at his watch. "Not enough steps. I'll have to do more later, but for now, I apologize. I have another appointment."

"This gives me a lot to think about. Before I go, would you mind summing up for me how this relates to near death experiences?"

Loretta pulls out her phone and starts recording again just as students surge into the brick courtyard for the switchover between class periods.

"Yes, of course, that's why you are here."

She strains to hear his words, half lip-reading over

the youthful shouting and laughter, once again moving the phone closer, trying not to hit his teeth.

"Near death experiences offer an insight into the sense of self. Understanding how the self shuts down or transmutes at death gives us clues to how it forms, but frankly, near death experiences are of limited use from a scholarship perspective because these people are one-offs and the experiences cannot be predicted, or replicated, and therefore reliable data about them can never be obtained. We are at the mercy of the memory of those reporting the experiences and humans are, alas, unreliable witnesses in almost all regards."

"Theoretically, what if someone is having lots of near death experiences, you know, like every week or so?"

"It would provide a rare opportunity to test multiple hypotheses about the origins of human consciousness, but that's unheard of so not a useful question. Which might make it perfect for *60 Minutes*, of course."

THIRTEEN

The metal detector at the courthouse beeps as Loretta passes through. The guard points at the decorative buckles on her yellow shoes and smiles. She slips them off and goes back through. It beeps again. Likely, the underwire in her bra. She looks down at her chest and the officer waves her through. Behind her, the Black woman who also set off the metal detector is stopped for a bag search. Loretta feels like she maybe should say something, ask why she's being searched when Loretta wasn't, but isn't sure the woman would want attention drawn to her. Loretta would hate that kind of attention. She walks on.

The docket office is in the basement at the end of a dusty, barely lit corridor that smells like mildew and chemicals. Probably insecticide. Or rat poison. Two people are in line ahead of her. She doesn't recognize them as reporters. That's good.

After a short wait, she is assigned a monitor and waits for the case file to load. She moves past the first few pages of administrative information quickly, eager to get to the narrative description of the case. Flipping through the docket, she reads faster and starts using her phone to take photos, unsure it is allowed. Unwilling to risk hearing no, she doesn't ask.

After leaving the courthouse, she stops outside the front doors to call Mona. "It's all there, every bit of it, some stuff we didn't know about. Now all formally public record."

"What's there, exactly?"

Loretta hears traffic sounds through the phone. "Call me back when you aren't driving."

The workday is almost over. Lawyers, courthouse staff, defendants, people looking for a bathroom, lost souls and jury members stream out the doors of the downtown building; standing there in the middle of the crowd, her body is like a mid-river boulder, splitting the flow of hurried and irritated people into two channels.

Tired of fighting the current, Loretta crosses the street to a little park. She hands a crumpled dollar to a man holding a cardboard sign that says *Veteran, anything helps, God bless.* A woman wearing threadbare clothes walks by, hair sticking up like a crown of thorns, pushing a battered stroller with a dirty rag doll inside. On the other side of the Korean War Memorial at the park's center, Loretta sits on an empty bench. To her right, a businessman drinks from a can in a brown paper bag. The hems of his gray pants are frayed, and she remembers the sewing her mother took in for extra money.

A pigeon lands next to Loretta's bench. She fishes in her bag and finds the uneaten almonds Matthias packed for her yesterday. Do pigeons like almonds? She crushes a nut and tosses the crumbs on the ground. Six other pigeons come in for a landing.

Mona calls back. "I'm parked. What did it say?"

"Everything. Transcripts of clinic phone calls and texts, depositions of an on-duty nurse that said the sperm sample was dropped, got mixed up, the donor's so-called traumatized reaction when he learned the truth."

"That's not so bad, we've owned up to the error."

"The filing makes clear he also knows about the pregnancy. So that fact will be public now."

"Nothing unexpected there either. We informed him of that. But he doesn't know, at least not from us, that a child was born."

"It says the University offered to pay the woman an undisclosed sum if she would take a morning-after pill."

"Shit," Mona says. "How could he know that?"

"Is it true?"

The seven pigeons puff up their chests and feathers as Loretta raises her voice.

"A suite of options was provided," Mona says.

"It says that the University offered to provide an abortion free of charge and that when she refused, we pressured her to have it. Is that true?"

"Of course that's bullshit. The sperm donor was the one demanding an abortion."

"It gets worse," Loretta says.

"What could be worse than a legal document asserting a publicly funded University tried to force an abortion on a woman who conceived a child after being knocked up with the wrong sperm?"

"That we did it because of racism, that's what could be worse. It says we were motivated to offer a generous settlement in exchange for an abortion because the child would be biracial."

"How does the sperm donor know the woman isn't white?"

"Good question."

"That's the attorney throwing big fat chunks of red meat to conservative reporters and his client's followers to rile things up. Not an unexpected strategy for what they hope to gain."

"It's sick and gross."

"What about the request for damages?"

"Twelve million for emotional distress. And if any child was born, it must be presented, genetic testing must be completed and if his paternity is proven, he wants custody."

"Again, no surprise. His lawyer told us that would be in the filing. It's his only play."

"The wording suggests they see this as a potential challenge to current sperm donor case law."

"While not a direct impact to the University, likely something we'd have to monitor for years," Mona says. "An unwelcome expense."

"The one bit of good news is there's no information about identities of either the man or woman."

"Maybe the timing is right for that to change."

"Leak something?"

Mona doesn't answer, and Loretta realizes she should not have asked that so overtly. They agree to touch base later. A barely-there rain is falling, dusk is coming fast. A man carrying a skateboard asks her for a cigarette. Loretta shakes her head no. Then she closes her eyes, listening, separating the sound of water from air. After a few minutes, her phone vibrates. *Where are you? Come home soon.*

Loretta stands; the pigeons hop away, even as they keep watching her, hopeful. Loretta shivers a little. Her ass is damp from the bench. She walks by the spiky haired woman who has parked the battered stroller next to the Korean War Memorial and is now bathing her dirty rag doll in the non-functional fountain while singing. *Hush little baby don't you cry.* Loretta pulls her jacket tighter and walks faster.

But then she stops. Jenny's words echo. We are one. We are indivisible.

She fishes out a five-dollar bill from her pocket and takes the few steps back to the woman. Loretta speaks quietly, trying not to be threatening. "I wonder if you could use a little—"

"Get away from me and my baby, you bitch!" the woman screams. "Don't hurt us! I'll kill you!"

The money floats from Loretta's hand onto the ground as she hurries from the park.

FOURTEEN

The drizzle has cleared. The sharp, after-rain smell of wet rocks seeps into the drafty porch-room. Matthias pours Loretta a glass of chardonnay as she sits on the sofa.

"How was the beach?" she asks.

"A little cold, but nice," Jenny says. "Your husband is good company."

"You aren't so bad yourself," Matthias says. Turning to Loretta, he asks, "How was your day? How goes the quest?"

Before she can answer, Loretta's phone vibrates. Toni has sent a link to the article filed by an Associated Press reporter: *Clinic that gave sperm to wrong woman defends itself from lawsuit seeking $12 million in damages.* She reads the article out loud.

"Is this good for you?" Matthias asks. "Honestly, I can never tell."

"Moderately good. They hinted at the pregnancy but focused on the damages. It means I have a reprieve to enjoy your company this evening, might sleep decently, fingers crossed, but need to be ready for an avalanche in the morning."

"Is your life always like this?" Jenny asks.

"What do you mean?"

"Consumed by your job."

"Yes," Matthias interrupts, giving Loretta no pause to answer herself.

"Must be tough on both of you."

"It is," Matthias says, again too quickly.

"It's a demanding job, without question," Loretta says, mostly keeping the irritation from her voice. She doesn't want to be the person who gets angry at a sick husband and her perpetually almost-dying friend for being insensitive to the fact that it is her job that pays the bills, including the medical bills. She slouches into the cushions, exhausted not by her full day but by the effort it takes to ignore a sudden urge to flee. "Don't mind me, and please don't be offended, but I'm going to rest my eyes for just a sec."

"Long day for you, honey, I know. Working while we're gallivanting to the beach." Matthias gets up to rub her neck.

"Gallivanting is a good thing," Loretta says. "And stop, Matthias, really, that's not necessary—"

He doesn't stop and Loretta can't keep herself from swooning into the sense of release as he presses her muscles with exactly the right amount of familiar force. She shuts her eyes, her mind wanders to the philosophy department meeting and she decides to test herself, to push her brain outward, to experience the world as if she is Matthias. If I can't be a bat, can I at least imagine what it is like to be him, someone I know so well?

She visualizes pressing her mind into his body, pictures a white vapory ghost-like substance that is her essence, her soul or self or whatever, breaching his skin, wrapping around his bones and slipping into his brain. Looking out from behind his eye sockets, like his mind is a pair of binoculars, she sees the back of her own head, her graying hair, her tired shoulders, watches his kneading hands, her hands now, and tries to feel them feeling her. Then she imagines his thoughts, thinking that he is probably wondering why she has a knot on the right side of her neck. She thinks his question using the words he would, "I wonder why Loretta is so tense in this part of her neck? Maybe she should get a standing desk at work. I bet the knot is related to when she broke her collarbone last year." She realizes she is imagining Matthias's thoughts in his actual voice, or rather, a stilted stage-struck version of his voice. Does an interior voice sound the same as an exterior voice? Would it even have a sound? As she is trying to identify the sound of her own thoughts, the vaporous self becomes detached from his mind. Stay with it, stay inside his mind. What is his experience of this moment? Is his skin cool in the drafty room? She pulls a throw blanket across her lap. It's going to be a frigid night. Dammit. She is back in her own head. Concentrate harder. But just as fast as that thought arrives, another overtakes it; the act of concentration is uniquely of her mind, she cannot extract it from the will to experience Matthias's qualia.

She can't believe she just used that crazy word.

Loretta sits up straight. "You can stop now."

He kisses the top of her head in that way she's always hated, what she imagines a dad-kiss would be like. Back in his chair, Matthias fishes around in the pocket of his denim work shirt, and pulls out a bag of tobacco and rolling papers. He dribbles tobacco onto a single sheet and skillfully rolls a cigarette, pinching off both ends.

"What are you doing?" Loretta asks, knowing full well what he is doing, so her question should be why, not what.

"I'm having a smoke."

He lights a match to the cigarette tip.

Matthias was a hard-core smoker when they first met, a habit picked up during his time in the military, and because she wanted to share everything with him in the heady days of first love, she took up smoking. Now, in the instant of registering the scent, distant echoes of joy wash over Loretta as she is transported back to the languid hours spent in bed, the volcanic elation, the feeling they wanted to crawl inside each other and never be apart. Even though it had been hard to quit, hellish even, and the nicotine-deprived arguments were epic, when Loretta became pregnant with Sally-Anne they both took the plunge and never looked back. Until now. This minute.

"Why?"

"I feel like it."

"It's a foul habit," Jenny says.

Matthias is blowing smoke rings, a game they used to play post-sex. He manages three rings successively and looks at Loretta, challenging her. Holding the cigarette in place with his teeth, Matthias rolls another. He tosses it and the matches to Loretta.

"It *is* a foul habit," Loretta says, lighting up.

The heat braises the back of her throat like a prickly embrace. She puffs out a smoke ring bigger than any of Matthias's and now it's his turn to laugh. Jenny waves her hand in front of her, and the ring collapses.

"Whoops, sorry."

"It's a silly game anyway," Loretta says.

"And terrible for your health."

"Yeah, there's that."

It's nearly night, the sky mottled blue and black like fresh spilt ink soaking through a white tablecloth. Something scratches beneath the old deck turned drafty sunroom.

"Raccoons," Matthias says, lighting a new cigarette. "Probably settled in for the winter. Might have to do something about that. Mean, destructive little bastards."

"Lolo, what did you find out today?" Jenny asks.

The wine and the neck rub and the cigarette have unwound Loretta. She tells them about the brain bank and how simultaneously unsettling and thrilling it was to watch the young man's brain as it was sliced up.

"Who was it?" Matthias asks.

"Twenty-six and the funeral was today. That's all I know."

Matthias pulls out his phone and taps on the screen. After a minute, he looks up.

"Found one person matching gender and age with a funeral today. The burial was at Lone Fir Cemetery."

"What was his name?" Jenny asks.

"I'm not sure we should be doing this," Loretta says.

"Why?" Jenny asks.

"Feels like a violation of privacy."

"No one will know but us," Matthias says as he begins to read from the obituary.

"Nelson Bargrove. Loved astronomy, the beach and hiking. Two years as a junior park ranger at Yosemite and a summer at Denali where he was in charge of sled dogs. Leaves behind two younger sisters. Parents predeceased him."

"Tragic," Loretta says.

Matthias and Loretta drink more wine, cigarette smoke accumulates like a ghostly shroud in the high reaches of the room. Jenny sips water. Each drift into private thoughts about Nelson Bargrove. Jenny has a mental image in which she and Nelson are laughing at a joke together. Loretta animates the brain slices and they grow into a Nelson who is Sally-Anne's friend and has come for one of Matthias's weekly spaghetti dinners. Matthias wonders how Nelson killed himself, stops himself from imagining multiple scenarios and just asks Loretta. She tells him.

"That takes courage," he says. "Intentionality."

"This is getting morbid. Let's talk about something else," Loretta says. "Jenny, who is in the tunnel when you have one of your things?"

"The cast changes some each time, but my dad is almost always there, and my grandma."

"I don't remember your grandma. Did I meet her?"

"Probably not. She died when I was young and my own memories of her are sketchy, but over the years my mother told me stories. She lived a wild life."

"Tell us," Matthias says.

"It's kind of a downer."

"Can't be more of a downer than Nelson Bargrove."

"You might be wrong about that. But if you want me to I will."

"Sure, go ahead," Loretta says.

"Her name was Helen. She was born in rural Pennsylvania. She came from a long line of chicken and turkey farmers and she spent her childhood collecting fresh eggs from under their bodies."

"The chickens, not the farmers, right?" Matthias asks, exhaling.

"Yes, the chickens," Jenny says. "Although who knows, maybe the farmers too."

"Keep going," Loretta says.

"My grandma married way too young, like sixteen or something. A child bride. No surprise, the marriage was a disaster. He cheated on her from nearly the first week and then after five pregnancies and three births, all girls, he abandoned her. Just up and left. At the time, divorce was a dirty word, which is to say it was okay for men but not for women."

"Is that so wrong?" Matthias asks.

"Stop with the un-clever distractions," Loretta says.

"Long story short, after that, Helen spent a few years painting, trying to carve out a creative identity but pretty much everyone turned their backs on her. Out of anger, or maybe despair, she isolated herself, including from her three daughters, leaving my mom, the oldest, to raise her two younger sisters. Then one day, out of the blue, Helen decided she could get another man to marry her if she lost weight.

"She wasn't fat. I've seen photos, so who knows what was going through her mind. Some quack doctor prescribed diet pills, promising they would melt away the pounds. They worked, she got model-thin, also hyperactive, irrational and super unpredictable. It was basically speed, but since she was losing weight she kept taking the pills. Two months later, after she walked naked down the street in front of the house one night, to celebrate the full moon, I think, her parents committed her to an asylum. The sheriff arrived to take her away on what was Helen's thirty-fifth birthday."

Matthias rolls another cigarette and offers it to Loretta. She declines. The pleasant mix of smoking and wine are ganging up into what she fears is likely to be a memorable headache, and she is now resigned to being unable to sleep tonight.

"Helen moved in and out of the Wernersville State Hospital for the Insane for the rest of her life, mostly in. My mother and her two sisters lived with an aunt, until they could leave at eighteen. When I was little, my mom took me to visit Helen at the asylum."

"That must have been scary as a little kid," Matthias says.

Loretta imagines the asylum. Cavernous and dark. Patients lined up outside of rooms in the corridors. A big kitchen, a workhouse, a vegetable garden. She has never been to an asylum, so the images must be lifted from a movie or a novel.

"It wasn't scary but it was a little weird. When we arrived, Helen had just finished a round of electroshock therapy. She didn't recognize my mother but she held me in her arms, rocking me, and whispered she would give me her magic." Jenny touches her head and then her heart. "I just thought of something. Given what's going on now, maybe she did."

"Did what?" Loretta asks.

"She thought her mental illness was a gift, that it gave her unique insight, at least that's how mom explained it. I keep hoping Grandma, I mean Helen, will say something about the magic in the tunnel but she never says anything, she's just there, a welcoming and super-loving presence."

"How did she die?" Matthias asks.

"Helen lived at the asylum for like twenty more years, until she was old. Well, probably our age, but back then fifty-five seemed ancient. They forced her out a few years before she died, even though she begged to stay. By that time, it felt like home. Plus, the shock therapy had completely wrecked her long-term memory. Only the asylum was real to her. But it was a time when they were emptying out those kinds of places, some new policy, I guess. Her daughters, all grown-up now with their own families, couldn't take her in, too stressful, so they pooled money to rent her a little apartment."

"That was good of them. Most people kicked out of mental health facilities in the Reagan era ended up homeless," Loretta says, thinking about the old woman at the park near the courthouse washing and singing to her rag doll in the war memorial fountain. "There's still no place for them."

"What was her diagnosis?" Matthias asks.

"At first, it was manic depression, later changed to bipolar disorder. By the end, that changed. After Helen died, Mom found a copy of the release paperwork from when they booted her out of the asylum in the bottom of her bathtub under a mountain of unread books and old National Geographic and Life magazines."

"What did it say?" Loretta asks.

"It said that she suffered from the consequences of

profound loneliness."

This hits Loretta hard, harder than the wine, and she fights back tears. Why is she crying? What is wrong with her? It's not her grandma. This kind of reaction isn't supposed to happen to zombies.

"Okay, you were right. That's a tie with the Nelson Bargrove story," Matthias says.

"I warned you it was a downer."

"I vote we end this day," Matthias says, standing.

"Seconded," Jenny says.

Loretta isn't sure if they don't notice her upset or if they're being polite, giving her space. She decides there probably isn't an important difference between the two. Sitting there alone for a few minutes, she recovers her balance, and stops thinking about Jenny's grandma.

Later in bed, Matthias reads a book of poetry as Loretta writes a strategy memo for Mona and the University general counsel for the next round of media inquiries about *The Case of the Misplaced Sperm*. Finally, she closes her laptop, changes into a nightshirt, and slips under the covers. He puts the book down. Loretta turns out the light.

"We've got to get you a vacation soon," he says.

"We can't afford that, not with Sally-Anne's tuition." And your cancer co-pays, she thinks, but doesn't say it out loud.

"I'm thinking of changing my ranking, the whiplash ranking," he says.

"Oh yeah, to what?"

"A zombie-threat level. Well, not precisely a threat level exactly because that would mean, based on zombie culture, how many zombies are poised to eat your brains."

"Maybe something along the lines of how much self I can detect?"

"A measurement of the density of self, that's good," he says. She rests her head on his chest. "Assuming two days ago, when you first told me about the zombieness, you were at ten, maximum zombieness, when you can't detect a self at all, what is it today?"

"An eight?"

"Excellent, it's trending in the right direction."

Loretta is not sure why Matthias thinks more-self is the preferred direction, but is too tired, or maybe too uninterested, to argue. Instead, she asks, "Why are you smoking?"

"I'll stop if it bothers you."

Matthias pushes up her nightshirt and strokes the curve of her hips with his palm.

"After all we've been through?"

"Here's the truth," he whispers. "Seeing Jenny the other day, watching her go through her near death experience in the bathtub in that golden light, I swear I saw her cross over, and then when she returned, she was peaceful, so overjoyed. It emanated from her."

"Matthias, what does that even mean?"

"I don't know, but it was incredible."

She starts to ask why that would make him smoke but the answer comes to her before the words get out. He doesn't see the value in constraining himself in this world.

"Please don't make me regret helping Jenny."

"I promise you, I'm not giving up."

Loretta is silent against his chest; his breathing lifts her and then brings her back down every few seconds, a metronomic rhythm. She looks up at the ceiling, at the darkness hovering there. "I love you."

"Me as well."

Hours pass. Loretta is awake, staring at the same darkness, trying to trick herself into sleeping in its swirl. Matthias snores. Loudly. A band of light sweeps across the carpet like the beam from a tiny lighthouse. Jenny tiptoes inside until she stands over Loretta. Her eyes are wide and frightened.

"Did you just have one?" Loretta asks.

Jenny nods and whispers, "I'm caught, in between."

Loretta gets up, careful not to wake Matthias, and helps Jenny back to her room who then curls into a fetal position on Sally-Anne's bed.

"Sometimes, they're not so good."

Jenny shivers and cries and pushes her face into the pillow. Loretta doesn't know how to help, but then she remembers when Sally-Anne was an infant, crying and crying, when nothing would comfort her, they started wrapping her up in blankets so tight she could barely move. Matthias figured it out. He said being born is a traumatic event, imagine floating peacefully inside your mother, no conscious awareness of your body, existing outside of gravity. And then suddenly, to be thrust into this chiseled world, limbs transformed from weightless sensors into dense, fleshy anchors hanging, flailing, stretching. Swaddling turned back time, Matthias said, sending Sally-Anne back to the instant before a miniature big bang created the tiny universe of her.

Loretta wonders if it could help Jenny too. She tugs off the quilt, leaving Jenny exposed on the top sheet, soft and pilled from use; she grabs the left corner and tucks it beneath Jenny's right shoulder. She does the same from the other side. Loretta wraps the dangling bottom edges snugly around her feet. Jenny smiles weakly in between tears, moving when prodded, trying to be cooperative but not understanding. When Loretta is done and Jenny is held tightly inside the makeshift cocoon, she calms.

"Does that help?"

"Yes."

"The darkness is gone?"

"Yes."

"Good."

"I was afraid I would be stuck like that forever."

"Like what?"

"Floating in nothingness."

"I don't understand."

"It's so hard to explain but who I am disappears, or not so much disappears but is shattered, and the pieces are taken in...maybe dispersed is better...I don't know what to call it. I'm sorry, Lolo, I can't describe it any more than that."

"All that matters is you're okay now."

"I am. Thank you." Jenny struggles to keep her eyes open.

"Should I stay?"

"You can go back to bed."

Loretta loosens the sheet around her hands.

"I'm not crazy, I'm not like my grandmother." Jenny grabs Loretta's wrist. "You have to believe me."

"I believe you, I do. And your grandma wasn't crazy, she was lonely, there's a difference, I think. We're going to get through this together. Don't worry."

"You're going to have to change the title now."

"What title?"

"The notebook. It's twenty-four now, not twenty-three," Jenny whispers. "*The 24 Near Death Experiences of Jenny Black.*"

Loretta smiles. "I'll stay here a little longer."

Jenny nods. Loretta sits on the bed's edge. It doesn't take long for Jenny to fall asleep and when she does, Loretta tiptoes back to her bedroom. Matthias lifts the blanket and she crawls under.

There, in the darkest part of night, when the sky is now an impenetrable shade of indigo blue, Matthias and Loretta make love for the first time in more than a year, the first time since the chemotherapy. The passion is tempered, the touch is careful, even tentative, but for the briefest of moments, the world falls away and they are one.

FIFTEEN

Looking through the window of the tallest building on the upper campus, Loretta is drawn into the subdued dawn light, following the flight of a lone bird gliding in the distance, wondering if it's the eagle she spotted last week nesting near the top of the tram. Even though she woke feeling unrested from the drinking and smoking last night, and in her rush to make this early-morning appointment hasn't yet processed the implications of Jenny's late-night near death experience, the feeling of connection to Matthias, having him inside her after so many long months, eclipses everything and this private joy pulls her into the raptor's flight.

The door creaks as it swings open mechanically. Loretta slips back into her body and turns around. The chair of the Department of Physics, Dr. Swift, navigates her wheelchair around the desk, pulls back on the armrest joystick, swivels and comes to a stop in front of Loretta. She wiggles in the seat, leans down and repositions her calves into the footholds. Loretta smells baby powder. The gentleness of her tiny tan face and wide eyes are offset by the cheekbone-sculpted swales reaching ear to lip. She invites Loretta to sit down. Loretta looks at the pile of manuscripts on the nearest chair, a question in her eyes, and Dr. Swift nods. Loretta places the pile of papers on the floor, thinking maybe the next big scientific discovery is somewhere in this mess, and then sits. Dr. Swift apologizes for being late and gets right to the point. "I would be a nervous wreck on *60 Minutes*. A total embarrassment for the University and me."

Loretta is surprised by her feeling of relief. The *60 Minutes* lie feels denser today, but still, as part of her real task, the quest as Matthias calls it, she must not waste this precious time with Dr. Swift, so she plunges forward with a partial truth. "Given that we both dragged ourselves here at the crack of dawn, why not reframe our time as you providing background rather than as auditioning to appear on camera?"

"That I can gladly do. Where should we begin?"

Loretta has been thinking about the information she's collected so far, and feels a missing chunk is figuring out something more, anything really, about human consciousness. She skips over her usual opening question.

"From my departmental interviews so far it's clear that no one agrees about the meaning or even the cause of near death experiences," Loretta says, "but there is agreement, sort of, around the idea that understanding near death experiences requires an understanding of, or maybe better to say a position on, the nature of human consciousness or, as others call it, the sense of self. Could you talk to me about that?"

"That's an unexpected direction for our discussion," Dr. Swift says. "My research is in theoretical physics, focused on gravity. Consciousness is not my area of expertise." As Loretta is wondering why the Dean sent her to the physics department, the professor adds, "but

I do keep up with the topic."

"Are you willing to share?" Loretta asks.

"I won't be quoted?"

"Just on background."

"No taping? A dawn conversation among friends?"

"Sure," Loretta says, warming to the professor's casual tone and pleased to be put into the category of friend, even if it's only conversational politeness.

"Well, as you say, we're both already here," Dr. Swift says with a delicate shrug. "But I will come at it from an atypical perspective. Are you a patient person?"

"Not always, but for this I am."

"Good, you'll need it."

Professor Swift twists, trying to get comfortable in her wheelchair. Her coltish legs, encased in tight-weave dark red tights, don't move in alignment with her upper body, hostage to both biology and gravity; she leans down to adjust their position again with her hands. She tugs at a faded green and black plaid blanket spread across her lap, tucking the cloth into the gap between her thighs. Settled, she returns her attention to Loretta.

"At the level you and I exist, the air we breathe, our bodies, the earth, even the way planets move through space-time, we in physics have a satisfying theory. Applying this theory, which is largely a set of equations, we can predict how living or inanimate objects will act when subjected to various vectors, be they gravity, energy and the like. There are gaps in this knowledge —for example, our theories at this level of macro reality do not explain the nature of time—but by and large we can predict effect from cause in ways that are aligned with our direct experience of how the world operates."

She opens her hand to reveal a small blue rubber ball, the kind used for physical therapy to strengthen muscles. "For instance, we can accurately predict what will happen when I throw this ball in the air, how it will fall and so on." She tosses the ball and it falls onto her lap. "Understanding gravity and force and friction, we can predict how matter, in this case, the ball, is going to behave in ways that make intuitive sense, are accurate and also, as I noted, predictable."

She pauses. "I am simplifying decades of thought and discoveries to make a point, which will be shortly forthcoming, but this background is important for what comes next because things get complicated. Are you with me so far?"

"So far, so good."

"Okay, so when we move to the micro level, where atoms and their component particle parts bump around, we have another theory called quantum mechanics, which is unintuitive. Indeed, it makes a mockery of what we observe in our day-to-day lives. This theory suggests the behavior of things at this micro level is influenced, in part, by how we interact with these things. For instance, whether a light wave collapses into a particle or maintains its wave function depends on our behavior in relation to it."

"I've heard about this. I think what you are saying is the thing or person doing the measuring determines if it's a particle or wave by how they measure it."

"It's perhaps more accurate to say that this micro-world is best described as a collection of probabilities awaiting manifestation."

"Does this micro theory imply there's no reality to reality? That it all depends on human interaction?"

"It's an easy path to interpret it that way but rather than deny reality, most physicists would answer that the theory is incomplete. However, the predictive value of quantum mechanics is exceptionally accurate, much of what we have today in terms of computing power, for example, is due to this theory. This suggests it must be true in some sense, even if it requires a conclusion that reality is to some degree participatory."

"That's a lot to take in so early."

"And for completeness's sake, I'll add that there are other aspects of quantum theory beyond this interactive measurement problem, such as how the theory predicts that particles, once manifested, maintain a sort of memory of prior interactions with other particles, and can exert an influence on each other at a distance."

"They remember their past lives?"

Her laugh is like the sound of a harmonica. "I see why you're in communications," Professor Swift says.

She wiggles in her wheelchair again and the blue ball slides an inch or so down her thighs, like a miniature bowling ball in a gutter lane, but stops midway. Loretta crosses her own legs at the ankles, feeling an acute awareness of the miracle that her legs move in a manner united with her thoughts.

"From a predictive standpoint, both theories work well within their realms, with problematic caveats that, frankly, are becoming more problematic of late, but that's a story for another dawn conversation.[17] For our discussion, you need only know that neither theory is helpful outside its particular realm. They don't play well together."

"So, there are two different theories in physics that describe our world?"

"Yes. And finding a theory that unifies the macro and the micro, or quantum, has consumed the careers of countless physicists. With little success, thus far."

"Where's the boundary?"

"Where does the application of one theory stop and the other begin? An excellent question. On one level, the answer is simple. We don't know."

Loretta likes her frankness.

Dr. Swift continues. "But on another level, it's more complicated. Because what we don't know is what the late great Stephen Hawking called the 'fire' of matter.[18] What is the fire that causes atoms to bind themselves together into the forms that make up our experience of macro reality? How and why does reality at the macro level manifest from the micro level in the way it does? Understanding this is key to unifying the theories, and their underlying equations, one way or the other."

She stops talking and looks at Loretta as if expecting her to have an idea about how to unify the theories. Loretta does not have an idea and stays silent, although she mentally notes the similarity of parts of this interview to the philosophy department discussion.

"I've established the background now, so let me try to articulate my main point. I'm enjoying talking to you, but please keep in mind that what I'm about to say is entirely my view, although I'm certainly not the only one thinking about things in this way. I articulate these thoughts in response to your earlier inquiry about consciousness, but also because sometimes it helps to refine one's thinking to say things out loud. I hope you don't mind."

"Quite the opposite," Loretta says, leaning in, not wanting to miss a single word.

"Nobody believes there are two ways that matter operates at different levels of reality, so something is amiss with our two theories. As I mentioned, the search is on for a unified theory in physics, or something that bridges them. But what intrigues me is there are also two currently dominant theories in the study of human consciousness."

"The biology-based brain-is-mind concept and the other way that says the subjective nature of human experience can't be explained by the laws of biology."

Dr. Swift nods her head approvingly. "You've done your homework. And to articulate your response somewhat differently, there are those who believe that science can, eventually, uncover the mystery of how the brain creates this wonderful sense of awareness that allows each of us to experience the world in a uniquely personal way. These thinkers are what we call materialists, those who believe that brain-is-mind. By contrast, there is the other group who think about—"

"—what it's like to be a bat."

"Yes, that's right, and this contingent believes we're overlooking something, although precious few will, or can, identify what exactly is being overlooked. Still, they assert that the subjective nature of self and experience is unlikely to be explained by biology, perhaps being unreachable entirely in the way we conduct science."

"I feel like I'm beginning to understand the position of these two camps, at a simple, basic level, at least."

"Simple is good enough because everything said or written about consciousness is largely wordplay among academics from the two camps. And my, oh my, the words being thrown around. If you can believe it, some scholars deny the very existence of consciousness. Our awareness is the most real thing of our existence. But they say we imagine it, but who is doing the imagining? I suppose this is a theatrical tactic to draw attention to those who have staked their reputations on the brain-is-mind model."

This time when she shifts around in the wheelchair, Dr. Swift lets out a sigh, like a tire deflating, but she doesn't seem smaller afterward, the air loss seems to sturdy her. "Academics rather desperately seek approval from one another, when it would be more constructive to measure success by the effect of our public service."

"If that was the measure of success, we wouldn't have things like the atomic bomb."

"I don't follow your logic and your conclusion seems unjustified to me. When something can be envisioned theoretically, such as the bomb, as well as art or music, humans are compelled to demonstrate it in practice. To manifest it, if you will. How could it be otherwise?"

Which is one way of saying humans are compelled

to render thought into matter, Loretta thinks. She feels a stony hardness in her mind, an unnamable certainty, which makes her believe there is something important in this concept, a thread she is unable to pull out right now. Maybe later.

The ball rolls off Dr. Swift's lap and wedges in the footholds. Loretta bends forward, grabs it and hands the ball to her.

"Thank you. Now, going on. Some scholars hold that the two positions in consciousness research can be resolved by staking out a middle ground. For example, certain scientists postulate the existence of biological particles inside the brain, giving them the name of microtubules, a special environment in which the micro theory of quantum mechanics operates and controls, or creates, consciousness."[19]

"But still inside the brain, so brain-is-mind wins out over the bat question."

Dr. Swift nods. "Others expand the definition of the mind to include its external interactions with objects or people, but again achieving the effect of creating a unique environment in which to consider subjective experience.[20] What I find particularly fascinating is that in these two examples and others like them is an intriguing parallel with the effort to integrate the two incompatible theories of physics, macro and micro. Are you still following?"

"Yes, completely and on the edge of my seat."

"At last I arrive at my point. It is possible that the stuff, so to speak, of consciousness, whatever it is, is fundamental." Dr. Swift pauses. Loretta recognizes the pause; it means the scholar is articulating an idea that must be understood to continue the journey. Usually at this point, Loretta fakes her way through an interview, nodding knowingly while furiously scribbling notes so she can research the concept later for whatever media release she's writing, but that won't work this time.

"Do you know what this means in the context of science?" Dr. Swift asks.

"No," she admits.

"Being fundamental means it is irreducible, can't be further broken down. Gravity and light, as we currently understand them, are fundamental forces. The particles of atoms are fundamental units of matter."

"I get that, I think."

"If consciousness is not a product of biology but instead is fundamental, like light or gravity, I am intrigued by the idea it may somehow represent the boundary, or at least operate at the boundary we discussed earlier, between macro and micro-quantum worlds. Perhaps consciousness supplies the missing fire that connects all matter and provides a path to integrate the two theories of physics. Because when you think about it, the self and the world observed by the self both dissolve at death."

Loretta remembers that the philosophy chair said being unable to prove that mind emerges from biology would require a reconsideration of the foundations of human knowledge. Is this what he meant? A whole new theory?

Dr. Swift pushes the joystick on the arm of her wheelchair, spins around and nods in the direction of a print hanging on her office wall, the largest of a dozen or so framed reproductions.

"Do you know art?"

"A little," Loretta says, wondering why Dr. Swift is abruptly changing the discussion, but trusting. She follows her gaze to a reproduction of Van Gogh's *Starry Night*—swirls of blue and yellow fleeing the dark sky above the honey-colored thatched rooftops of a French village. When she was twelve or so, Loretta saw the original with her mother on one of their regular Sunday museum outings. Standing in front of the canvas, her mother believed Van Gogh saw the world as he painted it. Loretta remembers feeling dizzy as she imagined this swirling reality.

"There is evidence to suggest that the appearance of the autobiographical mind in humans, which is to say the ability to remember past events and project them forward to imagine a future outcome, a hallmark of the subjective experience of consciousness, what some call qualia, was simultaneous with the first human art, cave paintings and such.[21] When I was a little girl—"

Loretta tries to picture Dr. Swift as a little girl. Was she in a wheelchair or did it happen later?

"—I would stare at Van Gogh paintings, wondering if the artist saw the world as he painted, whether he was painting his personal reality. I know that's a rather fashionable observation now and may seem lacking in freshness, but long ago as a child, it felt new to me, and so very revelatory."

Loretta isn't surprised by the synchronicity of Dr. Swift's words with her own memory; she thinks maybe she should find this coincidence odd but doesn't.

"To this day, that question intrigues me. Perhaps art shows us not only the arrival of human consciousness and the attendant sense of self but also presents a map of its evolution. Maybe some artists have the ability to see through the veil of our macro reality all the way to the micro, understanding viscerally how the former manifests from the latter."

"Wouldn't the concept of consciousness evolving in this way lend credence to the idea it's biology-based?"

"That's a possibility. But it could also mean humans were evolving the biological capacity, the tools so to speak, to integrate the stuff of consciousness, whatever it might be."

Loretta flashes on childhood days poring over her mother's collection of art books as she pointed out the differences between representational, and religious, paintings and centuries-later work of modern artists, asking Loretta to think about the minds of Basquiat, Mapplethorpe or Krasner compared to Renaissance-era masters painting the stories of God. What does it mean that art changed so dramatically over the centuries, her mother asked?

"You believe the human brain is still evolving and art is the proof."

"Evolution didn't stop just because Darwin and his contemporaries named it."

"Evolving how?"

"Maybe certain brains are evolving to better experience the boundary between the macro and micro worlds, to understand, or at least to comprehend, to somehow feel, how consciousness, if it is fundamental, could be playing a role manifesting the physical world. And we must be clear here. By evolving, I am not suggesting these people are better, only different."

Loretta notes similarities with the whole cosmic consciousness thing the chair of religion talked about. This would also answer the Dean's original question about why not everyone who dies and then comes back has a full-on near death experience. Only those with the evolutionary variance would have them.

"Do you think near death experiences are evidence of an evolved brain?" Loretta asks.

"I have no idea."[22]

Dr. Swift's assistant comes in the office and fusses around the desk, cleaning up papers and rearranging journals. Loretta understands the signal but ignores it.

"You said consciousness might be fundamental, irreducible. Why do physics, science, math or whatever start with an assumption of a common denominator, that all things must be reducible? Doesn't that lead to, in a way, a preordained answer?"

This assumption, she realizes now, is what's behind Occam's razor, the idea that the most beautiful, simple theory is always right.

"By and large, scientists no longer call it reduction, as that implies one thing leads to another, like nesting dolls. But even with that caveat, to address the essence of your quite reasonable question, I don't have a good answer except to say that it provides a path to unify human knowledge. Imagine for a moment if there was no such assumption. How would we ever make sense of the chaos? What would be our goal? By contrast, if everything ultimately leads back to a single answer, or more accurately to a single mathematical model, we can explain something profound about our universe and, presumably, ourselves, maybe everything, in fact."

Dr. Swift pauses, and her next words are more halting, cautious. "I also find it intriguing that the very idea of reality being contained in the structures, mathematical or otherwise, of a single entity, whatever that entity, is stunningly similar to the idea of God."

"I'm not tracking anymore."

"Science as we know it today, including the precepts controlling its conduct, originated some 400 years ago during an era in which a monotheistic God was omniscient. Isn't God, by definition, irreducible?"[23]

SIXTEEN

Loretta closes her office door, drops her bag onto the cluttered desk and pulls out the Jenny notebook. The edges are warped from the misty weather. She opens to a dry page in the middle, writes Department of Physics in pink ink, underlines it twice and starts to write— about the strangeness of there being two theories of physics, about the possibility that consciousness might somehow bridge them, and if so, how the missing "fire" explaining how physical reality manifests from the quantum world could have something to do with consciousness being fundamental. She writes about how Dr. Swift believes the brain is still evolving and perhaps these evolved people are the ones who see beyond the macro world into, well, she isn't honestly sure what they would be seeing into which, of course, is the whole conundrum, what everyone wants to know.

As she writes, a thought flutters in. If the story underlying science isn't that different from the story underlying most religions, neither of which is really a story, rather more akin to a quest to uncover something core about reality, what they both might be trying to unravel is the thing Jenny is experiencing, that oneness she describes. For religion that would be their heaven and for science it would be that fundamental aspect of bedrock reality, whatever it turns out to be.

Loretta closes the notebook and thinks back to what Jenny said last night. *The notebook. It's twenty-four now, not twenty-three.* She takes out a marker and changes the cover to *The 23 24 Near Death Experiences of Jenny Black.*

Loretta walks down the corridor to Toni's corner cubicle. Toni is an all-weather bike commuter; her gear is draped over a table, drying out from the morning slush. She is laughing at something on her phone. When Loretta knocks on the half-wall, Toni puts the phone down and after good-morning niceties, fills her in on where things stand.

"The AP piece is getting picked up around the country. We're getting follow-up calls for comment."

"Is the abortion rumor coming up?"

"Not yet."

"Comments on the all-employee email?"

"Mostly stupid jokes, but a few say we did right by apologizing."

"Social?"

Toni looks at her screen.

"Not much Twitter action. A hundred and thirteen Facebook comments, all the expected snarky stuff, juvenile humor. The regular trolls going on about awful experiences in our hospital, mistrust of science and the elite ..." Toni uses air quotes as she says the last word. "Those are mixed in with lots of supportive comments about what a great asset the University hospital is to the state, doctors are human, that kind of thing." She scans the feed. "Oh wait, here's a new one that just posted this sec saying the University tried to force the woman to have an abortion because the baby is Black. Oh crap, and another one right below now posting who wants a half-breed baby? This is gross."

"Delete those comments."

"With pleasure. Who would post stuff like that?"

"The sperm donor's attorney."

"You think *he's* commenting? That's crazy unethical. And gross. He should be reported to the state Bar."

"Not him directly. But they're making it happen for sure, to benefit him and his client."

She figures the lawyer hopes seeding racism in their public relations push will keep the University off balance and a little frantic, especially if the media takes the bait. Her immediate inclination is not to respond, thinking if they ignore the whole thing it won't gain traction because it's so ludicrous. Facts are on their side because race is irrelevant in *The Case of the Misplaced Sperm*.

But maybe she shouldn't ignore it because maybe race isn't irrelevant. Maybe she is naïve to think race is, has ever been, or ever will be irrelevant in America. Why is she always so hesitant to call people out? Maybe it's because she's never been on the receiving end of racism and so it's not her problem, really. But that's not who she is, is it? She hopes not. Or maybe it's because of her distaste for the spotlight, a wariness of being noticed. She's spent most of her life trying to hide but then why in the world is she in this job, more to the point, why is she so good at this job?

On each of those Facebook comments, she *should* call it out, say something. But what? Any response will juice up the posters, giving salacious fodder to media outlets that at this point don't know anything about the race of the man or woman. One thing she has learned in this job, the hard way, is winning a public relations battle sometimes means knowing when to stay silent. But silence comes with its own price. Loretta looks out the window at three crows flying low against the wintery sky. She wonders if birds fly closer to the ground to stay warm in cold weather.

Caron pops her head in the door. "KGWN is on the line for you. And a producer from *Good Morning America* and another from *60 Minutes*."

"I'll call back from my office," Loretta says.

"Is *60 Minutes* calling for the near death experiences story?" Caron asks.

"What story is that?" Toni asks.

Loretta's phone vibrates. She reads the text from Matthias. *Taking Jenny on my favorite hike along the river. A good distraction.*

Matthias's favorite hike is a basalt-lined trail named Angel's Rest that winds through multiple waterfalls and ends on a steep cliff overlooking the river. Even though it's usually way over-crowded, the views are expansive when it's not cloudy, making up for what it lacks in solitude. But the reason it's his favorite trail is because he proposed to Loretta at its crest. Every year on their anniversary, they hike the trail. Or they used to. They've missed the past two years.

She returns to her office without answering Toni's question. She looks over the front page of the print edition of the local paper. The sperm article is below the fold and largely a rehash of the AP article, with a few new flourishes—two fresh patient quotes and a photo of the University hospital. She reviews the local news websites and online video for broadcast coverage. The story leads on all three channels. Mostly fact-based and sticking to the statement, but on the Fox channel in the cross talk, they posit the possibility of a child. "If so, who does that baby belong to?" the female anchor asks. She's white with long blonde hair that reaches to her bust line.

Loretta's cell phone buzzes. It's Jamie. "What can I do for you?" Loretta asks, keeping her voice flat and a little nice.

"I'm running a story today at noon that a publicly funded state institution tried to force a patient to have an abortion."

Crap.

"If you don't get me someone to put on camera, I will bring my crew to your campus and follow your president around like a starving poodle after a bone until he comments. Or maybe I'll follow the Dean, your golden boy, that would really piss you off."

"A starving poodle?"

"I just got my daughter a dog."

"Aww, what's its name?"

"Buttons."

"Not sure I deserve the starving Buttons treatment. Also, you know better than that. We would never try to force anyone to do anything they didn't want to do. It's wrong and, as you know, incredibly illegal. It doesn't work that way."

"Yeah, well, something is going on. And while *you* are trying to kill this story, I'm trying to milk it for all it's worth, which will be a damn lot for me. So get me someone for an on-camera interview. You are a public institution. My viewers are taxpayers and they deserve your transparency."

"Our patients are also taxpayers and they deserve their privacy."

"What about you?"

"I don't appear on camera. You know that."

"Someone has to."

Loretta quickly processes the situation. Refusing to give Jamie a talking head will force her hand and she'll go for some sort of reality-TV stunt, wandering around campus, and who knows what a random student or a faculty member with a chip on their shoulder might say, which means it has the chance of going viral like Jamie hopes. Jamie is probably angling for a job in a bigger market and intends this to be a splashy audition reel.

"First, tell me how you knew about this story before anyone else."

"And?"

"I'll get someone for you to interview."

"Just me?"

"Just you."

"Someone with legal credentials tipped me off, that's all I'll say."

As suspected. The sperm donor's lawyer.

"Meet me in two hours and I'll have someone."

"Who?"

"Trust me." Loretta disconnects.

She collects her thoughts and then calls *Good Morning America*. She can tell within half a minute that the producer is on the fence. Let's keep it that way, she thinks, or better yet, shove him off. She cannot let this become a national media story. That would be the worst outcome possible.

"Who is your spokesperson?" the producer asks, his voice low-pitched. Loretta lowers her own, meeting his tone.

"We don't have one," she says. "Because we're not commenting beyond the statement. We are deeply sorry for this situation and are doing our best to make things right. That includes respecting the privacy of everyone involved. They wish to remain anonymous."

She's a wind-up robot, no wait, she is a zombie, on repeat mode.

"Filing a lawsuit is a funny way to be anonymous. Pretty juicy stuff in that court document."

She doesn't respond, letting the silence build enough until he breaks it. "Okay, you win. I'll check in later this week. To be frank, I need either the mom or the baby-daddy on camera to make this story work for us. But my bet is on the anonymous aspect breaking and when it does, we'll be there."

"You've got my number. Call me anytime. And if I

have more information, you'll get it."

The next conversation is with Wendell, the *60 Minutes* producer, and it goes about the same, except he says they might use the situation as a springboard for a deep dive into the ramifications for sperm donor law. "If the plaintiff wins the custody case, it could open up the door for every sperm donor in the world to sue for parental rights."

"I never said there was a baby."

"That's true, but we both know that's going to pop," Wendell says. They banter a few more minutes, he says they'll dig around on their own and he'll let her know what they decide.

Thinking ahead, Loretta knows whoever she puts on camera for Jamie's broadcast today has to be incredibly boring and unappealing. She needs to put these national primetime producers to sleep.

Loretta hustles down three flights of stairs to Mona's office. She is meeting with the communications director from the primate center where the University keeps hundreds of Macaque monkeys as stand-ins for humans in medical research studies. Last week, a monkey escaped its pen and ran around the city for almost three hours, turning into a fifteen-minutes-of-fame local celebrity. Someone set up a Twitter account for the missing monkey and it had 702 followers by the end of that day, far more than Loretta's account.

Mona and John, the primate comms director, are catching up on the coverage from that debacle. As she listens, Loretta remembers John was on-camera for the missing-monkey story. He was calm, didn't ruffle easily and stayed on message. John is also a plump middle-aged white man, slightly bald, not too tall, not too handsome, but not ugly. (No offense, John, she apologizes inside her head).

"Sorry to interrupt," Loretta says.

"What's up?" Mona asks.

"I need an on-camera talking head to read our fertility clinic statement, stick completely to the talking points and deny any involvement in an abortion."

"What abortion?" John asks.

"We aren't providing a spokesperson," Mona says.

"KGWN needs a warm body," Loretta says. After she recounts her conversation with Jamie, she looks at John, then back to Mona, eyebrows raised. Then they both look at John. Mona also raises her eyebrows and flutters her crazy-long lashes. John grins.

"Point me at the camera and tell me what to say."

"Thank you. I owe you. Her crew will be here in two hours. Meet me back here in ninety minutes and I'll fill you in," Loretta says.

"Where are you going now?" Mona asks. "I want an update on the situation."

"I have a meeting."

As she leaves the office, Loretta feels Mona staring at her back. She pictures Mona's curiosity as a fly buzzing around her head and swats it away.

SEVENTEEN

Cars zoom past on the left. Matthias, Jenny has now learned, never drives above the speed limit. Mostly, he drives under it, plus he hits the brakes for no apparent reason, causing the car to randomly lurch.

The car window is down an inch, cold air streams in; she unrolls the sleeves of her denim shirt by two folds. Matthias takes a sip from a cup of take-out coffee.

"What are those rocks over there, do you know?" Jenny asks, pointing to a curtain of thick hexagonal columns forming black cliffs.

"Old lava. This whole area was once covered in a lake of the stuff, hundreds, maybe thousands, of feet deep."

"Why do they look like columns?"

"Thick lava sometimes cools into a hexagonal shape. The same way mud dries, and you get mud flats with the six-sided cracks. Salt flats do that too. This is like that, it's called columnar basalt and the expressions of it here are among the best in the world."

"How do you know all this?"

"I'm a fount of useless information."

She watches the cliff features glide by silently. "Were people around when the lava was coming out of the earth?"

"No, it was too long ago. People came later."

"Seems odd to me."

"Odd how?"

"They're so beautiful, those columns, like the organ pipes in a church. And no one was here to witness all that beauty coming into existence. Not odd, but sad, I guess. Or a wasted opportunity. Are you sure?"

"I'm pretty sure there's no evidence of people so far back." Matthias finds this a peculiar way to think about the world, that a witness is required to make it real, or appreciate it. "But who knows? The lava would have burned up all traces."

That seems to cheer her up.

The gunmetal gray sky exaggerates the peaks, valleys and crags marking the columnar cliffs on either side and reflects off the lacy white-capped waves whipped up by the wind blowing across the river.

"Is this near where you and Loretta were married?"

"Yes, good memory."

"That was a nice ceremony, super fun. What ever happened to Walter?"

"My best man? Walter died a few years after the wedding. A freak windsurfing accident."

"That must have made you sad."

"It did."

"Did Loretta ever tell you?"

"About what?"

"Walter and I ... we had some fun with each other at your wedding."

"Really? Huh. No, Loretta didn't tell me."

"It was in the bathroom, clumsy, drunken sex, but it turned out well, if you know what I mean. We were young and it was easy. After, I couldn't find my left shoe, and people started banging on the door because it was the only bathroom. I panicked, gave up looking. When Walter opened the door, I was hopping on one foot, and the people waiting, your friends, clapped and cheered. Everyone was fairly drunk by that time. I can't believe no one told you."

Matthias smiles. "He was a lucky man."

"He was nice to me. Maybe I should look for him at the end of the tunnel next time."

They are quiet for a few miles, separated by their memories of that day more than twenty years ago, and also watching the scenery rush by: waterfalls knifing through rocks; towering ancient conifers; a hawk catching an air current.

"This truly is a magnificent area," Jenny says. "I would love to see it in the springtime but winter has its charm as well."

"What's the best place you've ever visited?"

"The way the light is hitting the black rock columns, it's turning out to be right here, right now. But Iceland and Turkey were nice too."

"What did you like about them?"

"Iceland is so rugged and new and beautiful, a lot like this area, and the people believe in magic and elves. I could live there but I love Turkey, only for a different reason. I fell in love with a cat there."

"A cat?"

"Not one cat, a type of cat, a Lake Van cat. They live in eastern Turkey. They're large for cats, almost like small dogs, with a white coat, but what's cool is their eyes. One is blue and the other is amber."

"Two different eye colors on the same cat?"

"Yes, and they swim in Lake Van. Swimming cats with different colored eyes, isn't that incredible? They run wild all over the city by the lake. I stayed for a month and swam with them every morning."

Matthias eases the car off the Interstate onto a

narrow old highway with no shoulder and lined with crumbling stone walls. Whenever he is out this way, he imagines the heavily muscled workers from a century ago blasting through the dense rock and cutting down trees in what would have been a wilderness, lugging boulders along the base of the cliffs to build this road that long preceded the Interstate.

"Swimming with cats," Matthias says. "That's a one-of-a-kind experience."

Jenny doesn't say anything else. He glances sideways; her eyes are closed and she is leaning her head back.

"You okay?" he asks.

"Just remembering the swimming cats."

Rounding a bend in the old road, he says, "Must be hard on you, never sure when one is coming."

She says, "Yeah, it is. I can be anywhere and boom, I'm gone. It's made me a cautious about traveling alone. Still, I'm not complaining. I wouldn't change anything, I really wouldn't, no matter how it turns out. Even the bad ones, like last night, are good in a way. And by the way, thanks for taking me in. Your very own stray cat."

He says, "But with boring, same-colored eyes."

She laughs.

He parks the old banged-up light blue Mercedes—a car Matthias has owned and tinkered on for sixteen years—by the trailhead and grabs a canteen from the trunk. They bundle up in fortified rain gear. Jenny bends down to check the laces on her hiking boots.

"The trail is pretty steep, especially toward the end, but it's just a couple of miles. And only half a mile or so of the really steep stuff. Might be muddy in some places. You still game for this?"

"Sure, absolutely."

They walk, Matthias in the lead and Jenny behind, feet cushioned by a matted layer of wet pine needles. The leaves from the mid-canopy deciduous trees are long gone, the limbs now naked, skeletal, surrounded by withering underbrush ferns. Wind moving at the very top of the tallest conifers makes a faint whistling sound. After a few yards, Matthias turns and faces Jenny.

"Can you really do that?" he asks.

"Do what?"

"Find people in the tunnel. Like you said earlier, about maybe looking for Walter."

"I've never tried, to be honest."

He turns back and continues along the trail. His footfalls are heavy and rapid. Jenny catches up to him and slips her gloved hand inside his. "I'll try if the time comes, Matthias. I promise, I'll try to find you."

They walk hand in hand until they reach a stream fifty yards or so down the trail. As they cross the water, she lets go of his hand.

EIGHTEEN

The door is mirrored and as Loretta approaches, she watches her reflection grow larger and larger until she and it merge. When she opens the Department of Neuroscience door, her frazzled doppelganger in scuffed yellow shoes spins off. Inside the room, a dark-skinned Black man, thirty-something, closely cut hair, perches on the edge of a red sofa. Dust motes float in a gauzy lattice of sunlight behind his head.

"Am I in the right place?" she asks.

"Guess that depends on where you want to be," he says, standing. He is tall, easily more than six feet, about the same as Matthias.

"I'm Loretta Sparkman, from the Dean's office."

"Then you're in the right place. Devlin Richardson."

He sticks out his hand. After shaking, he slips both hands into the slouchy side pockets of his stiff white lab coat, the uniform—and armor—of a scientist.

"I'm supposed to meet the chair of the Department of Neuroscience here."

"He sent me instead. I'm a post-doc in neurological

imaging. He had a conflict, asked for volunteers."

"You were left holding the short straw."

"Untrue. I wanted to meet you."

"Why?"

When she meets his eyes, she sees a spark, a reined-in eagerness there.

"I know a thing or two about your subject."

"Really? Well, okay, Dr. Richardson, let's get going."

"We can start with the 2T."

"What's that?"

"An MRI. Magnetic Resonance Imaging. The one in this building is for scanning the brains of large animals, not people, but it's easier to get access to it than to the two for patients over in the hospital."

"Why do I need to see the MRI, Dr. Richardson?"

"Ground zero. It's advances in MRI technology that have caused neuroscience research to take off this past decade, the field is going crazy, just killing it. And call me Devlin."

"What does the 'T' stand for?"

"Tesla. A measurement of power. And an homage, I suppose."

"To the car?"

He smiles, uncertain if she's joking. "To the man. The original brilliant, one-of-a-kind man."

She follows him to the rear of the room. "Why did you want to meet with me? Is it because you want to be on *60 Minutes*?"

"Oh, hell no."

Devlin is growing on her.

"I wanted to talk about near death experiences."

He holds open a door that leads to a staircase. She looks down. Each step is painted a different color: gold, lavender, dark green, orange. The contrast forces her to focus on the steps as individual components and for an instant she loses sight of the whole, becoming hyper-aware of her body's position relative to each step. She grabs the railing for balance.

"Don't worry, it throws everyone at first," he says.

"Is this some sort of research experiment?"

"Not a bad idea. Measure the effect of color on spatial orientation. But no, the truth is mundane. An art project gone awry. We've got a request into facilities to repaint the stairs one solitary color, but who knows how long that will take. Here, I'll go first, in case you need me to break a fall."

Break a fall? Really? Still, she holds onto the railing with a death grip until the middle of the staircase where she regains her balance and most of her confidence.

"Are near death experiences real?" she asks Devlin's descending back.

"Most definitely."

His confident response is a surprise and Loretta asks what seems like the only logical follow-up question.

"Have you had one?"

"Not me, but my mom did."

At the bottom of the stairs, she follows him down a short corridor. He stops in front of a pair of swinging doors.

"Take off any jewelry and your watch. Leave it and your phone out here." She isn't wearing jewelry or a watch. He drops his phone onto a table and Loretta does the same. They pass through the doors, a hum reverberates inside the compact room and Loretta feels a faint, tickling vibration travel through the soles of her feet up her calves and into her thighs.

Early on after Matthias's diagnosis, he underwent a full-body MRI but Loretta wasn't allowed in the exam room during his scan because of the possibility of spillover radiation. This machine is smaller than the one Matthias was in, by half, maybe more, but with the same basic elements. A polished metal rectangular box with a tunnel in the middle and a little stretcher that slides in and out of the tunnel. The on-off switches and a dashboard full of monitoring dials are off to the side inside a windowed control room.

"Is it safe?"

"Yes. It's in background mode."

"Why did you bring me here?"

"Dramatic. Could be a backdrop for *60 Minutes*."

"A little snug for the cameras, but maybe. So, what's your research area?"

"I'm working with my faculty advisor to identify the neurological basis of autism. But on my own time, I research near death experiences."

"Because of your mother?"

"Yes. And I've got results you may find interesting."

"First, you said earlier that neuroscience is just 'killing it' because of this technology. How so?"

"Do you know how an MRI works?"

"A little, but pretend I don't."

Devlin places a small metal wrench, no bigger than a child's toy, on a plastic table near the machine and then backs away from it. The wrench wriggles slightly, which builds to a tremble and then full-on movement as it scoots itself closer to the MRI on its own.

"What's going on?"

He smiles, his expression like that of a satisfied magician. "I love doing that to people. It happens because the MRI generates its own magnetic field. Think of it like a giant magnet rotating really fast. See, the human body is made up mostly of water. Inside the water molecules is hydrogen …"

He stops to gauge her response. The familiar pause to check if she understands.

"Water. Two hydrogen atoms and one oxygen," Loretta says.

"Yes, that's right."

She wishes he sounded less surprised.

"The magnetic field causes the insides of the hydrogen atoms to line up like little soldiers and emit a signal, and the strength of the signal is different depending on if the hydrogen is in blood or bone or something else. The whole thing hinges on the fact that when any specific part of the brain is active, when it goes into action to direct some human behavior or respond to a stimulus, blood rushes to that spot in the brain. And blood has tons of hydrogen atoms in it, so that's what the MRI registers."

"You put people in the machine, you look at their brains while they do things or think about things, you watch where the blood flows, which is really watching where the hydrogen atoms flow, and then take pictures of it," Loretta says.

"You said you don't know how the MRI works."

"I said *pretend* I don't know."

She doesn't mind his surprise this time.

"Well, okay, good. It's worth calling out that it takes an army of computers to reconcile the amount of data that even a single trip through the tunnel generates, but we have the computational power to do that and these tools are also getting better all the time. In fact, while the MRI technology is vital, the ability of computers to analyze mountains of data is as important, maybe more."

"How reliable are the outcomes?"

"Pretty crude, to be honest, but the potential is there. Plus, a lot of this MRI analysis is being done on non-human primates, and that has some limits."

"Monkeys and such?"

"Yeah. We alter their brains and then take pictures of them inside the MRI to test various hypotheses."

Alter, of course, means surgically modify or damage the parts of monkey brains that might be linked to risk-taking or maternal affection or addiction of whatever hypothesis a scientist comes up with, and then observe how, if, monkey behavior changes and take a bunch of MRI brain images of that whole process. Or genetically engineer the monkeys to get neurological diseases, like Parkinson's. And see how the monkey brain changes over time due to that condition. Or surgically implant lab-grown human brain cells into apes or chimps or macaques, like the biology chair described, to grow next-gen Frankenstein primates to test ideas about consciousness. And take MRI monkey brain pictures from start to finish. She knows it's necessary to improve human lives, but that doesn't make it less gross and heart-breaking.

"For both non-human primates and humans, the MRI shows hot spots in the brain," Devlin says.

"Hot spots?"

"That's what we call the brain areas that flood with blood when a person, or non-human primate, is doing something or thinking, when the concentration of hydrogen-filled blood registers on the MRI scan. We can correlate language, for example, with a specific area of the brain because it gets 'hot' when people talk, although it's not refined much beyond that, with a few exceptions. But we'll get there. With better imaging and upgrades in computing capacity, someday we'll be able to map the neural correlates of behavior, including emotion."

"Neural correlates. I should take that literally? The parts of the brain that correlate to a particular behavior or emotion."

"That's right, but it's a work in progress, for sure. But what will be super cool is when we can connect data from scans around the world. Right now, it's an imaging study here and there, you know? But when we can pull data together from entire populations, billions of brain scans, then you get seriously meaningful data. A full brain map. That could translate into cures for Alzheimer's, reversing brain damage so people can walk, even talk, again, figure out schizophrenia or—"

"—incite love, or tamp down its less pleasant side

effects, like lust or jealousy. Or otherwise muck around with people's emotions," she says.

He pauses, and then says, "Well, sure, there's always a potential downside. I mean if the wrong people get ahold of the controls."

She wants to say not if but when, because the wrong people always get ahold of the controls, but she decides that conversation won't help Jenny and it's probably better if this young scientist feels optimistic for as long as possible about the applications of his research. Maybe it will turn out as he hopes, or at least, the benefits will outweigh any negatives.

"Although would it be so bad if we could shorten grief, for example? People would like that." His Adam's apple moves as he swallows. She wonders why grief came to mind and if it's impolite to ask, but he quickly changes course. "Consider the possibility of telepathy."

"Telepathy."

"You'll like this. A healthy man is placed inside an MRI and asked a bunch of questions, all with a binary yes or no answer. For yes, he is told to imagine himself playing tennis. For no, he is to imagine the face of his newborn child. The hot spots in the brain for physical activity and affection are in different areas, so the brain scans will light up differently for each answer. Basically, he was asked to communicate only with his mind. And it worked. He answered yes or no questions without using words from inside an MRI like this one right here. That's telepathy, right? Communicating with the mind."[24]

"Wow, what an inventive use of the technology."

"The concept is being expanded to the alphabet now. Assign an action or emotion with a unique neural hot spot to each letter and people could spell things out without ever talking."

"A Ouija board of the brain. Amazing. The potential for people who can't speak is mind-boggling, no pun intended," she says. "What about unraveling the neural correlates of human consciousness?"

"That's where a lot of the research is aiming even though we're a crazy-long way from working that out, probably not in my lifetime, but some day."

"You don't believe in the hard question of human consciousness?"

"That we can't understand the brain because of the subjective nature of human experience?"

"Yes, that the focus on what can be measured, the objective methods of science, can't penetrate the unique way we each experience the world. You know, the famous what's-it-like-to-be-a-bat question."

He laughs and says, "I think that question might be famous in a pretty small circle."

"But what's your answer?"

"I don't see a point in framing the discussion in either-or terms, or for that matter, what I 'believe.' It makes it seem like a person must choose in souls or biology as the explanation for consciousness. To me, that's out-of-date thinking. I'd rather plod along, ask questions, conduct the MRI tests and see what comes out of that."

"Don't you need a theory to drive the questions?"

"That's what we're taught, and I would say that all researchers, well, probably all people, frame questions aligned to some prevailing theory or belief system, it's how humans process information. But neuroscience is in the early days in understanding these things, so many possibilities are still out there, and even though every full professor in the field is throwing their pet theory against the wall like spaghetti hoping it sticks, I'm cool working with the current model. Meaning, we'll likely be able to answer most questions about the relationship between mind and brain by assuming biology is in charge of what we now call consciousness. But I'm fine with being wrong if that's where the data leads."

Loretta looks at the wall clock. She can't be late to brief John before his interview with Jamie about *The Case of the Misplaced Sperm*.

"Sorry to rush things but could we please switch to near death experiences now?"

"Sure. Come on, I have some scans to show you."

Loretta follows him into the side control room. He sits down in front of an oversized computer screen and clicks the space bar. Two oval lobes connected by a dark band in the middle pop up on the screen, a cross-section of a brain, with splashes of shades of gray and yellow interspersed with black dots and splotches.

"This is the brain at rest, a DMN image, otherwise known as the default mode network,[25] meaning what the brain does when it's theoretically doing nothing or doing nothing of which the mind is aware because really, the brain is never doing nothing."

"Like when we're daydreaming."

"Yes, that's the baseline. Now, let's compare this brain scan with another." He clicks the space bar a second time and another brain image slides into position. In this one, both lobes are lit up along their edges in pastel colors, rimming the skull bone barrier.

"Remember, the brain on the left is what we call an average brain under resting conditions." She leans in to see better. Devlin smells like cloves. "The brain on the right is the same brain, but the image was taken under, well, unusual circumstances. It was dying."

"Dying?"

"I took this scan of a person just as she died."

"How did you scan a dying person? I haven't heard about that kind of study going on at the University. I would know about something so unusual."

"I took these scans privately."

Loretta looks at him curiously.

"It was my mom. Don't worry, she signed all the paperwork."

"Your mom."

"Yes."

"As she was dying."

"Right."

"You scanned your mom as she was dying, right here in this lab, in this machine for large animals?"

He shrugs. "She wanted to make a difference."

Loretta pictures him sneaking his mother in late at night, placing her inside the machine, holding her hand and scanning her brain as she suffocates on her last pull of breath. She wonders how he got the body out, but then realizes it wouldn't have been too difficult. The University hospital has its own morgue. Still, no matter how he disposed of his mother's body, this is ethical quicksand. She should say something. She has to say something.

"This scan could get you kicked out of your field, you know that? Using relatives as research subjects, especially under those conditions, it has serious ethical considerations. If anyone finds out ..."

"I trust you."

"This isn't about trust."

"Should I stop talking?"

She should say *yes*, stop now, immediately. Let's go talk to the ethics officer and get you some remedial help before you ruin your career.

Then she thinks about Jenny. Maybe the career that will be ruined will be her own.

"Keep going."

"I took this scan to find out if previous studies on rats could be extrapolated to humans." Devlin points at the colored edges around the edge of his mother's brain scan. "As I hoped, this scan reinforces those results."

"Explain the rat study." Loretta talks fast, trying to outrun her ethics.

"Cardiac arrest was induced in a group of rats. And then their brains were scanned."

"How were the rats scanned?"

"The researchers implanted electrodes in the rodent brains. The rodents were clinically dead, without breath or heartbeat, but their brains still showed signs of consciousness and then after a few more seconds their brain activity became more synchronized, even though they were clinically dead, and it as very hot in the same areas that human MRI studies have suggested are responsible for perception and the ability to undertake complex tasks."[26]

"And so?"

He points to the colored edges around the scan. "My mother's scan shows the same thing. The same flash. As we, or at least the rats and my mom, die but before moving into permanent unconsciousness, the brain dances around for a while in the areas that may be responsible for higher level activities."

Maybe she can find a loophole, some way to not report Devlin to the Office of Research Integrity. She'll figure out how later. Or just ignore it. No one will ever find out unless she says something. And she could keep quiet. Keeping quiet is definitely a zombie strength.

"When someone is near death, on the brink, the scans show an instant of heightened consciousness and connectivity across the neural pathways of the brain that we see at no other point during life," he continues.

"Could this hyper-connected state explain near death experiences?"

"That's my hunch. But to be fair, at this stage, it could mean anything, even a soul escaping through the brain, although I doubt many scientists would travel down that path."

"Do people who are doing psychedelics also have this hyper-connected state?"

"The research on that is thin, but growing. What it shows so far is that the brain on psychedelics is hyper-connected but not in precisely the same way. What's also interesting is that when terminally ill patients take mushrooms or other forms of psychedelics, and then have trips or whatever they're called in the scientific jargon, the patients largely lose any fear of death."[27]

"Because of what they experience on those trips."

"Right."

Loretta flashes on the Good Friday experiments the chair of religion told her about but then refocuses on the rat study and Devlin's mother. "It will be tough to replicate the rat research at a level needed to collect human data. Your mother is only one data point."

"Impossible, really. It would require a lot of humans on the verge of death to spend their final moments in an MRI machine instead of surrounded by their loved ones."

Multiple dying people or one having repeated near death experiences, Loretta thinks.

"I don't want to give you the wrong impression," he says. "She did it willingly, she wanted me to have the scan. A long time ago, before I was born, my mom had her near death experience after a bad car accident, my interest in them now, even in neuroscience at all, is because of what she told me about the tunnel, the life review, floating above her body. She said it taught her we are all connected. Mom wanted me to use her death to gain more knowledge about them."

His voice is sincere and earnest, and Loretta knows he understood the risk describing his unapproved research to her. And yet he did it anyway. The power of a mother's love.

"What was your mom's name?"

"Martha Richardson."

"Martha Richardson. Maybe she'll be a twenty-first century Phineas Gage."

"Phineas Gage. I wonder what he would think if he could have predicted his scientific infamy, a century later, all because he survived when a railroad tie went straight through his skull."

"I think it was a crowbar. It's called the American Crowbar Case."

"Whatever," Devlin says.

"Maybe the world's next Phineas Gage will be someone experiencing near death experiences over and over again, multiple times."

"Do you know someone like that?"

"Possibly."

"Is that all you're going to say?"

"For now."

"You are describing a research gold mine, a brain I would love to scan." Devlin closes the computer files. "What would be incredibly valuable would be to have other people in adjacent MRI machines who had already had a near death experience to see if the hyper-connectivity flash showed up on those brains."

"Do you think it would?"

"Maybe people who've had near death experiences are changed neurologically by the experience, or maybe they were different to begin with. Can't know yet. But identifying a change or congenital commonality might allow something special to be observed between them."

"You think the brains of people who have had near death experiences would respond in some measurable way when someone nearby is having one? Why? I mean, it seems a bit of a stretch, especially for a scientist."

"Thinking outside the box, that's all. I'm wondering if they're wired, or get re-wired, differently to be receptors of whatever is beyond consciousness."

"You mean the oneness-place they all describe?"

"Yeah, that. My other goal for this research is to figure out a way to induce near death experiences without putting people in any danger. Maybe a drug or an electro-shock or something else."

"That would be amazing," Loretta says, imagining

the ripple effect of everyone in the world having the experience of losing their sense of self, to feel part of something greater, even just for a few seconds. "How would you know if that drug was creating a hallucination or somehow opening a door to another reality?"

"It may not matter but answering that question is kind of the whole point," he says.

"I suppose so." She remembers the question the Dean asked. "Did the MRI show that all the rats have the heightened connectivity?"

"Yes."

"But not every human who comes back from being clinically dead has a near death experience."

"An anomaly worth exploring. It could be that how we define death is wrong."

"How old is your mom's scan?"

He leans back in his chair, and when he does, his pants ride up an inch or so; his socks are mismatched, like the stairs.

"She died three months ago. Cancer."

"My husband has cancer."

Loretta doesn't know why she tells Devlin about Matthias. It is something she rarely talks about because speaking the truth out loud squeezes her chest to the point where she can barely breathe.

"It doesn't have to end like it did for my mother."

"No, it doesn't. Thank you. I appreciate that. He's fine now, totally fine." They are quiet for a few beats.

"Did you know that before he died, for real, I mean, Phineas Gage was reduced to begging on the steps of Harvard Medical School?" he asks.

"I didn't know that, but somehow it's not a surprise. Used and discarded."

He twists a dial. The hum of the machine grows.

"Want to go for a ride?" he asks, tilting his forehead toward the MRI. "Get your brain scanned?"

"Is that allowed?"

"According to you, it's okay since you're not related to me. As long as you sign the consent paperwork."

"This machine is for large animal research."

"Aren't we all large animals in the grand scheme of things?" Devlin asks, grinning.

NINETEEN

The two-person elevator, original to the century-old building, bumps into place and the door creaks open; a young woman pushes out a metal cart carrying a plastic tub covered with a blue dish towel. Tiny paws scratch against the inside of the plastic. Loretta knows that the tub carries a litter of mice, maybe rats, perhaps piglets. University researchers don't use dogs or cats anymore, too much public pressure against that. Plus, what would they tell their own kids?

Loretta points at the towel, which has slipped off the left side of the tub. The secret is never let anyone outside the scientific realm see the eyes of research animals, she's been told. The lab tech says, "Oh my gosh, thanks," and quickly pulls the cover into place. Loretta get on the elevator and the doors close.

Three floors later, the doors slide open. John is waiting to get on. He looks rattled.

"Another fucking Macaque got out, the police have it cornered behind Starbucks at the mall. All hell is breaking loose on social media. They're calling it Apeuccino, for Christ's sake. I need to go. Really sorry, but I can't go on camera for you."

"Oh shit," Loretta says, her tone sounding as if she's commiserating with John but really, she's sliding into a panic because there's not enough time to find anyone else. She runs through a list of candidates in her mind, and knows none of them are available. The only other option at this late moment is a very bad option.

A phobia of being on camera, live or taped, would typically be disqualifying for her job, but Loretta didn't discover this fear until well after her assimilation into the University public relations machine, and so far, it's been accommodated as a quirk. But she has always known the day would come, and dreaded its arrival.

Okay, she thinks, I can do this. She dashes down the back stairs, stopping at the restroom to wash her face and run a comb through her rain-frizzed hair. She leans on the sink, looks in the mirror and spits out a pep talk at her reflection: Cede control to your inner zombie; no fear, no anxiety, just pure reaction.

A few minutes later, Loretta swings open the door to the University media relations bullpen, her face partially rejuvenated with a fresh application of pale pink lipstick and too much face powder.

Jamie is waiting for her, with her peach-white, smooth, young skin, waist-pinched custom tailored suit and sleek on-camera blonde bob. She looks at Loretta. Her expression is not friendly.

"Well?"

Malcolm, the cameraman, is next to her, surrounded by equipment. A Black, middle-aged man with a salt and pepper beard and a widening belly, his primary job is to be sure Jamie looks perfect in all lighting circumstances. After that, it's to get the news.

"There's a spot out back near a Douglas fir grove. It will catch the mid-day sun nicely," Loretta says, hoping Jamie can be tricked into a shot without any iconic

University attributes in the background, minimizing its future use as stock footage.

"Outside? In this weather?"

"Why not? We've got a sunbreak. Maybe you'll get a rainbow."

"It's cold."

"We've got coats."

"Who's on camera?" Jamie asks, looking behind Loretta at the empty hall.

Loretta pauses. "Me."

"Well now, what a surprise." Jamie smiles and picks up her bag. "We'll shoot wherever you want."

Next to the dark green conifer branches, Malcolm sets up a camera tethered to a remote broadcasting van parked on the lawn, sinking slightly into the mud. Loretta will get an earful from University maintenance later about the tire tracks.

Jamie checks the framing through the lens. "Looks like we're in a goddamn forest. But you're right, the light is nice. It's fine. Let's just get this done before Loretta chickens out. I guess it is a scoop of sorts. Veteran University PR flack makes her first on-camera appearance."

The filming attracts passersby, a handful linger to watch. Loretta shifts from one foot to the other, paces a little, recites the media statement in her head and predicts the questions Jamie will ask. A canary lands on the low branch behind her. Just as Loretta is processing the improbability of the presence of the domesticated bird, it flies away. She hopes it finds its cage. Or maybe not. Why should she assume that being in a cage is better than the bird living life on its own terms? Well, she argues with her non-self, the caged bird would live longer, right? But why would that matter if a bird isn't aware of its life, or its inevitable death? What's it like to be a canary? She almost laughs, then stops cold. Uh-oh. Her mind is ricocheting. Breathe, Loretta, breathe. Give in to the zombie. React, don't think.

Jamie looks at Loretta. "You're a little flushed. Want some powder?"

"No, and can you please just start? Let's get this over with."

"I'll ask the questions, put the microphone toward you. You answer, then I'll follow up. You know the drill."

"Of course."

"We're live for this broadcast but I may edit it back, depending on how it goes, for the after-work segment. I'll for sure run it again at the ten o'clock slot."

Jamie straightens Loretta's collar, shoos an insect away from her hair and then pulls a handkerchief from her pocket and dabs the sweat beading up on Loretta's forehead.

"Are you running a fever or something?"

"Jamie, come on, start the damn interview."

Jamie looks at her watch and then over at Malcolm. Malcolm is talking into his headset and puts up his palm to wait, talks some more, and after a minute or so, he holds out his fingers, counting down—three, two, one, thumbs up. Jamie looks straight into the camera and does the setup introduction. Then she pivots to Loretta but not so far that she is in stark profile; she knows her best angle. Loretta wishes she knew her best angle.

"We are talking with Loretta Sparkman, University spokesperson, about this challenging situation." Before Jamie can get the microphone over to her mouth, Loretta begins talking, creating a brief transition echo. From the corner of her eye, she sees Mona on the edge of the group of gawkers, her expression materializing into what Loretta registers as concern.

Loretta says, "We're very sorry for this situation. In decades of operation, nothing like this has ever happened at the fertility clinic. This is a complicated situation, and we are very, very sorry."

Shit, Loretta thinks, I said we're sorry twice, very, very sorry. We're not double sorry—we're only the right amount of sorry, single sorry. Panic rises in her chest like a cresting wave of nausea, but she pulls it back. Stay focused. Stick with the media statement. "It is our responsibility to do everything we can to support the patients in this difficult situation and that includes respecting and protecting their privacy."

"Did the University clinic try to force the female patient to have an abortion?"

Loretta gets caught up in the wording of the question. Female patient? What? Why would anyone ask a male patient to have an abortion? But she keeps it together, she doesn't falter. "Under no circumstances would the clinic or a health care provider employed by this University ever force decisions about health care."

"Are you denying that the University recommended an abortion?" Jamie asks, poking the microphone closer to Loretta's mouth, almost hitting her teeth. Loretta hopes her lipstick isn't smeared over her teeth; she doesn't want to look like a crazed clown on television.

"Health care decisions are always up to the patient. Under all circumstances, we answer patient questions and provide information about the suite of options."

Okay, I'm doing fine, she thinks. Only need to get through another minute.

"Was an abortion performed? Did you use public taxpayer funds to pay for an abortion?"

"Come on, Jamie, you know we would never breach patient confidentiality in this or any situation."

Crap, too casual, exactly what she always advises against in these types of situations. Familiarity translates as a dodge, like someone is trying to hide something. And straighten up. She can feel her shoulders slouched like an old woman. Jamie tilts her head down slightly, the way one might if they were going to smile but no smile appears; she knows she just got under Loretta's skin. She's coming in for the kill. Shit, shit, Loretta says inside.

"Are you confirming that a child was born?"

"I didn't say that."

"Are you denying it?"

Before Loretta has a chance to answer, Jamie barrels ahead. "Was it because the child was mixed race that the University tried to force an abortion?"

A collective inhale from the small crowd watching the interview pulls at the air, warping the space around Loretta; her thoughts become thin. And then the worst happens. Loretta imagines herself on camera, as if she is floating above the scene and she is horrified by her unrecognizable appearance.

"State taxpayers have a right to know if their money, the money that funds this University, is being used in illegal or unethical ways," Jamie says.

Loretta fights her way back into the moment, but now she is fumbling her words. "How, how could you think that, I mean, how could you even make such a charge? It's ridiculous."

Jamie is ready. "This state has a long history of racist laws, laws which prevented Black people from residing or owning land in this state. Exclusion laws, also called sunset laws, established at the same time this University was founded more than a century ago. The same time. No one at this University has ever spoken out about these laws, not then, not now, not once. Why shouldn't I ask a question about racism at this University? It would be irresponsible not to ask. And so, I ask again, did the University try to force this woman to have an abortion?"

Loretta has thoroughly lost her place and timing. From the sidelines, Mona catches her eye. *We are sorry*, she mouths.

She takes Mona's cue and somehow it comes back

together, the same as when she writes something she knows is perfect. Her words are pure. Real.

"We are sorry for this situation. Truly sorry. What can I say beyond that? No matter what you say, no matter what you ask, I will not breach the privacy of these people. Something happened that put them in a difficult situation. We can't change that, but we can take responsibility and from this moment do whatever is needed to protect their privacy, to protect their futures, to reveal absolutely nothing about them or the circumstances beyond what is required by law."

"But in the lawsuit—" Jamie counters.

"You'll have to speak to the lawyers for additional comment about the lawsuit, but I ask you and your viewers to consider the type of person who would take this difficult, morally complex situation and throw racism into the mix to advance an agenda."

Even in the chilly weather, Loretta feels the heat rippling from the back of her neck across her face. She is thinking about that man, the sperm donor, the shock jock radio guy who she met once years ago at some philanthropic event where everyone ate goat cheese and baguettes, and feeling awful that whoever this mystery woman is out there who doesn't know she made a baby with this terrible, hateful man. The University has dealt her a bad fucking hand. And she, Loretta, is the mouthpiece for this University still dealing that bad hand. No, not mouthpiece. Storyteller. Loretta is the storyteller for the University. She is telling the story.

But she is also the one who created the story.

That means she can change the story.

Jamie tries to say something, but Loretta looks directly, and intently, at the camera and talks over her.

"I am sorry. I am deeply sorry for everything. I can't change the past, but I will do my best to help change the future, to make the future better. For you."

The camera lingers on Loretta's face. She is crying.

Crying? Why the hell is she crying? Loretta lets the tears fall without wiping them away. Jamie quickly regains control, walking toward the camera, sidelining Loretta, mimicking an exaggerated sense of slow motion like a CSI episode without the cleavage.

"Viewers, this is an ethically complex situation and one that raises issues that can be painful to discuss. We will have more on this developing story in our evening broadcast. This is Jamie Ignatius reporting live from the University. Back to you, Trent."

Malcolm waves his finger across his neck signaling he has stopped recording.

"What the hell?" Loretta says. "You ambushed me."

"You're supposed to be better at your job."

Loretta looks over at Malcolm to be sure he's no longer recording; he's winding up the unplugged cable around his thumb and elbow. "We are not responsible for what happened more than one hundred years ago. *I* am not responsible," Loretta says.

Jamie places her hands on her hips, the microphone dangling by her side. "You didn't live back then but you are responsible for how the legacy of those racist laws and, at best, indifference by the University plays out now, how they're embedded into the roots of this place, going back centuries, sunk into the foundations of knowledge itself."

"You're straying pretty far afield from a lawsuit about misplaced sperm. What are you talking about?"

But Loretta knows what Jamie is talking about. It's not so far removed from when she was trying to figure out the origins of academic departments. Who or what makes the call to prioritize knowledge, now and across history? What's the ripple effect of that decision? If white people have been doing that since Universities were established, and actively keeping anyone else out of that process, certainly their interests have been prioritized in the hierarchy and pursuit of knowledge.

"I like you," Jamie says. "I really do. And you're in a position of serious influence, even if you don't act like it, or even seem to realize it. Who knows how long you'll have that influence. Use it. Get that white faculty, all those white administrators, to look in the mirror. People need to speak up. It's long past time to look the other way, to fear being uncomfortable."

Jamie abruptly turns her back on Loretta and walks over to Malcolm. She wobbles a few times as her towering heels get stuck in the soft ground. Jamie helps Malcolm and together they finish packing up the gear.

Mona pulls Loretta aside and hands her a Kleenex. "Your mascara is running."

Loretta wipes her eyes, smudging them even blacker. "Mona, I'm sorry. I should have found someone else to be on camera. I ran out of time."

"Don't beat yourself up, not yet at least. This could work for us. Empathy is gold in crisis communications and you were very empathetic, plus a little pitiful."

"Pitiful? I looked like a sweaty, crazed raccoon clown," she says. "Rambling incoherently."

Mona puts her arm around her shoulders. "Let's not jump all the way to incoherent raccoon clown until we see how it plays out."

They pass through a back door into the cafeteria overflowing with students and staff. A student crossing in front of Loretta stumbles and drops her tray of food. A tuna melt splatters onto Loretta's yellow shoes. The clattering noise makes the room to go quiet and in that narrow valley of silence, Loretta covers her mouth as a surge of nervous bile climbs up her throat. The three students sitting at a nearby table jump out of the way as she loudly vomits into the garbage bin. Mona hands her a wet napkin.

"I'm glad you didn't barf on air though," she says.

Loretta wipes her face. Her phone vibrates—a text from Matthias. *You looked so beautiful on camera.*

TWENTY

At the midway point between Loretta's office and the Department of Anthropology, a falling-down gazebo perches unsteadily on the banks of a widening stream in a field covered mostly with hibernating ferns and over-wintering shrubs. An acre or so of land overgrowing its once-promising garden plans, the area abandoned by the dwindling University landscapers who now are paid to focus their efforts on clipping, mowing, planting and watering the expansive front green lawn, a place for well-heeled donors to gather for charity appreciation functions. Ignored and free, the area is reverting to wildness, now a favored spot for birds, mostly finches and crows, but she occasionally spots a heron or hawk. During the summer, Loretta often eats the lunch Matthias packs for her out here. He includes a small bag of birdseed during the warmer months.

But today as Loretta walks past, she hardly notices the landscape, obsessing on her on-camera debacle (a story she has provisionally titled *Loretta's Broadcast News Debut Disaster*), trying but not succeeding in putting it out of her mind. She was silently grateful when Toni pushed her out of the Dean's office suite saying she would finish the needed responses to emails and phone calls, along with the explosion of comments on social. *"Go to your appointment,"* she said. *"I got this."*

Loretta arrives at the door just as a student catches up from behind. He carries a cage with two fluffy yellow ducklings inside. With his free hand, he holds the door for Loretta to pass through. The young man is exuberantly welcomed at the far side of the reception area by students sprawled on orange beanbag chairs; one, a red-headed white woman wearing a blue scarf, squeals happily, pulls a baby duck from the cage and cuddles it to her cheek.

"Therapy ducks," the receptionist says, following Loretta's gaze.

"No way."

"Exam time can be very stressful."

Even though Loretta thinks this is totally crazy, she fights the urge to grab a baby duckling, imagining the hypnotic softness against her cheek.

"Loretta from the Dean's office?" a woman asks, stepping into the reception area. "Professor Kinzer, chair of the Department of Anthropology," she says, holding out her hand to shake. A white woman, she is about Loretta's age and height. Her blunt-cut shoulder-length gray hair is flecked with purple and lime green tint, and there is a tattoo around her wrist, a rainbow braided bracelet. "Come, come, let's make our way to the seminar room. I've asked two doctoral students to join us, if you don't mind."

"Not at all. Never too early to get future scholars up to speed on the needs of your friendly University public relations office."

"Speaking of which, that was some interview. Is that the sort of thing you're envisioning for *60 Minutes*? I have to say upfront, I'm not comfortable crying for an audience, and doubt I could do it on cue."

Loretta groans. "Please, let's not talk about that."

"Better get used to it. I suspect by the end of the day everyone on campus will be talking about it. It was oddly powerful. And memorable. You'll be, what do the young people call it, a viral sensation."

"The last thing I need," Loretta says, covering her mouth, worried about a still-lingering vomit scent, even though she brushed her teeth twice, chugged two mini-cans of Diet Coke and chewed a half-pack of gum in the last thirty minutes. Not in that order.

Professor Kinzer introduces Stanley and Megan, the doctoral students. She places four paper cups and a bottle on the conference table. "Wine? I'm thinking you need it."

"I won't turn it down." Loretta sinks into the chair, suddenly feeling bone tired and defeated from the earlier events, but maybe from life overall. Despite the exhaustion, or maybe because of it, Loretta sloughs her phone onto the table, clicks record and auto-asks the first question.

"Are near death experiences—"

"Our brains are in the business of fooling us," Professor Kinzer interrupts.

"Don't ever trust your brain," Stanley adds.

"Neurons are liars," Megan says.

A disruptive start. It appears the trio has rehearsed. She is suddenly a little less tired. "Okay," she says. "My brain is a liar. Interesting. Please, go on."

"My focus as an anthropologist is the study of how society is shaped by the collection of meta-stories that cultures use to define themselves," Professor Kinzer says. "I've had no prior reason to review near death experiences, but after receiving your *60 Minutes* request, I called colleagues, and Stanley and Megan undertook a literature search. We've prepared a brief PowerPoint presentation."

Loretta's sparked interest rearranges itself into mild dread, recalling the standard coma-inducing academic presentation style. She should be drinking coffee, not wine. Still, the opening about a liar brain *was* promising.

Stanley dims the lights. Three large screens flash to life; on the middle screen is a photograph of a tunnel, on the right a body floats, suspended in mid-air, on the left a cartoon of a bearded white-male God welcoming the newly deceased through ornate pearly gates. Ten beats, eight too long, Loretta thinks, and the right and left images fade to black, replaced by a man floating above a hospital gurney on the middle screen, as if his belly is tethered to an invisible celestial lasso. They must really, *really* want to be picked for the fake *60 Minutes* episode, she decides.

"A tunnel, a bright light, out-of-body elements, the welcoming from relatives, a life review, and the sense of being enveloped in love or a greater power, that iconic sense of oneness," Professor Kinzer says. "Similar attributes of near death experiences are found in nearly all cultures, with few exceptions. Generally, although not always, those who have an experience report more positive feelings about life and a diminished fear of death. In fact, fear of death is often erased."

She loses her place in the slide deck, clicks through a series of images (why is there a vampire in this, Loretta wonders as Dracula whizzes past), going backward by one, then forward by three, apologizes, and then lands on the right slide: a marble bust of a man with a beard like white steel wool floating in a yellow background. Letters forming the name swirl and grow, capitalized neon green font pulsating across the top.

"The earliest known description of a near death experience was recounted by Plato in 420 B.C. in *The Republic*."

The name *Plato* carries Loretta back to high school; a teacher, a man with long scruffy hair, leads the class in a thought experiment. Consider this, he says: A group is chained inside a cave their entire lives, facing the wall, their backs to the entrance. They see their shadows cast on the cave wall from the light of the fire behind them and this is all they can see; the shadows are their reality. Then one day, the prisoners break free, escape the cave and discover reality is something else entirely different than their cave shadows. The teacher asked if this story caused them to think differently about their own perceptions of reality. Loretta wonders if Plato came up with this thought experiment because of his near death experience. Could that be?

The middle screen fades into a pale-faced, golden-haloed Jesus standing over an open grave, holding out his hand to help a man step out. The picture is stylized, like someone used a drawing app to modernize an old-style Sunday school poster. On the left and right are images of the bible in the same style.

"Some believe the biblical story of Lazarus, the man Jesus brought back from the dead, was a metaphor for the near death experience," Professor Kinzer says.

A dozen more slides slip by—of Christ ascending into heaven on a cloud of light in all kinds of artistic styles, from wildly abstract to chubby cherub-baby rococo. The contrast is surprisingly beautiful.

The professor continues narrating. "Studies of early Christianity indicate the resurrection itself was believed by some people, later categorized as heretics, to be symbolic of spiritual awakening. Non-canonical gospels include descriptions of a swell of heavenly light at the time of the resurrection like the kind reported in a near death experience."

She jumps ahead a few centuries. "Throughout history, highly credible people have reported near death or out-of-body experiences, for example, Carl Jung." An image of Dr. Jung, spectacles balanced on his nose, gives way to a lurid painting of Dracula hovering over an innocent maiden, bright red blood dripping down her punctured neck. It's a ghastly depiction, so much so it's almost comical. "Some scholars suggest the original vampire myth originated in the near death experience."

That's a novel take, Loretta thinks.

"Hemingway's short story *The Snows of Kilimanjaro* describes the main character's slow death, a white hunter on safari in Africa, using the elements of a near death experience."

"Suggesting Hemingway either had one himself—"

"—or was made aware of the phenomenon from someone else, yes, this is an inescapable conclusion," Professor Kinzer agrees. "He certainly found the near death experience worthy of exposition to his audience."

After the professor clicks through a dozen or so more vampire images but oddly none of Hemingway, she lands on a cheerful middle-aged white man, glasses propped up on his bald head. "Raymond Moody helped bring the near death topic into the mainstream with his book *Life After Death*, a bestseller in 1975. After Dr. Moody's book, many people came forward with similar stories and the topic exploded."

An audio kicks in. Is that wind? Why add wind sounds to PowerPoint? Loretta suppresses a laugh. A movie poster for *Flatliners* leaps onto the center screen, flanked on the left by a young Julia Roberts and on the right by even-younger Kiefer Sutherland. "Accounts of near death experiences are prevalent in popular culture. This film is one of dozens."

Professor Kinzer clicks off the projector. The three screens fade out; no one gets up to switch on the lights and she keeps talking in the dark conference room. "The question for us to consider is while most cultural meta-stories disappear over time, even entire religions vanish, why has the near death experience not only persisted throughout recorded history but seems more ubiquitous than ever?"

Loretta starts to answer but the professor holds up her palm. "Let's table that question. I'll end this section by calling the ubiquity of the near death experience across time as our first lesson. Bookmark that."

Bookmarked, Loretta says to herself, finishing her cup of wine and wondering if it's too soon to ask for a refill. The middle screen resurrects brightly into a gold-framed antique photograph of a white man with dark hair holding a metal rod. On the screen next to the man is a sketch of a skull with a rod poking through from the chin up to the top of the head. On the third screen, letters circling in a vortex finally arrange themselves into *The American Crowbar Case*.

"Allow me to tell you the story of Phineas Gage ..."

For the next five minutes, with the aid of another dozen slides, Professor Kinzer describes the accident and follows with the now-familiar information about how the medical tragedy of Phineas led to the discovery that brain-is-mind. But then, as other departments did, she adds a twist to that big-picture interpretation.

"When you dig into the details, it is difficult to track down the facts as many neuroscientists wish them to be. There is no agreement in any documentary evidence that this poor man's personality changed because of his injury. Rather, scholars increasingly believe Phineas Gage provided a useful template at a unique moment in scientific history to apply pre-formed ideas evolving from phrenology ..."

In the summer between eighth and ninth grades, Loretta obsessed over a set, less one, of encyclopedias her mother got from Goodwill and stacked up in a lower kitchen cabinet so Loretta could reach them. In the 'P-Q' volume there was an entry about phrenology, how people once thought the topography of the skull could predict certain character traits. After reading the article, Loretta asked Jenny, who happily obliged, to shave off her hair so she could try to correlate the hills and valleys of her skull to her personality. Their moms were not pleased.

"We believe it's possible that phrenology is the unacknowledged precursor meta-story leading to the brain-is-mind theory," Professor Kinzer says.

"Wait, what? The quack theory of bumps-on-the-head revealing your personality led to the idea that the human mind is rooted in biology?"

"Physicians in that era, the mid-nineteenth century, were looking for something to replace the story of phrenology, which was increasingly being debunked for lack of correlative behavioral evidence. Mr. Gage and his fluctuating personality appeared right at the precise historical moment to construct the needed bridge from phrenology directly to materialism."[28]

Professor Kinzer hands the clicker to Stanley, a white man with thick black hair hanging down to his broad shoulders. He clicks to illuminate an image on the middle screen of a brain colored red, blue and yellow, each color defining a distinct labeled region.

"Are we done talking about Phineas?" Loretta asks.

"We'll circle back to him at our closing," Professor Kinzer says. "Stanley now will describe another way of considering the brain, a more recent concept."

Stanley's head is backlit by the image of the brain on the screen, giving the appearance of a corrugated halo.

"For years, decades even, the most common brain model has followed the prevailing concept of ontology recapitulates phylogeny, which posits that the growth and development of an organism is a mirror of its unique evolutionary path, including humans," he says. "Within this framework, we can uncover aspects of, for example, the evolutionary trajectory of a specific fish by observing it from embryo to adult forms."

"A blueprint to our origins hidden inside our own growing bodies," Professor Kinzer adds.

She rolls a laser pointer across the long conference

table. Stanley picks it up, turns it on but then struggles to orient the thin red beam to the projected images; as the dot careens across the screen, a waterfall of internet cats chasing lasers cascades through Loretta's head. He gets the laser pointer under control and begins to talk, his tone serious, like a formal lecture.

"This is a diagram of what is referred to as the triune brain. This model posits that the brain's anatomical structure provides clues to its evolution, which in turn can be applied to the brains of lesser species." He points the red laser at the bottom of the image. "We begin at the brain stem, categorized as the most ancient part of the brain, from an evolutionary standpoint, controlling primal behaviors assumed to be an aspect of early human evolutionary forms focused on basic survival. In other words, according to the triune theory, the stem part of the brain houses our instincts, things shared with our reptilian ancestors."

"An example?" Professor Kinzer prompts.

"Fear of snakes. No matter what you rationally think about snakes or despite never having seen one before, when we see one, we respond with an urgent need to flee or kill."

"Good, very good. We can identify other examples perhaps even more universal. The urge to procreate and the accompanying lustful feelings are presumed to exist in the brain stem, for example."

Stanley clears his throat, coughs twice into his elbow and continues in his deep monotone voice. "Sitting on top of the brain stem is the emotional system, known formally as the limbic elements. In the triune model, this part of the brain originated in mammals, and controls more sophisticated aspects of existence that are shared to varying degrees across the animal kingdom, including humans. Think of examples such as parental behavior and crude attachment emotion."

Stanley moves the red laser dot to the top of the

brain image.

"Third, on top of and enveloping the entire brain is the cortex, with the rational parts that provide humans with language, abstraction, planning and similar higher-order functions," he says. "This triune reptile-mammal-human model was popularized by none other than Carl Sagan."

He pauses. Loretta can sense the question. "I know who Carl Sagan is but honestly, I'm more surprised that you do. He's been dead a long time."

"He has a certain legacy, fraught as it is," Professor Kinzer says.

Stanley clicks and a smiling Sagan pops into the right screen, a universe of stars flickering behind him. "This triune paradigm has guided scientific thinking for many decades, a dominant model against which inquiries have been formulated."

"I'm familiar," Loretta says. "Sometimes people fall back on this idea of a reptilian brain to make excuses for acting in a child-like way, blaming their primal instincts."

"There's just one problem," Professor Kinzer says. "It's wrong. These anatomical brain divisions are present in animals, not just humans. If this triune model were true, and our cortex houses all the special hardware we need to be human, then animals would talk and have self-awareness too."

Stanley looks surprised when she steals his punch line, but he doesn't let the disappointment linger on his expression. "This story is so pervasive that scientists have relied on it for nearly a half-century, and as you point out, humans across cultures use it to justify their own behavior,"[29] he says.

"Further, recent neurological imaging with MRIs shows what we have been calling primal attributes are not in fact located in the brain stem, also disputing this triune model," Megan says, her soft and slow-paced voice a contrast to Dr. Kinzer's hyper efficient pacing.

"This turns out to be just one of many examples of how the broader recapitulation concept, the idea that we can understand something of value about the adult from the development of the embryo, is wrong and now largely discredited," Stanley says.

Dr. Kinzer says, "We arrive at lesson number two, as revealed through a more careful look at the evidence regarding Phineas Gage along with the triune brain model. Lesson two. The stories we have told ourselves in the past about our own brains, what some call theories, are inevitably fallible, even as they run deep."

Loretta says, "Influenced by the prevailing cultural winds."

Dr. Kinzer replies, "And the prevailing scientific evidence. Now let's dig deeper into the implications of our second lesson, shall we?"

Professor Kinzer nods at Stanley who clicks through to three new images: an early computer—a large bulky one filling up an entire room, a second cheesy photo of an office worker wearing giant headphones using the internet, and a third of a hipster at a coffee bar scrolling through an iPhone.

"Loretta, you are old enough to remember an era before computers, I'm guessing?"

"I am."

"Before their appearance, did you think of your brain as a computer?"

"No, how could I? They didn't exist. If I thought much about my brain, which I didn't, I suppose I saw it as more like a theater in my mind, directed by a little mini-me."

"Like a television show," Dr. Kinzer says.

"I guess," Loretta says.

"Before television, people generally thought of their mind as a ghostly presence, able to receive and process information," Stanley says. "Like electricity or radio waves."

"How do you think of your mind today? Still like a little theater?" Professor Kinzer asks.

I think of my mind like a zombie, empty except for a functional presence, largely devoid of a core identity. This is what she'd like to say, but it would undoubtedly divert this presentation down an unproductive path.

"The same as most people, like a computer."

"Today, as you say, most people in our culture default without much thought to the metaphor of brain as computer, a biological machine crunching through equations and probabilities to make decisions. More recently, scholars have loaded the computer metaphor with the story that our sense of self, or consciousness, emerges from all that data crunching. Even more recently, we have adapted this model to accommodate the idea of the mind, and consciousness, being akin to a series of connected apps."

"With the advent of cloud computing," Stanley says, "we are witnessing a renewed interest in the idea that consciousness may be external, perhaps shared in some way."

Megan chimes in. "Imagine how we will describe our brain and its relationship to mind when we reach the point of implanting nodes inside the brain to read other people's thoughts."

"Or in a future world run by adaptive artificial intelligence," Stanley says.

"Hold up," Loretta says. "You're saying the way we characterize our brain is influenced by technological trends that may have nothing at all to do with the brain?"

"We're the ones who create technology. Perhaps what we create are inventions that reflect the ongoing evolution of the human mind," Stanley says.

"But that's not the only way to look at it, or even the simplest," Loretta says. "It seems more likely that the stories we tell ourselves about our brains are shaped by our inventions."

"Either way, it is intriguing but for our purposes immaterial," Professor Kinzer says. "We arrive at our third lesson, which is that the contemporary stories we tell ourselves about the brain are linked to technology."

"How does this relate to the near death experience? Because, you know, that's what *60 Minutes* is interested in," Loretta asks.

"Please bear with us a little longer," Dr. Kinzer nods at Megan and Stanley passes the clicker. "Megan will bring us back to the beginning, to the idea that our brains are liars. Megan is with us only for this term. Her doctoral studies are in neuro-engineering."

"Have you heard of blind sight?" Megan asks.

Loretta says no. She holds out her paper cup, no longer caring if the gesture is rude. Professor Kinzer pours more wine.

"When a blind person is put in an unfamiliar space with large obstacles, usually they can navigate the room without bumping into the obstacles, and they do so far more effectively than a sighted in a blindfold."

"I don't understand," Loretta says, meaning both blind sight and how it relates to near death experiences.

"The mind receives and responds to signals from our environment of which we are entirely unaware of from a consciousness standpoint. An example from the game of baseball shows this."

Megan points the remote and clicks, and each screen fills up with the same image: a pitcher getting ready to throw a ball, his face fiercely concentrated and looking directly at Loretta.

Backlit by the screen, Loretta sees that Megan is strikingly attractive and, atypically for academics, is wearing makeup, lots of it, including a brown-red glossy lipstick that complements her dark skin.

"The speed of a pitched ball in a professional game

is faster than the brain's conscious ability to calculate that speed to mechanistically position the swing of the bat," Megan says. "That means the unconscious mind is doing that work for the batter, using data gathered on the position of the pitcher and past experiences about ball speed to make a best guess of where to aim the swing. Batters are literally swinging at probabilities. But after the swing, the brain backtracks and creates a story, rewrites the internal playback so to speak, allowing the athlete to feel they were consciously in control and aiming the bat at the ball as it approached. Athletes often refer to the phenomenon as being 'in the zone.'"

Professor Kinzer asks, "What do we take away from this?"

Loretta says, "I have no idea."

Megan answers. "We must assume that some degree of our everyday behavior is similarly controlled by reactions to external stimuli of which our thinking self is entirely unaware."

Loretta asks, "Our unconscious mind is doing most of the work of living?"

Megan says, "I didn't say *most* of the work. The degree of involvement is unknown. We can say with some certainty that our unconscious mind is in control, for example, of our ability to walk. If we had to think about walking all the time, we wouldn't be able to do anything else. But the degree to which our unconscious mind is involved in driving our self to respond in any given way, be it to hit a speeding baseball or react to political concepts or to feel attraction for someone or, for our purposes, to create stories about the brain, is poorly understood."

"I'm guessing that's lesson number four," Loretta says.

Professor Kinzer finishes her wine in an exaggerated gulp, purple-red half-moons now at the corners of her mouth. "Let's put the lessons together now, shall we?"

Megan clicks to a slide with four bulleted points. The professor launches into a summary.

"First, ubiquity. The near death experience story is ubiquitous across time. Second, there is a clear influence of prevailing culture and beliefs on what we agree, at any given moment, to be facts, including those about the brain. We provided the examples of Phineas Gage and the triune brain. Third, the modern story of technology. The prevailing model of the brain that drives inquiry into the mysteries of the mind and self-awareness is rooted in the culture of technology, and we can witness in real time across our own lives, at least those of us of sufficient years, the subtle shift of these stories as our technology has rapidly evolved. Fourth, the brain is a liar. Our unconscious brain is, to a degree we do not yet understand, in control of actions that appear to us as self-directed."

"How are we supposed to know what to believe is real if everything is linked to a story that eventually goes out of date, told by a self that is being covertly run by our unconscious mind?" Loretta asks.

"You have articulated the conundrum well. Here is my answer. To know what to believe, we must find ways to rise above our liar-brains, to outsmart them, to tease the truth from ourselves. How can we do this?"

"It all sounds very complicated," Loretta says. "But here is a truth I'm sure of. When a baseball hits me, it will hurt. I can believe that. It's an objective fact, no matter what."

"The persistence of pain. Is there a way to apply that same logic to discerning something real within the meta-stories we tell ourselves about our minds? We believe a safe tactic is to look for what transcends time, culture and technology."

"The near death experience," Loretta says.

Everything collapses into place from this disjointed presentation, which Loretta thinks she may have to retroactively recast as insidiously brilliant. "Your first lesson. Its ubiquity."

"The near death experience is a rare phenomenon, an ancient story persisting across time and cultures that bumps headlong against every story about our minds, past and current, challenging each, be they religious, scientific, philosophical or technological. A persistent, ubiquitous non-conformist. It is the survivalist story in the grand collective quest to unearth the meaning of human existence."

"A near death experience must mean *something* because of its stubbornness as a story? Is that that the takeaway?"

"More or less. There is a clue there."

There's a commotion outside the conference room. The receptionist pokes her head in the door. "The baby ducks got loose. Best to stay put while we round them up."

Professor Kinzer laughs. "We'll wait."

Megan and Stanley return to their seats. No one turns on the lights. Loretta leans back in her chair and closes her eyes. Far inside her mind's theater, in the distance, a glimmer flashes across the darkness there, like a vague Independence Day sparkler, and as she watches the distant light, Loretta is startled. She hears and sees and tastes and feels words as they come into being, and in those strands of light the knowledge from the departments begins to arrange itself, to weave itself into a story. Loretta concentrates on the dancing light, mesmerized and awed by what seems to be happening.

"Loretta, what did you think of our presentation?"

She opens her eyes. The light disappears.

"I'm sorry, were you napping? Oh dear, that's not a good sign."

"My apologies. It's been a long day."

"Yes, of course it has. But how did we do? What are our chances for appearing on *60 Minutes*?"

"Your chances are as high as any other department, probably higher. Especially if you top off my wine."

"Excellent," Dr. Kinzer says with a smile, reaching for the bottle.

TWENTY-ONE

Matthias sits alone in the living room, a bowl of popcorn balanced on his thighs. With the window shades drawn the room is dark, save for the flickering television. When Loretta comes in, he lowers the volume and stubs out a cigarette. She sits next to him on the couch and grabs a handful of popcorn.

"Where's Jenny?"

"Upstairs."

They eat popcorn in silence for a minute, watching the black and white program. "What is this?" she asks.

"An old zombie movie, one of the classics." When she laughs, he adds, "Need to keep up with my wife's state of mind, or lack thereof."

"Not my mind, exactly. More like my sense of self."

"Explain the difference."

Loretta sighs. "Honestly, I'm not so sure anymore. The problem is when you try to define these things, they slip away, they resist being tied to words."

A zombie clutch lumbers through a cemetery, clothes shredded, moaning, faces and skins sliding off in chunks. A non-zombie woman, a Marilyn Monroe lookalike, blonde hair tussled, screams and the effort causes her blouse buttons to pop open. Desperately, she barricades herself inside a farmhouse. Sirens blare. Police storm in. Shotguns blast. Barns burn.

"Can zombies be killed?" Loretta asks.

"They're already dead, strictly speaking. The walking dead. So, no, but they can be made *more* dead, or at least less mobile, by beheading or fire. Then they, I guess, revert to being the dormant dead."

"You know a surprising amount about zombies."

The woman screams again and runs into the arms of a handsome policeman after he battles his way through the zombies and the farmhouse door with an axe.

"How was the hike?" Loretta asks.

Matthias mutes the sound. "Good. Took the new canteen to test. Damn thing leaks."

"I'll get you another one." She leans in to kiss his cheek.

"Decent weather for this time of year, crisp, clear and the view when we crested, just incredible. The river was white-capping with the wind, the sky was so blue."

"Sorry I missed that."

"The best was when a raven landed on the edge of the cliff, a few feet from where I sat, just hanging out. Hopping around and hoping for something better than my trail mix."

"Ravens remind me of you," she says.

"Why?"

"Smart and sleek, curious about the world. Always tilting their heads and looking like they are perplexed and intrigued. Irritated and mischievous."

"It's all an act."

"For you or for ravens?"

He laughs. "Both."

"Did Jenny have an episode up top?" Loretta asks.

"Not that she told me, but we did our own thing. I

stayed close enough to keep an eye out near the drops. Mostly she was meditating or communing with nature or whatever. I was hanging out with my raven friend."

"What else?"

"Odds and ends on the drive out about living with the episodes, some reactions to the lava fields, how she swam with cats in Turkey." He rubs his palms together. "It was nice."

"I want to swim with cats."

"Can zombies swim?"

"As well as cats."

"On the way home, she talked about sometimes feeling disembodied."

Loretta scrapes the bottom of the bowl for the last kernels, some hard and only half-popped, coated in butter and salt. She swirls them around in her mouth. "During the near death experiences or all the time?"

"She wasn't clear on that point," he says. "But I was struck by the fact that what's happening to her sounds similar to what's happening to you, how you say your sense of self is fading away."

"I guess there's overlap but different reasons."

"What exactly are your reasons again?"

"I don't have any new way to describe it, Matthias, it's the same as what I said before," she says, feeling a little defeated by her inability to explain. "All I know is the part of me that's supposed to be in charge seems, well, less and less there, and less and less important."

They watch the soundless zombies fight it out as the farmhouse goes up in flames.

"I've been thinking about this and for the record, I'm not going to let you pretend this situation away. You can't push it aside, we have to figure out what it all means," he says.

She spits out the kernels into a napkin.

"But to get back to your question about Jenny, she said in that disembodied state, she exists outside her own body, sometimes shadowing and other times partially there, ghost-like. Then she said she can usually coax herself back into her body, except for last night. What is extraordinary, her word not mine, is there seems to be two distinct parts, her body and her self."

"That sounds a little unbalanced."

"Literally."

"Have we made a big mistake in not getting Jenny to a doctor right away?" Loretta asks.

"She went to a doctor early on, right?"

"Yeah, but they didn't believe her."

"You're doing what she asked."

"I could be more adamant about medical help."

"What advice have the department chairs given you about seeing a doctor?"

"I haven't asked them, specifically. Only the Dean knows about Jenny, and I didn't tell him how many near death experiences Jenny has had."

"I don't understand. Under what pretext have you been gathering all this information?" Matthias asks.

"I lied. I made something up about appearing on *60 Minutes*."

"Why?"

"I didn't think the chairs would talk to me if I told them the truth. Well, they might talk to me but only to get an introduction to Jenny."

"Again, why? Why make that assumption?"

"Every single person I've talked to, when I hint about her, sees a walking research gold mine. I don't want Jenny becoming another Phineas Gage."

Matthias turns his full frame toward Loretta.

"Who the hell is Phineas Gage?" They hear muffled sounds of movement upstairs. "Tell me later. I don't want to be talking about her when she comes down. But quick, who's on tap for the interviews tomorrow?"

"Psychiatry and the hospital chaplain."

"Promise me you'll ask the psychiatry chair about

Jenny seeing a doctor."

"I promise." She grabs his hand as he stands. "I wish I could have gone on the hike with you today."

"We'll do it, just the two of us, or maybe with Sally-Anne the next time she's home, after you get Jenny's thing figured out."

He lightly kisses her on the forehead, that dad-kiss again, and steps into the kitchen to make dinner. Jenny tiptoes down the staircase and takes Matthias's spot on the couch, first brushing popcorn crumbs into her palm and then placing them back into the bowl. Loretta watches as the last remaining living humans finally set the lumbering undead ablaze and then turns away from the gray-scale zombies to face Jenny.

"How was the hike?"

"Really great. On the way down, I took off my shoes and stuck my bare feet in the creek. So cold, glacial melt, Matthias said, my toes nearly fell off."

"That sounds fun."

"It was. Hey, thanks for helping me last night. I was kind of a mess."

Loretta clicks off the TV. "We'll get through this."

Jenny bites her thumbnail and then runs her hand across her forehead, swiping away errant hairs. "Are you making progress? I don't mean to pressure you or anything."

"I think so."

"What's left?"

"A shrink and a preacher."

"Imagine if they walked into a bar together."

Loretta is relieved by Jenny's joke, but then asks, "Are you worried about what happened last night?"

"Not worried so much as surprised that it was so hard to get back. It's never been that bad. It doesn't change how I feel, I'm blessed to be seeing into this other realm, but still, I'll be glad when you have enough information for us to make a decision on what to do."

Later, after a meal of leftover pasta, Matthias teases Loretta about her on-camera performance, hoping to rub the edge off her embarrassment. Loretta tells them what she learned about MRI technology, but holds back the fact that Devlin has a brain scan of his dying mother. She also describes the presentation from the Department of Anthropology, and they fall into a light-hearted debate about the role of stories in shaping perspective.

That leads to Jenny proposing they play a game she learned camping in New Zealand with a group of ex-pats. A shortcut way of getting to know each other, she says. Each player writes a three-sentence description of their own life story and makes up three sentences about the other players, and then reads them aloud to see how they compare. Loretta is tired and games are not her thing, and she doesn't understand this one because if it's about getting to know a new person, how could anyone write three sentences about a stranger's life? But she agrees because it seems to lighten Jenny's mood.

After scribbling with a worn-down pencil for a few minutes, Loretta is the first to read her sentences. "I was born and raised by an amazing woman. The two best days in my life were when I met Matthias and when Sally-Anne was born. I wish I could watch the sunrise every day."

"You are never up early enough to see the sunrise," Matthias says. "At least not by choice."

"You wake every morning disappointed and go to sleep each night hopeful," Jenny says. "Not a bad way to live, Lolo. I think you're onto something."

"Doesn't that also mean my happiest time is when I'm asleep? Maybe I'd better work on that. Your turn Jenny."

"Here goes. One. Ever since I can remember, I've been searching for something bigger than me, and the sureness it's out there has driven all major decisions of my life and that's why I'm growing old alone. Except for the both of you. Two. I think am close to the end of my search and that kind of scares me. Three. I have learned we are all one, so no one is really alone."

There's a silence as they take that in.

"Matthias?" Loretta says, trying to bridge the serious turn the game took, hoping Matthias will toss in some humor.

"I don't need three sentences for my story."

"Those are the rules of Jenny's game."

Jenny says, "I'm flexible. Make your own rules."

"There's one story, for me, both you and everyone. All other stories are a derivative or a distraction from that," he says and then lights a cigarette.

Loretta is annoyed he is still smoking even though she wants one. Matthias lingers in the moment, lighting and exhaling dramatically, like a ghost-piano man in a fedora singing in a rundown alley bar, his form shadowed by a veil of translucent smoke.

"Come on!" Jenny and Loretta exclaim at the same instant.

He takes a drag, slowly, enjoying their impatience, and exhales, before continuing. "The story of my life, of every life, is that life is a remission from death."[30]

"The point of this game isn't the story of everyone's life," Loretta says.

"Like I said, it's the only story that matters. We are nothing, briefly become something, and then return to nothing again."

"That's two sentences." Loretta stabs at the words on the paper, irritated because he's being too serious when she wanted funny. "Add one more."

"Who made you game sheriff?" Matthias says, but he starts writing with his hand over the slip of paper, hiding his words, mimicking a student protecting his quiz answers, letting the cigarette dangle from his lips. Finally, he reads a third sentence out loud, the cigarette now clenched between his teeth. "The fact that we die makes me doubt we exist."

"You're ridiculous," Loretta says. "And weird."

"Weird? Or honest?"

"Weird. Definitely weird."

"Okay, come on, no fighting, please," Jenny says. "Let's skip ahead to the part where we read what we wrote about each other."

"I wrote that for both of you, so I'm done. Like I said, my story is everyone's story, I'm sticking to it."

"Your answers may be true for everyone, but how it plays out from birth to death is different for everyone," Jenny says with gentle but firm authority. "The whole point is for a person to choose their own answer to the question of why we exist."

"I'm not buying that. As far as I can tell, the most humans have done to answer that question is figure out new and novel ways to deny death. At least that's the story of religion, and science killed that."

"But has it, really? Science has replaced one fable with another," Loretta says. "Evolution."

"Evolution is not a fable," Matthias says.

"Maybe not a fable, but a miracle. The improbability of everything coming together over billions of years randomly in the perfect sequence to create not just life but our experience of life is a fucking miracle."

"There are no miracles in science, just steadiness through the enormity of time," Matthias says, coughing.

"That's the answer to your sad-sack story that the only meaningful thing about life is death? Scientific steadiness through the enormity of time? Who's the audience for *that* story?" Loretta takes his cigarette and stubs it out. "Stop chain smoking. It's gross."

"I will if you get busy making up a new story for me, for the audience of all humanity. You're a storyteller, right?"

"You are getting more ridiculous by the minute."

"Seriously, why not use all this stuff you're learning in the Jenny quest?"

Loretta is wondering if it's too early to go to bed.

"Maybe *that's* why I keep getting sent back," Jenny says. "To help you come up with a better story for all of us. I love that idea."

"These department chairs are so goddamn smart and have about a hundred doctorates among them. I'll be lucky if I can sort out what they are saying to even meet the basics of helping Jenny," Loretta snaps, but then realizes her impulsive response might cause Jenny to worry, make her think this is all for nothing, that no answers are coming, and so she adds, "I mean, I'll be able to figure out next steps for you for sure, but I'm not the right person to figure out some grand new story for humanity. Leave that to the experts."

"No one who's ever come up with a grand story was steeped in expert or academic qualifications," Matthias says. "In fact, that's probably the least likely person to come up with a grand story."

Loretta rubs her temples. "You're making my head hurt. I'm a nobody."

Jenny and Matthias turn to look at each other, and then burst into laughter at the same instant.

"Lolo, we're all nobodies. And anyway, think of it as just an extension of my three-sentences game."

"We didn't finish the game."

"Forget the game," Matthias says. "Honey, I know you're doing it, coming up with a grand narrative to fit what you're learning, a tidy architecture so that all the puzzle pieces of near death experiences lock into place. You can't help it. It's the same process you use for your crisis public relations stories, just this time with real meaning."

Loretta looks at their faces. Jenny's expression brims with optimism, eyes wide. Matthias, on the other hand, looks stern, a taskmaster pushing her to be her best. In both their eyes she sees a ferocious love, and in that warmth, she relents. Why not? Why not try to describe what she saw in that burst of light at the end of the meeting with the Department of Anthropology earlier?

"All right, I'll play your game."

Jenny claps her hands together with joy.

"If you believe in the big bang—"

"I do believe in the big bang," Matthias says.

"Then it means you believe there was something close to a single instance of creation and therefore you must logically assume everything in our reality is reducible, or traceable, to that single event, the cause of the universe. What story does that sound like?"

"Like God creating the universe," Matthias says.

"Right, exactly, so the origin story of both science and religion has a core assumption that reality is reducible to a common property. In the case of science, that being atoms or some subset of them along with some forces and other stuff I don't understand. In the case of religion, or most of them at least, that being God, the singular power underlying reality."

"This is like that phrase I've read, you know the one, that the big bang is God dressed up in math," Matthias says, nurturing a small diamond of hope that this moment might represent the beginning of the reversal of Loretta's zombieness. She's engaged, really thinking about things this time.

"Yes, but not quite. That feels like another sleight of hand denying the basis of religions. Because if it turns out that many religious stories originate from visions associated with an advanced human consciousness, what Dr. Orr in religion called cosmic consciousness, and those stories were handed down and twisted up over centuries, maybe as we evolved we unconsciously tell the same story through a modern biological lens with the metaphor of the big bang. Maybe religion and science will turn out to be flip sides of the same coin, the same stuff."

"But how does it answer the what-it's-like-to-be-a-bat question you told us about?" Matthias asks.

"That's where Jenny comes in."

"That's right," Jenny says. "I know."

"You do?" Matthias asks.

"Not exactly what it's like to be a bat. But I can see, especially when I'm having trouble getting back into my body, something in the space between the bat and me where we exist simultaneously, where I am creating and being created, and the bat too. You know, what I keep saying, where we are all one."

Loretta's phone vibrates. A text from Mona. *Confirming you will be at the court hearing tomorrow? And still waiting for updated comms plan.*

"Goddamn it," Loretta says, texting back. *Yes. I'll be at hearing. Will send new plan shortly.*

"*The Case of the Misplaced Sperm*?" Matthias asks.

"Yes, although tomorrow, it seems likely the world will find out it wasn't misplaced at all."

TWENTY-TWO

Loretta is tired after a night of spinning through a chaotic dreamscape—chasing Matthias, wading in a rushing, overflowing river, something about a giraffe with radioactive eyes—all collapsing into the sinkhole-sound of the alarm. She flashes back to younger years, before Sally-Anne was born, when she was a prolific dreamer, when they seemed to make sense, as if her dreams were mysteries of her own mind waiting to be solved. Back then, she spent the first ten minutes of wakefulness every morning faithfully transcribing her dreams into a dedicated notebook she kept next to her bed. Loretta was determined to extract meaning from the dead zone of sleep. She doesn't remember exactly when she stopped recording her dreams or what became of those dream journals. Why, and when, did she stop caring? She has no idea, no recollection. Maybe that's just part of aging, she decides. Gradually realizing everything you thought was important actually isn't, and the fact you can't even pinpoint the moment this became true somehow makes it more profound.

She flips on the right turn blinker, exits the interstate and follows the signs for The State Hospital. Minutes later, she pulls the car into the half-circle cobblestone driveway, a decaying waterless stone fountain in its center. The hospital was once known by a longer name, The State Hospital for the Terminally Insane, but at some point, those last four words were dropped. She wonders who made that decision. There's probably a good story there.

After smoothing down her hair and zippering up her coat, she crosses the parking lot and tugs open the timbered front door of what used to be the actual mental hospital, a century-old brick building, now full of administrative offices and dwarfed by the adjacent new ten-story warehouse-style inpatient hospital. The University uses the hospital, and its patients, for medical student training, which is why the office of the Department of Psychiatry is housed off-campus in an insane asylum.

Dr. Peaker meets her in the corridor and shakes her hand enthusiastically. He is a plump triangle-shaped white man somewhere in his sixties, or seventies more likely, with fine hair combed over his balding head into a wisp of left-behind hay. Loretta follows him into his office and sits in the wide-back wicker chair that looks like it was borrowed from a poolside patio. Dr. Peaker slides into the corner of a crackled brown leather sofa. His office is in a prime location with a view onto an old-style garden, probably original to the hospital's early days. Antique wrought iron gating encircles the garden topped with modern barbed wire, all camouflaged by a grove of drooping willows, and inside is a maze of walkways lined with boxwood where she imagines patients taking their daily exercise, now and in decades past. She remembers the story Jenny told about her grandmother living in an insane asylum and adds that to her imaginary picture, an old woman walking the cobblestone path holding the outstretched hand of a toddler, talking about magic, fresh from her session of electroshock therapy.

"Near death experiences, you say?" Dr. Peaker asks.

Loretta rattles off the *60 Minutes* cover story and opens the interview with her first question. "Are near death experiences real?"

"As real as anything else that occurs in the mental realm, although we may need to spend time agreeing on a definition of reality."

She is about to ask her second interview question when she remembers her promise to Matthias last night to ask the psychiatry chair if Jenny should see a doctor.

"What would you say to a person who came to you seeking advice about treatment for their own near death experience?"

"This is what you expect *60 Minutes* to ask? I admit I have not seen the show in some time but that sounds quite specific."

His brown eyes, the openings hooded and narrowed by age, are kind and inside that warmth infused by the blue-tinged morning light sliding through the bent venetian blinds, Loretta changes course without any sense she is about to do so the second before.

"*60 Minutes* isn't true. I mean the show exists, of course, but their interest in near death experiences is a lie. I made it up so I could get information for a friend without having to tell anyone the truth, because she is having lots of near death experiences. Twenty-four of them so far. I think that's how many though I've lost count. I know that may sound crazy, and I thought so too at first, but I believe her. I really do. My husband witnessed one, and he saw a golden light but he's not so sure about that anymore. I saw the after-effects two nights ago but not the whole thing, I mean not the whole near death experience. Anyway, the Dean said I should try to understand current research on near death experiences so I'm asking all the chairs of departments that have some relevance what they think, to tell me what to think, so I can be like a bridge between all this knowledge to help my friend because I love Jenny and my husband thinks somehow this will keep me from turning into a full-blown zombie, but that's another story. What I'm really asking is what should she do, is this departmental quest on my part ridiculous, and maybe instead should she just get to a doctor?"

His expression stays flat; he takes a sip from a white coffee mug, his fingers partially obscuring an image of Albert Einstein sticking out his tongue.

"Oh, my god, I'm sorry, I don't know what came over me," Loretta says, catching her breath.

Where the hell *did* all that come from, she thinks, but then as Loretta struggles to tame the rising wave of embarrassment for her outburst, she notices Dr. Peaker is having a hard time swallowing. He places the coffee cup on the low table between them. He bends forward at the waist, rests his elbows on his knees and covers his face with his palms. He is crying. Crying! Why on earth is he crying? It makes her want to cry too but she holds it in. After a few seconds, he lifts his head. Watery tears sparkle between the small map of broken veins on his translucent old-man skin.

"You say she has regular near death experiences?"

"Yes. Are you okay?"

"Does she leave her body?"

"Yes."

He wipes his face with the sleeve of his lab coat, and then blows his nose into a rumpled cloth handkerchief.

"Dr. Peaker, are you okay?" Loretta repeats.

"Yes, yes, I'm fine. Sorry about the waterworks."

"I'm sorry about the *60 Minutes* lie."

He laughs, a little snort, which makes his nose run more; he blows again, and then stuffs the handkerchief between the sofa cushions. "I'm not upset about *60*

Minutes." He rubs the remaining tears from his face with two swooshes of his index finger. "Do you mind if I tell you a story? A story about my first patient."

"Sure," she says gently, wishing she could rewind to the beginning of this interview, have a fresh start.

He turns to look out the window; as he talks she is watching him in profile, mostly his right ear. A wild hair sprouts from the lobe. Dr. Peaker must live alone.

"During my early training years, at least thirty years ago, maybe it was thirty-five, even forty," he says, and then shaking his head adds softly, "God, am I really that old? For fuck's sake."

The sharpness of 'fuck' surprises her; she doesn't let it show.

"Back then," he waves his hand around, "this was the extent of the hospital, this small old brick building and two dormitories, not the sleek facility it is today."

She doesn't find the adjacent brushed metal building sleek at all, it looks like a prison, but there is no reason to contradict his point.

He stands and pulls a thin book from the shelf behind his desk and hands it to Loretta. She reads the cover: *Report on the Defective, Dependent, and Delinquent Classes of the Population of the United States. June 1, 1880.*

"Must be a valuable book, so old," she says, keeping her voice purposefully soft.

"This book, put together by government census staff, defined seven types of idiocy or insanity, two of which were epilepsy and paralysis. Think of that, epilepsy and paralysis defined as mental illness. We humans have an urgent need to categorize, especially ourselves, even when data are sparse."

Loretta hands the book back. He flips through the pages, running his finger along their dried-out edges.

"Up until the mid-1900s, books of this type were used to share information and data, to find common ground, to discuss tactics that worked to help patients in distress. But this purpose shifted during World War Two when our government identified a pressing need to formally categorize men as suitable, or not, for war. And equally important, they needed a framework to categorize and rank the various mental traumas suffered by soldiers after war, for treatment and compensation."

He pulls out another book and hands it to Loretta. It's thick, with an overly serious academic binding, but not so old. She opens the book to the title page.

He says, "And behold, the *Diagnostic and Statistical Manual of Mental Disorders*, also known by its acronym DSM, was born. A perpetually growing manual issued every few decades since that war, with the latest iteration a few years ago, in which a well-meaning group of elite psychiatrists informs those in trenches of everyday practice, as well as the rest of society, who is normal and who is not against a baseline for normalcy they themselves agree on."

"I feel like I should have heard of this book," she says, thumbing through its pages.

"Let's consider what I've said. The original entrance fee, so to speak, for being categorized as normal was an ability to disassociate from your morals well enough to overlook, or recast, our cultural taboo on murder. From that, the baseline has evolved and today the definition of normalcy is agreed to be, by and large, the degree to which someone is persistently economically productive."

"It says that?" she asks, incredulous. "Productivity is the baseline for normal?"

"Not directly but the logic is unassailable."

"A person needs shelter and to eat. Maybe it makes sense that not being able to take care of yourself is abnormal." But even as she says it Loretta's flawed logic becomes clear. Wouldn't that make babies and toddlers insane? Well, maybe they are, in a way.

"The deference to money as the normalcy baseline is

more insidious. Consider this. Why does the recent DSM define the symptoms of collecting piles and piles of newspapers, cupboards full of teacups, mounds of paper clips and all manner of other things under the diagnosis of 'hoarding disorder,' but fails to extend this diagnosis to people who obsessively hoard money? Instead, we laud their status."[31]

"That is something to think about," she says. "I assume there is a type of informed expert judgment that goes into these determinations."

"You'd think so, yes. And to a degree, there is. But with the benefit of hindsight, we see that transcending prevailing culture and the concurrent bias has proven challenging."

Loretta considers what she heard yesterday from the anthropology department about the persistence of stories across time. Presumably, observing symptoms of mental illness with historical tenacity plays a role in overcoming cultural influences.

"Consider diseases outside of the mental realm," Dr. Peaker says. "For instance, we connect a broken arm, a cancerous tumor or high blood pressure to a biological basis, thus giving it a sense of reality. But there is little biological evidence for depression or narcissism or hoarder's disease. Decoupling observation in this realm from cultural influence is tricky."

The radiator makes a loud banging noise and then falls into a graceless hum. Dr. Peaker ignores it. He runs his palm along the spines of all the books on the top shelf. He pauses at the last volume, the thinnest. "One hundred and three disorders in the first edition, homosexuality among them. Oh, the things we have gotten wrong over the years. Drapetomania.[32] Look that one up sometime and prepare to be appalled." He lets out a long sigh like the whistle of a distant teakettle on a low simmer.

"It will be of interest to you that the DSM to this

day, and throughout its iterations, categorizes out-of-body experiences as an aspect of a psychological disorder known as depersonalization, or unreality of self."

He sits back down, sinking into the couch. Loretta isn't particularly surprised to learn that the DSM captures her zombie state as a disorder.

"Her name was Dorothy. My first patient."

He turns his eyes away from Loretta, gazing again into the asylum yard, falling into the past. "She arrived at The State Hospital for the Terminally Insane at seventeen. It was the late seventies. She ran away from home and landed in San Francisco. She met a young man, a boy really, fell in love, and consumed a cornucopia of drugs, tuned in, turned on and dropped out, as they said back in the day. After a year or so, she returned to the rural town of her birth, broke and pregnant. Her parents wanted to put the child up for adoption. She resisted, but it became a moot point because the infant died hours after birth."

"Maybe a blessing given her drug use," Loretta says. "Still, it must have been terrible for Dorothy."

"It was terrible. She was given over to our care. And in my own youth, still blinded by the hierarchy of the academic world, its parochial rewards system and, frankly, excited to be deemed ready to care for my first patient, I did not question the basis upon which her parents and the town doctor committed Dorothy to our asylum. I assumed they made the correct decision and affirmed their observation that she met four of the symptoms for severe depression then listed in the DSM. For about a month, we talked. It was the era of talk therapy and I got to know Dorothy. I remember like it was yesterday even though in this moment I can't remember your name—"

"Loretta Sparkman."

"Right, yes. Thank you, Loretta Sparkman."

He moves his gaze to her. "When I was trained, long ago, most of us believed, to one degree or another, that the brain at birth was a blank slate with some capacities hard-wired, like grammar. Back then, we psychiatrists stayed in our lanes, putting aside thoughts about the nature of the mind or its relationship to the brain, relying on the work of the DSM and other publications, along with the giants of our discipline, to guide us in pragmatic ways to help patients. We believed people had control over their impulses, by and large, and that those who behaved outside of the norms as defined by the DSM could be coaxed back into socially acceptable behavior and productive labor with a combination of talk, drugs and psychosurgery."

"None of that seems unreasonable," she says, now feeling like this interview may be heading someplace relevant.

"Today, we've made advances in understanding the brain and its relationship to the mind. Recent studies, especially advanced MRI mapping combined with sophisticated computing, have begun to refine the idea of a blank slate at birth, or rather, how our biology builds a sense of self from birth onward. In turn, this will hopefully help us begin to establish a more rigorous foundation for categorizing mental illness."

There it is again, the sense of self. Loretta is increasingly persuaded that the story of self, what it is, where it comes from, how it drives behavior, is pivotal to pinning down what's happening to Jenny, and maybe her own non-self issues as well. While she hates to divert Dr. Peaker from Dorothy, the more perspectives on this topic the better.

"Can you say more on the current thinking about the sense of self?"

"It's a fascinating topic."

He doesn't mind, or notice, the diversion.

"How is it formed?"

"During infancy, the brain receives stimuli and patterns are laid down. Think of a mother's smile. A baby learns to associate that smile with affection and care. The infant's neurons establish a link between a human expression and fulfillment, so the next time the baby, and eventually the adult, sees a smile, the brain predicts positive outcomes. The same process takes place for, say, exposure to fire. The brain learns to avoid it. And so on, layer after layer of interactions from birth through the years while the brain is growing and developing, until an effective predictive model for interacting with the world has been built from scratch. Like snowflakes or fingerprints, each predictive model is unique, because no two people ever experience the same things in precisely the same sequence in those formative years. The self is some mysterious total of all our individual early experiential inputs."[33]

"At what point is that sense of self fully formed?"

"Impossible to know. Maybe never."

"What about babies or kids who experience abuse when their layers of self are being laid down? Does this story about how a self develops mean they are forever consigned to a dark world?"

"Also unclear. But possibly, and an insight that opens entirely new avenues into understanding mental illness in adults, even criminal behavior."

"Maybe, in a way, this accounts for the crazy state of the world," Loretta says. "As the world becomes more crowded and information blows like a tornado through so many channels and sources, what infants and children are exposed to becomes more complex too. The fingerprint of each mind, collectively speaking, is increasingly jumbled."

"An intriguing thought, although it's important to acknowledge this model remains conjecture. But unlike the concept of the soul, for example, this is the type of conjecture that leads to rich lines of research and may help us develop a landscape of the mind, and mental illness, to allow us to transcend things like the DSM. Still, there are reasons to question this model."

"Reasons like Dorothy?"

"Like Dorothy, yes. I think about her case, as I have done every day since then, and in hindsight conclude that this sense of self we describe didn't seem to exist in her. I mean, she had a personality, of course, and the ability to interact but she was not attached to that identity the way most of us are, the way we feel it defines who we are, confers agency in the world. You see, Loretta Sparkman, Dorothy admitted to me that her parents committed her to this hospital because of visions she was having of her infant at the end of a tunnel, bathed in golden light, and because she told them she could float above her body. She had these visions almost every day."

Loretta is stunned. "Dorothy was having near death experiences?"

He nods slowly, gravely. "Such experiences were poorly documented and not always called by that phrase then. But yes, I believe she was having repeated near death experiences."

"What happened when you found out?"

"We undertook a regimen of talk therapy to address what I diagnosed as a psychotic break caused by grief-induced depression, although I also considered she may have been undergoing severe post-partum depression, which wasn't recognized by the DSM until 1994, but many of us had already begun to talk about these symptoms informally. But Dorothy insisted she was not sad, that she would see her baby, that she saw him now, that she could see her baby and herself in everything. Everything is connected, she said, I am one with my child and you and everyone—"

"What?" Loretta feels a rising euphoria hearing that Dorothy used the same words as Jenny. "What did she say exactly?"

"We are indivisible. I am the world, and the world is me. When you show kindness to one, you show it to all. She sounded crazy, frankly, to use a word we frown on in my profession."

"Where is Dorothy now?"

He takes a deep breath before continuing. "On the advice of my chair, I informed Dorothy her release would be contingent on us working together to end the visions, either organically or with medication."

He pulls himself up on the sofa into a stoic posture, cleft chin tilted up. He is stone-faced, expressionless.

"She agreed to be medicated, became obedient. She swore the visions had disappeared and stopped talking about them altogether. Dorothy seemed to, I don't know, become luminous. I attributed it to improving mental health and a healthier diet. After a few months, we discharged her into the custody of her parents."

The pacing of his words slackens. Loretta waits. Her initial excitement about Jenny being able to meet and talk with someone like Dorothy is giving way to dread.

He closes his eyes, sliding deeper into the past. "I was a hero. My chair congratulated me on the success of her therapy and medication regime. I hoped it would result in a jump in faculty rank as I intended to publish a scholarly paper on her case."

A door opens and shuts from somewhere outside, two feminine voices speak softly in an outer office, and a machine whirs to life, probably a printer.

"She killed herself a day after her release. With her father's shotgun. A few days later, I received a postcard in the mail. She'd mailed it before, you see. 'It's all one, everything, I will see my baby now, I will become my baby. Don't be sad for me, Dr. Peaker. I'll wait for you in the tunnel.'"

He exhales, as if something vile has been expunged.

"My God," Loretta whispers. "I am so sorry."

She wonders if he still has the postcard and if so, where he keeps it and what picture was on it, but of course she won't ask these questions. Instead, while she hates to push Dr. Peaker at this emotional moment, she has to know more.

"Was there anyone else like Dorothy?"

"Not that I am aware of, until your friend."

Loretta digs her fingers into the reedy arms of her chair, speechless, but again hears Matthias reminding her to find out if Jenny should see a doctor.

"What would you tell Dorothy if she arrived here today? What should I tell my friend Jenny?"

He answers quickly, as if he has been preparing for decades, perhaps hoping he would have the chance to rewrite the past.

"I'd rule out dangerous things, then make sure she has a safe and happy life, a way to be taken care of when she has the visions, and only then, if she agreed, see if we could learn useful things from her in a way that honors her experience. With Dorothy, not only did we lose a precious young life, we lost a person whose brain had the potential to reveal important things about human consciousness. What is self? What happens to that self when we die? What is human consciousness and where does it come from? What role does it play in furthering the species?"

"I'm scared for Jenny."

"You should be. But you can help guide her. And your friend has important information, even if we can't understand it at this moment. If she is willing and feels safe, what she is, what she experiences, should be shared as widely as possible to inspire us to seek answers, to be curious, to do the science. I would also tell her to be wary of those who want to *fix* her because it presumes she is broken. Remember, it wasn't that long ago when we fixed depressed people with icepick lobotomies."

An assistant pokes her head into the office to say his first patient of the day is ready. Dr. Peaker stands and shakes Loretta's hand, and then tenderly puts his other hand on top. "I can refer you to a therapist if you need help navigating your own response to what's happening with your friend. And I'd be happy to help your friend directly, if she wishes. You are clearly a good person and she is lucky to have you." He releases her hand. "But keep a close eye, guard her. The temptation from the other side can be strong." A shadow passes over his eyes as he says this.

Twenty minutes later, Loretta is back on the road, processing this new information. A phone call comes in; she connects through the dash but before she can muster a greeting, Mona spits out, "Loretta, what the hell is this story about near death experiences and *60 Minutes* the Department of Neuroscience chair called me about? How is it possible I would not know about something this big?" Her voice is high, reaching the rare pitch Loretta recognizes as anger. Mona does not often lose her cool.

"I have to go to the courthouse, but I'll come by your office right after—"

Mona disconnects without another word. Loretta pulls the car onto the shoulder to think. Gravel slides under her tires as she brakes. A red jeep passes; the driver honks and gives her the finger. She looks at the nearby field, turned-under plowed rows covered by a barely-there ice lattice reflect the sunlight. A turkey vulture glides over the barren landscape. She considers how to explain the *60 Minutes* lie to Mona. This is not going to be easy or pretty.

Then an idea comes to her. Loretta scans her call list, finds what she is looking for and hits send. He picks up on the first ring.

"Wendell Holland, *60 Minutes*."

"Wendell, this is Loretta Sparkman."

"Hey there, how's it going? That sperm story still sticking around? No pun intended," he adds. "Do you have someone willing to speak on camera yet, other than you? No offense."

"You saw that."

"Yeah, you did okay. A little weepy for someone in your position, but also probably effective for your needs. But we need a doctor or reproductive specialist or scientist or something, or better yet, the woman who was impregnated."

"I never said she was impregnated."

"Come on, the University wouldn't have its crisis communications staff, meaning you, assigned to this if there wasn't a baby. By the way, we've been digging into the father's identity. A rumor made it to me he's a celebrity type. What exactly does it mean to be a celebrity in your neck of the woods?"

"Not much, really. It's a small pond. You'll let me know what you find out?"

"You don't know who the dad is?"

"I make it a practice not to pollute my brain with unnecessary information," she says, which isn't a lie but isn't the truth either.

"Good tactic. Keeps you from lying to the press."

"I've got something else to pitch you."

"Yeah? What's that?"

"Ever hear of near death experiences?"

"Sure, who hasn't?"

"What if *60 Minutes* could be first in the history of the world to broadcast an MRI of the brain of someone as they are having a near death experience?"

"I'm listening."

TWENTY-THREE

Loretta sits in the last seat on the last row of wooden benches inside the county courtroom. The sparse audience is made up of what she assumes are law students, court workers and friends or family of people appearing in court today. She is waiting for the attorneys to question the jurors, figuring she might glean insights to help guide the next phase of the University's misplaced sperm story.

The lawyer for Tom Thomas, the MAGA-loving shock jock radio minor celebrity sperm donor who to the rest of the world remains Mr. Anonymous John Doe, is a forty-plus-something white man with dense brown hair and a face tanned two shades past the edge of healthy. He wears a pinstriped gray suit tailored to his tall athletic body. His shoes shine like black mirrors.

To his left at the scratched-up table facing the judge's bench is the attorney for the wrongfully inseminated woman. No, she thinks, not wrongfully. Mistakenly. That distinction matters. This attorney is a young, broad-shouldered man, Asian heritage, wearing a mix-and-match off-the-rack suit; the hems of the navy blue slacks bunch up at the ankles and thin accordion pleats splay out over new-looking white canvas deck shoes.

Signs posted on either side of the gallery explain that the judge doesn't allow cameras or recording devices in her courtroom. Jamie, intrepid reporter and, as Loretta learned via yesterday's on-camera humiliation, closet activist, is in the front row. Her knees knock up against the partition between the gallery and the courtroom. Next to her are three people with notebooks. Loretta recognizes one as an Associated Press stringer.

A group files in from the adjacent sequestered room. Each wears a plastic identity card on a lanyard around their neck with JUROR in black capital block letters, a warning to lawyers and staff and reporters to keep quiet around them lest they risk a mistrial. The clerk stands and asks them to take a seat in the jury box; the judge will arrive in due course. A few look nervous, others irritated, two beam with undisguised pride, or maybe arrogance, it's sometimes hard to tell the difference.

In the waiting lull, Loretta thinks more about the sense of self. Sifting through the department interviews, sorting, categorizing and ranking the information, she detects a common denominator. Except for religion, which didn't have much to say about this subject, all the departments more or less told her that the self is a product, or maybe artifact is a better way to say it, of evolution, created by the developing brain to elevate the story of an executive-in-charge so humans can cooperate in ways that lead to lots of baby-making. This executive, so to speak, has the "job" of evaluating incoming data to make decisions about big-ticket items, ranging from what to have for lunch to allowing an aging doctor to squirt sperm inside your vagina using basically a high-tech turkey baster. By contrast, lower-level events happen in pulses of mind-bogglingly small increments of time without the need for direction from the self-boss—things like how to put one foot in front of the other, what tastes good, the images that pop up during sex, how to react to a snake—all things for which the perception of agency, or self, is unnecessary, maybe even detrimental, for optimal performance.

But where is the dividing line? That's the part she can't figure out. What relegates some decisions to the state of non-self and others to the self-state? Certain things like how to walk, as Megan said in anthropology yesterday, are obvious. If the self were contemplating and making a judgment call on every step, any stray thought would send us stumbling. And if conscious thought were required for breathing or heart-beating or digesting, we'd never accomplish anything else, and certainly not reproduction. But how much of my life, she thinks, of anyone's life, is being lived in a zombie state and then recast retroactively with a story that allows us—or tricks us—into thinking we are in charge, like the baseball player hitting the phantom of the speeding fastball?

Even as she is thinking all this, she is aware of falling into a rabbit hole of circular language—what self is thinking about Loretta's self in this very instant? To even consider the concept of self, you need to split yourself into two or more selves. A conversation about the self requires another self, but who or what is the self that is examining the other self? Which is the true self? How many selves nest inside or below the next self? It's a Russian doll problem.

A fresh thought breaks through the swirl.

What if the inadequacy of language in describing a self is a signal, like a flare in the distance, sending a message that something is missing in this evolutionary explanation? Because how could this possibly be merely a problem of vocabulary? If the story of self is the story of what it means to be human, why don't humans have the language to tell it?

"All rise," the clerk says as the judge swooshes into the courtroom from the adjacent chambers.

Dammit, bad timing, Loretta thinks, feeling as if she was on the cusp of something important, something fundamental. With difficulty, she switches focus to *The Case of the Misplaced Sperm*.

The judge doles out a litany of instructions to the potential jurors with a low voice. A frail white woman upward of sixty with short dark hair and wire-rimmed glasses, she is striking enough. She ends her brief remarks by instructing the plaintiff's attorney to begin voir dire.

"Juror thirteen, have you ever been artificially inseminated?" the attorney for the misplaced sperm donor asks, standing behind the wide desk.

Juror thirteen is a tattooed twenty-something white man ... hold on. Now that she is looking more intently, Loretta realizes that every person in the jury box is white. How can that be? That doesn't seem right. But then, an embarrassed laugh from juror thirteen brings her back into the moment. He answers no. The rest of the jurors also laugh along with half of the onlookers. The attorney is too smart to ask such a dumb question. What's he fishing for? Two jurors, women about her age, don't laugh, not even a smirk. One holds her arms tightly crossed against a pastel cardigan and the other jots something down in a yellow notepad balanced on her knees. The attorney looks at his jury box diagram and makes two swift marks, covering the sheet with his hand.

"Juror ten, is artificial insemination a sin?"

The attorney for the misplaced sperm donor continues along this line, questioning the jurors about their experiences of pregnancy without the benefit of sex, and after that he zeros in on their views on the health care system. He is trying to identify jurors who hold negative views of both, people who have been, as he calls it, victims of a medical error or have knowledge of someone else in that category. Stacking the jury with Luddites and doctor-haters is apparently advantageous to men with misplaced sperm, she concludes. That's good information for the rest of the communications planning, and could help strengthen the University's 'we're sorry' story arc.

After almost an hour, with a flourish of his left palm he passes off the questioning to the opposing attorney. The young lawyer steps out from behind the desk, stands directly in front of the raised wooden jury box and speaks so softly the jurors collectively lean forward to hear him.

"Juror two, were you raised by a single mother?"

The juror, a young woman who reminds Loretta of her kindergarten teacher, looks surprised. "Yes, I was."

The attorney turns to the woman sitting next to her. "Was your relationship with your father positive?"

"Positive enough," she says, and without prompting adds, "That man is awful for what he is doing to that woman. She's the victim in this. He's a son-of-a- bitch."

The courtroom erupts in nervous laughter. Loretta watches as the attorney surveys the jurors, a shadow of dismay crossing his suntanned face as most nod in agreement. The judge bangs her gavel, asks for quiet and reminds the potential jurors to answer only the questions asked and to refrain from expressing unsolicited opinions.

Loretta eavesdrops on the whispered conversation of two women sitting in the row in front of her.

"She's right, you know," one says. "They ought to leave that poor woman alone."

"No kidding, hasn't she gone through enough? And after the dust settles, I'm sure the mother will find it in her heart to have the child meet the dad. And how many times does that University have to say sorry?"

Loretta wants to lean forward to remind them that no one has confirmed a baby was born, but that feeling is checked by the impulse to jump up and throw a victory fist in the air. The story, her story of the University's heroic journey to seek redemption, has taken hold.

Score one for the zombie.

The jury questioning continues into the afternoon. By its close, each attorney has dismissed two jurors including the woman who called the sperm donor a son-of-a-bitch, and the judge grants the hardship petitions of two others, leaving twelve jurors. The judge says the day is ending, so they will recess and begin the case in earnest next week. Loretta exits the courtroom before Jamie or any other reporter can corner her and slips into the bathroom to call Mona.

"The mood is turning against the sperm donor."

"That's good," Mona says. "But we can't count on his attorney to convey that information, given his financial incentive to keep the case going. Ideas?"

Loretta sits on a toilet inside a stall with a swinging wooden door, probably original to the old courthouse building, strategizing with Mona and peeing at the same time.

"A few snarky comments on social media?"

"Too risky, can be traced back," Mona says.

"An op-ed under the byline of a community leader."

"Same problem. Has to be organic."

"Hold on, I just thought of something, but I need to quickly catch Jamie."

The noise of the flushing water drowns out Mona's question about *60 Minutes*.

Jamie is in the corridor outside the courtroom with Malcolm, packing up her bag to head back to the news van. Loretta says, "I've got an angle for you."

"If it includes putting you on camera, I'll pass."

"Now you know why I never go on camera. I'm

strategic but media-awkward."

Jamie laughs. "That was beyond awkward. What's your angle?"

"I overheard a few ladies chatting in the courtroom gallery about their views on this situation. Maybe you ought to interview them, give your story the woman-on-the-street treatment." Loretta nods in the direction of the two who were whispering earlier, now standing near the courtroom door, looking over at Jamie.

Jamie glances over at them. "You're terrible."

"It's a good angle and you know everyone loves to be on television," Loretta pushes gently. "Except me. Seriously, check it out. They're looking at you now, they recognize you. You're a local celebrity."

"I assume this won't help the University at all."

"Depends. It's not like they're plants or anything."

"You swear?"

"I'm kicking myself for not thinking of that."

Jamie walks over to the women, hand outstretched. Malcolm trails behind with the camera on his shoulder. "Jamie Ignatius from KGWN. May I get your opinion on this situation?"

A few minutes later in front of the courthouse, Loretta puffs up a little thinking maybe, just maybe, she has shut this one down for good, but she won't know for sure until she watches Jamie's broadcast later and hears what the ladies end up saying.

Her phone buzzes. It's Toni. "Calling is never a good sign," Loretta says into her phone.

"The medical students are planning a sit-in at the Dean's office tomorrow. There are flyers all over."

"Read one to me."

"We the medical students and future caretakers of public health believe the University has been lacking in transparency regarding the fertility clinic incident. We demand the truth about how patients were treated and to know if race played a factor in that treatment."

TWENTY-FOUR

Loretta sits at the kitchen counter reading the news on her phone and watching Jamie's interview of the two women in the courtroom as they bitch up a storm about the sperm donor. It's the third time she's watched it, marveling at how well it turned out for the University. She's feeling triumphant and also stupid for feeling triumphant about such a trivial thing. It's an internal conflict that's plagued her since the start of this job. She leans back in the counter stool, sips her wine and watches Jenny.

Jenny opens the oven door and slides out a tray of cookies; a light maple smell circulates through the room. She places the tray on the counter to cool and then stirs the egg noodles in the pot of boiling water on the stovetop. Matthias comes downstairs, dad-kisses Loretta and opens a bottle of wine. Loretta tells them about her visit to The State Hospital for the Terminally Insane and Dorothy and her near death experiences, which as she says it out loud sounds like the name of a heavy metal band.

"This happened thirty years ago?" Matthias asks, setting down plates and silverware on the table.

"Maybe even longer. Jenny, tell me the absolute honest truth, do you ever feel suicidal?"

"Not directly, no." Jenny thrusts her hands inside oven mitts and pours the noodles from the boiling pot into a colander to drain. Loretta is surprised at how easily this question lands. Steam swamps Jenny's face. "But I do understand why Dorothy would choose to leave this world to stay in the connected one. Wait, that's coming out wrong." She pauses, searching for the right words as she dumps the slippery noodles into a mixing bowl. "What I mean to say is the bonds to this world are weaker when you know something else is waiting, something good. That was probably doubly true for her, with her baby gone. But don't worry, I'm in no rush to leave."

"Promise?"

"Promise."

Jenny mixes the noodles with milk, a can of condensed mushroom soup and a can of drained tuna and then pours it all into a blue casserole dish. She sprinkles shredded cheddar cheese over the top and covers the whole thing with aluminum foil.

"Dr. Peaker said the advice he wishes he had given Dorothy, and what he would say now to you, would be to rule out bad things being the cause of the experiences and then determine what can be learned from your brain in a way that honors your experiences. What do you think about that?"

"Pretty straightforward," Jenny says. "And not very specific or helpful, frankly." After slipping the casserole into the oven, she uses a spatula to slide the warm, still-soft cookies from the tray onto a cooling rack. One slips onto the floor, splattering into chunks. "Oh, rats. I lost one. Sorry. I'll clean that up in a sec."

"What tests would be needed to find out if there are

any bad things?" Matthias asks.

Before she can answer, the doorbell rings. Matthias looks at Loretta questioningly and she shakes her head no, indicating she's not expecting anyone or a delivery. They infrequently have visitors, and never after dark.

"I'll get it, you guys keep talking," he says.

"Your bell sounds like a broken flute," Jenny says.

When Matthias returns, a Black woman carrying a baby is with him. She's attractive, mid-thirties with dark brown skin; her hair is piled on top of her head in a plaited coil. At first, Loretta has no idea who she is but then it hits her. Standing in her kitchen next to a rack of freshly baked cookies is the female protagonist from *The Case of the Misplaced Sperm*.

"This is Ava and Emanuel Longstreet," Matthias says. "Ava, this is my wife, Loretta, who you may know from recent television infamy, and our friend Jenny."

Despite the shock, or maybe because of it, Loretta's mind leaps into action, analyzing the various public relations outcomes associated with the fact that a main actor in a lawsuit against her employer is standing in her embarrassingly messy house with an adorable baby. In all of her public relations scenario predictions of the past week, not one included this plot development, not even at the extreme end of the outcome probability spectrum.

Loretta stands and forces her brain to construct sentences from words, defaulting to auto-politeness, even though she is reeling. "It's a pleasure to meet you. Well, maybe pleasure is not the right word under the circumstances, at least not for you, and I apologize in advance if this sounds rude, but I have to ask given my position at the University and the potential conflict of interest, why are you here?"

Standing behind Ava, Matthias is looking over her shoulder, smiling and making googly eyes at the baby, who is snug in a lavender-colored flannel body-carrier wrapped around Ava's waist and over her shoulders. Jenny pulls off the oven mitts and leans against the counter's edge to listen.

"On that news show you said you were sorry. You cried, you looked me straight in the eye." Ava's tone is firm and confident. "You said you couldn't change the past, but you would try to change the future. I felt like you were talking right to me. And you seemed sincere."

I looked everyone in the whole city straight in the eye, Loretta thinks, but she realizes on some level she had been talking directly to Ava.

"So why are you here exactly?"

"When I got home this evening, two reporters were sitting on my porch."

"Shit," Loretta says. "That asshole."

"Excuse me?" Ava says.

"The attorney for the donor. Who else would leak your address? Although how he has your address, given no one, or very few people, know your name, I couldn't say."

"Maybe good old-fashioned investigative journalism tactics," Matthias says. "From the reporters, I mean."

"Maybe," Loretta says. "Doubtful though."

"I don't want to deal with them, and I don't know how to handle this. I need help," Ava says. "From someone who understands this media stuff. Isn't that your job?"

Jenny wipes her hands on her apron and then reaches out to touch the baby. Ava reacts instinctively, placing her own hand protectively over the child's head and taking a step back. The baby lazily turns his face toward Jenny and smiles. Ava softens at the interaction. Jenny's eyes glaze over, her knees suddenly buckle and she slumps sideways, collapsing to the floor, banging the edge of the stove with her shoulder. She lands in a crumpled heap, her cheek pressed into the warm cookie still on the floor.

"Jenny!" Loretta rushes around the kitchen counter island and drops to her knees next to Jenny.

Jenny's eyes are wide open, staring up at Loretta. An expression like nothing Loretta has ever seen—of total joy or ecstasy, something otherworldly—illuminates Jenny's face. Her eyes roll backward into her head, leaving only the whites visible. She shudders and within seconds the movement grows into a full wave that racks her body. She begins to shake and seize, her head knocking against the floor.

"I'm a nurse," Ava says, unsnapping the carrier holding Emanuel and handing the baby to Matthias. He pulls the infant in close.

Ava grabs a wooden spoon from the counter, still coated with tuna casserole, and kneels next to Jenny and Loretta, gently inserting the spoon between Jenny's chattering teeth. Jenny bites down as she continues to shake. Ava rolls Jenny on to her side and cradle's her head in her lap, carefully supporting her neck. "Hold her feet, gently but firm," she says to Loretta.

After what feels like a lifetime but is only a half-minute, the shaking slows to a vibration and a few seconds later, her movement becomes sound. Jenny emits a low hum that seems, impossibly, to be emanating from her entire body. After another few long seconds, Jenny slips into silent stillness, her eyes return to normal, her blue irises and dilated pupils again visible.

"There it is," Matthias whispers. "The light, can you see it? It's all around her. Amazing, right?"

Loretta does not see the light.

The baby whimpers and Matthias rocks the child in his arms.

"Please get me a cool towel," Ava says.

Loretta soaks a dishtowel under the faucet, wrings it out and hands it to Ava, who wipes Jenny's forehead. Jenny closes her eyes and feels the coolness against her temples. Ava cleans cookie splatter from her cheek.

"I can get up," Jenny whispers.

Loretta helps her stand and guides her to the armchair in the living room. Matthias, still holding the infant, and Ava follow.

"Are you okay?" Loretta asks as Jenny sinks into the chair. "Should we get you to a hospital?"

"I'm okay, I just need to be still," she says quietly. Loretta tries to hide how stunned she is by the violence of this near death experience. Jenny takes Loretta's hand. "Stop worrying. I'm in the clear, back from the dead, and totally embodied this time."

"Coming here was a mistake. You have your hands full," Ava says. She gestures and Matthias hands the baby to her.

"No, the opposite, it was a miracle," Loretta says, turning around. "You saved her life. You were so cool, so calm."

"Like I said, I'm a nurse."

"I'm so grateful for your quick thinking."

"I'm glad I was here to help. But I should go. As long as Jenny is okay. Jenny?"

"I am. Okay, I mean."

"Please stay," Loretta says. "Let's sit and calm down, well, at least I can calm down, and together figure out what to do with those reporters on your doorstep."

Ava agrees and they sit in the living room, making do with a single soft lamp—the bright light stings Jenny's eyes—that casts a subtle golden glow across their faces.

Matthias doles out bowls of tuna casserole followed by cookies and another bottle of wine. Emanuel cries and Ava lifts her shirt. As she breastfeeds the baby, Jenny, Matthias and Loretta watch silently, reverently, all on the cusp of old age, long past the possibility of creating or sustaining life. When Emanuel is finished, Ava asks Matthias to hold the baby again while she uses the bathroom. Matthias presses his nose into the tiny curls covering his little head. When Ava returns, she shakes her head when Matthias starts to hand Emanuel back.

"Do you mind keeping him a bit longer? It feels good to have my arms free. He seems comfortable with you."

"I'll hold this beautiful child as long you like."

Ava takes a seat next to Loretta, crosses her legs at the ankles and looks over at Jenny huddled in the big chair, wrapped in a quilt and sipping a glass of water. Jenny is luminous, almost glowing, as if all the light in the universe is tenderly moving through her. Loretta watches Matthias rubbing his nose against the baby's nose and remembers when Sally-Anne was a baby, how happy they had been. Loretta is suddenly aware of, and heartbroken by, the breakneck passing of time.

"So, what do you suggest I do?" Ava asks.

"I need to know a little more to be able to advise you. The full story, or as much as you're willing to tell. I don't mean to be nosy or anything, but if I don't know what to plan for, anything I suggest will be guesswork."

Emanuel lets out a little yawn that sounds like a kitten's mew. Matthias grins and stands, moving his body back and forth, rocking the boy in the cradle of his sway and softly humming a lullaby into the infant's ear. Ava starts her story.

"About two years ago, my husband and I admitted we would never conceive on our own. It took some hard soul-searching before we decided to go ahead with the University fertility clinic services, mostly because he felt guilty."

"He was why you couldn't conceive," Loretta says.

"He said we could break up, even offered to annul our marriage, so I could have a chance with someone else, but of course that was not what I wanted. We managed, did the emotional work, made our way through the difficult process of using an anonymous donor. After we learned about the mix-up, he couldn't get past it. He wanted me to, you know, not have the baby. When the lawsuit was filed, it was too much. We split up. For now. That could still change. I hope it changes."

"That must be hard."

"He didn't want to raise another man's child."

"Wasn't he going to do that anyway?"

"It was different when the donor was anonymous. And not white. I told him he was being a fool, that we were blessed with a beautiful child of our own."

"Oh, and he is beautiful," Matthias says, still rocking Emanuel. "So very, very beautiful."

"I want to protect my husband from any bad media coverage. He doesn't deserve that."

"Is he in this area?"

"No. He's gone back to, well, it doesn't matter."

"You're right to worry. If this suit continues, it's only a matter of time before the reporters on your doorstep are joined by media from around the country, and they will dig hard for his side of the events."

"That can't happen. No one knows what we did. His family is deeply religious and would not approve." She pauses, choosing her next words carefully. "And while I worry about their reaction, there is one more thing that is more important to me. I don't want my child's life to start out by being subjected to this kind of reporting, this salacious bullshit."

"Let's work backward then, starting with what you would want to see happen if you could design the near-term future," Loretta says.

"To raise my child without interference, to have no one interested in me or Emanuel."

"For that to happen, the donor would have to drop the suit and cease all efforts to find out Emanuel's biological paternity, a long shot, but one that dovetails with what the University would like to see happen. But saying you don't want to see the sperm donor has risks. The public might feel sorry for him, and turn on you."

"Why does it matter what anyone thinks?" Matthias asks. "Who cares?"

"It doesn't matter in any grand sense. But it does have an impact in today's hyper-connected world, to Ava's sense of security and the introduction of Emanuel to the world. Ava, what's your second-best scenario?"

"That Emanuel is introduced to the world in a joyful and strong way, despite our circumstances. Interest in us is positive and then, hopefully, dies down fast."

"Let's talk about that one. It's more achievable. To make that happen, though, you will have to tell your story on your own terms before the court case gains momentum. You'll have to open up to the public soon, maybe in the next few days." Loretta's voice is soft. "Are you up for that?"

"What's involved?" Ava glances at Matthias and the baby. Emanuel has fallen asleep in his arms. Matthias is beaming.

"I can create controlled opportunities in which you will be interviewed or otherwise share your story. Local and national. We can rehearse those interviews."

"Won't that get you in trouble at the University?" Matthias asks. "You're supposed to make the story go away, not make it bigger."

"Let's put that aside for now."

But Matthias is right, of course. This approach will not sit well with Mona or the University attorneys. She can deal with that later.

"Could you tell my story, you know, as a proxy?" Ava asks.

"I don't think so. That could give the appearance that the University is trying to control things, which would backfire, maybe turning the public against you and adding fuel to the fire. You could have someone else, a friend or family member, be your spokesperson but you're the best choice. If you're not the one to tell your story, the other side, the donor's side, will tell it for you. And that side will have people on the payroll to do that, just like the University has me, well, much better paid people than me and far better and more ruthless—"

"Hence, their better pay," Ava says.

Loretta shrugs. "Maybe. But what these well-paid people will do is shape your persona through the lens of him being wronged, being victimized and, well, I hate to say it, but the issue of race."

"Why do you hate to say it? Race and racism permeate pretty much everything in this country. It may be a surprise to you, but certainly not to me." Loretta doesn't say anything because she doesn't know what to say. Ava continues. "Thanks for this, but I need to think about being on television, my face splashed all over social media—"

"You don't have to do this. But I'm being honest when I say if you stay silent the odds of a scenario in which you and Emmanuel are seen positively and then interest dies down are very low. But if you want to stay private, I'll do my best to counter the stories they put out. His notoriety will make that hard, since he's got a pretty huge social media following."

"Who is he?" Ava asks.

"You don't know?"

"No."

There are so many breaches of legal confidentiality here, Loretta thinks, but the fact that she knows the identity of the father and the mother does not gives her a sick feeling, and makes Loretta think that perhaps everything she has done with *The Case of the Misplaced Sperm,* even naming it so carelessly, has somehow been wrong.

And shallow.

And reactive.

And selfish.

"Tom Thomas."

Ava looks at her with a trace of confusion. "Are you sure?"

"That's what I was told, and that's who is bringing the suit."

"I've never actually listened to his program. Is he as awful as people say?"

"Worse. His audience is long-suffering mediocre white men, and the women who depend on them who want to return us to the 1950s when their dominance was unquestioned, who think Trump and his kind are their ticket to stay on top," Loretta says.

Ava lets out a sigh. "So, that is Emanuel's father."

"I'm sorry. I can't imagine how you feel."

"Are you a mother?"

"She's grown up, away at college."

"Then you probably can imagine, at least to a degree. Will you set up a meeting between me and him?"

"Really?"

"Really."

"Your lawyer should do that."

"This is not about law," Ava says. "You said you would try to change the future. To help me."

The baby starts to fuss. "My skills are no longer adequate," Matthias says, handing Emanuel to Ava.

Ava stands with Emanuel in her arms, "Jenny, is there anything I can do before I go?"

"Won't the reporters still be there?" Jenny asks.

"There's a hotel near the courthouse."

"Stay here," Jenny says. "I can clear out of the guest room and sleep on the couch."

"That's too much to ask. You just had a seizure."

"Not a seizure. A near death experience."

"A what?" Ava asks.

"Please stay," Loretta says. "It's not too much to ask. The opposite."

"I'll dig out that crib from the basement we bought when my cousin was visiting," Matthias says.

Later, after everyone is settled into their sleeping arrangements, Matthias and Loretta stretch out on the bed. Matthias is asleep in minutes. Loretta is rigid, unready for sleep. Yet again. There, in the darkness, thoughts come unbidden, untethered and lacking logic, tumbling and banging and slamming into each other like corn in a hot air popper. What self, she wonders, is responsible for her thoughts? Is it wrong to help Ava? How can it be wrong to do the right thing? Did the zombieness keep her from considering or imagining Ava as a person? Or is there something else, something even worse, wrong with her? She casually categorized Ava and the child as a University mistake that needed cleaning up. But what if helping Ava gets her fired? She won't be able to pay Sally-Anne's tuition.

Matthias lets out a snort-snore and rolls over onto his other side.

Her thoughts race on. What happens to the self during sleep? Is sleep a preview of death? Is waking up a daily miracle, a recurring resurrection of self? And then Loretta thinks about her mother, which she rarely does because of the pain, remembering how in the days before she died her mother tried so hard to stay awake, to never sleep. *I'm afraid I won't ever wake again*, she whispered. That turned out to be true in the end.

At some point, Loretta's rattling thoughts become a dream. She and Matthias are on a cruise ship. He is vomiting, and she holds an empty can of mushroom soup in front of him to catch the throw-up. The small can overflows in seconds. He sits back on a weathered deck chair. Loretta paces worriedly, rubbing the vomit off her palms onto her pants, but then Matthias is playing shuffleboard, singing Sally-Anne's childhood lullaby. *Hush little baby, don't you cry.* Emanuel sits on the deck behind him, he is older, a toddler. Loretta looks down. In her hand is a slice of Nelson Bargrove's brain. She throws the brain slice into the ocean where a dolphin jumps up and swallows it whole before diving back into the water. The last part wakes her up.

Shit, she thinks, where did *that* come from?

She slips out of bed to get a glass of water. The light is on in the living room. Jenny and Ava are deep in quiet conversation.

TWENTY-FIVE

The chaplain's office is inside the University hospital across the hall from the surgical waiting room where families watch television and pass around dog-eared, celebrity gossip magazines and chew their nails as they wait for post-op conversations with surgeons in blue cotton scrubs and blood-splattered plastic clogs.

Loretta knocks and a booming voice from inside answers, "Come!"

He's a ruddy white man, with big brown eyes, and young, at least by Loretta's current standards, in the neighborhood of forty. He wears a traditional starched white collar on a gray button-down shirt, and sitting behind a banged-up metal desk he looks the part of a chaplain.

But when he walks in front of his desk to welcome Loretta, he is transformed. His pressed shirt is barely tucked into patched jeans cinched by a rainbow-striped belt, and he wears scuffed black leather motorcycle boots with bronze buckles. He extends his right hand to shake and she sees the word Love tattooed across the knuckle backs of his right four fingers. The word Holy is inscribed on his left hand knuckles. One of God's own Hells Angels in residence at the University. Who knew?

"You must be Loretta. I'm Father James."

"Thanks for meeting with me on such short notice."

A piece of stained-glass art hangs behind him inside the frame of the only window in his office; blue and gray and purple glass wedges are welded around the profile of a white dove winging upward to a cloudy heaven, a green olive branch in its beak, its eye a speck of obsidian.

"I apologize in advance but I have less time than expected today," Loretta says. "The medical students are staging a sit-in at the Dean's office in an hour and I need to be there."

"Bless their young hearts."

Father James fetches two folding chairs from the closet as Loretta's thoughts drift to home. It was hard to leave this morning, sitting at the table with Matthias, Ava and Jenny, drinking coffee, feeling renewed by the freshness of Emanuel's gurgles and giggles. Even his throw-up was charming. But she didn't want to cancel on the chaplain.

"Please." He points at the two chairs facing each other in the small space in front of his desk and Loretta sits. The metal is cold against the back of her thighs.

"Does anyone watch *60 Minutes* anymore?" he asks.

"It's still popular among a certain demographic."

"Would that be the get-off-my-lawn demographic?"

Normally she would laugh at this, but for some reason she's immediately skeptical about Father James; he's making the hair on the back of her neck stand up. So instead she nods politely and crosses her legs; her yellow shoe nicks his shin and her skirt slides up. She tugs it back into place and pulls her foot in closer.

"Can you please remind me of this episode's specific

focus?" he asks.

"The producers are convening a panel discussion about near death experiences and also maybe, if it can be worked out, conducting an MRI scan of someone while they have one."

Now that she's talked to Wendell, the *60 Minutes* producer about Jenny being in the MRI live on the show, she realizes she is no longer telling a lie and the accompanying sense of lightness that comes with this unburdening feels good, like an early spring breeze scented with pine blowing from behind, gifting her its quick push of promise.

"How would that be possible? How could anyone predict a near death experience?" He strokes his chin, darkened by stubble. "It's like an earthquake that way."

"We've got an angle."

He squints and his eyes express doubt, he seems to know she isn't being upfront. Loretta doesn't care; at this moment, she is only eager to get through this interview and then over to the student sit-in. Making sure any reporter that gets wind of the sit-in writes about it with an angle that favors Ava and Emmanuel is now her priority for *The Case of the Misplaced Sperm*. Plus, Father James was not on the list of departments the Dean gave her—applied religion is not a department, it's not really a thing at all, it's just church, as far as she can tell, but Babs, the patient advocate, insisted Loretta would find it worth the time.

"Are near death experiences real?" Loretta starts.

"Yes, absolutely."

"What do they signify?"

"That God is great. That the universe is bigger than we can ever imagine. That the dying brain panics. That aliens are sucking our souls into a giant neural harvester. They mean anything, everything or nothing. But one thing is clear: If you want to fully understand the experience, it's best to ask those who have had one."

"I agree. Do you know such people?

"Many." He leans back in the chair and stretches out his long legs, fencing her in on the left side. Dried mud caught in the grooves of the soles of his motorcycle boots flakes onto the tiled floor.

"I guess in your line of work, you're around death a lot. No offense."

He smiles; his teeth are crooked with a flash of gold. "None taken. And yes, I am around a lot of dying people. Sometimes, those on the edge of death describe things like the classic elements of a near death experience. But I'm not talking about them."

She waits, and then realizes he wants to be asked. "Who then?"

"I run a counseling group for veterans wounded in the line of duty. Many have had near death experiences, it's called a combat near death experience, a CNDE."

"Are they different than for non-soldiers?"

"The tunnel of light is olive drab." She looks at him blankly. "That was a joke."

A bad joke, she thinks. Stupid, really.

"But to answer your question, no, they aren't different. Why would they be?"

"Because you gave them a different name."

"The difference is how they react to the near death experience."

"And that is?"

"Stonewalling."

"Why?"

"The same reason soldiers don't like to talk about PTSD, or much of anything emotional. They don't want to be considered mentally ill or defective or weak, or let their squads down. Plus, it can come back to kick them right in their military benefits."

"That's a shame." Loretta thinks back to the books on mental disorders Dr. Peaker from psychiatry talked about. "For them personally, of course, but it also means scientists, especially biologists, are losing data."

"Is that your goal? To get to the supposed biological basis of near death experiences?"

"Not exclusively."

"Good. Taking God out of the equation would put us on different sides of the issue right from the get-go."

Loretta is about to say that she wasn't aware there were sides but is distracted by a flurry of text messages coming in from Toni and Caron, which she starts to read but then looks up to see Father James watching her with a mixture of curiosity and amusement. She sets her phone on airplane mode and puts it in her jacket pocket. "Sorry about that. This issue related to the—" she catches herself before saying *The Case of the Misplaced Sperm*. "The issue at the University fertility clinic is somewhat consuming."

"I'm praying for all parties involved."

A shadow passes behind the stained-glass dove, a fluttery motion, maybe a bird hovering on the other side. The tiny silhouette flickers, like a flame in reverse, and then the glass dove returns to stillness.

"What do you know about the so-called dying brain hypothesis?" he asks.

"I've talked to the biology chair about it extensively." An hour may not qualify as extensive, but she's not interested in prolonging this discussion by sitting through Father James's explanation. Loretta's scalp starts to itch; she refrains from scratching.

He continues anyway. "The dying brain hypothesis assumes that because the sense of self is constructed by the biology of the brain, people who come back from death remember an instant when the self was gone, which they mistakenly describe as a feeling of one with the universe."

"A selfless state."

"I don't believe it. The dying brain hypothesis, I

mean."

"I'm not surprised. You believe in heaven," she says.

"That's not why, although I do believe in heaven." He pauses and then says, "Did you know that twelve vets kill themselves every single day?"

"I have heard something along those lines before. It's heartbreaking."

"The suicide rate among veterans reporting a near death experience is zero."

"That is…" she searches for the right word, "…stunning." And she is stunned. "And cries out for someone to discover how to induce near death experiences in people suffering with suicidal thoughts."

She thinks back to what Devlin Richardson said, the neuroscientist who scanned his dying mother, at the end of their interview, almost as an aside. His dream, he said, was to create a drug to induce a near death experience. Maybe he's onto something, something that could change the world.

"That's a scientific breakthrough I could surely rally behind," Father James says. There's a light knock on the door. "If you don't mind, I've asked two friends to join us."

Without waiting for her answer, he stands and opens the door. Two men enter. "Welcome, welcome, gentlemen, and thank you for coming. Loretta, allow me to introduce Darren and Edward. They have volunteered to tell their stories about combat near death experiences. I believe this approach will be more constructive for your *60 Minutes* research than hearing me drone on."

Again, before Loretta can respond, he smiles and assumes her agreement; two more metal chairs squeak as he unfolds them for his guests. He arranges the chairs in a tight triangle with the three men facing Loretta, trapping her in the corner of the small office. She notices the plastic edge of a prosthetic leg when

Edward's khaki slacks ride up as he fits his tall frame into the too-small chair; the skin tone of the fake limb is dark brown, which is not the same as the ruddy redness of the rest of him.

"Loretta is a busy woman, so let's just stick to the stories themselves. Edward, why don't you start?"

Edward is the older of the two. His bright eyes seem out of place on his weathered face, as if a younger person is looking out from behind a worn-out mask. He wears an oversized Seattle Seahawks jacket and smells of cigarette smoke mixed with sweat. He speaks haltingly, with heavy breaths between short sentences.

"I was drafted. I tried for a deferment. No college; no dice. It was my 345th day. We were on the move, from one damn muddy place in the jungle to some other damn muddy place in the jungle. I'll never forget the sound, the feel of the click under my boot, that's crystal. When I came to, my mouth was full of dirt and I couldn't hear nothing. My buddies were screaming at me, their lips opening and closing like hooked catfish, but it was all quiet in my head. They carried me to the chopper, my leg dangling below my knee, held on by skin, my foot gone. Didn't really hurt then, not like later. I thought they'd dropped me or we was crashing or something because after they got me on board the chopper, it was like I was falling, but I wasn't. I was floating up outside my body. I saw everything. The medic shook his head all sad and moved on to the next guy. I didn't care because I was inside the light. That sounds weird, I know, but that's the only way to say it. I knew I was supposed to be inside it, and part of it. But then another medic wrapped a tourniquet around my leg, and I got pulled back into my body."

He stops talking. Father James nods and puts his hand on Edward's shoulder. "Thanks for that. Darren, will you tell us your story now?"

Darren is a young Black man, probably about thirty.

His umber cheeks and forehead are pocked by what look like old acne scars, or maybe chickenpox. He keeps his gaze focused on the floor as he speaks, his voice flat, steady. "We were on patrol and tripped an IED outside Mosul. When the charge went off, it blew me clear across the road and I landed in a pile with three of my buddies. We'd been laughing and joking the minute before, and then just blood and body parts all tangled up. It still wakes me up at night, so I won't describe that pile because there's no reason to keep you up at night too. I didn't know it then, but there was shrapnel in my chest. It was bone shards mostly, not even mine. I don't know for sure if I was conscious or not, but suddenly I lifted off and was above my body. I floated up, like Edward said, into a tunnel of light. I heard voices. My grandma was there. She told me I was brave, she was singing this song from when I was a kid. But then she said not just yet, D-lite. That's what she called me when I was little. Not yet, she said, you ain't done. I'm expecting good things from you, D-lite. The next thing I remember my chest was on fire and blood was going everywhere. I didn't want to go, I wanted to stay with my grandma. It was beautiful."

"Same for me," Edward says. "Didn't want to come back."

Loretta is still. Father James holds out a Kleenex box but she is not crying. Loretta takes a tissue out of politeness. The men look at Loretta for a reaction. She is helplessly furious for what the world, what America, has done to them. Father James stands. Loretta twists the tissue back and forth, shredding it into little pieces that land on her lap. She doesn't know how to bridge the divide between her small inconsequential life—hiding from everything—and theirs.

"How did the experience change you?" she finally asks.

Father James claps his hands together, and then

holds them together, as if in prayer. "This is exactly the right question. You get it! Gentlemen, what's the answer?"

Edward starts to say something then shakes his head, pulls his arms and legs in tight, making himself small. Darren watches him, giving the older man deference but when it's clear Edward doesn't intend to answer, Darren speaks up.

"When I came back, I got into bad stuff, drugs and alcohol, my wife left me because, well, I am ashamed to say it but it's best to be honest, I hit her. I couldn't cope. Right when I was about to put a bullet through my head, I remembered my grandma's voice saying I had things to do. I heard it over and over, and I knew I hadn't been brought back to just fuck everything up, excuse my language, ma'am, and kill myself, so I looked for help. I found Father James."

"My role was very minor," he says. "Darren now works with vets from Iraq and Afghanistan. I can't tell you how many soldiers credit him with helping turn their lives around."

"Whatever it was out there that happened to me, it gave me a reason to live, even though I didn't want to be here anymore."

"What do you mean?"

"It was better, inside that tunnel. And I knew it was leading to someplace even better. Not a place, more like a feeling. Like being inside a good feeling. Forever. I wasn't alone, I was surrounded by love, you know? I knew that everyone is connected, all one, and when you know we're all one, well, it means you got to live your life in a different way. It was…good."

Father James touches Edward's shoulder. The old man keeps his head down, still unable to respond, and then pulls out a pack of cigarettes. Marlboros. Loretta can't tell if his hand is trembling due to disease or from emotion.

"Is it okay if I tell Loretta what you are doing now?" Father James asks. Edward nods, and then pastes his eyes on the stained-glass dove. "Edward works at a clinic with people getting used to artificial limbs, mostly veterans but also those who have lost arms or legs for other reasons. He shows them life goes on and can get better."

"Thank you for telling me this, for sharing your stories," she says

The chaplain turns to the men. "I also appreciate how helpful you have been. I'd like to speak to Loretta for a few minutes alone but if you wait outside, we can go for a coffee and doughnut at the hospital cafeteria. My treat."

After Edward and Darren leave, Father James stands with his back to the closed door, facing Loretta. She pushes away the reaction of being trapped. "I invited Edward and Darren because I want you and *60 Minutes* to understand the transformative effect of a near death experience, the ripple effect. That's the important part."

"It definitely seems to have impacted their lives."

"Many combat vets, some living alone, too many homeless, have had these experiences but are afraid to come forward. They feel crazy. If Darren or Edward were to appear on *60 Minutes*, we could reach a lot of these people, encourage them to get help, to get mental health services. And we can learn from them."

"It's not up to me to choose who gets on *60 Minutes*, but I understand what you are saying," she says.

"I'm not sure you do. I want these proud, scarred vets to believe in the spiritual power of their near death experience, regardless of what science says."

"With respect, is it right for you to encourage them to believe in something that isn't known or understood, even if it's emotionally helpful?"

"You've basically described all religions. And yes, it is right. If we can help people deal with trauma, to put

272

it behind them and live their lives aligned with a story infused with gratitude and mutual love, that's worth it. Think about how the world would change if everyone felt and believed we are all connected."

"That's ostensibly how religion is supposed to work, and yet we still fight and kill and hate," she says.

He nods. "I understand your frustration, but there has to be a unifying story, one that shows people these connections. For me and millions more, that story is God. You can't take that story away just because some experiments track back to a dying brain."

"I'm not trying to take anything away, as if I had that power. I just want to make sure I do this small thing, this inquiry into near death experiences, the right way. I'm only trying to be thorough."

"My sense is that you may be inclined to prioritize a biological explanation ahead of, or even exclusive of, the spiritual."

"I'm don't think I'm the one doing the prioritizing."

He looks at the ceiling, and she figures he is deciding how to manage her. When he looks down, his crooked teeth form a big smile.

"Could you at least suggest to the *60 Minutes* team that they explore the question you asked earlier, how the experience changes people? What is it about the near death experience that causes people to adopt a more empathetic worldview?"

Even though the *60 Minutes* segment could be real now, it's likely the producers will only want to talk with Jenny. She is the one with the amazing story to tell.

"I'll try," she says. And she means it, sort of.

"If these two soldiers, these heroes, believed their near death experience was a biological event, little more than a giant brain fart, do you think they would have had an easier or harder time surviving the trauma of war?" he asks.

"Wouldn't it make more sense to help people avoid

the trauma of war by not having any more wars?"

He laughs quietly. "That is something on which we definitely agree."

"I should go. Thanks so much for everything."

He doesn't move aside, he is still blocking the door.

"Let me leave you with one more thought. The near death experience gives these combat veterans a reason to believe in love, a reason to find purpose in kindness and emotional generosity." There is a low urgency in his voice, close to a growl. "The near death experience gave new meaning to their lives. Science can't do that."

She knows Father James is doing good and kind things in the world, certainly far better than anything she has ever done, or probably will do, but she is irritated by his blind certainty. What gives him the right to decide what's true?

"I appreciate your commitment, it's truly wonderful that their near death experiences, under such awful circumstances, have helped them find meaning. But people find meaning in many ways, based on all their experiences throughout life, and how they add up. You've chosen God. Darren and Edward have chosen helping others. Others choose science. Or nature."

"What do you choose?" In his eyes, Loretta sees a mixture of accusation and pity, and it pisses her off.

"I choose writing and storytelling. I choose love and family. Pizza and popcorn. That's the whole point, we *can* choose. I choose looking for common ground, being objective about knowledge, science, religion, philosophy, anthropology, neuroscience, art, music, comic books, all of it. Why guess what meaning is, why not work together to prove what it is, where it comes from, or why we even need it in our lives?" Loretta pauses, surprised by the forcefulness of the words.

Father James looks hard at her with a flinty stare. "Where is the hope in that? For any common reality to provide an existence worth living, there needs to be hope in it, a vision that encourages us to be our best selves, to transcend our embodied self, to act in a way that is selfless, if you will."

The way he says the word startles Loretta back into the moment and into an awareness of the difference between the literal and metaphorical meaning of the word selfless—to be utterly giving is also to be without a self, to be self-less. As this thought free floats through her mind, she looks at the wall clock. Shit. "I'm sorry, I really have to go. This was all very moving, I appreciate you connecting me with Edward and Darren."

Father James sticks out his hand. She takes it. "I welcome you back anytime for further discussion." He moves away from the door, freeing Loretta.

Outside, walking to her office, she nods at Edward and Darren who are smoking on a bench in front of the emergency room. Her lungs reach out like a thousand tiny grasping hands at the acrid tobacco smell. Dammit, how fast the addiction comes back. She takes a few more hurried steps, but then changes her mind, spins around and walks back. "Can I bum one?"

"Smokes are kind of expensive," Edward says.

"Of course." She fishes a dollar from her pocket.

He moves over, making space on the bench. Darren lights her cigarette. She hopes the Dean doesn't walk by but then forgets that thought entirely, as she is drawn into the color of the flame, brilliant orange, a beautiful, all-consuming color, a hue she's never seen before. She sucks in a drag and, closing her eyes, exhales, focusing on the memory of the brazen color. Now, inside the darkness of her mind, she sees the same starburst lights that appeared at the end of the anthropology meeting, only now closer, bigger, blazing. The light shatters into a constellation of sparks, and as she stares into the void between the shards, her consciousness is swept out of the current of the present, and Loretta finds herself in a place where time doesn't flow, separate and alone; she hears the silence and at the same time her own voice inside a golden light. She is inside a vortex of words, sorting, listening, understanding and experiencing a story, *the* story beneath all stories. She feels the inside of her mind tremble, and shakes and slips back into the present moment. She looks around. The cigarette between her fingers has not burned down at all. Only seconds have passed.

"You okay, lady?" Darren asks.

"Yes. I'm okay."

Loretta stubs out the cigarette, pulls *The 24 Near Death Experiences of Jenny Black* notebook from her bag and opens it to a new page, the color of fresh-fallen snow. And there, between the two battle-scarred, chain-smoking men, Loretta begins to write quickly, furiously, desperate to capture everything she just saw and felt. Her hand flies across the paper, hurried, fearful it will be like a dream, fleeting and irrevocably collapsing into nothingness.

TWENTY-SIX

Loretta rushes up the stairs to the Dean's office suite, energized by her breakthrough and eager to get past the sit-in so she can get in touch with Jenny.

Caron is at the top of the stairwell. She looks serious and pale. "Where have you been and why aren't you answering your phone or texts?"

"I was in a meeting—"

"You need to get to the ER right away," Caron says. "Matthias was brought by ambulance an hour ago. He collapsed."

Her heart rate explodes. Matthias was inside the ER the entire time she was writing and smoking on a bus stop bench just outside? She pulls her phone from her pocket, takes it off airplane mode and sees dozens of unanswered text messages. Ava comes up the stairs behind Loretta; the baby is snuggled against her chest in its shoulder carrier.

"What are you doing here?" Loretta asks.

"I rode with Matthias and Jenny in the ambulance."

"Is he okay?" Loretta's voice breaks.

"Whatever it was seems to have passed. Still, best to be cautious, given his health."

"But why are you here now in the Dean's office?" Loretta asks, but doesn't wait for her answer. She turns to Caron. "How many students so far?"

"A dozen or so."

"No bike locks?"

"Not that I saw, why?"

"To chain themselves together."

"I don't think people do that anymore."

Loretta hears the students chanting, "We demand the Dean! We demand the Dean!" She wonders how many of them are live-streaming.

"Shit, shit," she says, even though part of her wants to laugh at how silly they sound. "I can't do this right now. Are there any real reporters?"

"Go on," Ava says. "Jenny told me about this sit-in, what it's about. Won't they be surprised to see me as their special guest."

"This is an uncontrolled situation, you can't be sure how it will turn out, this is not what we talked about, not at all," Loretta says, already backing down the stairs. "I won't be here to help."

"I've got this. Your husband needs you."

Dashing across campus, Loretta's University ID gets her through the crowded ER, and a nurse tells her Matthias is in an exam room toward the back. Loretta pulls back the curtain. Jenny steps away from him.

"What's going on?" She's trying to keep the panic out of her voice.

"It's nothing, I feel better now. Some kind of fluke," he says.

"What happened?"

"I felt a weird heaviness in my chest and it was hard to catch my breath. I got a little dizzy."

"And he was coughing," Jenny says.

A doctor in blue scrubs pushes aside the privacy

curtain, says a friendly hello and then runs through the possibilities: a sudden onset of extremely low blood pressure; fatigue and dehydration, a known residual effect of chemotherapy; a nutritional deficit; stress. The doctor recommends staying overnight for more tests but Matthias flat-out refuses. She relents and prescribes super-charged vitamins, rest and lots of fluids and asks them to stay put until the exit paperwork is finished.

Matthias leans all the way back, his body flat, his head resting on a small foam pillow. Loretta pulls the visitor's chair close enough to hold his hand. Jenny picks up scissors, puts them down and then grabs a roll of adhesive tape with her left hand and fiddles with a thermometer with the other.

"I'm sorry I wasn't here," Loretta says.

"I'm fine. Go back to work. No extra whiplashes on my account."

"It's not *my* stress we should be concerned about."

"I can go home with Matthias and watch over him," Jenny says, now examining the stethoscope the doctor left behind on the counter. "No problem."

"Absolutely not. I'm taking my husband home."

Loretta sits still for a minute, recovering from the toxic rush of terror-fueled adrenaline.

"Stop worrying. It was nothing," he says.

"It wasn't nothing, and you know goddamn well it was the smoking. You have to stop."

"To be fair, you kind of smell like smoke," he says. "Who have you been smoke-cheating on me with?"

"It is so foul," Jenny says.

"It's stupid, for both of us. Promise you'll stop. Your body can't take it," Loretta says.

"I promise."

Jenny picks up a bottle of generic hospital antiseptic and pumps it twice onto her hands. "I love the smell of hospitals, so clean and distinct. Lolo, put some on for your smoke stink." She hands the bottle to Loretta.

Through the gaps in the privacy curtain they watch the silhouette of a man on a gurney being wheeled into an exam cubicle as doctors shout incomprehensibly. A woman's sobs trail in the wake of the wounded moans.

"This is depressing as hell. How long is this going to take?" Matthias asks.

"Could be a while," Loretta says. "They're so busy."

"Can't you pull some strings?"

"Let's give it a little bit longer before I do that."

"What happens if I just leave?"

"One of us ends up spending a bunch of time on the phone figuring out how to get reimbursed without the approved paperwork."

"This is a barbaric and inefficient system."

Loretta smiles. His irritation means he's feeling better. She looks up at the ceiling and wonders if this is the room where that old man who lost his dentures floated out of his body. She tells Matthias and Jenny the story and they stare up at the corner, their necks craned back as if they might be able to see some lingering impression of the denture-less man floating there.

"I think I understand what's happening with the near death experiences. Or what might be happening," Loretta says.

Matthias and Jenny look down from the ceiling.

"You've put it together?" Matthias asks.

"Maybe."

"Well, come on, don't leave us in suspense," Jenny says.

"Now?"

"What better place than an ER to talk about death?" Matthias asks.

"I agree. And we do have time to kill," Jenny says.

Loretta pauses to gather her thoughts, eyes on the floor. Jenny and Matthias keep staring at her. She looks up at them. "Come on, give me a second here," she says. They laugh, and look back up at the corner but only for a few seconds. Loretta rolls her eyes and then plunges in.

"I've said that an area of agreement related to near death experiences is how the departments all define human consciousness and, by extension, the sense of self. I mean, they don't agree about those things, but they agree that how we interpret near death experiences is shaped by the theory, or story, of self, whatever it may be."

Loretta is nervous but she keeps going because she knows it's important to Jenny and because suddenly this story about near death experiences seems like it may end up being the most consequential thing she will do in her life.

"Let's assume human consciousness is fundamental, like what the chair of physics brought up, and the chair of philosophy too in an indirect way, meaning it's like atomic particles or gravity, irreducible, something new to be discovered or understood. We don't have the tools to detect it, yet, maybe because we don't have the language that lets us imagine it as a separate thing."

Matthias props himself up on the bed, swinging his legs around to bring him into a sitting position. He pats the spot next to him and Jenny lightly hoists herself up. Together, they wait for more.

"The next part is how consciousness as this distinct fundamental entity interacts with other irreducible things, like the component particles of atoms, the things science tells us everything is made of. So, here is what I think is happening."

She looks at Matthias and Jenny and the sight of two of her favorite people, side by side, hanging on every word, sends a flood of joy washing over her, so strong she wants to stop talking, to experience it completely, but the impatience in their eyes keeps her going.

"The stuff of consciousness manifests in humans as a sense of self and this self serves as, well, an interface for lack of a better word, between human life and the micro-components on the other side. Consciousness is what allows us to experience the physical world, to move in it, exist in it, and so on rather than as the swirl of atoms, or whatever, that makes up this room, this floor, the white color of the sheets, the smell of that lotion Jenny likes."

"Even us?" Jenny asks.

"Even us. Consciousness creates the, um, words are problematic here, and interface is not great. You could say consciousness creates the self as an avatar. Yuck, that's awful but the word is familiar because—"

Because it's a word from current technology, Loretta thinks, finishing the sentence in her mind. Exactly like what was discussed in the anthropology interview. One more piece of the puzzle clicks into place. Outside, the siren of an approaching ambulance gets closer.

"It's more than an interface. Consciousness is what creates matter from the underlying microscopic reality, it's the organizing force. We don't walk around seeing atoms and neutrons and gamma bits or whatever is spinning and buzzing and emitting energy signals or becoming a wave or a particle, because consciousness is the filter connecting all that."

"Are you saying reality isn't real?" Matthias asks.

"No, it's completely real, but consciousness is what allows us to experience it at this macro level rather than at some deeper atomic particle level."

"Assuming atoms are on the other side," Matthias says.

"Sure, maybe not atoms but something, or some things, is on the other side and maybe consciousness is the fire, as Stephen Hawking said, that brings it all together. When you die, you lose your sense of self and the interface disappears, your consciousness as that fundamental force is released, and you become one with whatever is beneath the reality as we experience it day to day, you are that microscopic reality again."

Jenny and Matthias don't say anything, and Loretta feels panic rising and then she remembers something Matthias said a few months back after reading a book about wolves.[34]

"Matthias, you told me scientists think wolves may experience their world predominantly through smell."

"Yes. And there is evidence that the world they move through may look—or be experienced—radically different than ours because of that."

"And fish, salmon for example, who find their way back to where they were born to give birth and then die. Or butterflies who fly hundreds of thousands of miles in a seasonal migration to the same place, over and over, some having never done it before."

"Possibly because they sense the electromagnetic field. How does that connect to consciousness or near death experiences?" Matthias asks.

"These animals experience the world differently than humans. The consciousness interface of animals, that first level of consciousness the religion department chair talked about, creates a different reality than what we experience. And that gives credence to the idea that reality might be a function of biology, but not like it *comes* from our biology, not strictly brain-is-mind, but rather how we integrate the consciousness stuff into our biology while we're living."

Loretta is a little breathless, and stands up, but doesn't stop talking. "We understand that interface through the story of self. Our sense of self is constantly creating and recreating reality from what lies beyond, every instant, every second. What you experience may not be exactly the same as I experience, like I can't know if my red is the same as your red, but it doesn't matter. It doesn't have to be the same, it just has to allow us to exist cooperatively even though reality is continuously manifesting uniquely for every living thing. We're creating reality, each of us, and we are all connected through it."

"There is no common reality?" Matthias asks.

"It could be common, or not, but it doesn't matter. That's the point. How can we ever know if it's the same? Even if I describe this table as silver, your definition of silver could be what I define as brown. Every second, every nanosecond, our consciousness interacts with the stuff of reality, a bunch of firing atoms or whatever the hell it is, to create our unique personal diorama. And while each diorama may be unique, enough common elements mean we can relate to each other through our shared experiences. Reality is constantly coming into being for each of us as we move through the world, creating a feedback loop of shared, or shared enough, experiences that link and bind us together."

"Consciousness is creating the macro environment from the micro because it's necessary for species reproduction?" Matthias asks.

"Right, exactly. And that's happening at whatever level of consciousness, or maybe it's the amount of consciousness, we embody."

The siren reaches a peak outside the ER and then goes silent, like the abruptness of a door slammed shut.

"Jenny, you're not saying anything," Loretta says.

"It's interesting, really."

"But?"

"What about love?"

"Love?" Matthias asks.

"The most important part when I have these things is the love, the oneness with everything and everyone, that sense—"

The *sense*. That's it, Loretta realizes. We are evolving, always evolving, and one aspect of that is we are evolving the sense to see beyond this macro-curtain. Beyond the curtain, what a stupid phrase, or even in this context, 'see.' Why can't she find better words?

Loretta thinks about what Father James said, that an explanation about near death experiences should not destroy the hope they engender. Now she understands what he meant because in a way, that is the most important part. Father James is right. Darren and Edward are the evidence of that.

Loretta says, "Love, it's love, the love we feel, if we're lucky, for others and from others, is an indicator of a new sense, the sense that would allow us to see past the limits of our consciousness interface."

"Are you saying reality beyond the interface is made up of love?" Matthias asks.

"No. I'm saying that love on this side of that interface is a signal, no, not a signal but an expression of that indivisibility, a glimmer of what's on the other side. It's our evolving ability to experience oneness, like a butterfly senses electromagnetism. Love is what we've named the emerging human sense that may allow us to experience reality in its raw, pre-manifested state."

"Love is irreducible," Jenny says.

"Love *is* irreducible. And durable, the most enduring thing in human existence, the strongest force."

"There are some obvious questions," Matthias says.

"Big, giant gaping questions, for sure," Loretta says.

"But it's something to think about," he says.

He isn't convinced, Loretta thinks, but that's okay, she isn't advocating, she's only opening a door.

"Here's one question I keep coming back to. Why do people who have near death experiences only see people who are already dead?" Loretta asks.

"That is a very good question," he says, cocking his head left, recognizing its implications. "Can your theory explain that?"

"It's not a theory, just some ideas," Loretta says.

"Still, can it?"

"Can it what?"

"Explain why there are only dead people in the tunnel, I mean, if it's not heaven, why would that be, how could that be?"

"Maybe something happens to our embedded consciousness-stuff as we die," Loretta says, talking slowly now, as she tautly paces the four steps allowed by the dimensions of treatment room. "Somehow, that change is marked within this micro-reality swirling around beyond the consciousness interface. That marking remains there, like an echo."

"Then when I die, I'd sense those echoes and recognize them in my tunnel, as my dead people?" Matthias says. "Yeah, I'm trying to stay with you, but that's pretty far out there."

"Remember the other night when I said religion and science could be stories describing the same thing?"

"Meaning the selfless state of consciousness is actually what people mean when they talk about God?" Jenny asks.

"Let's not go that far yet—"

"I'll go that far," Jenny says.

Matthias starts coughing.

"Maybe we should stop, talk about this later," Loretta says as she pulls a paper cup from a dispenser, fills it with water from the sink and hands it to him.

"No, don't stop, this is rejuvenating," he stutters in between coughs and sips. "Please, go on."

"You sure?"

"Dead sure."

"Okay. What I like about this idea is that it blends the different departmental perspectives. Religion called it cosmic consciousness, philosophy called it qualia, biology saw it exclusively from the physical side but still recognized that something about consciousness was unaccounted for, and in physics it was somehow wrapped up with the goal of bridging two theories, and so on."

"How does this explain what's happening to Jenny? And why?" Matthias asks.

"Somehow, the subset of people who have the near death experience when clinically dead must have a genetic predisposition, a free-rider, like the flirty Irish evolutionist speculated—"

"Flirty?" Matthias asks, arching an eyebrow.

"I'm sure I imagined that."

"I doubt that." He smiles and she continues.

"Anyway, a free-rider might let them see past our arranged world, between all the individual dioramas, into where everything is indivisible, connected. That genetic anomaly only expresses itself at death, or near death, so we only know about it from the very few who come back. In Jenny, I guess that genetic predisposition is something new, something we haven't seen before, well, not often anyway," Loretta adds, thinking of Dorothy.

"Where did these ideas come from?" Matthias asks.

"I've been thinking about this stuff kind of nonstop since Jenny got here."

"But when did it all come together?"

"Twice now, first after the anthropology interview and then again today, just before I got here when I was sitting in between two vets, Darren and Edward, who had near death experiences. With my eyes closed, I saw the words in the distance, surrounded by light, or maybe I felt them. It was like fireworks, first a tiny spark, then all lit up."

"You saw through to the other side," Jenny says.

"Maybe, I don't know. But I did feel removed from the present, like I was all encased by something beyond how we describe our world now."

She pauses, unsure if now is the right time to ask, but events are collapsing around them and not only does she need to get an answer to *60 Minutes*, it also seems like a big opportunity to get people talking about a new story about human consciousness, to get people thinking about the ramifications. "Jenny, how would you feel about getting an MRI scan while you are experiencing an episode?"

Before Jenny answers, Matthias asks, "What would an MRI scan show?"

"I'm not sure. But maybe evidence of that other sense being opened, achieving awareness? An effect on neurons? We won't know until it happens but it's an incredibly rare opportunity, no, not rare, that's the wrong word. It's brand new, never been done."

"If you think I should do, I'll do it," Jenny says.

"Would you do it live on *60 Minutes*?"

"Will Scott Pelley be there?"

"It's possible.""

"Then sure."

An orderly in faded green scrubs and white clogs swooshes open the curtain of the examining room.

"Your discharge paperwork is ready. Rest, lots of water and a round of vitamins are in your immediate future. You have a low-grade fever so keep an eye on it and if it gets higher, give us a call but other than that, you're free to go."

"That's it?" Matthias shouts. "You kept me here for nearly an hour to say the same thing the doctor said? What kind of bullshit is that?"

TWENTY-SEVEN

Loretta tucks Matthias into bed, a mug of chamomile tea on the nightstand next to a pitcher of water, and extracts a promise he will rest until she gets home with his prescribed uber-vitamins in a few hours. "I have to run by work first."

"It was nothing. I'm already feeling better."

He coughs three times, dry and shallow.

Loretta sighs. "Please, don't scare me like that again. And for fuck's sake, stop the smoking."

"Done, done. Now get out of here, do your work. I'll call Sally-Anne for a nice long chat and Jenny will look in on me."

Loretta kisses him and Matthias holds her embrace longer than usual. "Don't pick today to run away with the Dean."

"Well, it is getting closer to the weekend ..."

He laughs.

Loretta drives to the pharmacy to pick up the prescription. She pulls into the underground lot, parks and before going inside, calls work to find out what happened with the student sit-in.

"It was crazy," Toni says.

"Good crazy or bad crazy?"

"See for yourself, I'm sending the video. But I didn't start recording until about five minutes in. I didn't know who she was right away. None of us did."

As the file downloads, Loretta watches an old man wearing a red baseball cap, a purple jacket and pants held up by twine feed a grocery cart full of can returns one-by-one into a recycling machine. He'll get about six bucks for those returns, Loretta calculates, maybe enough for supper. She looks down at her phone, hits play and bumps up the volume.

About twenty students, all white except for two who are Black, the only two in the 223-member medical school class, all wearing their short white lab coats, sitting in a circle on the checker-board patterned brown and tan carpet. Ava stands in the center of the circle, holding Emanuel. Loretta should be relieved that so few students showed up, but somehow, she isn't. She's disappointed. Why do so few students care?

The clip starts mid-sentence.

"... glad you are here today, honored in fact, that you want to stand with me, a stranger, to protect my interests, your willingness to take a stand against the University administration and its propaganda machine is commendable."

Propaganda machine? Okay, Loretta thinks, not sure I deserved that.

"You are showing the courage needed to confront how your chosen discipline, medicine, has been an active participant in dehumanizing Black Americans from the moment my ancestors were violently brought to this country centuries ago."

What the hell? Why isn't Ava talking about being the wronged party in *The Case of the Misplaced Sperm*? Why isn't she telling everyone that the University didn't try to force her to have an abortion?

"Now that I have your attention, I want to challenge you to take another step, to a place more challenging than spending a few hours of your time, a different place, where you confront your own history, your own culpability, either by intent or inaction. As a medical professional, you need to ask yourself, really ask yourself, why Black infant mortality is higher than for whites, why more Black women die in childbirth, why lifespan is lower for Black people. Do you ask yourselves these questions?"

Loretta sits back, now understanding what Ava is doing, what she meant last night when she said she wanted Emanuel's introduction to the world to be strong and positive.

The students have been joined by the Dean's office staff, all standing now in the reception area, leaning in to hear Ava's words. Loretta notices, not for the first time but more sharply now, that every single person working in the Dean's office is white, just like the jury earlier and the University communications team. How is that possible? What role has she played in this outcome, even if only by inattention?

"Do you look at surveys and statistics that show how doctors, and medical students such as yourselves, dismiss the symptoms Black men and women describe? Do you allow yourself to default to an assumption that the past has no bearing on the present ...?"

The video goes wobbly and Loretta hears Toni say 'oh, shit.' The picture bounces into a disorienting close-up of the carpet weave. Ava's voice is barely audible; Toni picks up her phone and after a few seconds, voice and image realign.

"... the past of your University, of most American universities and scientific establishment. It's not only the overt tragedies like forced sterilizations and non-consenting experimentation, it's the justification of such horrors with what they insisted was science. They said Black people don't experience pain, that injuries hurt us less, we have thicker skin and slower brains than white people. Was there evidence? Not a shred. An entire body of pseudoscience, a belief system, was created in the halls of learning to justify white supremacy, a toxic legacy still coloring our world today, still part of the foundations of academic institutions. Indeed, the entire edifice of medical education was structured to exclude black people from becoming healers, to teach you how to practice a medicine for whites that was different than for Black people.[35] What is wrong with white people that so many cannot feel whole unless they dehumanize people of color? You must answer this question, you white students, you must demand your University take a hard look at its role in sustaining racist systems. If we cannot look honestly at the past, how can we change the future?[36]

If we cannot look honestly at the past, how can we change the future? It's what Loretta said when she was crying and looking straight at the camera during her broadcast news debacle. Is Ava saying something meant for her?

"I'm glad you showed up here today. Really. Thank you from the bottom of my heart, thank you for caring about my child and me, about what happened at this University. What happened to me was a mistake. I bear no ill will due to a mistake. Humans make mistakes. But racism is not a mistake, it is a choice, a choice made by too many white people because it benefits them, even when they look away, unable to acknowledge it, even when they are silent. You cannot look away any longer. I challenge you to keep fighting, because this is America's fight, not just my fight or the fight of people of color. Until you work to destroy the racism built into the very fabric of this nation's founding, and the bedrock of medicine, none can be free. Together, we can rewrite the story of America, together we can live up to the ideals, because looking forward, our story is, our story must be that we are all one."

The recording swivels to the Dean. His face is pink, a possibly-having-a-heart-attack shade of bright pink. Toni return the lens to Ava. Emanuel wriggles in her arms. The Dean walks into the frame.

The video stops.

We are all one.

Loretta taps her fingers on the steering wheel. She can't believe she wants a cigarette, but damn, she does. She watches the stooped old man still loading cans into the recycling receptacle. And then she decides.

Loretta texts Toni: *Post the video on our official social accounts. Fast. Get Ava's permission first.*

She's with the Dean. His office door is shut.

Interrupt them. We need it up now. And tell her I want to tag Tom Thomas.

Toni texts back: *The radio host? Why?*

She'll understand.

Loretta waits a minute. Toni texts two thumbs up.

What are they talking about?

A new committee? She laughed when I said you wanted to tag Tom Thomas. Asked if this was what you meant by a controlled opportunity.

Loretta sends a smiley face.

Are you sure I should post it? I cursed in it.

No worries. And share to all subaccounts.

Okay, here goes.

Twitter too. He's got close to a million followers.

Loretta punches in a number on her cell.

"Jamie Ignatius."

"Jamie, it's Loretta at the University. You were right."

"About the abortion? You tried to force that woman to have an abortion. I knew it. Self-entitled fucking academic elite—"

"No, not about that. You were totally wrong about

that. The other thing."

"You can't even say it, can you?"

"Yes, I can."

"Go on then."

"Check the University Facebook page. Not sure if it will stay up long, but maybe you can help with that. And Twitter."

"Racism, the other thing is confronting the legacy of racism at your University. Active, passive, indifferent, whatever, it's all built on a racist foundation."

"Just check our page."

She disconnects. Loretta starts the engine.

Next stop, the Dean.

TWENTY-EIGHT

Loretta knocks on the Dean's open office door. He looks up from the computer. "Loretta, you missed an exciting afternoon. Ava made quite an impression on the students, on all of us, really. But first things first, how's Matthias?"

"He's okay but the doctors don't know why he collapsed. Said it might be a vitamin deficiency, or dehydration."

"I imagine that's not very satisfying. Do you want me to see what I can get from them?"

"I think bed rest will do the trick. But thank you. He's home now."

"Did the ER staff treat him well?"

"Well enough."

"Go home, be with him. It'll be tough but we can get by without you until tomorrow." He smiles good-naturedly.

"Actually, do you have a few minutes?"

"Yes, although not too much longer than that. I have a meeting with the President. Maybe something positive can come from the fertility clinic mess."

Loretta sits down at his meeting table. He comes out from behind the desk and takes the chair across from her.

"Ava came to my home last night."

She knows him well enough to understand that the flatness of his expression is a practiced reaction, a way of not giving away his viewpoint, and it means he is concerned. He waits a few beats before responding.

"Do you know her?" he asks, his voice even.

"No."

"Then why would she come to your home?"

"She wanted my help dealing with some reporters camped out at her house."

He pauses again and then says, "You're aware this potentially puts the University in an awkward legal position."

"It happened so fast, and then when she came with Matthias to the ER, it was her idea to come up here on her own to talk to the students. I didn't ask her to do that."

The Dean looks out the window. A pigeon lands on the sill, poking around on the edges looking for food. After a minute, the Dean returns his gaze to Loretta. She knows he's decided something.

"I don't doubt you for an instant. We'll get it sorted out. In the end, what happened today will, I hope, be good for the University, so let's look at the situation from that vantage. I'll talk to Legal. Nothing for you to worry about."

Loretta doesn't say anything.

"Is there something else?"

"Do you ever wonder who you are?"

"Not really." He shows no surprise at her question. "I'm the Dean at a University. A surgeon. A husband, father, son, soon-to-be grandpa. I contain multitudes, as Whitman wrote. Why do you ask?"

"That's not quite what I mean. Not what you do in life but who that person is, the one inside you, directing the doing, the thinking, feeling the feelings, tasting the cherry pie."

"Help me understand where you're going with this question."

"You remember my friend having the near death experiences?"

"Of course. Have the visits with the department chairs been useful?"

Loretta thinks about how to explain to the Dean what's happened, wondering how much he needs to know. Probably everything, she decides. He deserves that much.

"I'm going to start at the beginning. And this time, I'm not going to leave anything out."

He arches his eyebrows, his expression now a mix of concern and curiosity. Loretta knows she is about to test the strength of their bond.

"I came to you a week ago, or was it more, gosh, so much has been going on I've lost track of time. Anyway, what I didn't tell you was my friend, Jenny, had twenty-two near death experiences, although since then there have been three more, so it's up to twenty-five—"

"You told me there had been a few. I distinctly remember you saying the word 'few.' Twenty-five is considerably more than a few. This information would have had a bearing on my response. Why didn't you tell me?"

Loretta isn't sure if he's irritated that she left out a crucial fact or hurt that she didn't trust him. Maybe both.

"I honestly don't know. At the time, I was worried for her, feeling protective. I wanted to go slow, figure out what was happening. And the truth is that Jenny's near death experience situation coincided with some sort of, well, I don't know what to call it, some sort of existential crisis I'm having—"

"Loretta, what's going on?"

"It will be easiest if you just let me get this out."

He nods and she continues. "I had been feeling as if I'd lost my identity, and I gave it a silly name, saying I had turned into a zombie. In part, it was because of this job, nothing to do with you personally, I think the world of you, but it has zapped so much of me. Now I'm not even sure that's true. Because if I'm honest, my disintegrating identity first started when Matthias got sick, and suddenly, the idea that he might not be part of my life anymore, well, it was easier to shut down. The thought of him dying, of being gone, was too painful, so I froze. At least, that's what I thought. But now I believe the zombieness is possibly the beginning of something important, not something I should try to end."

The Dean's assistant knocks softly on the door three times, their private signal to tell him to wrap up whatever he's doing or boot out whoever is in his office and get moving along to his next meeting. He stands and opens the door. "Would you let the President know I'll be late?" He shuts the door, sits back down and says, "Go on, Loretta, take your time."

"Thank you," Loretta says. "Just when I was at the lowest point, feeling like I'd never find myself again, Jenny showed up and I decided to help her because Matthias thought it would cure my zombieness and because I genuinely wanted to help my friend. So, that's when I started this quest, as some people meaning Matthias and Jenny call it. I call it *The 24 Near Death Experiences of Jenny Black*. No wait, I forgot to change it. *The 25 Near Death Experiences of Jenny Black*."

"You gave it a name?"

"It's a habit. I name everything, even the fertility clinic crisis."

"Let's hear it."

"*The Case of the Misplaced Sperm.* Sounds sort of like a terrible Nancy Drew mystery, right?"

The Dean says, "It's your imagination that makes you good at this job. But I wish you had told me earlier that it was causing you this degree of stress."

"I don't think there is anything you could have done about that."

Loretta hopes their relationship is strong enough for what's coming next.

"I met with the chairs you suggested about near death experiences. I learned a lot."

"I'm glad it helped."

"I grounded the entire inquiry in the question you identified right off the bat: Why is it that some people return from clinical death having had this life-changing experience and others don't? Each department gave me a different answer, but the common thread was that the near death experience offered clues into the nature of human consciousness and, by extension, the nature of self."

"Near death experiences are both self-reported and unpredictable, making them impossible to study with scientific rigor thus allowing for vastly differing interpretations of their meaning," he says. "And this is made more difficult because they generally occur only once in any individual life."

The light in his eyes shifted. He saw it. She knew he would see it.

"Your friend Jenny could change that," he says.

"She's agreed to have an MRI scan and any other tests while she is having a near death experience. But the condition, my condition, is we move forward only if you approve and are involved." Loretta didn't know until this minute that was her condition, but she realizes now the Dean's involvement is the only way to be sure Jenny is protected. "Before we talk about that, there's one more thing you have to know."

"This is definitely not the day I was expecting. What else?"

"I told all the chairs that *60 Minutes* wanted to do a segment on near death experiences and that they might be featured on it. That wasn't true."

"You didn't tell them about Jenny?"

"No," she says.

"You solicited information from the chairs based on the false premise that they would appear on *60 Minutes*. Why?"

That familiar pink flush creeps up his neck.

"So they would talk to me."

"You didn't think a request from the Dean would suffice?"

"You know faculty love media attention, to raise their profile for research funding, maybe attract a tech billionaire as their guardian angel."

"And?"

"If I dangled *60 Minutes*, I knew they wouldn't stop talking. You, on the other hand, you scare them. No offense, but they might have only said things that would impress you. But now they want to be involved."

"In a lie?"

"It's no longer a lie. *60 Minutes* actually wants to do a segment on Jenny having a near death experience during an MRI. And have a bunch of scientists and other experts on the show to talk about it."

He shakes his head, confused. "How did that come to pass?"

"I pitched the idea for real and they love it."

He cocks his head to the left. "Let me be sure I understand. Your made-up story about *60 Minutes* is now real?"

"Yes. Only here."

He looks out the window again. His neck flush is receding. He is considering his words, and Loretta does nothing to interrupt his thought process. She examines his expression while he is thinking and wonders what he looked like as a boy. Did his neck flush easily when he was little?

"Is she willing to have this done at our University?"

"Yes."

"And our department chairs would be featured?"

"I can arrange that."

"The scientific implications could be profound." Loretta recognizes cautious excitement in his tone. "A scan might show things related to what happens to consciousness at death. The data would be invaluable."

"Right, and also possibly show us if something is altered in the brains of people who have near death experiences," she says.

"Why would you think that might have happened?" the Dean asks.

They are back on solid footing now. "Think about it, maybe if consciousness is fundamental—"

His assistant knocks on the door again and pokes her head inside. "Dean, the President's office called a second time."

"I'm on the way and call ahead please to tell the President I have two items for our agenda now, urgent items."

Five minutes later, Loretta knocks on Mona's door. Mona waves her in as a shred of lettuce from the taco she is eating gets lodged in her throat, and she coughs repeatedly until her eyes drip tears. She takes a long swallow from a water bottle, wipes her eyes with a napkin, looks at the fake eyelash inside the crumpled paper and then up at Loretta.

"I must look crazed with one eyelash," she says.

So, the lashes are fake, Loretta thinks.

"Are you going to finally tell me why the chairs are asking me for an update on *60 Minutes*? What the hell is going on?"

Even with her asymmetrically lashed raccoon eyes overpowering her expression, Loretta knows Mona is angry. She does not like being out of the loop.

"I was talking to the *60 Minutes* producer, trying to get them off the sperm story and I pitched something else," Loretta says.

"Good strategy. A distraction. What did you pitch?"

"I have a friend who has spontaneous and repeating near death experiences. *60 Minutes* wants to shoot her having one during an MRI, and then have doctors and scientists talking about what happens during a near death experience."

"Why does anyone care what happens?"

"Some people think it shows heaven. Others think they're hallucinations, maybe from oxygen deprivation as the brain shuts down at death."

"Those 'some' people being the religious types and the 'others' being our faculty," Mona says.

"Yes. A modern update to the battle between God and science." That isn't the ideal way to describe where Loretta stands now on near death experiences, but it's a story that will sell public interest, at least initially. Still, she'd better seed the more constructive version she hashed out with Jenny and Matthias in the ER earlier.

"Plus, it's possible near death experiences provide an insight into the nature of human consciousness, or at least provide a basis for asking the next set of questions."

"Our University on *60 Minutes* with our scientists talking about the insights into human consciousness," Mona says. "That would be fantastic. I might even forgive you for all the mice shit you've been throwing around."

"The Dean is talking to the President this minute about it."

"You went over my head?" She is less excited now. She pulls off the remaining fake lash and puts it on the desk. The lash sits there—limp, alone, wildly out of place. In any other situation, Loretta would make some sort of joke, but not this time.

"Not intentionally. It happened so fast that things got out of control."

Mona considers whether the possibility of national coverage for the University is worth whatever motive Loretta is holding back.

"Let's do it," she finally says.

Okay, she's in the place I want her to be, Loretta thinks. Here we go. "I'm setting up a meeting between the two parties in *The Case of the Misplaced Sperm*."

"The case of the what? Why are you calling it that? And you can't do that, it's for Legal to handle."

"We said that we would do anything needed to help in this, what did we call it, this 'ethically complex situation,' and this is what's needed."

"You'll violate your confidentiality agreement, you could be fired."

"I'm not asking permission. I'm telling you so you have a heads-up for any possible media ramifications."

Mona's phone vibrates and she looks down at it. "What the hell is this about a video on our social feeds going viral? Loretta, where are you going? Loretta!"

TWENTY-NINE

Loretta, Jenny and Matthias sit in the enclosed back porch. Fading pewter clouds hang lightly across the late-evening indigo sky, slowly fading into night. Jenny and Loretta sit shoulder to shoulder on the couch, reading the papers inside an open folder spread across Loretta's lap. Matthias looks out the window, watching their reflections in the glass, the edges of their mirrored bodies shimmer and tremble as they flip pages.

"What is all that?" he asks, speaking to the glassy window versions of Loretta and Jenny.

"The Jenny protocols," Loretta says, handing a page she's just finished to Jenny.

"The what?"

"Research protocols for Jenny's near death experience. All the individual experiments and data the scientists and other experts want to get out of those few minutes."

"Like what?"

Loretta holds up a sheet of paper. "This one is from the Department of Anthropology in partnership with the Department of Religion. It says, 'We will establish a prior baseline of neurological readings from the MRI regarding discrete religious symbols. We will then compare these readings to those measured during the near death event to evaluate our hypothesis that prior cultural conditioning influences the self-reported symbology of the near death experience.'"

"What they don't say is establishing that baseline took forever," Jenny says. "While I was inside the MRI tunnel, they read from the bible, the Koran, then some Buddha stuff and at one point, someone was singing old-timey church hymns into my headphones."

"Wouldn't that experiment need someone with a different cultural background from Jenny to compare?"

"Yes, it would," Loretta says. "But they'll collect the data now in anticipation of that someone coming along. That's science. One step at a time. Or what did you call it the other night? The slow march of knowledge through the enormity of time."

"Steadiness, not slow march. Steadiness through the enormity of time was what I said. What else is in that pile of papers?"

As she pages through the stack, Loretta summarizes others. "Biology is doing a full data sweep to test the dying brain hypothesis, looking at what happens to inner ear fluids, also measuring respiration, heart rate, oxygen levels in the brain and such. There are another three that will generate data to better understand brain-death, what it is, when it occurs, if it's even a useful way to define death. Those are from neuroscience."

"Are any taking on the hypothesis of heaven?"

"Not directly. How could you? But two will collect data on markers of a type of electrical brain activity that could shed light on whether Jenny is experiencing something real or a hallucination."

"What about cosmic consciousness, that thing the religion department thinks is happening, about moving to a higher level of consciousness?" Matthias asks.

She flips through more papers, finally pulls one out and reads. "Religion's hypothesis is that Jenny's brain or genes are altered either by the near death experiences or that she was born with some sort of difference that causes the events, like we talked about when we were waiting in the emergency room. They're partnering with neuroscience and biology to collect data to inform future studies. They've already done a full genetic mapping of Jenny, along with resting-state MRI scans."

Matthias stops talking to their window reflections and turns around.

"Do any of these experiments address your theory?"

"It's not a theory, just some ideas."

"You can still answer."

Loretta closes the folder. "Honestly, I don't know what data would be needed or how to design that experiment. I'm hopeful that with all this information coming together, once I get up the nerve to talk to the scientists about it, maybe they'll have an idea about how to parse the data around these ideas."

"I wonder how the world would change if we adopted a new meaning for the concept of self," Jenny says. "Like in your theory."

"Again, not a theory, just some ideas."

"We'd all be zombies," Matthias says. "Or some new version of zombie, maybe a neo-zombie, or zombie-innovatus."

"Clever," Loretta says. "But I have been puzzling over that question. The story of self is everything about who we are, about how society is organized, how we interact with each other, the organizing principle, at least in our culture."

"That is something to think about," Matthias says.

"It's mind-blowing to consider it from the vantage point of history," Loretta says. "The concept of self emerges ultimately from the thinking of a breed of ancient male philosophers grounded in religious ideas. Was the entire idea of self, even the precursor concept of soul, linked to the need for people to justify exerting dominance? The ripple effect is huge. I mean, think about it. Our society, our economy, our government, all organized around the idea of a unique and permanent individual sense of self. What if that need for one group to exert control over others is baked into the current concept itself? It requires an impermeable self with agency to first elevate one group of selves and then demand other selves do their bidding."

"You'd have to study how people across the world and throughout history have defined self," Matthias says. "Something for your anthropology department."

"This is all wasted on me," Jenny says.

"What do you mean?" Loretta asks, putting down the files.

"Assuming this ends up being about genetics, which I think it might, evolution made a mistake with me."

"That's all evolution is, a bunch of mistakes that turn out not to be mistakes in hindsight," Matthias says.

"But I have no children to pass this on to, it's a full stop with me."

"Consider it more broadly," Loretta says. "Lots, maybe even most, people throughout history whose mystical experiences have changed how we look at the world didn't make change happen through their kids."

"Well, there is that beloved son of the Christian god to consider," Matthias says.

"What I meant is that Jenny just being Jenny is enough to have an impact, if it turns out that way."

Jenny leans in to kiss Loretta's cheek. "I'll sleep on that. See you both in the morning. Big day tomorrow."

After Jenny leaves, Matthias and Loretta sit quietly, the only sound the hum of the laboring space heater. Matthias switches off the light and as their eyes adjust to the fullness of the night, the stars begin to pop out.

"Does any of what's happened mean you're not feeling so zombie anymore?" Matthias asks.

What she wants to say but can't find the right words is that a sense of joy is washing through her, again and again, like waves against the shoreline of a mountain lake, and it doesn't matter who or what is feeling the joy. It's the joy that matters, a joy without cause, free floating. She suspects the act of relinquishing the permanency of self, or at least the idea of it, which she is in the process of doing, might be responsible for this incomparable joy, this unexpected sense of liberation, and connection. She will try to explain this to Matthias later, maybe tomorrow. Right now, she just wants to be with it. Be with him.

"Let's just say it may not matter so much anymore."

He takes her hand and she feels the warmth of his skin. They stare up at the night sky in silence.

THIRTY

The set inside the hospital MRI suite is crowded with cameras, lights, miles of cable and a small army of crew members. The chairs of religion, biology, philosophy, physics, neuroscience, anthropology and psychiatry, along with the Irish evolutionist, the patient advocate and three department chairs—neurosurgery, literature and anesthesiology—that she missed in the first set of interviews, hover around the set, excited and nervous about witnessing scientific history or getting the chance for a celebrity-making turn on *60 Minutes*.

The program director and two assistants check equipment, block out shots and conduct interviews with the chairs, conferring and making quiet judgments about who the viewers will fall in love with and who they will hate, and how those naturals can be pitted against each other, reality-TV style. The elbow-throwing defense of the dying brain theory from Dr. Mitchell, the biology chair, means she'll rocket to the top of their list, paired off against Dr. Orr, the quirky religion chair and cosmic consciousness champion. Dr.

Peaker, psychiatry chair, and his tear-jerker story about Dorothy surely will be in the running. But she's not ruling out Dr. Thill, the chair of philosophy who believes the study of consciousness will upend everything known about the material world, although that might be too complex for *60 Minutes* or, from the director's perspective, too boring.

Loretta stands against the back wall, watching Mona mingle and charm. Her phone buzzes; a text from Devlin Richardson, the post-doc in neuro-imaging who scanned his mother while she died. *We're all set. Darren and Edward are in the machines and the chaplain is here. He's a talker!*

Loretta is about to send back a smiley face but she feels the energy in the lab shift and knows without looking that the Dean has entered the imaging suite. The department chairs at the far end of the room all stand a little taller, except Dr. Swift, the physics chair, who Loretta has decided is her favorite. Dr. Swift sits in her wheelchair, observing the lemming-like reaction of these academics, a wry smile on her face.

Loretta waves and the Dean walks over.

"The campus is buzzing about a mystery woman with near death experiences being scanned here today."

Loretta sighs. "So much for confidentiality."

He leans in closer so his words are exclusive. "I have other news. Tom Thomas dropped the lawsuit."

"That is very good news. Why?"

"Don't know. No explanation. But take comfort in the fact your, what did you call it, the case of the mistaken sperm, has been solved."

If he wasn't her boss, she would punch him good-naturedly on the arm and tell him it wasn't mistaken sperm, it was misplaced. But he is her boss, so she just smiles. He charges ahead with his next piece of news.

"Another thing. With full buy-in from the President, I've charged a new task force to look at the University's role, directly or by inaction, in systemic racism in this state. Now and in the past, and how we make amends for our role."

"That's great."

"It's long overdue. I suppose I wasn't ready, or maybe if I'm honest, didn't understand, but now I'm trying. And listening. I want our process to be fully transparent. I'm thinking of having a member of the media embedded. Any ideas?"

Loretta glances at the far end of the room where Jamie and Malcolm are setting up. "I know just the person."

"Good. Time for this University, and me, to show a little backbone here."

"Thank you."

"What for? You did the work, and I come up smelling like roses."

"Thank you for everything, for encouraging me to find out about near death experiences, for lending your reputation to my credibility, for always trusting me and for not being irritated by the whole *60 Minutes* lie." Mostly, she wants to say, thank you for being such a good person, but she doesn't say that part. It might embarrass him.

"That little ruse of yours turned out okay in the end." He glances at the notebook Loretta carries in her left hand. "What's that?"

"Keeping track of everything, so I can tell the story." She holds up the notebook for him to see the title: *The 25 Near Death Experiences of Jenny Black.*

"Let's hope you have to change that title today." Before Loretta can say anything else, he walks toward the chairs and claps Dr. Peaker on the back. "A banner day for research, eh?" he says loudly, and the group nervously laughs as each chair begins to talk over each other.

"I guess I'm ready," Jenny says, appearing next to

Loretta. She is wearing a short denim skirt with a black leotard shirt.

"Jenny, you surprised me. Where's Matthias?"

"Parking the car. Tell me again, how will all this work?"

Loretta motions over the *60 Minutes* director—a tall, thin woman in her forties, holding a clipboard tight against her chest like a shield—and introduces Jenny. The director explains the anchor will arrive shortly, and the first thing they'll do is record an interview with Jenny and then put her inside the MRI machine.

"What happens if it takes a while?" Jenny asks. "Maybe even days?"

"We'll leave a crew behind to shoot it, however long it takes. After it happens, whenever it does, we'll fly you and the University experts to New York to tape the full segment."

"Can Loretta come?"

"You're our star, you call the shots."

The door swings open and Scott Pelley enters. He is more handsome than he appears on television, Loretta thinks, and he is very handsome on television.

"Wow," Jenny says. "How is it possible he is more handsome in person?"

Jenny and Loretta giggle like children, but only for an instant. The director rushes over to welcome him. They shake hands and whisper and then Scott Pelley makes a beeline for Jenny, ignoring everyone else in the room. He sticks out his hand and Jenny takes it, and then he puts his other hand on top of hers.

"I'm honored to meet you. I'll be interviewing you today for our little show. Are they treating you okay?"

"Sure, everything is great so far," Jenny says. "And getting better."

The director asks if Jenny is ready to start.

"Will you stay?" Jenny asks Loretta.

"To the bitter end."

Loretta watches the director lead Jenny toward two armchairs in front of a green screen. The crew is fine-tuning the lights and camera angle. The makeup artist shadows Scott, discreetly dusting face powder across his cheeks and forehead. Jenny stops, turns and looks back at Loretta. Her eyes are wide, panicked. Loretta recognizes the look from the kitchen last week. "Is one coming?" Loretta asks.

Jenny nods, as her body begins to go limp. Loretta rushes forward, grabs her beneath her armpits and half-drags, half-pulls her to the machine. "It's happening, now, it's happening!" she yells.

The director is shouting, "Roll tape, run sound, places everyone, the event is coming, now! Go!"

The group jumps into action. A videographer hoists a mobile camera onto his shoulder and leans into the machine. A second and third camera, each on a tripod, blink red. The soundman lifts the boom microphone. Imaging technicians turn dials and computer screens flare to life. Loretta starts to help Jenny onto the stretcher but she is pushed back, politely but firmly, by lab staff. They take over, sliding Jenny into the MRI tunnel. Loretta texts Devlin Richardson. *She is having one. Get it all going now!*

The room drops into silence. Phones are held aloft, a small forest of arms recording the scene. After about three minutes, a low hum, like what Jenny emitted at the end of the kitchen near death experience, flows from the machine. The soundman slides the boom microphone inside the tunnel trying to capture the odd audio. Another minute passes. The soundman takes off his headphones. "She said she's done. She is asking for Loretta."

The stretcher slides out. Loretta gently pushes through the moat of people to get to Jenny's side.

Tears stream down Jenny's face.

"Jenny, what's wrong? Are you hurt?"

Jenny throws her arms around Loretta's neck and pulls her close, now sobbing. "I saw him. Oh, Loretta, I'm sorry. I saw Matthias in the tunnel."

THIRTY-ONE

The last mile is the toughest.

A steep incline where before it was mostly flat. Fractured basalt slabs and chunky gravel, ankle-twisting terrain if attention wanders. In this final stretch, the towering trees give way to scrappy shrubs, some with hard white berries. The sun is hidden behind fat gray clouds. Rain threatens.

Loretta looks up-trail at Sally-Anne, twenty feet or so ahead, hopping across the rocky path like an elf. Loretta wants to shout *Be careful. Oh, please, stay away from the ridge!* but she stops herself.

"I need to catch my breath. Can we stop for a sec?" Jenny asks.

Loretta stops, pulls a canteen from her backpack, unscrews the top and hands it to Jenny. The bottom of Loretta's pack is moist from the canteen's slow leak. She checks the seal of the Ziploc bag. It's holding tight.

"It's good to be outside," Jenny says, pulling the blue mask down to her chin to sip the water. "See something beyond the walls of your house, no offense, it's a nice enough house."

"None taken."

They stand without talking, drinking the water, their hearts adjusting to the demands of the trail's elevation. Loretta tries to call up the day Matthias asked her to marry him on this trail, so long ago. It was cloudy, which was okay because Matthias loved clouds, thought they were mysterious. He bought the ring at an antique thrift shop. She twists the ring around her finger now but as she does the memory is pushed aside, replaced by the seared image of Matthias collapsed over the steering wheel, the horn of the banged-up old classic Mercedes making a pitiful sound, a thumping low hummmm-click-hummmm, like a dead car battery trying one last time to turn itself over.

"Is it hard for you to be here?" Jenny asks.

"No harder than being everywhere."

Something went haywire in his heart, that's what the coroner pronounced after the autopsy. But later, about seven weeks later, after a tracer called, his doctor raised the possibility that Matthias died of complications from the virus, an undiagnosed early case, noting that fast-tracked research results suggest coronavirus exacerbates heart issues.

All that wasted time worrying about cancer.

Loretta peers into the distance at the Douglas fir trees stretching across the foothills, the forest green punctuated by brown, likely last year's burn or maybe beetle infestations. A darkness is there in those spots. From her vantage, Loretta imagines them as black holes and that by falling into one she might find eternity, or just escape from the pain for a little while.

"Come on, Mom, Aunt Jenny! You're almost at the top," Sally-Anne shouts.

"Let's go, Lolo, let's go," Jenny chants, clapping her hands together like a cheerleader. "We got this."

"Was it this tough when you were here before with

Matthias?" Loretta asks, starting back up the trail.

"We weren't trying to keep pace with your twenty-year old daughter."

They walk. And walk some more. A woman coming down from the peak approaches. The trail is narrow. Loretta slips her mask back on, and Jenny covers her face. The woman wears no mask. As she passes by them, Loretta decides not to be irritated by this. Not now. Not today.

"When was the last time you had one?" Loretta asks.

"Twelve days ago."

"And?"

"He wasn't there."

"So, that makes thirty-one?"

"Yes."

"Was it okay? Did you come back easily?"

"Yes, it was okay. I haven't had a bad one since, well, not for a while."

Jenny had two more near death experiences inside the machine during the *60 Minutes* taping back on that day more than three months ago. Each time she saw Matthias in the tunnel. But since then, he hasn't been there. This surprises Loretta. It seems like he should always be there. She's pinned her hopes on the idea that something in all the data coming out of those studies will help her understand why he's disappeared from the tunnel. But it may be a while before that data makes it into the public realm.

The experiments outlined in the University research protocol, what she still calls the Jenny protocols, were mostly successful and lots of data were generated. The chairs and faculty and a battalion of post-docs were working nonstop to analyze it all, until the pandemic hit. The entire worldwide research machine, including at the University, pivoted to finding treatments or a vaccine. There hasn't been time, or money, to focus on near death experiences.

Even so, *60 Minutes* ran the segment without the data analysis, using a bunch of experts and a few new-age types offering ad-hoc commentary, as the footage rolled of Jenny in the MRI machine. Scott Pelley put on his most serious face to ask about the meaning of the MRI results, which showed blood levels in her brain soaring as they had on the MRI of Devlin Richardson's dying mother. Something was clearly happening, as it was "hot" all along the rim of the blood brain barrier. The experts gave Scott Pelley a dozen answers—mostly various spins on the dying brain theory—but a few weighed in with optimism, even tempered excitement, about how the data might lead to breakthroughs related to understanding human consciousness.

After dragging everyone through this segment, Scott pivoted to what his viewers really wanted to hear about. Loretta refused to be interviewed about Matthias appearing in the tunnel, of course, but Jenny's interview was pure brilliance, describing Matthias the three times she saw him after he had died as well as describing what he was like when he was alive. The video was the most shared on social ever from a news organization. Afterward, the entire world fell a little in love with Jenny. And by extension with Loretta because Jenny said that everyone watching had to be concerned about Loretta, that her grief was as important as the fact that they had been blessed to witness the miracle of her husband appearing in the tunnel as he was dying in real time. A few crackpots claimed they had staged the whole thing, but the evidence just didn't hold up. Loretta received a mountain of invitations for talk shows, podcasts and the like. She refused them all.

Even so, Loretta was buoyed by all the well-wishes, as was Sally-Anne. But they did not penetrate, in any meaningful way, the grief that gripped Loretta since that day, although it's full-bodied harshness has abated to the degree that she finally recognizes the need to function, even if minimally. And the first step, she and Sally-Anne agreed, now that the lockdown has been partially lifted, is spreading Matthias's ashes.

"I'm sorry I've left you mostly on your own these past few months," Loretta says.

"It's me who should be sorry."

They've talked about Jenny's guilt, how she feels she should have paid closer attention to the weariness Matthias expressed that morning as they drove to the University. Loretta only blames herself and there's no point in reliving that today, out in the world for the first time in months, so she doesn't respond directly to Jenny. Better to focus on the future. Or at least try. Or make the pretense of trying, she thinks.

"The virus sidetracked things," Loretta says. "Does that bother you?"

"In a weird way, I think it's better. I needed space to think about what's next and I got that time and space. I have things planned, but I'll need your help."

"That's good, about the plans."

"This pandemic crisis is a big change and during big-change moments, people open themselves to new ways of thinking," Jenny says. "More is coming, I can feel it, the world is changing, the change may bring difficult birthing pains, but it's coming. And in that new space, there is room for your theory."

Loretta starts to say *It's not a theory, it's just some ideas,* but doesn't have the energy. She hasn't given a great deal of thought to her ideas since Matthias died, except to wonder if they provide hope of seeing him again. She doesn't think they do, not in the way she thinks of being alive now, but she believes in a distant possibility, a different kind of hope, if she can keep thinking about the concept of self differently.

She has this hope because of what happened with the scans of Darren and Edward. Even though the virus has prevented anything official from coming out from the University about the Jenny protocols, some information has leaked. And what has everyone talking is the outcome of the simultaneous MRI scans of the two combat vets.

While the Dean was initially reluctant, he agreed to allow the vets to be scanned while Jenny was having a near death experience. Given the size and weight of an MRI machine, there was no way to move two machines into the same suite where Jenny's *60 Minutes* filming took place, so the two vets were secured in another area of the University, awaiting a signal to start, with Devlin Richardson's oversight and Father James's enthusiastic encouragement.

The brains of the vets lit up like fireworks during each of Jenny's three near death experiences, meaning somehow the brains of people who have had near death experiences are connected. So, either people are permanently imprinted from the experience or there *is* a genetic underpinning. Either way, when it happens, their neurons are rewired, always ready to echo the experience of being on the other side of our physical reality.

"Loretta, what will you do with the notebook?"

"Sally-Anne is bugging me to turn it into a book."

"That's a super idea. I'll use it when I start touring."

"Touring?"

"I'll explain all that another time. What will you call the book?"

"*The 31 Near Death Experiences of Jenny Black*, of course. That's its name."

"Where will it begin?"

"I suppose when you came to the house and told us about your near death experiences."

No, Loretta thinks, not then. Earlier.

Matthias, I am becoming a zombie.

Right this second?

No, not this second. It started a while back, and it's definitely a work in progress, but I'd say it's pretty close to done."

Loretta, what exactly does 'becoming a zombie' mean?

Loretta scrambles up the final twenty feet or so of trail with Jenny close behind. Sally-Anne is already on the ridge, looking out over the river. Loretta sets down her backpack and offers another drink from the canteen. They are quiet as they sip and look at the landscape. Blue skies, fluffy clouds, ancient slabs of lava pooled beside the river, towering conifer stands sprinkled with sloping yellow aspens.

"Here?" Sally-Anne asks.

"This is good," Loretta says.

Loretta pulls the Ziploc out of her pack. Matthias's body—blazed white fragments and sand-size grains mixed with pebbles and the skeletal parts that don't burn and fizzle, any piece that doesn't vaporize into nothing—fills the plastic bag. It's heavy, a few pounds easy, maybe more.

"How should we do this?" Sally-Anne asks.

Jenny takes a few steps back. This is for them. She is a bystander in this experience.

"Scoop and throw?"

"It's chunkier than I expected," Sally-Anne says, eyes sparkling with tears. "We'll have to throw pretty hard."

"The wind should catch most of it."

Loretta opens the bag.

Sally-Anne takes a handful and throws wide.

It's a good throw, the ashes create an arc a few feet out from the cliff's edge, hover there in the curve's pinnacle for an instant, and then drop, the big pieces landing fast, the dusty parts floating into the rocks and brush, some catching the wind and disappearing quickly.

Sally-Anne grabs a second handful and throws in the opposite direction. Another good throw.

Loretta gives the bag to Sally-Anne and brings her

hands together, forming a cup ready to receive.

Sally-Anne empties the last ashes into Loretta's palms. Loretta bends at the knees and heaves the ashes up and out as hard as she can with both arms.

A raven cuts across the sky in the distance.

About the author

F.E. Shearer traces the origins of her interest in near death experiences to a car wreck. As a teenager, she was thrown head-first through the windshield of a Chevy van. Traumatically injured and near death, she vaguely remembers a light-filled tunnel but little else. She's been writing or thinking about near death experiences, and this book, ever since. In addition, she grew up, fell in love, became a mother, and worked nearly every kind of job related to writing starting with dawn delivery of *The Washington Post* and moving on to speechwriting, journalism, media relations, and recently, a lengthy stint as a public relations director at a biomedical research university. *The 31 Near Death Experiences of Jenny Black* is her debut literary fiction novel.

ENDNOTES

¹ The Dean is referring to a 2001 article published in *The Lancet,* a medical research journal founded in 1823. The article, *Near-Death Experience in Survivors of Cardiac Arrest: a Prospective Study in The Netherlands,* is by Pim van Lommel, Ruud van Wees, Vincent Meyers and Ingrid Elfferich.

² Several publications—scientific and mainstream—have covered the link between epileptic seizures and out-of-body experiences. A starting point for learning more is a study funded by the National Institutes of Health with results published in the 2014 issue of *Frontiers of Neuroscience,* titled *Out-of-Body Experiences Associated with Seizures* by Bruce Greyson, Nathan Fountain, Lori Derr and Donna Broshek.

³ This discussion is drawn in part from *Cosmic Consciousness: A Study in the Evolution of the Human Mind* by Richard Bucke, published in 1901. In 1872, Bucke experienced a fleeting mystical event that caused him to see the universe as a living presence. This event inspired him to research the world's literature on mysticism and enlightenment, culminating in his theory about the evolutionary nature of consciousness. While a compelling analysis, there are problems with Bucke's framework that reflect the biases of his era (he didn't believe women could attain cosmic consciousness, for example).

⁴ The idea that religions have mystical origins, and that these origins have been altered over time by people in (or seeking) positions of wealth and power, is by no means unique to this novel. An entry to understanding how this transformation occurs over long (and short) periods of history can be found in the collected works of scholar Elaine Pagels, especially *The Gnostic Gospels* and *Adam, Eve, and the Serpent: Sex and Politics in Early Christianity.*

⁵ Two titles that explore the topic of bridging the mind-body barrier are *Why Buddhism is True: The Science and Philosophy of Meditation and Enlightenment* (2017) by Richard Wright and *Why God Won't Go Away: Brain Science and the Biology of Belief*

(2008) by Andrew Newberg and Eugene D'Aquili.

[6] This idea is covered eloquently in *Prophets, Cults and Madness* (2001) by John Price and Anthony Stevens.

[7] The academic paper that Loretta reads is Pahnke's *Good Friday Experiment: A long-term follow-up and methodological critique* by Rick Doblin, originally published in *Journal of Transpersonal Psychology* in 1991.

[8] This compelling psychological history is captured well by Don Lattin in *The Harvard Psychedelic Club: How Timothy Leary, Ram Dass, Huston Smith, and Andrew Weil Killed the Fifties and Ushered in a New Age for America* (2010).

[9] The story of the social and economic consequences of the evolution of the Harvard MBA curriculum is told in *The Golden Passport: Harvard Business School, the Limits of Capitalism, and the Moral Failure of the MBA Elite* by Duff McDonald, published in 2017.

[10] A database of first-person near death experience stories is maintained by the International Association for Near-Death Studies; this anecdote and others in the novel are inspired from these and other sources; the final descriptions herein, however, are entirely fictional.

[11] Many books have been written about the current and shifting state of knowledge regarding human consciousness. The writings of Susan Blackmore are an excellent place to start, with her highly accessible explanation about a complex topic plus the many suggestions for follow-up readings she provides.

[12] Rene Descartes, one of the most enduringly influential philosophers on the topic of the mind-body problem (which extrapolated represents the core question and battle over human meaning), posited that the "stuff" of the mind was different than the stuff of the body and that the mind-stuff interacted with the body through the small pineal gland in

the center of the brain, designating it the "principal seat of the soul." In this way, Descartes was able to designate the physical body as the realm of the emerging sciences while maintaining the soul as separate from it and belonging to the realm of God (church), thereby liberating science from the intellectual tyranny of religion in his era (16th/17th century). But in turn, this tidily set aside issues that now have become pressing in the modern world. Recent reconsiderations of Descartes suggest that he may have set back "progress" in the consideration of self significantly by creating this dualist framework. Not only has this made considering the concept of materialist brain-is-mind broadly challenging, because non-academic people may construe this biology-based model as negating free will, agency, individuality, etc., but more importantly for the ideas in this book, it doesn't allow for a third way. Descartes's construct set up the battle inherent in dualism, a proxy for religion versus science still raging today, with no obvious off-ramp to other paradigms.

13 This is a focus area of neuroscience research; search the keywords *brain* and *stem cells* for a robust list of lay and scientific articles. To get started, check out *Cerebral Organoids at the Air-liquid Interface Generate Diverse Nerve Tracts with Functional Output* from the lab of Madeline A. Lancaster at Cambridge, published in *Nature Neuroscience*, March 2019.

14 A search of PubMed will turn up studies linking vestibular imbalance to out-of-body experiences. To start, have a look at *Out-of-Body Experience in Vestibular Disorders—A Prospective Study of 210 Patients with Dizziness* by Lopez and Elziere (2017).

15 The implications of the "hard problem" of consciousness for the scientific enterprise as a whole has been articulated by Thomas Nagel in several places, but his 2012 book *Mind & Cosmos: Why the Materialist Neo-Darwinian Conception of Nature is Almost Certainly False* covers the topic succinctly. In prior work, Dr. Nagel coined the now infamous (in some circles) 'what-it's-like-to-be-a-bat' question.

16 David Chalmers was among the first (if not the first) to coin the phrase "the hard problem." If you are at ease with philosophically structured arguments and writing, learn more in his 1997 book *The Conscious Mind: In Search of a Fundamental Theory*. The opposing argument of materialism is covered in Daniel Dennett's 2017 book *Consciousness Explained*. Taken together, these two books represent the current guideposts of philosophical debate regarding the nature of human consciousness. I found them both tough to read. There are other more accessible books on the topic, but these two are core source materials.

17 Sabine Hossenfelder's 2018 book *Lost in Math: How Beauty Leads Physics Astray* is a mostly jargon-free overview of current challenges facing physics theories at the conceptual level, and in particular, those associated with the concept of theory elegance.

18 From Stephen Hawking's *A Brief History of Time* (1988): "Even if there is only one possible unified theory, it is just a set of rules and equations. What is it that breathes fire into the equations and makes a universe for them to describe?"

19 Roger Penrose created the concept of microtubules, explained in his 2016 book *The Emperor's New Mind*.

20 An April 2018 *New Yorker* article is a good place to start on the concept of the expanded mind and its relationship to consciousness models: *The Mind-Expanding Ideas of Andy Clark* by Larissa MacFarquhar.

21 Many thinkers have wrestled with the idea of how art may provide clues to unraveling the history of God and gods; an example is *Evolving Brains, Emerging Gods: Early Humans and the Origins of Religion* by E. Fuller Torrey (2015).

22 Aspects of this chapter are derived in part (mistakes or misinterpretations are mine) from one of the most understandable books about physics I've encountered: *Seven Brief Lessons in Physics* by Carlo Rovelli (2016). Another

source, and one that provides an eye-opening discussion of the influence of white patriarchy on physics (and science, generally), both in terms of the cosmological limitations of a singular cultural perspective and the punishing academic culture it spawns for anyone other than white men, is *The Disordered Cosmos* (2021) by Chanda Prescod-Weinstein. The author also articulates a clear framing of the "problem" of merging the theoretical underpinning of the micro world with the macro world of everyday human experience, in a way that allows readers to share both in the mystery of physics and the joy its study brings Dr. Prescod-Weinstein.

[23] This is not a novel concept; in the early days of what we now identify as science, most scientists, Galileo and Keppler to name two, along with philosophers (such as Descartes) believed God to be the one true creator, and the goal of any inquiry, scientific or otherwise, was to seek out the rules that God made manifest within nature. The second chapter in Sabine Hossenfelder's *Lost in Math* (2018) provides a nice overview of this intellectual trajectory.

[24] This fascinating study about MRI telepathy, and more, is discussed in *Into the Gray Zone: A Neuroscientist Explores the Boundary Between Life and Death* by Adrian Owen (2017).

[25] The concept of DMN is contained in Michael Pollan's book *How to Change Your Mind: What the New Science of Psychedelics Teaches Us About Consciousness, Dying, Addiction, Depression, and Transcendence* (2018).

[26] This study from the University of Michigan Health System was widely covered in scientific and mainstream media. An accessible summary, *Electrical Signatures of Consciousness in the Dying Brain*, appeared in *ScienceDaily*, August 2013. Of note, Loretta would be critical of this paper title for not including the phrase "in mice."

[27] This hyper-connectivity topic along with the loss of fear of death are covered in Michael Pollan's book *How to Change Your Mind: What the New Science of Psychedelics Teaches Us About*

Consciousness, Dying, Addiction, Depression, and Transcendence (2018). While this is a nice summary of this topic in Pollan's engaging first-person based writing, others go deeper. One I found particularly illuminating is *Why God Won't Go Away: Brain Science and the Biology of Belief* by Andrew Newberg, Eugene D' Aquili and Vince Rause (2002).

[28] John Fleischmann covers the American Crowbar Case, providing historical and scientific context in his 2013 book *Phineas Gage: A Gruesome but True Story About Brain Science.*

[29] The triune brain is a long-standing model, and references to it can be found in many places; the inspiration for its inclusion in the anthropology chapter comes from a concise discussion by Lisa Feldman Barrett in her excellent book *How Emotions Are Made: The Secret Life of the Brain* (2017).

[30] I don't know the origin of this phrase regarding life being a remission from death (maybe Kafka?). Barbara Ehrenreich covers it in her 2018 book *Natural Causes: An Epidemic of Wellness, the Certainty of Dying, and Killing Ourselves to Live Longer.* In her earlier 2014 book *Living with a Wild God*, also well worth reading, she muses about the overlap of science and religion, and ponders the cultural evolution of the concept of self as an outgrowth of the soul metaphor.

[31] To learn more about the history of the DSM, have a look at the excellent *The Book of Woe: The DSM and the Unmaking of Psychiatry* by Gary Greenberg (2013). It was in Greenberg's book that I first learned about drapetomania (see note below) and also encountered the revelatory commentary about the mental illness of hoarder-billionaires.

[32] The sole symptom of drapetomania, once recognized as a mental illness exclusively diagnosed in Africans, was the impulse to flee one's enslavement. A horrifying example of scientific and academic racism, American physician Samuel Cartwright "defined" this condition in 1852, insisting that any African not wishing to be enslaved must be mentally ill.

---

[33] Once again, *How Emotions Are Made: The Secret Life of the Brain* by Lisa Feldman Barrett, published in 2017, is a cut-to-the-chase overview of current scientific thinking on the development of "self" and also provides additional source material for those who wish further excavation.

[34] *Wayfinding: The Science and Mystery of How Humans Navigate the World* by M.R. O'Connor, published in 2019, is a fascinating look at the intrinsic capacities of animals and humans to navigate their physical worlds.

[35] The sheer scope of racism in medical practice—and medical education—is breathtaking. One place to begin is the 1910 *Flexner Report*, which was the basis upon which the scientific model for most U.S. medical schools were established. The report embedded and institutionalized racism in medical education and, by extension, how medicine is practiced that persists today. Changing this requires that medical education itself changes. See the Sept. 1, 2021 New York Times article *"The Black Mortality Gap, and a Document Written in 1910"* by Anna Flagg.

[36] See endnote #32 and also conduct an Internet search on "scientific racism." You'll be shocked, and depressed, at the extraordinary lengths to which white scholars went (and still do—witness the backlash in some scholarly quarters to *The 1619 Project*) to provide an "evidentiary" paradigm to justify racism. From Thomas Jefferson all the way to the DNA discoverer James Watson, the willingness of scholars to traffic in pseudoscience for the purpose of upholding white supremacy calls into question aspects of science itself given the ease with which this bias was/is embraced and evidence ignored. If the intellectual foundations of science (as well as philosophy) are steeped in racism, what parts of these paradigms must be overtly reconsidered? Also, search for the work of Dan-el Padilla for an example of the historical entanglement and possibly inseparability of white supremacy in the Classics field, and the ripple effect of this truth on other disciplines and society more broadly.